ALSO BY

ALLY CONDIE

Matched
Crossed

REACHED

ALLY CONDIE

REACHED

DUTTON BOOKS
An imprint of Penguin Group (USA) Inc.

TEEN
F
CONDIE, A

11/12
dry

DUTTON BOOKS
An imprint of Penguin Group (USA) Inc.

3 1257 02409 4673

Published by the Penguin Group
Penguin Group (USA) Inc., 375 Hudson Street, New York, New York 10014, U.S.A. | Penguin Group (Canada),
90 Eglinton Avenue East, Suite 700, Toronto, Ontario, Canada M4P 2Y3 (a division of Pearson Penguin Canada
Inc.) | Penguin Books Ltd, 80 Strand, London WC2R 0RL, England | Penguin Ireland, 25 St Stephen's Green,
Dublin 2, Ireland (a division of Penguin Books Ltd) | Penguin Group (Australia), 707 Collins Street, Melbourne,
Victoria 3008, Australia(a division of Pearson Australia Group Pty Ltd) | Penguin Books India Pvt Ltd,
11 Community Centre, Panchsheel Park, New Delhi—110 017, India | Penguin Group (NZ), 67 Apollo Drive,
Rosedale, Auckland 0632, New Zealand (a division of Pearson New Zealand Ltd.) | Penguin Books, Rosebank
Office Park, 181 Jan Smuts Ave, Parktown North 2193, South Africa | Penguin China, B7 Jaiming Center,
27 East Third Ring Road North, Chaoyang District, Beijing 100020, China | Penguin Books Ltd,
Registered Offices: 80 Strand, London WC2R 0RL, England

"Poem in October"—By Dylan Thomas,
from THE POEMS OF DYLAN THOMAS, copyright © 1945
by The Trustees for the Copyrights of Dylan Thomas, first published in POETRY.
Reprinted by permission of New Directions Publishing Corp.

"Do Not Go Gentle Into That Good Night"—By Dylan Thomas,
from THE POEMS OF DYLAN THOMAS, copyright © 1952 by Dylan Thomas.
Reprinted by permission of New Directions Publishing Corp.

"They Dropped Like Flakes"—By Emily Dickinson,
reprinted by permission of the publishers and the Trustees of Amherst College
from THE POEMS OF EMILY DICKINSON, Thomas H. Johnson, ed., Cambridge, Mass:
The Belknap Press of Harvard University Press, copyright © 1951, 1955, 1979, 1983
by the President and Fellows of Harvard College.

"I Did Not Reach Thee"—By Emily Dickinson,
from THE POEMS OF EMILY DICKINSON, Thomas H. Johnson, ed., Cambridge, Mass:
The Belknap Press of Harvard University Press, copyright © 1951, 1955, 1979, 1983
by the President and Fellows of Harvard College.

"The Single Hound"—By Emily Dickinson,
reprinted by permission of the publishers and the Trustees of Amherst College
from THE POEMS OF EMILY DICKINSON, Thomas H. Johnson, ed., Cambridge, Mass:
The Belknap Press of Harvard University Press, copyright © 1951, 1955, 1979, 1983
by the President and Fellows of Harvard College.

"In Time of Pestilence, 1593"—By Thomas Nashe

The publisher does not have any control over and does not assume any responsibility
for author or third-party websites or their content.

Library of Congress Cataloging-in-Publication Data

Condie, Allyson Braithwaite
Reached / Ally Condie.—First edition.
pages cm
Sequel to: Crossed.
Summary: "In search of a better life, Cassia joins a widespread
rebellion against Society, where she is tasked with finding a cure to
the threat of survival and must choose between Xander and Ky"—Provided
by publisher.
ISBN 978-0-525-42366-9 (hardcover)
[1. Government, Resistance to—Fiction. 2. Fantasy.] I. Title.
PZ7.C7586Rd 2012
[Fic]—dc23   2012031916

Published in the United States by Dutton Books,
an imprint of Penguin Group (USA) Inc.
345 Hudson Street, New York, New York 10014
www.penguin.com/teen

Designed by Irene Vandervoort | Printed in USA | First Edition
10 9 8 7 6 5 4 3 2 1

for Calvin,
who has never been afraid to dream of places Other

REACHED

～

A man pushed a rock up the hill. When he reached the top, the stone rolled down to the bottom of the hill and he began again. In the village nearby, the people took note. "A judgment," they said. They never joined him or tried to help because they feared those who issued the punishment. He pushed. They watched.

Years later, a new generation noticed that the man and his stone were sinking into the hill, like the setting of the sun and moon. They could only see part of the rock and part of the man as he rolled the stone along to the top of the hill.

One of the children became curious. So, one day, the child walked up the hill. As she drew closer, she was surprised to see that the stone was carved with names and dates and places.

"What are all these words?" the child asked.

"The sorrows of the world," the man told her. "I pilot them up the hill over and over again."

"You are using them to wear out the hill," the child said, noticing the long deep groove worn where the stone had turned.

"I am making something," the man said. "When I am finished, it will be your turn to take my place."

The child was not afraid. "What are you making?"

"A river," the man said.

The child went back down the hill, puzzling at how one could make a river. But not long after, when the rains came and the flood flashed through the long trough and washed the man somewhere far away, the child saw that the man had been right, and she took her place pushing the stone and piloting the sorrows of the world.

This is how the Pilot came to be.

The Pilot is a man who pushed a stone and washed away in the water. It is a woman who crossed the river and looked to the sky. The Pilot is old and young and has eyes of every color and hair of every shade; lives in deserts, islands, forests, mountains, and plains.

The Pilot leads the Rising—the rebellion against the Society—and the Pilot never dies. When one Pilot's time has finished, another comes to lead.

And so it goes on, over and over like a stone rolling.

In a place past the edge of the Society's map, the Pilot will always live and move.

PART ONE

PILOT

CHAPTER 1

XANDER

Every morning, the sun comes up and turns the earth red, and I think: *This could be the day when everything changes. Maybe today the Society will fall.* Then night comes again and we're all still waiting. But I know the Pilot's real.

Three Officials walk up to the door of a little house at sunset. The house looks like all of the others on the street: two shutters on each of its three forward-facing windows, five steps up to the door, and one small, spiky bush planted to the right of the path.

The oldest of the Officials, a man with gray hair, raises his hand to knock.

One. Two. Three.

The Officials stand close enough to the glass that I can see the circle-shaped insignia sewn on the right pocket of the youngest Official's uniform. The circle is bright red and looks like a drop of blood.

I smile and he does, too. Because the Official: is me.

In the past, the Official Ceremony was a big occasion at City Hall. The Society held a formal dinner and you could bring your parents and your Match with you. But the Official

Ceremony isn't one of the three big ceremonies—Welcoming Day, the Match Banquet, and the Final Celebration—and so it's not what it used to be. The Society has started to cut corners where they can, and they assume Officials are loyal enough not to complain about their ceremony losing some of its trimmings.

I stood there with four others, all of us in new white uniforms. The head Official pinned the insignia on my pocket: the red circle representing the Medical Department. And then, with our voices echoing under the dome of the mostly empty Hall, we all committed to the Society and pledged to achieve our Society-designated potential. That was all. I didn't care that the ceremony wasn't anything special. Because I'm not *really* an Official. I mean, I am, but my true loyalty is to the Rising.

A girl wearing a violet dress hurries along the sidewalk behind us. I see her reflection in the window. She's got her head down like she's hoping we won't notice her. Her parents follow behind, all three of them heading toward the nearest air-train stop. It's the fifteenth, so the Match Banquet is tonight. It hasn't even been a year since I walked up the stairs of City Hall with Cassia. We're both far away from Oria now.

A woman opens the door of the house. She's holding her new baby, the one we're here to name. "Please come in," she tells us. "We've been expecting you." She looks tired, even on what should be one of the happiest days of her life. The Society doesn't talk about it much, but things are harder in the Border Provinces. The resources seem to start in Central and then bleed outward. Everything here in Camas Province is kind of dirty and worn out.

After the door closes behind us, the mother holds out the baby for us to see. "Seven days old today," she tells us, but of course we already know. That's why we're here. Welcoming Day celebrations are always held a week after the baby's birth.

The baby's eyes are closed, but we know from our data that the color is deep blue. His hair: brown. We also know that he arrived on his due date and that under the tightly wrapped blanket he has ten fingers and ten toes. His initial tissue sample taken at the medical center looked excellent.

"Are you all ready to begin?" Official Brewer asks. As the senior Official in our Committee, he's in charge. His voice has exactly the right balance of benevolence and authority. He's done this hundreds of times. I've wondered before if Official Brewer could be the Pilot. He certainly looks the part. And he's very organized and efficient.

Of course, the Pilot could be anyone.

The parents nod.

"According to the data, we're missing an older sibling," the second in command, Official Lei, says in her gentle voice. "Did you want him to be present for the ceremony?"

"He was tired after dinner," the mother says, sounding apologetic. "He could barely keep his eyes open. I put him to bed early."

"That's fine, of course," Official Lei says. Since the little boy is just over two years old—nearly perfect spacing between siblings—he's not required to be in attendance. This isn't something he'd likely remember anyway.

"What name have you chosen?" Official Brewer moves closer to the port in the foyer.

"Ory," the mother says.

Official Brewer taps the name into the port and the mother shifts the baby a little. "Ory," Official Brewer repeats. "And for his middle name?"

"Burton," the father says. "A family name."

Official Lei smiles. "That's a lovely name."

"Come and see how it looks," Official Brewer says. The parents come closer to the port to see the baby's name: ORY BURTON FARNSWORTH. Underneath the letters runs the bar code the Society has assigned for the baby. If he leads an ideal life, the Society plans to use the same bar code to mark his tissue preservation sample at his Final Celebration.

But the Society won't last that long.

"I'll submit it now," Official Brewer says, "if there are no changes or corrections you want to make."

The mother and father move closer to check the name one last time. The mother smiles and holds the baby near the portscreen, as if the baby can read his own name.

Official Brewer looks at me. "Official Carrow," he says, "it's time for the tablet."

My turn. "We have to give the tablet in front of the port,"

I remind the parents. The mother shifts Ory even higher so that the baby's head and face are clearly visible for the portscreen to record.

I've always liked the look of the little disease-proofing tablets we give at the Welcoming Day ceremonies. These tablets are round and made up of what looks like three tiny pie wedges: one-third blue, one-third green, and one-third red. Though the contents of this tablet are entirely different from the three tablets the baby will carry later, the use of the same colors represents the life he will have in the Society. The disease-proofing tablet looks childish and colorful. They always remind me of the paint palettes on our screens back in First School.

The Society gives the tablet to all babies to keep them safe from illness and infection. The disease-proofing tablet is easy for babies to take. It dissolves instantly. It's all much more humane than the inoculations previous societies used to give, where they put a needle right into a baby's skin. Even the Rising plans to keep giving the disease-proofing tablets when they come to power, but with a few modifications.

The baby stirs when I unwrap the tablet. "Would you mind opening his mouth for me?" I ask the baby's mother.

When she tries to open his mouth, the baby turns his head, looking for food and trying to suck. We all laugh, and while his mouth is open I drop the tablet inside. It dissolves completely on his tongue. Now we have to wait for him to swallow, which he does: right on cue.

"Ory Burton Farnsworth," Official Brewer says, "we welcome you to the Society."

"Thank you," the parents say in unison.

The substitution has gone perfectly, as usual.

Official Lei glances at me and smiles. Her long sweep of black hair slides over her shoulder. Sometimes I wonder if she's part of the rebellion, too, and knows what I'm doing—replacing the disease-proofing tablets with the ones the Rising gave to me. Almost every child born in the Provinces within the past two years has had one of the Rising immunizations instead of the Society's. Other Rising workers like me have been making the switch.

Thanks to the Rising, this baby won't only be immune to most illnesses. He'll also be immune to the red tablet, so the Society can't take his memories. Someone did this for me when I was a baby. They did the same for Ky. And, probably, for Cassia.

Years ago, the Rising infiltrated the dispensaries where the Society makes the disease-proofing tablets. So, in addition to the tablets made according to the Society's formula, there are others made for the Rising. Our tablets include everything the Society uses, plus the immunity to the red tablet, plus something more.

When we were born, the Rising didn't have enough resources to make new tablets for everyone. They had to choose only some of us, based on who they thought might turn out to be useful to them later. Now they finally have enough for everyone.

The Rising is for everyone.

And they—we—are not going to fail.

Since the sidewalk is narrow, I walk behind Official Brewer and Official Lei on our way back to the air car. Another family with a daughter wearing Banquet attire hurries down the street. They're late, and the mother is not happy. "I told you *again* and *again*—" she says to the father, and then she catches sight of us and stops cold.

"Hello," I say as we pass them. "Congratulations."

"When do you next see *your* Match?" Official Lei asks me.

"I don't know," I say. "The Society hasn't scheduled our next port-to-port communication."

Official Lei is a little older than I am: at least twenty-one, because she's celebrated her Marriage Contract. As long as I've known her, her spouse has been out in the Army stationed somewhere at the edge of the Borders. I can't ask her when he's due back. That kind of information is classified. I don't think even Official Lei knows when he'll return.

The Society doesn't like us to get too specific when we talk about our work assignments with others. Cassia's aware that I'm an Official, but she doesn't know exactly what I do. There are Officials in all different departments in the Society.

The Society trains many kinds of workers at the medical center. Everyone knows about the medics because they can diagnose and help people. There are also surgics who operate, pharmics who make medicines, nurses who assist, and physics like me. Our job is to oversee aspects of the medical field—for example, administrating medical centers. Or, if we become Officials, we're often asked to serve on Committees, which is what I do. We take care of the distribution of tablets to infants and assist in collecting tissue at Final Banquets. According to the Society, this assignment is one of the most important ones an Official can have.

"What color did she choose?" Official Lei asks as we approach the air car.

For a second, I don't know what she means, and then I realize she's asking about Cassia's dress. "She chose green," I say. "She looked beautiful."

Someone cries out and the three of us turn in unison. It's the baby's father, running toward us as fast as he can. "I can't wake my older son," he calls out. "I went in to see if he was still asleep and—something is wrong."

"Contact the medics on the port," Official Brewer calls back, and the three of us move as fast as we can to the house. We go inside without knocking and hurry to the back where the bedrooms always are. Official Lei puts her hand on the wall to steady herself before Official Brewer opens the bedroom door. "You all right?" I ask her. She nods.

"Hello?" Official Brewer says.

The mother looks up at us, her face ashen. She still holds the baby. The older child lying on the bed doesn't move at all.

He rests on his side, his back to us. He's breathing, but it's slow, and his plainclothes hang a little loose around his neck. His skin color looks all right. There's a small red mark in between his shoulder blades and I feel a rush of pity and exultation.

This is it.

The Rising said it would look like this.

I have to keep myself from glancing at the others in the room. *Who else knows?* Is anyone here part of the Rising? Have they seen the information I've seen about how the rebellion will proceed?

Though the incubation period may vary, once the disease is manifest, the patient deteriorates quickly. Slurred speech is followed by a descent into an almost comatose state. The most telltale sign of the live Plague virus is one or more small red marks on the back of the patient. Once the Plague has made significant inroads into the general populace, and can no longer be concealed by the Society, the Rising will begin.

"What is it?" the mother asks. "Is he ill?"

Again, the three of us move at the same time. Official Lei reaches for the boy's wrist to take his pulse. Official Brewer turns to the woman. I try to block her view of her child lying still on the bed. Until I *know* the Rising is on the move, I have to proceed as usual.

"He's breathing," Official Brewer says.

"His pulse is fine," Official Lei says.

"The medics will be here soon," I tell the mother.

"Can't *you* do something for him?" she asks. "Medicine, treatment . . ."

"I'm sorry," Official Brewer says. "We need to get to the medical center before we can do anything more."

"But he's stable," I tell her. *Don't worry,* I want to add. *The Rising has a cure.* I hope she can hear the sound of hope in my voice since I can't tell her outright *how* I know it's all going to work out.

This is it. The beginning of the Rising.

Once the Rising comes to power, we'll all be able to choose. Who knows what might happen then? When I kissed Cassia back in the Borough she caught her breath in what I think was surprise. Not at the kiss: she knew that was coming. I think she was surprised by how it felt.

As soon as I can, I want to tell her again, in person: *Cassia, I'm in love with you and I want you. So, what will it take for you to feel the same? A whole new world?*

Because that's what we're going to have.

The mother edges a tiny bit closer to her child. "It's just," she says, and her voice catches, "that he's so *still.*"

CHAPTER 2
CASSIA

Ky said he'd meet me tonight, by the lake.

When I see him next, I'll kiss him first.

He'll pull me so close that the poems I keep underneath my shirt, near my heart, will rustle, a sound so soft that only the two of us will hear. And the music of his heartbeat, his breathing, the cadence and timbre of his voice, will set me to singing.

He will tell me where he has been.

I will tell him where I want to go.

I stretch out my arms to make sure that nothing shows underneath the cuffs of my shirt. The red silk of the dress I'm wearing slips neatly under the unflattering lines of my plainclothes. It's one of the Hundred Dresses, possibly stolen, that came up in a trade. It was worth the price I paid—a poem—to have such a piece of color to hold up to the light and pull over my head, to feel so bright.

I sort for the Society here in their capital of Central, but I have a job to do for the Rising, and I trade with the Archivists. On the outside, I'm a Society girl wearing plainclothes. But underneath, I have silk and paper against my skin.

I have found that this is the easiest way to carry the poems; wrap them around my wrists, place them against my heart. Of course, I don't keep all of the pages with me. I've found a place to hide most of them. But there are a few pieces I don't ever like to be without.

I open my tablet container. All the tablets are there: blue, green, red. And something else besides. A tiny scrap of paper, on which I've written the word *remember*. If the Society ever makes me take the red tablet, I'll slip this up into my sleeve, and then I'll know that they've made me forget.

I can't be the first to have done something like this. How many people out there know something they shouldn't—not *what* they have lost, but that they *have* lost?

And there's a chance I won't forget anything—that I'm immune like Indie, and Xander, and Ky.

The Society thinks the red tablet *does* work on me. But they don't know everything. According to the Society, I've never been in the Outer Provinces at all. I've never crossed through canyons or run down a river in the night with stars sprinkled overhead and a silver spray of water all around. As far as they know, I never left.

"This is your story," the Rising officer said to me before they sent me on into Central. "This is what you say when people ask where you've been."

He handed me a sheet of paper. I looked down at the printed words:

The Officers found me in the forest in Tana, near my work camp. I don't remember anything about my last evening and night there. All I know is that I ended up in the woods somehow.

I looked back up. "We have an Officer who is prepared to corroborate your story and claim she found you in the woods," he said.

"And the idea is that I'd been given a red tablet," I said. "To forget that I saw them take the other girls away on the air ships."

He nodded. "Apparently one of the girls caused a disturbance. They had to give red tablets to several others who woke up and saw her."

Indie, I thought. She's the one who ran and screamed. She knew what was happening to us.

"So we'll say that *you* went missing after that," he said. "They lost track of you for a moment, and you wandered off while the red tablet was taking effect. Then they found you days later."

"How did I survive?" I asked.

He tapped the paper in front of me.

I was lucky. My mother had told me how to identify poisonous plants. So I foraged. In November, there are still plants on the ground that can be used for food.

In a way, that part of the story was true. My mother's words did come back to help me survive, but it was in the Carving, not in the forest.

"Your mother worked in an Arboretum," he said. "And you've been in the woods before."

19

"Yes," I said. It was the forest on the Hill, not the one in Tana; but hopefully it would be close enough.

"Then it all adds up," he said.

"Unless the Society questions me too closely," I said.

"They won't," he said. "Here's a silver box and a tablet container to replace the ones you lost."

I took them from him and opened the tablet container. One blue tablet, one green. And one red, to replace the one I'd supposedly taken at an Official's command in Tana. I thought about those other girls who really did take the tablet; most wouldn't remember Indie, how she cried out. She'd have disappeared. Like me.

"Remember," he said, "you can recall finding yourself alone in the forest and the time you spent foraging for food. But you've forgotten everything that *really* happened in the twelve hours before you went on the air ship."

"What do you want me to do once I'm in Central?" I asked him. "Why did they tell me I could best serve the Rising from within the Society?"

I could see him sizing me up, deciding if I really *could* do whatever it is that he wanted. "Central is where the Society planned to send you for your final work position," he said. I nodded. "You're a sorter. A good one, according to the Society's data. Now that they think you've been rehabilitated in the work camp, they'll be glad to have you back, and the Rising can make use of that." And then he told me what kind of sort to look for, and what I should do when it happened. "You'll need to be patient," he said. "It may take some time."

Which was a wise piece of advice, it seems, since I haven't sorted anything out of the ordinary yet. Not that I remember, anyway. But that's all right. I don't need the Rising to tell me how to fight the Society.

Whenever I can, I write letters. I've made them in many ways: a *K* out of strands of grass; an *X* with two sticks crossed over each other, their wet bark black against a silvery metal bench in the greenspace near my workplace. I set out a little ring of stones in the shape of an O, like an open mouth, on the ground. And of course I write the way Ky taught me, too.

Wherever I go, I look to see if there are new letters. So far, no one else is writing, or if they are, I haven't seen it. But it will happen. Maybe even now there's someone charring sticks the way Ky told me he did, preparing to write the name of someone they love.

I *know* that I'm not the only one doing these things, committing small acts of rebellion. There are people swimming against the current and shadows moving slowly in the deep. I have been the one looking up when something dark passed before the sun. And I have been the shadow itself, slipping along the place where earth and water meet the sky.

Day after day, I push the rock that the Society has given me up the hill, over and over again. Inside me are the real things that give me strength—my thoughts, the small stones of my own choosing. They tumble in my mind, some polished from frequent turning, some new and rough, some that cut.

Satisfied that the poems don't show, I walk down the hallway of my tiny apartment and into the foyer. I'm about to open the door when a knock sounds on the other side of it, and I start a little. Why would anyone be here now? Like many of the others who have a work assignment but who have not yet celebrated their Marriage Contract, I live alone. And, just like in the Boroughs, we aren't encouraged to visit one another's residences.

An Official stands at the door, smiling pleasantly. There's only one, which is strange. Officials almost always travel in groups of three. "Cassia Reyes?" she asks.

"Yes," I say.

"I'll need you to come with me," she says. "You're required at the sorting center for extra work hours."

But I'm supposed to see Ky tonight. It seemed that things were, at last, aligning for us—he was finally assigned to come to Central, and the message he sent telling me where we could meet arrived just in time. Sometimes, it takes weeks instead of days for our letters to go through, but this one came quickly. Impatience floods over me as I look at the Official, with her white uniform and her impassive face and her neat insignia. *Don't bother with us anymore,* I think. *Use the computers. Let them do all the work.* But that goes against one of the Society's key tenets, one that they tell to us from the time that we're small: *Technology can fail us as it did the societies before ours.*

And then I realize that the Official's request might hide something more—could it be time for me to do what the Rising has asked? Her face remains smooth and calm. It's impossible to tell what she knows or for whom she really works. "Others will meet us at the air-train stop," she says.

"Will it take long?" I ask her.

She doesn't answer.

As we ride in the air train, we pass by the lake, dark now in the distance.

No one goes to the lake here. It still suffers from pre-Society pollution and isn't safe for walking in or drinking. The Society tore out most of the docks and wharves where people long ago used to keep boats. But, when it's light, you can see that there are three piers left in one spot, jutting out into the water like three fingers, all equal length, all reaching. Months ago, when I first came here, I told Ky of this place and that it would be a good spot to meet, something he could see from above that I have noticed from below.

And now, on the other side of the air train, the dome of Central's City Hall comes into view, a too-close moon that never sets. In spite of myself, I have a little stirring of pride and hear the notes of the Anthem of the Society singing in my mind whenever I see the familiar shape of a Hall.

No one goes to Central's City Hall.

There's a tall white wall around the Hall and the other buildings nearby. The wall has been here since before I came. "Renovations," everyone says. "The Society will open the stillzone back up again soon."

I'm fascinated by the stillzone, and by its name, which no one seems to be able to explain to me. I'm also intrigued by what's on the other side of the barrier, and sometimes after work I take a small detour on my way home so that I can walk next to the smooth, white surface. I keep thinking of how many paintings Ky's mother could have put along the length of the wall, which curves back in what I imagine is a perfect circle. I've never followed it all the way around, so I can't be sure.

Those I've asked are uncertain about how long the barrier has been here—all they say is that it went up sometime in the last year. They don't seem to remember why it's really here, and if they do, they're not saying.

I want to know what's behind those walls.

I want so much: happiness, freedom, love. And I want a few other tangible things, too.

Like a poem, and a microcard. I'm still waiting for two trades to come in. I traded two of my poems for the end of another, one that began *I did not reach Thee* and tells of a journey. I found the beginning of it in the Carving and knew I had to have the end.

And the other trade is even more expensive, even more risky—I traded seven poems to bring Grandfather's microcard from my parents' house in Keya here to me. I asked the trader to approach Bram first with an encoded note. I knew Bram could decipher it. After all, he'd figured out the games I made for him on the scribe when he was younger. And I thought he'd be more likely to send the microcard than either of my parents.

Bram. I'd like to find a silver watch for him to replace the one the Society took. But so far the price has been too high. I rejected a trade for a watch earlier today at the air-train stop on my way to work. I will pay what's fair, but not too much. Perhaps *this* is what I learned in the canyons: What I am, what I'm not, what I'll give, and what I won't.

The sorting center is filled to capacity. We are some of the last to arrive, and an Official ushers us to our empty cubicles. "Please begin immediately," she says, and no sooner have I sat down in my chair than words appear on the screen: *Next sort: exponential pairwise matching.*

I keep my eyes on the screen and my expression neutral. Inside, I feel a little *tick* of excitement, a tiny skip in the beat of my heart.

This is the kind of sort the Rising told me to look for.

The workers around me give no indication that the sort means anything to them. But I'm sure there are others in the room looking at these words and wondering *Is it finally time?*

Wait for the actual data, I remind myself. I'm not just looking out for a sort; I'm also looking out for a particular set of information, which I'm supposed to mismatch.

In exponential pairwise matching, each element is ranked by assigning an importance to each of its properties, and then paired to another element whose property rankings fit optimally. It is an intricate, complicated, tedious sort, the kind that requires every bit of our focus and attention.

The screen flickers and then the data comes up.

This is it.

The right sort. The right data set.

Is this the beginning of the Rising?

For a brief moment, I hesitate. Am I confident that the Rising can bug the error-checking algorithm? What if they didn't? My mistakes will all be noted. The chime will sound, and an Official will come to see what I'm doing.

My fingers don't tremble as I push one element across the screen, fighting the natural impulse to put the element where my training says it should go. I guide it slowly to its new location and slowly lift my finger, holding my breath.

No chime sounds.

The Rising's bug worked.

I think I hear a breath of relief, a tiny exhalation somewhere else in the room. And then I feel something, a cottonwood seed of memory, light and flitting on the breeze, floating through.

Have I done this before?

But there's no time to follow the wisp of memory. I have to sort.

It's almost more difficult to sort incorrectly at this point;

I've spent so many months and years of my life trying to get things right. This feels counterintuitive, but it is what the Rising wants.

For the most part, the data comes through quick and relentless. But there's a short lag while we wait for more of it to load. That means that some of it is coming from off-site.

The fact that we're doing the sort in real time seems to indicate that there's a rush. Could the Rising be happening now?

Will Ky and I be together for it?

For a moment I picture the black of ships coming in above the white dome of the Hall and I feel the cool air through my hair as I rush to meet him. Then the warm pressure of his lips on mine, and this time there is no good-bye, but a new beginning.

"We're Matching," someone says out loud.

He breaks my concentration. I look up from the screen, blinking.

How long have we been sorting? I've been working hard, trying to do what the Rising asked. At some point I became lost in the data, in the task at hand.

Out of the corner of my eye, I catch a glimpse of green—Army Officers in uniform moving in on the man who spoke.

I saw the Officials when we first came in, but how long have Officers been here?

"For the Banquet," the man says. He laughs. "Something's happened. We're Matching for the Banquet. The Society can't keep up anymore."

I keep my head down and continue sorting, but at the moment they drag him past me I glance up. His mouth is gagged and his words unintelligible, and above the cloth his eyes meet mine for a brief moment as they take him away.

My hands tremble over my screen. Is he right?

Are we Matching people?

Today is the fifteenth. The Banquet *is* tonight.

The Official back in the Borough told me that they Match a week before the Banquet. Has that changed? What has happened that would make the Society in such a rush? Data culled so near to the Banquet will be prone to errors because they won't have much time to check for accuracy.

And besides, the Match Department has its own sorters. The Matches are of paramount importance to the Society. There should be people higher than us to see to it.

Perhaps the Society doesn't have more time. Perhaps they don't have enough personnel. Something is happening out there. It almost feels like they'd done the Matching before, but now they have to do it again at the last minute.

Perhaps the data has changed.

If we're Matching, then the data represents people: eye color, hair color, temperament, favorite leisure activity. What could have changed about so many people so quickly?

Maybe they haven't changed. Maybe they're gone.

What could have caused such a decimation in the Society's data? Will they have time to make the microcards or will the silver boxes stay empty tonight?

A piece of data comes up and then gets taken down almost before I see it at all.

Like Ky's face on the microcard that day.

Why try to have the Banquet like this? When the margin of error is so high?

Because the Banquet is the most important celebration in the Society. The Matching is what makes the other ceremonies possible; it's the Society's crowning achievement. If they stop having it, even for a month, people will know that something is very, very wrong.

Which is why, I realize, the Rising added the bug, so that some of us could Match incorrectly without getting caught. We're causing further havoc with an already compromised data set.

"Please stand up," the Official says. "Take out your tablet containers."

I do, and so do the others, faces appearing from behind the partitions, eyes bewildered, expressions worried.

Are you immune? I want to ask them. *Are you going to remember this?*

Am I?

"Remove the red tablet," the Official says. "Please wait until an Official is near you to observe you taking the tablet. There's nothing to worry about."

The Officials move through the room. They're prepared. When someone swallows down a red tablet, the Officials refill the containers right away.

They knew they'd have to use these, at some point, tonight.

Hands to mouths, memories to nothing, red going down.

The little seed of memory floats past again. I have a nagging feeling that it's something to do with the sort. If I could only remember—

Remember. I hear footsteps on the floor. They're getting closer to me. I wouldn't have dared to do this before, but trading with the Archivists has taught me to be stealthy, sleight of hand. I unscrew the lid and slip the paper—*remember*—into my sleeve.

"Please take the tablet," the Official tells me.

This isn't like last time, back in the Borough. The Official standing in front of me isn't going to look the other way, and there's no grass beneath my feet to grind the tablet into.

I don't want to take the tablet. I don't want to lose my memories.

But perhaps I *am* immune to the red tablet, like Ky, and Xander, and Indie. I might remember everything.

And, no matter what, I *will* remember Ky. They're too late to take him from me.

"*Now,*" the Official says.

I drop the tablet into my mouth.

It tastes like salt. A drip of sweat running down, or a drop of tears, or, perhaps, a sip of the sea.

CHAPTER 3
KY

The Pilot lives in the Borders, here in Camas.

The Pilot doesn't live anywhere. He or she is always on the move.

The Pilot's dead.

The Pilot can't be killed.

These are the rumors that people whisper in the camp. We don't know who the Pilot is, or even if the Pilot is male or female, young or old.

Our commanders tell us that the Pilot needs us and can't do this without us. We're the ones the Pilot will use to take down the Society—and it's going to be soon.

But of course the trainees can't help but talk about the Pilot any chance they get. Some speculate that the Chief Pilot, the one who oversees our training, is *the* Pilot—the leader of the Rising.

Most of the trainees want to please the Chief Pilot so badly you can feel it rolling off them in waves. I don't care. I'm not in the Rising because of the Pilot. I'm here because of Cassia.

When I first came to this camp, I worried that the Rising

might use us like decoys the way the Society did, but the rebellion has invested too much in our training. I don't think they've trained us to die. But I'm not sure what kind of life they've trained us for either. If the Rising works, what happens next? That's the part they don't often talk about. They say that everyone will have more freedom and that there won't be Aberrations or Anomalies anymore. But that's about all they'll say.

The Society is right about Aberrations. We're dangerous. I'm the kind of person a good citizen imagines coming up behind them in the night—a black shadow with hollow eyes. But, of course, the Society thinks that I already died in the Outer Provinces, another Aberration cleared away.

Dead man flying

"Give me a couple of steep turns," my commander says through the speaker on the panel. "I want a left turn to a south heading and a right turn back to the north heading—one hundred and eighty degrees on each."

"Yes, sir," I say.

They're testing my coordination and mastery of the ship. A coordinated turn with sixty degrees of bank exerts twice the force of gravity on the air ship and on me. I can't make any abrupt corrections or changes or the ship might stall or break apart.

As I perform the turns, I can feel my head, my arms, my whole body sinking into the seat beneath me, and I have to strain to hold myself upright. When I finish, my heart pounds and my body feels unnaturally light at the lifting of the extra pressure.

"Excellent," my commander says.

They say that the Chief Pilot watches us. Some of the trainees think they've ridden with the Chief Pilot—that he's disguised himself as a trainer. I don't believe that. But it's true he could be watching.

I pretend that she is too.

I turn the air ship in the sky. When I first came up it was raining but now all of that is below me.

She's far away right now. But I've always hoped that through some trick of distance and desire she might look up and see something black against the sky and know it's me by how I fly. Stranger things have happened.

And soon I'll be finished with my practice flight and they'll send me out on my real assignment for the night. When they handed out the assignments last week, I couldn't believe my luck. Central. At last. Later tonight, she really could see me flying, if she looks up at the right time.

I bank again and then begin to climb. We only fly alone like this when we're on a training run. Usually, the Rising has us work in groups of three: a pilot, a copilot, and a runner who rides in the hold and takes care of the errands—the forays into the Society that the Rising conducts as stealthily as possible. I like it best when they let the pilots and copilots help the runners and we sneak through the streets of a City on a mission for the Rising.

Tonight, I'm assigned to stay with the ship, but I'll find a way around it. I'm not getting that close to Cassia and then staying on board the whole time we're in Central. I'll find some excuse to leave and run to the lake. Maybe I won't come back, even though in some ways I do fit in with the Rising better than I have anywhere else.

I've had the ideal upbringing to work with the rebellion. I spent years perfecting the art of being unnoticed in the Society, and I had a father who didn't accept the way things were. I understand him better up here, where he has never been, than I ever did on the ground. Sometimes a line from the Thomas poem comes to mind:

And you, my father, there on the sad height,
Curse, bless me now with your fierce tears, I pray.

If I could do what I *really* wanted, I'd gather up everyone I care about and fly them away. I'd swoop down first in Central, for Cassia, and then I'd get everyone else, wherever they might be. I'd find my aunt and uncle, Patrick and Aida. I'd find Cassia's parents and her brother, Bram, and Xander and Em and all the others from the Borough where we grew up. I'd find Eli. Then I'd soar back up again.

You could never fly with that many in this ship. It's too small.

But if I could, I'd take us somewhere safe. I don't know where yet but I'd know it when I saw it. It might be an island somewhere out in the water, where Indie once believed you could find the Rising.

I don't think the Carving itself is safe anymore—but I think out in the old Enemy territory there must be some other secret place where we could run. If you go to a museum now, you see that the Society has changed the Outer Provinces—made them smaller on the map. If the Rising fails to overturn the Society, by the next generation the Outer Provinces might not show on the maps at all. It makes me wonder what's out there that I know nothing about and how else the Society might have altered maps over the years. There must be a world past the Enemy territory. How much has been erased and taken away?

I wouldn't care how small the world became as long as I had Cassia at the center of mine. I joined the Rising so we could be together. But they sent her back to Central and now I keep flying because that's the best way I can think of to get to her, as long as the Society doesn't shoot me down.

There's always that risk. But I'm careful. I don't take unncecessary chances like some of the others who want to impress the Chief Pilot. If I die, I'm no good to Cassia. And I want to find Patrick and Aida. I don't want them to think that they've lost another son. One is enough.

They think of me as their own, but they always saw me

as who I was. Ky. Not Matthew, their son who died before I came to live with them.

I don't know much about Matthew. We never met. But I know that his parents loved him very much, and that his father thought Matthew would be a sorter someday. I know that he was visiting Patrick at work when an Anomaly attacked them.

Patrick survived. Matthew did not. He was just a kid. Not old enough to be Matched. Not old enough to have his final work assignment yet. And certainly not old enough to die.

I don't know what happens after we die. It doesn't seem to me like there can be much past this. But I suppose I can conceive that what we make and do can last beyond us. Maybe in a different place, on another plane.

So. Maybe I'd like to take us somewhere higher, above the world entirely. It's colder the farther up you climb. It could be that if I flew us high enough, all the things my mother painted would be waiting, frozen.

Dead man breathing

I remember the last time I saw Cassia, on the bank of a river. The rain had turned to snow and she told me that she loved me.

Dead man living

I bring the ship in fast and smooth. The ground comes up to meet me, and the sky shrinks down from being all that I can see to a line on the horizon. It's almost completely dark.

I'm not dead at all. I've never been more alive.

The camp feels busy tonight. "Ky," someone says as they pass by me. I nod in return but keep my eyes on the mountains. I haven't made the mistake of getting too comfortable with people out here. I've learned my lesson, again. The two friends I had in the decoy camps are both gone. Vick's dead and Eli's in those mountains somewhere. I don't know what happened to him.

There's only one person here who I'd call a friend, and I knew her from the Carving.

I see her when I push open the door to the meal hall. As always, even though she stands near some of the others, there's a little circle of isolation around her, and people look at her with admiring, perplexed expressions. She's widely regarded as one of the best pilots in our camp. But there's still space between her and everyone else. I've never been able to tell if she notices or cares.

"Indie," I say, walking up to her. I'm always relieved to see her alive. Even though she's an errand pilot like me, not a fighter pilot, I always think she might not make it back. The Society's still out there. And Indie's as unpredictable as ever.

"Ky," she says without preamble. "We've been talking. How do *you* think the Pilot's going to come?" Her voice carries, and people turn to look at us. "I used to believe that the Pilot would come on the water," Indie says. "That's what my mother always told me. But I don't think that anymore.

It's got to be the sky. Don't you think? Water isn't everywhere. Sky is."

"I don't know," I say. This how it always feels to be with her—a mixture of amusement and admiration and exasperation. The few trainees remaining around her mutter excuses and start across the room, leaving us alone.

"Do you have an errand tonight?" I ask her.

"Not tonight," she says. "Are you off, too? Want to walk to the river?"

"I'm on duty," I say.

"Where are you going?"

We're not supposed to tell each other where our assignments are, but I lean closer, so close that I can see the dark blue flecks in the light pools of Indie's eyes. "Central," I say. I waited until now to break the rules and tell her because I didn't want her to try to talk me out of going. She knows that once I get to Central, there's a chance I might find a way to stay.

Indie doesn't blink. "You've been waiting a long time for an assignment there," she says. She pushes her chair away from the table and stands up to leave. "Make sure you come back," she says.

I don't promise her anything. I've never been able to lie to Indie.

I've just started eating when the siren sounds.

Not a drill. Not tonight. This can't happen.

I rise with the rest of the trainees and head outside. Figures, fast and dark like me, run for the ships. By the looks of things, it's a full drill. The runways and fields are crowded with ships and trainees, all following procedure to prepare for the time when we all run one massive errand to take over the Society. I switch on my miniport. *Report to Runway 13,* the message reads. *Group Three. Ship C-5. Copilot.*

I don't think I've flown that ship before, though it doesn't really matter. I'll have flown something like it. But why am I the copilot? I'm usually the pilot, no matter who I'm flying with.

"To your ships!" commanders call out. The sirens keep on shrilling.

When I get closer to the ship I see that the lights are already on and someone's moving inside the cockpit. The pilot must already be on board.

I climb the steps and open the door.

Indie turns to look at me and her eyes widen in surprise. "What are you doing?" she asks.

"I'm the copilot," I say. "Are you the pilot?"

"Yes," she says.

"Did you know they were putting us together?"

"No," she says. She turns back to the panel to start up the engines on the ship, a sound familiar and unnerving at the same time. Then she glances over her shoulder at me, her long braid whipping around. She looks angry. "Why waste two of us on the same ship? We're both good."

The group commander's voice comes in from the speaker in the cockpit. "Begin final checks in preparation for departure."

I swear under my breath. It's a full drill. We're actually going to take flight. I can feel my trip to Central slipping away.

Unless they send us there on our drill. There's still a chance.

Indie leans forward to the speakers in the cockpit. "We're missing our runner," she says.

The door opens and another figure in black comes in. For a moment we can't see who it is, and I think *Maybe it's Vick, or Eli.* Why not? I'm paired with Indie, which feels almost as unlikely.

But Vick is dead and Eli is gone.

"You're the runner?" Indie asks.

"Yes," he says. He looks to be about our age, maybe a year or two older. I don't think I've seen him before, but we get new people all the time in the camp. I catch sight of a few notches on his boots as he walks over to the hatch.

"You were in the decoy villages," I say. There are a good number of us here who were decoys at one time or another.

His voice is flat. "Yes," he says. "My name is Caleb."

"I don't think I knew you there," I say.

"You didn't," he says, and disappears into the hold.

Indie raises her eyebrows at me. "Maybe they put him with us to equal things out," she says. "Two smart, one stupid."

"Do we have cargo for this drill?" I ask.

"Medical supplies," Indie says.

"What kind?" I ask. "Is it real?"

"I don't know," she says. "The cases are all locked."

Moments after Indie lifts us into the sky, the computer in the cockpit starts spitting out flight code.

I pull it out and read it.

"What does it say?" Indie asks.

"Grandia City," I say. *Not Central.*

But Grandia's in the same general direction. Maybe we could keep going past Grandia and on out to Central.

I don't say anything to Indie, not yet.

We leave behind the dark spaces near the mountains where our camps are located and soar over the Boroughs on the outskirts of Camas City. Then we move over the City itself. There's the river that goes through the City, and the taller buildings like the Hall.

A circle of white loops around them.

"How long has that been there?" I ask. I haven't flown directly over the City in almost a week.

"I don't know," Indie says. "Can you tell what it is?"

"It looks like a wall," I say. "Around City Hall and some other buildings."

My uneasiness deepens. I keep my eyes on the control panel, resisting the urge to look over at Indie. Why is there a wall around the center of Camas City? And Indie and I have never been paired up to fly together before. Why now?

Is this how Cassia or Xander felt when they found out they were Matched? *This can't be right. All the odds are against it. So how is it happening?*

Indie's thoughts must be running along the same track as mine. "The Rising matched us up," she says. And then, as Camas City disappears beneath us, she leans closer to whisper to me. "This isn't a drill," she says. "It's the beginning."

I think she's right.

CHAPTER 4
XANDER

The medic finishes examining the little boy and stands up. "Your son is stable," he tells the parents. "We've seen this illness before. People become lethargic and drift into a sleep-like state." He gestures to the other medics, who come forward with a stretcher for the child. "We'll take him to the medical center immediately, where we can give him the best possible care."

The mother nods, her face pale. The father stands up to help with the stretcher but the medics move around him. "You'll need to come with us," the medic says to the boy's parents. He gestures at the three of us Officials, too. "You'll *all* need to be quarantined as a precaution."

I glance over at Official Lei. She's looking out the window now, in the direction of the mountains. People who are from this Province do that, I've noticed. They're always looking to the mountains. Maybe they know something I don't. Is that where the Pilot is?

I wish I could tell the parents of the little boy that everything is going to be fine. The fear on their faces tells me that they're not part of the Rising. They don't know that there's a Pilot or a cure.

But there is. I'm sure of it. The Rising has it all planned out:

The Plague has been making inroads into the Provinces for months. The Society has managed to keep the illness contained, but one day it will break—and the Society will no longer be able to keep up with the spread of the disease. At this point, citizens will know what they have so far only suspected: there is a disease that the Society cannot cure.

When the Plague breaks, that is our beginning.

I'm part of the second phase of the Rising, which means that I'm supposed to wait until I hear the Pilot's voice before I take action. When the Pilot speaks, I'm to report to the main medical center as soon as possible. I don't know what the Pilot sounds like, but my contact within the Rising assured me that I'll recognize the Pilot's voice when the time comes.

This is going to be even easier than I thought. The Society's about to take me in for quarantine. I'll be ready and waiting when the Pilot finally speaks.

The medics hand us all masks and gloves before we climb into the air car. I pull the mask over my face even though I know none of the precautions are necessary for me. I can't get the Plague.

That's the other thing the Rising's tablets do. Not only do they make you immune to the red tablet, they also make you immune to the Plague.

The baby wails as they put on his mask, and I glance over at him in concern. He might get sick, since he was likely exposed to the illness before we could give him the tablet.

But if he does get sick, I remind myself, *the Rising has a cure.*

There's a river that winds through the middle of Camas City. During the daytime the water is blue. Tonight it looks like a broad black street. For a little while we hover along the dark surface of the water on our way into the center of the City.

The main City buildings, including the largest medical center in Camas, are all encircled by a high white wall. "When did that go up?" the father asks, but the medics don't answer.

The wall is new. The Society has built it to keep the Plague contained. It's one of many walls the Rising will have to tear down.

"Don't say you don't know," the father says. "Officials know everything." His voice sounds hard and angry now, and he looks first at Official Brewer, then Official Lei, then at me. I hold his gaze.

"We've told you what we can," Official Brewer says. "Your family is under enough distress. I'd prefer not to add a citation to your difficulties."

"I'm sorry," Official Lei says to the father. I hear almost perfect empathy in her voice. I hope that's the way the Pilot sounds.

The father turns around and faces forward again, his shoulders rigid. He doesn't say anything more. I can't wait to get out of this uniform. It promises more than we can deliver, and it represents something I haven't believed in for a while now. Even Cassia's face changed when she saw me wearing it for the first time.

"What do you think?" I asked her. I stood in front of the port and held my arms out to my sides and turned around, grinning, acting the way the Society would expect me to because I knew they were watching.

"I thought I'd be there when it happened," she said, her eyes wide. I could tell from the tight sound of her voice that she was holding something back. Surprise? Anger? Sadness?

"I know," I said. "They've changed the ceremony. They didn't bring my parents out either."

"Oh, Xander," Cassia said. "I'm sorry."

"Don't be," I said, teasing her. "We'll be together when we celebrate our Contract."

She didn't deny it: not with the Society watching. So there we were. All I wanted was to reach her and it was impossible, since she was in Central and I was in Camas and we were talking through the ports in our apartments.

"Your shift must have ended hours ago," she said. "Does this mean you left your uniform on all day to show off?" She was teasing back, and I relaxed.

"No," I said. "The rules have changed. We have to wear our uniforms all the time now. Not just at work."

"Even when you sleep?" she asked.

I laughed. "No," I said. "Not then."

She nodded and blushed a little. I wondered what she was thinking about. I wished we were together: face to face in the same room. In person, it's a lot easier to show someone what you really mean.

All the questions I had for her crowded my mind.

Are you really all right? What happened in the Outer Provinces?

Did the blue tablets help you? Did you read my messages? Have you figured out my secret? Do you know that I'm part of the Rising? Did Ky tell you? Are you part of the Rising now, too?

You loved Ky when you went into the canyons. So, was it the same when you came out?

I don't hate Ky. I respect him. But that doesn't mean I think he should be with Cassia. I think she should be with whomever she wants to be with, and I still believe it could be me in the end.

"It's nice, isn't it," she said, her face serious and committed, "to be part of something greater than yourself."

"Yes," I said, and our eyes met. Even with all that distance between us, I knew. She didn't mean the Society. She meant the Rising. *We're both in the Rising.* I felt like shouting and singing all at once but I couldn't do either. "You're right," I said. "It is."

"I like the red insignia," she said, changing the subject. "Your favorite color."

I grinned. She'd read the scraps I put in the blue tablets. She *hadn't* forgotten about me while she was with Ky.

"I've been meaning to tell you," she said. "I know I always said *my* favorite color was green. That's what it says on my microcard. But I've changed it."

"So what is it now?" I asked her.

"Blue," she said. "Like your eyes." She leaned forward a little. "There's *something* about the blue."

I wanted to think she was giving me a compliment, but that wasn't it. She wanted to tell me something more. I knew there was meaning beyond what she was saying: but what? Why the addition of the word *the*? Why not say "There's something about blue?"

I think she meant the blue tablets that I gave her back in the Borough. Was she trying to tell me that they saved her, the way we always believed they would? We all knew the tablets were meant to keep us alive in the event of a disaster. I wanted Cassia to have as many as possible when she left, just in case.

When I gave Cassia the tablets, I didn't tell her the truth about how I got them. I tried to find the explanation that would cause her the least worry. What I had to do to get the papers and tablets for her was worth it. I keep telling myself that, and most of the time I believe it.

I don't see any signs of rebellion as we arrive inside the white barricade. The Society appears to be in absolute control of the situation. A huge white tent marks the triage area, and they've set up temporary lights throughout the grounds inside the walls. Officials wearing protective gear oversee everything. Other air cars full of medics and patients land near us.

I'm not worried. I know the Rising's coming. And, without knowing it, the Society has delivered me almost exactly where I need to be. I wish Cassia and I could be together to see it all happen and to hear the Pilot for the first time. I wonder what she thinks of it all. She's in the Rising. She must know about the Plague, too.

"Infected to the right," an Official in a hazmat suit tells our medics. "Quarantine to the left."

I glance over to the left to see where he's pointing. Camas's City Hall.

"They must have run out of space in the medical center," Official Lei says softly to me.

That's a good sign: a very good sign. The Plague is moving quickly. It's only a matter of time before the Rising will need to step in. Already, most of the Society Officials look harried as they direct the traffic of people.

We walk up the steps and into City Hall. For a second I imagine that Cassia's walking next to me and we're on our way to the Banquet.

Official Lei pushes open the doors. "Keep moving,"

someone inside directs us, but I understand why people might stop in their tracks. The Hall has changed.

Inside the huge open area under the dome, there are rows and rows of tiny clear cells. I know what they are: temporary containment centers that can be constructed anywhere in case of an epidemic or pandemic. I've learned about them in my training but have never seen them for myself.

The cells can be taken apart and put together in different configurations, like the pieces of a puzzle. They have their own sewage and plumbing systems inside their floors, and the systems can be piggybacked onto those of a larger building. Each cell has a tiny cot, a slot for food delivery, and a small partition at the back, large enough for a latrine. The most distinguishing feature of the cells, besides their size, is the walls. They are, for the most part, transparent.

Transparency of care, the Society calls it. Everyone can see what is happening to everyone else, and medical Officials can watch their subjects at all times.

The rumor is that the Society perfected this system back in the days when Officials were on the move looking for Anomalies. Sometimes the Society had to set up centers to contain all the Anomalies they found in order to evaluate them, and so that's when they developed the cells. When the Officials from the Safety Department finished tracking down the majority of those they determined to be dangerous, they turned the cells over to the Medical Department for use. The

Society's official story is that these have always existed only for medical quarantine and containment.

Before I joined the Rising, I hadn't heard much about the way the Society methodically culled the Anomalies from the general populace—but I believe it. Why wouldn't I? They did something like it again years later, with Ky and other Aberrations.

I run a quick calculation as I look at all the cells. They're over half full. It won't be long before they're at maximum capacity.

"You'll be in here," an Official says, pointing to Official Brewer. He nods to us and goes inside the cell, sitting down on the cot obediently.

They move past a few empty cells before they stop again. I guess they don't want to put people next to those they know, which makes sense. It's disturbing enough to watch a stranger go down with the illness, even when you know they'll get better.

"Here," the Official says to Official Lei, and she walks inside the cell. I smile at her as the door slides shut and she smiles back. She knows. She has to be part of the Rising.

A few more cells over, and it's my turn. The cell feels even smaller on the inside than it looks on the outside. When I stretch out my arms, I can touch both walls at the same time. A thin sound of music comes through the walls. They're playing the Hundred Songs to keep us from going crazy with boredom.

I'm one of the lucky ones. I know that the Pilot's going to save us, and I also know that I'm not going to get the Plague. And when you're lucky, like my family always has been, it's your responsibility to do the right thing. My parents told us that. "We're on the right side of the Society's data," my father would say, "but it could just as easily have gone the other way. Things aren't fair. It's our job to do what we can to change that."

When my parents discovered that my brother, Tannen, and I were both immune to the red tablet, they became more protective because they realized that we were going to remember things that even they couldn't. But they also told us that this was something important, our immunity. It meant that we would know what *really* happened and we could use that knowledge to make a difference.

So when the Rising approached me, I knew immediately that I wanted to be a part of it.

Something thuds against the wall on the other side of the cell and I turn. It's another patient, a kid who looks like he's about thirteen or fourteen. He's lost consciousness and fallen against the wall without putting his hands out to catch himself. He hits the floor hard.

Within moments, the medics are at the door and inside the cell, masks and gloves on. They lift him up and take him out of the cell and then out of the Hall and, presumably, to the medical center. Some kind of liquid sheets down the walls and a chemical-laced steam boils up from the floor. They're sanitizing the cell to get it ready for the next person.

The poor kid. I wish I could have helped him.

I stretch out my arms again and press against the walls, pushing back so that I can feel the muscles extend all along my arms. I won't have to feel helpless much longer.

CHAPTER 5
CASSIA

A girl sits near me on the air train, wearing a beautiful full-skirted gown. But she doesn't look happy. The confused expression on her face mirrors the way I feel. I know I'm coming home from work, but why so late? My mind is foggy and very tired. And I'm nervous, on edge. Something feels the way it did in the Borough the morning they took Ky away. There's a sharpness in the air, an echo of a scream on the wind.

"Did you get Matched tonight?" I ask the girl, and the moment the words come out of my mouth I think, *What a stupid question.* Of course she did. There's no other occasion besides a Banquet where someone would wear a dress like this. Her dress is yellow, the same color my friend Em wore for her Banquet back home.

The girl looks at me, her expression uncertain, and then she glances down at her hands to see if the answer is there. It is, in the form of a little silver box. "Yes," she says, her eyes lighting up. "Of course."

"You couldn't have the Banquet at Central Hall," I say to the girl, remembering something else. "Because it's being renovated."

"That's right," she says, and her father turns to look at me, an expression of concern on his face.

"So where did you have it?" I ask.

She doesn't answer me; she snaps the silver box open and shut. "It all happened so fast," she says. "I'm going to have to look at the microcard again when I get home."

I smile at her. "I remember that feeling," I say, and I do. *Remember.*

Oh no.

I slip my hand inside my sleeve and feel a tiny scrap of paper there, one that's too small to be a poem. I don't dare take it out on the air train in front of so many eyes, but I think I know what's happened.

Back in the Borough, when the rest of my family took the tablet and I didn't, they all seemed like I do now. Confused, but not completely at sea. They knew who they were and understood most of what they were doing.

The air train slides to a stop. The girl and her family get off. At the last moment, I stand up and slip through the doors. This isn't my station but I can't sit any longer.

The air in Central feels moist and cold. It's not quite dark yet, but I see a hook of moon tipped in the dark blue water of the evening sky. Breathing deeply, I walk down to the bottom of the metal steps and stand off to the side, letting the others pass. I pull out the slip of paper from my sleeve, hiding my hands and their movements in the shadows under the stairs the best I can.

The paper says *remember*.

I've taken the red tablet. And it worked.

I'm not immune.

Some part of me, some hope and belief in what I am, dissolves and disappears.

"*No,*" I whisper.

This can't be true. I *am* immune. I have to be.

Deep down, I believed in my immunity. I thought I would be like Ky, like Xander and Indie. After all, I have conquered the other two tablets. I walked through the blue tablet in the Carving, even though it was supposed to stop me cold. And I've never once taken the green.

The sorting part of my mind tells me: *You were wrong. You are not immune. Now you know.*

If I'm not immune, then what have I forgotten? Lost forever?

My mouth tastes like tears. I run my tongue over my teeth, feeling to see if there's any trace of tablet left. *Calm down. Think of what I remember.*

My most recent memory before the air train is of leaving the sorting center. But why was I there so late? I shift and feel something under my plainclothes, something besides the poems. *The red dress.* I'm wearing it. Why?

Because Ky is coming tonight. I remember that.

I put my hand over my pounding heart and feel the whisper of paper underneath.

And I remember that I have poems to trade and that I carry them next to my skin.

I know how these papers came to me, back when I first got here. I remember it perfectly.

A few days after my arrival in Central, I walked along the edge of the white barrier circling the stillzone. For a moment I pretended that I was back in the Carving; that the barrier was one of the canyon walls and that the windows that lined the apartment buildings all the way up were the caves in the Outer Provinces; crevices in the stone of the canyon where people could hide, live, paint.

But, I realized as I walked, *the outside surfaces of the apartments are so slick and same that even Indie couldn't find a hold on the walls.*

The lawns of the greenspaces were covered in snow. The air felt like it did back in Oria in winter, thick and cold. The fountain in the middle of one of the greenspaces had a marble sphere balancing on a pedestal. *A Sisyphus fountain,* I thought, and I told myself, *I need to be gone by spring, by the time the water runs over it again.*

I thought about Eli. *This is his city, where he came from. I wonder if he feels about it the way I do about Oria; that, in spite of all that has happened, it's still home.* I remembered watching Eli go toward the mountains with Hunter, the two of them hoping to find the farmers who had avoided the Society for so long.

I wondered if the barricade was up when he lived here.

And I missed him almost as much as I missed Bram.

The branches above me were dry, dead, their fingers unleaved and bare. I reached up and snapped one down.

I listened. For something. For some sound of life in that quiet circle. But there were no sounds, really, beyond the ones that can't be stilled—like wind in trees.

But I realize that told me nothing.

In the Society, we don't call out beyond our own bodies, the walls of our rooms. When we scream it is only in the world of our own dreams, and I have never been sure who hears.

I glanced over to make sure that no one was watching, and then I bent down and in the snow near the wall I wrote an *E* for Eli's name.

When I finished, I wanted more.

These branches will be my bones, I thought, *and the paper will be my heart and skin, the places that feel everything.* I broke more branches into pieces: a shinbone, a thighbone, arm bones. They had to be in segments so they would move when I did. I slid them up into the legs of my plainclothes and down into my sleeves.

Then I stood up to move.

It's a strange feeling, I thought, *like my bones are walking along with me on the outside of my body.*

"Cassia Reyes," someone said behind me.

I turned around in surprise. A woman looked back at me, her features unremarkable. She wore a standard-issue gray coat, like mine, and her hair and eyes were brown or gray; it was hard to say. She looked cold. I couldn't tell how long she'd been watching me.

"I have something that belongs to you," she said. "It was sent in from the Outer Provinces."

I didn't answer. Ky had taught me that sometimes silence was best.

"I cannot guarantee your safety," the woman said. "I can only guarantee the authenticity of the items. But if you come with me, I'll take you to them."

She stood up and began walking. In moments she'd be out of sight.

So I followed her. When she heard me coming, she slowed down and let me catch up. We walked, not speaking, along streets and past buildings, beyond the edges of the pools of light from the streetlamps and then to a snarled wire fence enclosing an enormous grassy field, pitted with rubble. Ghostly white plastic coverings on the ground billowed and breathed in and out with the passing breeze.

She ducked through a gap in the fence and I did, too.

"Stay close," she said. "This field is an old Restoration site. There are holes everywhere."

As I followed her, I realized with excitement where I must be going. To the Archivists' *real* hiding place, not the Museum where they did superficial, surface trading. I was going to the place where the Archivists must store things, where they themselves went to exchange poems and papers and information and who knew what else. As I skirted the holes in the ground and listened to the wind rustle the plastic coverings, I knew that I should be afraid, and somewhere deep inside, I was.

"You're going to have to wear this," the woman said, once we were in the middle of the field. She pulled out a dark piece of fabric. "I need to tie it over your eyes."

I cannot guarantee your safety.

"All right," I said, and turned my back to her.

When she was finished tying the cloth, she held me by the shoulders. "I'm going to spin you around," she said.

A little laugh escaped me. I couldn't help it. "Like a game from First School," I said, remembering when we covered our eyes with our hands and played children's games on the lawns of the Borough during leisure hours.

"A little bit like that," she agreed, and then she spun me, and the world whirled around me dark and chill and whispering. I thought of Ky's compass then, with its arrow that could always tell you where north was no matter how often you turned, and I felt the familiar sharp pain that I always had when I thought of the compass, and how I traded his gift away.

"You're very trusting," she said.

I didn't answer. Back in Oria, Ky had told me that Archivists were no better or worse than anyone else, so I wasn't certain I *could* trust her, but I felt that I had to take the risk. She held my arm and I walked with her, lifting my feet awkwardly, trying not to step on anything. The ground felt cold and hard under my feet but every now and then I felt the give of grass, something that had once been growing.

She stopped and I heard the rasp of her pulling something away. *Plastic,* I thought, *that white sheeting covering the remains of the buildings.* "It's underground," she said. "We'll go down a set of stairs, and then we'll reach a long hallway. Go very slowly."

I waited but she didn't move.

"You first," she said.

I put my hands up to the walls, which were close and tight, and felt old bricks covered in moss. I scuffed my foot forward and took one step down.

"How will I know when I've reached the end?" I asked her, and the words and the way I used them made me think of the poem from the Carving, the one I loved the best of those I found in the farmers' library cave, the one that always seemed to speak of my journey to Ky:

I did not reach Thee
But my feet slip nearer every day
Three Rivers and a Hill to cross
One Desert and a Sea
I shall not count the journey one
When I am telling thee.

When I reached the last step, my foot slipped, just like in the poem.

"Keep going," she said from behind me. "Use the wall to guide you."

I dragged my right hand along the bricks while dirt crumbled among my fingers, and after a time I felt the walls open up into the space of a large room beyond. My feet echoed along the ground and I heard different sounds; feet shifting, people breathing. I knew we were not alone.

"This way," the woman said, and she took my arm to guide me. We moved away from the sounds of others.

"Stop," the woman said. "When I take off the blindfold," she told me, "you'll see the items that someone arranged to be delivered to you. You may notice that several are missing. They were the payment for delivery, agreed upon by the sender."

"All right," I said.

"Take your time to look things over," she said. "Someone will come back to escort you out."

It took me a moment—I was disoriented and the place underground was dim—to understand what I was seeing. After a moment, I realized that I was walled-in by two rows of long, empty metal shelves. They looked slick and clean, as if someone cared for them and smoothed away their dust, but even so they reminded me of the crypt of a tomb we saw once in one of the Hundred History Lessons, where there were little caves full of bones and people carved in stone on top of boxes. *So much death*, the Society told us, *with no chance of life afterward. There was no tissue preservation then.*

In the middle of the shelf in front of me, I saw a large packet wrapped in thick plastic. When I pulled back the top edge of the plastic, I found paper. *The pages I brought out of the Carving.* The smell of water and dust, sandstone, seemed to come up from the paper.

Ky. He managed to send them to me.

I put my hands flat on the papers, breathing in, holding on. *He touched these too.*

In my mind, a stream ran and snow fell, and we said good-bye on the bank, and I took to the water and he ran alongside it, bringing these words the length of the river.

I turned through the papers, looking at each page. And in that cold metal aisle, alone, I wanted him. I wanted his hands at my back and his lips speaking poems on mine and our journey to each other to be completed, the miles between us consumed and all distance closed.

A figure appeared at the end of the shelves. I held the papers against my chest and backed up a few steps.

"Is everything all right?" someone asked, and I realized it was the same woman who had brought me. She came closer, the yellow-white circle of her flashlight directed down at my feet and not at my face to blind me. "Have you had enough time to look?"

"Everything appears to be here," I said. "Except for three poems, which I assume are the price you mentioned for the trade."

"Yes," she said. "If that's all you need, then you can go. Come out of the shelves and cross the room. There's only one door. Take the stairs back out."

No blindfold this time? "But then I'll know where we are," I said. "I'll know how to come back."

She smiled. "Exactly." Her gaze lingered on the papers. "You can trade here, if you like. No need to go to the Museum with a cache like that."

"Would I be an Archivist then?" I asked.

"No," she said. "You'd be a trader."

For a moment, I thought she said *traitor*, which of course I was, to the Society. But then she went on. "Archivists work with traders. But Archivists are different. We've had specific training, and we can recognize forgeries that the average trader would never notice." She paused and I nodded to show I understood the importance of what she was saying. "If you bargain with a trader alone, you have no guarantee of authenticity. Archivists are the only ones with adequate knowledge and resources to ascertain whether or not information or articles are genuine. Some say the faction of Archivists is older than the Society."

She glanced down at the pages in my hands and then back up at me. "Sometimes a trade comes through with items worth noting," she says. "Your papers, for example. You can trade them one at a time, if you like. But they will have more value as a group. The larger the collection, the higher the price you can get. And if we see potential in you, you may be allowed to broker others' trades on our behalf and collect part of the fee."

"Thank you," I said. Then, thinking of the words of the Thomas poem, which Ky always thought I might be able to trade, I asked, "What about poems that are remembered?"

"You mean, poems with no paper document to back them up?" she asked.

"Yes."

"There was a time when we would accept those, though the value was less," she said. "That is no longer the case."

I should have assumed as much, from the way the Archivist in Tana reacted when I tried to trade with the Tennyson poem. But I thought that the Thomas poem, unknown to anyone except Ky and me, might have been an exception. Still, I had a wealth of possibility, thanks to Ky.

"You can store your items here," the Archivist said. "The fee is minimal."

Instinctively, I drew back. "No," I told her. "I'll find somewhere else."

She raised her eyebrows at me. "Are you certain you have a secure place?" she asked, and I thought of the cave where the pages had been safe for so long, and the compact where Grandfather kept the first poems hidden for years. And I knew where I'd hide my papers.

I've burned words and buried them, I thought, *but I haven't tried the water yet.*

In a way, I think it was Indie who gave me the idea of

where to hide the papers. She always talked about the ocean. And even more than that, it might have been her odd, oblique manner of thinking—the way she looked at things sideways, upside down, instead of straight on, seeing truth from unexpected and awkward angles.

"I want to trade for something right away, tonight," I told the Archivist, and she looked disappointed. As though I were a child who was about to spend all these fragile beautiful words on something shiny and false.

"What do you need?" she asked.

"A box," I said. "One that fire can't burn, and that won't let in water or air or earth. Can you find something like that?"

Her face changed a little, became more approving. "Of course," she said. "Wait here. It won't take me long." She vanished again along the shelves.

That was our first trade. Later, I discovered the woman's identity and learned that she was the head Archivist in Central City, the person who oversees and directs the trades but doesn't often execute them herself. But, from the beginning, she's taken a special interest in the pages Ky sent me. I've worked with her ever since.

When I climbed out from underground that night, clutching the box full of papers in my chilled hands, I paused for a moment at the edge of the field. It was silver grass and gray and black rubble. I could make out the shape of the white plastic that covered the other excavations, protecting them from a Restoration interrupted and not yet resumed. I wondered what that place used to be and why the Society decided to abandon any attempts at bringing it back.

And then what happened next? I ask myself. *Where did I put the pages after I took them from the Archivists' hiding place?*

For a moment, the memory tries to slip away like a silvered fish in a stream, but I catch hold of it.

I hid the papers in the lake.

Even though they told us the lake was dead, I dared to go into it because I saw signs of life. The bank looked like the healthy streams in the Carving, not the one where Vick was poisoned. I could see where grass had been; in a place where a spring came in and the water was warm, I even saw fish moving slowly, spending the winter deep below.

I crept out through the brush that went up to the edge of the lake, and then I buried the box under the middle pier, under the water and stones that pattern in the shallow part where the lake touches shore.

And then a newer memory comes back.

The lake. That's *where Ky said he'd meet me.*

Once I reach the lake, I switch on the flashlight I keep hidden in the brush at the edge of the City, where the streets run out and the marsh takes over.

I don't think he's here yet.

There are always moments of panic when I come back—will the papers be gone? But then I take a deep breath and put my hands into the water, move away the rocks, and lift out a dripping box filled with poetry.

When I trade the pages, it's usually to pay for the exchange of messages between Ky and me.

I don't know how many or whose hands the notes will go through before they get to Ky. So I sent my first message in a code I created, one that I invented during the long hours of sorts that didn't require my full attention. Ky figured out the code and changed it slightly when he wrote me back. Each time, we build upon the original code a little, changing and evolving it to make it harder to read. It's not a perfect system—I'm sure the code can be broken—but it's the best we can do.

The closer I get to the water, the more I realize that something is wrong.

A thick cluster of black birds has gathered out near the edge of the first dock, and another group of them is congregated farther down the shore. They cry and call to each other, picking at something, some *things*, on the ground. I shine my flashlight on them.

The black birds scatter and screech at me and I stop short.

Dead fish lap along the bank, catch in the reeds. Belly-up, glazed-eyed. And I remember what Ky said about Vick and the way he died; I remember that dark poisoned stream back out in the Outer Provinces and other rivers that the Society poisoned as the water ran down to the Enemy.

Who's poisoning the Society's water?

I shiver a little and wrap my arms more tightly around myself. The papers inside my clothes whisper. Underneath all this death, somewhere in the water, other papers lie buried. It's early spring, but the water is still frigid. If I go in to get the pages now, I won't be able to wait as long for Ky.

What if he comes, and I've gone home cold?

CHAPTER 6
KY

We're getting closer and closer to Grandia. It's time to tell Indie what I want to do.

There are speakers in the cockpit and down in the hold. The commander of our fleet can hear anything I say, and so can Caleb. So I'm going to have to write this out for Indie. I reach into my pocket and pull out a stick of charcoal and a napkin from the camp's meal hall. I always keep these things with me. Who knows when the opportunity to send a message to Cassia might come along?

Indie glances over at me and raises her eyebrows. Silently, she mouths, "Who are you writing to?"

I point at her and her face lights up.

I'm trying to think of the best way to ask her. *In the Carving, I said we should try to run away from all of this. Remember? Let's do that now.*

If Indie agrees to come with me, maybe we can find a way to get Cassia and escape with the ship. I only get one word written down—*In*—before a voice fills the cockpit.

"This is your Chief Pilot speaking."

I feel a little jolt of recognition, even though I've never heard him speak before. Indie draws in her breath, and I shove the charcoal and paper back into my pocket as if the Chief Pilot can see us. His voice sounds rich and musical, pleasing, but strong. It's coming from the control panel, but the quality of the transmission is much better than usual. It sounds like he's actually on the ship.

"I am also the Pilot of the Rising."

Indie and I turn to look at each other. She was right, but there's no triumph in her expression. Only conviction.

"Soon, I will speak to everyone in all of the Provinces," the Pilot says, "but those of you taking part in the initial wave of the Rising have the right to hear from me first. You are here because of your decision to join the Rising and your merits as participants in this rebellion. And you are also here because of another important characteristic, one for which you cannot take credit."

I look over at Indie. Her face looks beautiful, lit up. She believes in the Pilot. Do I, now that I've heard his voice?

"The red tablet doesn't work on you," the Pilot says. "You remember what the Society would have you forget. As some of you have long suspected, the Rising did this—we made you immune to the red tablet. And that is not all. You are also immune to an illness that is even now overtaking Cities and Boroughs throughout the Provinces."

They never said anything about an illness. My muscles tense. What does this mean for Cassia?

"Some of you have heard of the Plague."

Indie turns to me. "Have you?" she mouths.

I almost say *no* but then I realize that I might have. *The mystery illness that killed Eli's parents.*

"*Eli,*" I mouth back, and Indie nods.

"The Society intended the Plague for the Enemy," the Pilot says. "They poisoned some of the Enemy's rivers and released the Plague into others. This, combined with continued attacks from the air, completely eliminated the Enemy. But the Society has pretended that the Enemy still exists. The Society needed someone to blame for the ongoing loss of life of those who lived in the Outer Provinces.

"Some of you were out there in those camps. You know that the Society wanted to eradicate Aberrations and Anomalies completely. And they used your deaths, and the information they gathered from them, as one last great collection of data."

Silence. We all know that what he says is true.

"We wanted to come in and save you sooner," the Pilot says, "but we weren't ready yet. We had to wait a little longer. But we did *not* forget you."

Didn't you? I want to ask. Some of my old bitterness against the Rising fills me, and I grip the controls of the ship tightly, staring out into the night.

"Back when the Society created this Plague," the Pilot says, "there were those who remembered that what is water in one place becomes rain somewhere else. They knew that releasing this disease would come back to us somehow, no matter how many precautions were taken. It created a division among the scientists in the Society, and many of them secretly joined the Rising. Some of our scientists found a way to make people immune to the red tablet, and also to the Plague. In the beginning, we didn't have the resources to give these immunities to everyone. So we had to choose. And we chose *you*."

"He chose us," Indie whispers.

"You haven't forgotten the things the Society wanted you to lose. And you can't get the Plague. We protected you from both." The Pilot pauses. "You've always known that we have been preparing you for the most important errand of all— bringing in the Rising. But you've never known *exactly* what your cargo would be.

"You carry the cure," the Pilot says. "Right now, the errand ships, covered by the fighters, are bringing the cure to the most impacted cities—to Central, Grandia, Oria, Acadia."

Central is one of the most impacted cities. Is Cassia sick? We never knew if she was immune to the red tablet. I don't think that she is.

And why is the Plague in so many places? The largest cities, all sick at the same time? Shouldn't it take longer to spread, instead of exploding everywhere at once?

That's a question for Xander. I wish I could ask him.

Indie glances over at me. *"No,"* she says. She knows what I want to do. She knows that I want to try to get to Cassia anyway.

She's right. That *is* what I want to do. And if it were me by myself, I'd risk it. I'd try to outrun the Rising.

But it's not just me.

"Many of you," the Pilot says, "have been paired with someone you know. This was intentional. We knew it would be difficult for those of you who still have loved ones within the Society to resist taking the cure to your family and friends. We cannot compromise the efficiency of this mission, and we will need to bring you down should you try to deviate from your assigned course."

The Rising is smart. They've matched me with the one person in camp I care about. Which goes to show that caring about *anyone* leaves you vulnerable. I've known this for years but I still can't stop.

"We have an adequate supply of the cure," the Pilot says. "We do not have a surplus. Please don't waste the resources many have sacrificed to provide."

It's so calculated—the way they paired us up, the way they've made just enough of the cure. "This sounds like the Society," I say out loud.

"We are not the Society," the Pilot says, "but we recognize that we have to save people before we can free them."

Indie and I stare at each other. Did the Pilot answer me? Indie covers her mouth with her hand and I find myself, inexplicably, trying not to laugh.

"The Society built barricades and walls in order to try and contain the illness," the Pilot says. "They've isolated people in quarantine in the medical centers and then, when space ran out, in government buildings.

"These past few days have been a turning point. We confirmed that the numbers of those fallen ill have reached a critical mass. Tonight, Match Banquets all across the Society fell apart, from Camas to Central and beyond. The Society kept trying to reconfigure the data, right up until the last moment, but they could not keep up. We infiltrated the sorting centers to accelerate the problem. It wasn't difficult to throw the Matching into disarray. There were silver boxes with no microcards and blank screens without Matches all across the Provinces.

"Many people took the red tablet tonight, but not all of them will forget. The Match Banquet is the Society's signature event, the one upon which all the others rely. Its fall represents the Society's inability to care for its people. Even those who did forget will soon realize that they have no Match and that something is wrong. They'll realize that people they know, too many of them, have disappeared behind barricades and are not coming back. The Society is dying, and it is our time now.

"The Rising is for everyone." The Pilot's voice drops a little as he repeats the motto, becomes deeper with emotion. "But *you* are the ones who will begin it. *You* are the ones who will save them."

We wait. But he's finished speaking. The ship feels emptier without his voice.

"*We're* going to save them," Indie says. "Everyone. Can you believe it?"

"I have to believe it," I say. Because if I don't believe in the Rising and their cure, what hope is there for Cassia?

"She'll be fine," Indie says. "She's part of the Rising. They'll take care of her."

I hope that Indie's right. Cassia wanted to join the Rising, and so I followed her. But now all I care about is finding Cassia and leaving all of this behind—Society, Rising, Pilot, Plague—as soon as we can.

From above, the rebellion against the Society looks black and white. Black night, white barricade around the center of Grandia City.

Indie drops us lower to prepare for landing.

"Go first," our commander tells us. "Show the others how it's done." Indie's supposed to land the ship inside the barricade on the street in front of City Hall. It's going to be tight.

Closer to the earth. Closer. Closer. Closer. The world rushes at us. Somewhere, the Pilot is watching.

Black ships, white marble buildings.

Indie hits the ground smoothly, greasing the landing. I watch her expression. It's one of closely guarded triumph until the ship stops and she glances over at me. Then she smiles—pure joy—and hits the controls that open the door to the ship.

"Pilots, stay with your ships," the commander says. "Copilot and runner, get the cures out."

Caleb hoists up cases from the hold and we each shoulder two of them.

"You first," he says, and I duck through the door and start running the second I'm down the stairs. The Rising has cleared a path through the crowd of people and it's a straight shot to the medical center. It's almost quiet, except for the sound of the fighters covering us above. I keep my head down, but out of the corner of my eye I see Rising officers in black holding back the Officials wearing white.

Keep moving. That's not only what the Rising has asked us to do—it's my own personal rule. So I keep going, even when I hear what's coming across the ports in the medical center.

Now that I know the Pilot's voice, I can tell that it's him singing. And I know the song. The Anthem of the Society. You can tell by the way the Pilot sings it that the Anthem has now become a requiem—a song for the dead.

I'm back in the Outer Provinces. My hands are black and the rocks are red. Vick and I work on figuring out a way to make the guns fire back. The other decoys gather gunpowder to help us. They sing the Anthem of the Society while they work. It's the only song they know.

"Here," a woman in Rising black says, and Caleb and I follow her past rows and rows of people lying still on stretchers in the foyer of the medical center. She opens the door to a storage room and gestures us inside.

"Put them on the table," she says, and we comply.

The Rising officer scans the cases we've brought with her miniport and it beeps. She keys in a code to unlock the cases. The pressurized air inside makes a hiss as it escapes and the lid opens.

Inside are rows and rows of cures in red tubes.

"Beautiful," she says. Then she looks up at Caleb and me. "Go back for the rest," she says. "I'll send some of my officers out to help you."

On the way out, I risk a glance down at a patient's face. Blank eyes. Body still.

The man's face looks empty and undone. Is there even a person inside? How far deep has he gone? What if he knows what's happening but he's trapped there waiting?

My skin crawls. I couldn't do it. I have to *move*.

I'd rather die than be down like that.

For the first time, I feel something like loyalty to the Rising stir inside of me. If this is what the Rising has saved me from, then maybe I do owe them something. Not the rest of my life, but a few runs of the cure. And now that I've seen the sick, I can't compromise their access to the one thing that can help them.

My mind races. The Rising should get control over the trains and bring cures in that way, too. They'd better have someone good working on the logistics of getting the cure out. Maybe that's Cassia's job.

And this is mine.

I've changed since I ran off to the Carving and left the decoys to die. I've changed because of everything I've seen since then, and because of Cassia. I can't leave people behind again. I have to keep running in this damn cure even if it means I can't get to Cassia as soon as I'd like.

Back on the ship, I slide into the copilot's seat and Caleb climbs on board after me.

"Wait," Indie says. "What's that you have?"

Caleb's still holding one of the cases.

"They need *all* the cures," Indie says.

"This is cargo we're supposed to bring back with us," Caleb says, holding up the case for us to see, which doesn't prove anything. It looks exactly like the ones we just took out. "It's part of the errand."

"I didn't know about that," Indie says, sounding suspicious.

"Why would you?" Caleb asks. Something in his tone sounds dismissive. "You're the pilot. Not the runner."

"Indie," our commander says. "Come in."

"We're all here," Indie says, "but we've got some extra cargo. Our runner brought back a case."

"That's approved," the commander says. "Is there anything else?"

"No," Indie says. "We're all clear." She glances over at me and I shrug. Apparently they're not going to tell us anything more about Caleb's second errand.

We wait for the other ships to take their turns departing

from the street in front of the buildings. The computer sends us code again for our destination. Indie reaches for it first.

"Where now?" I ask her, even though I think I know what she'll say.

"Back to Camas," she says, "to get more of the cure."

"And then?" I ask.

"Then we come here again. This is our route, for now." There's a hint of sympathy in her voice. "Someone else will take cures to Central."

"They'd better," I say. I don't care if the Pilot hears. In fact, I hope he does. Why not? Long ago people used to say what they wanted out loud and hope that someone would give it to them. They called it praying.

Cassia has something tangible though—the papers from the Carving. She's only used a few of them to send messages. There must be plenty left for her to use for whatever she needs, maybe even enough to bargain for a cure. Cassia knows how to trade.

We start down the makeshift runway, building up speed.

The white and black uniforms on the ground grow smaller and smaller. We lift up. It's not long before the buildings disappear, too, and then it's all gone.

I can still hear the Pilot singing the Anthem of the Society.

I'm digging a grave for Vick. All day long, he talks to me. I know it means I'm crazy but I can't help hearing him.

He talks to me while Eli and I pull spheres from the stream. Over and over Vick tells me his story about Laney, the girl he loved.

I picture it in my mind—him falling in love with an Anomaly. Telling Laney how he felt. Watching the rainbow trout swim and going to speak with her parents. Standing up to celebrate a Contract. Smiling as he reached for her hand to claim happiness in spite of the Society. Coming back to find her gone.

Is that what's going to happen to me when I finally go to look for Cassia?

Cassia's changed me. I'm a better person now because of her, but it's also going to be harder than ever to get to her.

Indie brings us higher.

Some people think the stars must look closer from up here.

They don't.

When you're up here, you realize how distant they really are—how impossible to reach.

CHAPTER 7
XANDER

Something's happening. But, because the quarantine cells are soundproof, I can't hear anything except the tired sounds of the Hundred Songs.

Through the walls of my cell, I see Officials and Officers staring at the miniports in their hands and the larger ports arranged throughout the Hall. For a few seconds, everyone looks frozen, listening to whatever is coming from their ports, and then some of the people move. One walks over to a quarantine cell and enters a keycode. The person inside the cell steps out and heads for the main doors of the Hall. Another Officer moves into his path, trying to intercept him before he escapes, but right then the doors to City Hall burst open. Figures in Rising black swarm inside.

The Rising has begun. The Pilot's speaking and I can't hear anything.

The Officer releases someone else from a cell. That person heads for the doors, too, and the Rising officers in black hold back others to let her pass. Some of the workers look bemused. Most of them put their hands up in the air in surrender when they see the Rising.

It's got to be my turn soon.

Come on.

A Rising officer appears in front of my cell. "Xander Carrow," he says. I nod. He holds up the miniport, checking my face against the Rising's picture of me, and enters a code into the keypad on the cell. The door slides open and I'm out.

The Pilot's voice comes out over the ports. "This rebellion," he says, "is different. It will begin and end with saving your blood, not spilling it."

I close my eyes for a second.

The Pilot's voice sounds right.

This is the Pilot and this is the Rising.

I wish Cassia and I were together for the beginning.

I start for the door. All I have to do is leave City Hall and walk across the greenspace to the medical center. But then I stop. Official Lei is trapped inside her cell. No one has let her out.

She looks at me.

Is it a mistake that she's still locked in her cell? I pause at the door for a second. But she shakes her head at me. *No.*

"Come on," one of the officers says, pointing me toward the door. I've got to go. The Rising is happening *now.*

Outside, it's chaos. The Rising has cleared the way from City Hall to the medical center, but they're pushing back Officials, some of whom have decided to fight. An air ship screams overhead, but I'm not sure if it's ours until I see it spray warning shots down into an empty spot near the barricade. People scream and step back.

The Rising has thoroughly infiltrated the Army throughout the years. It's strongest in Camas, where most of the Army is stationed. Things should go smoothly here. It's deeper in the Society where we might have some infighting. But with the Pilot the only one speaking from the ports, the rest of the people should follow soon.

Another fighter ship comes over, protecting a heavier-looking ship that drops down to land. When I get to the door of the medical center, it's guarded by Rising officers. They must have already secured the inside. "Xander Carrow, physic," I tell one of the officers. He glances at his miniport to check my data. Runners wearing black sprint from the landing field where the ship came down. They carry cases marked with medical insignia.

Is that what I think it is?

The cure.

The officer waves me inside. "Physics report to the office on the main floor," he says.

Inside the medical center, I hear the Pilot's voice again, coming from the ports all over the building. He's singing the Anthem of the Society. *What would that be like?* I catch myself wondering. *To hear the music in your head and then have it come out sounding right?*

Two officers drag an Official past me. He's weeping and holding his hand over his heart, his lips moving along to the

Anthem. I feel sorry for him: I wish he knew that this wasn't the end of the world. I can see how it would feel that way.

When I get to the office someone hands me a black uniform, and I change into it right there in the hall like the others are doing. I roll up the sleeves because it's time to get to work, and I throw my white Official uniform down the nearest incineration tube. I'll never wear it again.

"We separate the patients into groups of one hundred," the head physic on duty tells me. He smiles. "As the Pilot said, some of the old systems from the Society will remain in place, for now." He points to the rows of patients, whom the Rising personnel have been referring to as the *still*. "You'll be in charge of making sure they get proper care and of overseeing the cure. Once they've recovered and moved on, we'll move new patients to your area."

The ports are silent. Right now they're flashing pictures of the still in Central.

Central: where Cassia is. For the first time I feel a hint of worry. What if she *didn't* join the rebellion and she's watching this? What if she's afraid?

I was so sure Official Lei was part of the Rising.

Could I be wrong about Cassia?

I'm not. She told me that day on the port. She couldn't say the words outright, but I heard it in her voice. I know how to listen, and I could tell she made the jump.

"We're waiting for more nurses and medics to come in,"

the head physic says. "Are you comfortable giving the cure for now?"

This is not like the Society. The lines are already becoming blurred. The Society would never have let me do the work of a medic after my promotion to physic.

"Of course," I say.

I scrub my hands and take one of the tubes from the cases. Next to me, a nurse does the same. "They're beautiful," she says over her shoulder, and I have to agree.

I remove the cover on the syringe and slide the needle into the line so that the cure flows into the patient's vein. The Pilot's voice comes over the ports in the medical center and I have to smile because his words fit perfectly. "The Society is sick," he tells us, beginning his message again, "and we have the cure."

CHAPTER 8
CASSIA

I can't wait here any longer. My whole body trembles with the cold.

Where is he?

I wish I could remember what happened earlier today. Did the Rising's sort come through? Did I do what they needed?

For a minute, anger shivers through me along with the cold. I never wanted to be here in Central. I wanted the Rising to send me to Camas like Ky and Indie. But the Rising didn't find me fit for flying or fighting, only for sorting.

That's all right. I am allied with the Rising, not defined by them. I have my own poems and I know how to trade. Perhaps it's time to use the papers from the Carving to bargain my way out of this place. I've waited long enough.

I look down at all the little fish bodies bumping along the shore, slapping into each other. I shudder at their glossy, dead eyes; their scaly, slick stink. They'll brush against my hands when I reach into the water to get the box. Their smell is so strong that I think I can taste their flesh in my mouth. It will linger on my skin when I've finished.

Don't look. Get it done.

I prop the flashlight on the ground under the dock and peel the papers from my wrists and set them down. I draw my hands up in my sleeves just enough to cover them over so I have a barrier between my skin and the water. As I wade out, I try not to feel the fish against my legs, the steady *bump-bump* of dead little bodies in a lake that used to be a safe place. I hope my clothes are enough to protect me from whatever poisoned this lake.

The smell is overpowering and I can't breathe as I put my hands in. I have to try not to throw up as I feel scales and fins and eyes and tails touching me.

The box is still there; I pull it dripping out of the lake as fast as I can, fish swarming my shins, pushed by the motion of the water. As I wade my way to the shore, little corpses part around and follow behind me.

I carry the box across the grass and away from the lake and crouch down for a moment, hidden in the tangles of brush. As I wipe my hands off on a dry spot on my shirt, I make sure not to drip on the papers I left here earlier.

Would I know the value of these fragile pages if I hadn't seen the place where they'd been hidden? If I couldn't picture Hunter looking through them to find a poem to write on his daughter's headstone? Perhaps that's why I wear them against my skin. Not only to hide them, but to feel them, to remember what it is that I carry.

I think of making myself a garment of words; something

tiled and layered like the scales of the fish behind me. Each page protecting me; paragraphs and sentences shifting to cover me as I move.

But the scales of the fish did not protect them in the end, and as I open the box I recognize something I should have noticed earlier, when I first lifted it. But I was too distracted by all the little bodies.

The box is empty.

Someone's taken my poems.

Someone's taken my poems, and Ky didn't come, and it is cold.

I know it's too late, but I find myself wishing I hadn't come here tonight. Then I wouldn't know everything I'd lost.

As I draw closer to the City and look up at the apartment buildings, I realize that something else is wrong, not just the lake.

It is the middle of the night. But the City has not gone to sleep.

The color of the lights seems strange—blue instead of gold—and it takes me a moment to realize why. The ports in all the apartments are on. I've seen Society-wide broadcasts like this on winter evenings before, when the sun goes down early and we are awake for part of the dark.

But I've never seen people watching ports *this* late.

At least, not that I remember.

What could be so important that the Society would wake everyone up?

I pass through greenspaces, now colored cool blue and gray, and I find my apartment complex and slip through the heavy metal door after entering the keycode. The Society will note my lateness; and someone will speak to me about it. An hour unaccounted for here or there is one thing; this is half a night, the kind of time that could be spent in a myriad of nonapproved ways.

The elevator slides as noiselessly as an air train up to my floor, the seventeenth, and the hallway is empty. The doors are well made, so none of the port light seeps through, but when I open the door to my apartment, the port waits in the foyer, as usual.

My hands fly to my mouth, my body anticipating my need to scream before my mind has taken in what's before me.

Even after my time in the Carving, I could never have conceived of this.

The portscreen is showing me bodies.

It's worse even than those burned, flung-aside, blue-marked corpses on top of the Carving. Worse than the stone rows of graves in the settlement where Hunter put his daughter down with care and farewell. The sheer numbers make this terrible, make it nearly impossible for my mind to take in. The camera goes up and down the rows so that we can see how many bodies there are. Up and down and up and down.

Why are we watching?

Because they're showing the faces. The camera lingers on each person, long enough for us to register either recognition or relief and then it moves on, and we are afraid again.

And then another memory comes to mind—the tubes inside the Cavern in the Carving, where Hunter took us.

Is that what they're doing? Have they found a new way to store us?

But I see now that the people on the screen are alive, though far too quiet and far too still. Their eyes are open and unseeing, but their chests move up and down. Their skin seems strangely dusky and blue.

This isn't death but it is almost as bad. They are here and not here. With us and gone. Close enough to see but out of reach.

Each person is tethered to a clear bag with a transparent tube running into their arm. Do the tubes run all the way through the patients' veins? Are their real veins gone and now they're threaded with plastic? Is this a new plan of the Society's? First they take our memories, then they drain our blood, until we are only fragile skin and haunted eyes, shells of who we used to be?

I remember Indie's wasp nest, the one she carried all through the Carving, the papery circles that used to contain humming, stinging creatures and their busy, brief lives.

In spite of myself, my eyes are drawn to the blank, unseeing gazes on the patients' faces. The people don't look like they are in pain. But they don't look like they are in anything.

The point of view shifts, and now I think we're watching from the ports mounted on the walls of whatever building houses these people. We're looking from another angle, but we're still looking at all of the sick.

Man, woman, child, child, woman, man, man, child.

On and on and on.

How long have the ports been showing this? All night? When did it begin?

They show the face of a man with brown hair.

I know him, I think in shock. *I used to sort with him, here in Central. Are these people in* Central?

The images keep coming, merciless, pictures of people who cannot close their eyes. But I can close mine. I do. I don't want to see anymore. I think about running and I turn blindly toward the door.

And then I hear a man's voice, rich and melodic and clear.

"The Society is sick," he says, "and we have the cure."

I turn slowly back around. But there is no face to put to the voice; just the sound. The ports show only the people lying still.

"This is the Rising," he says. "I am the Pilot."

In the tiny foyer the words echo from the walls, coming back to me from each corner, every surface in the room.

Pilot.

Pilot.

Pilot.

For months I have wondered what it would be like to hear the Pilot's voice.

I thought I might feel fear, surprise, exhilaration, excitement, apprehension.

I didn't think it would be this.

Disappointment.

So deep it feels like heartbreak. I brush the back of my hand against my eyes.

I didn't realize until now that I expected to recognize the Pilot's voice. *Did I think he would sound like Grandfather? Did I think the Pilot would be Grandfather, somehow?*

"We call this illness the Plague," the Pilot says. "The Society created it and sent it to the Enemy in their water."

The Pilot's words come into the silence like carefully selected seeds or bulbs, dropped into hollowed-out spaces in the soil. *The Rising has made these spaces,* I think, *and now they're filling them. This is the moment they come into power.*

The port changes; now we're outside following someone up the steps of Central's City Hall. The view is clear, even in the night, and though the building isn't lit up with special occasion lights, the look of the marble steps and the waiting doors make me think of the Match Banquet. Not even a year ago, I walked up steps much like those back in Oria. What lies behind the doors of Halls across the Society now?

The camera moves inside.

"The Enemy is gone," the Pilot says. "But the Plague the Society gave to the Enemy lives on with us. Look at what has happened in the Society's own capital, in Central, where the Plague first made inroads. The Society can no longer contain the Plague within the medical centers. They've had to fill other government buildings and apartments with the sick."

The Hall is filled, brimming, with even more of the patients.

And now we're outside, looking from above at the white barricade that encircles Central's City Hall.

"There are barricades like this in every Province now," the Pilot tells us. "The Society has tried to keep the Plague from spreading, but they have failed. So many have fallen ill that the Society can no longer keep up even its most important occasions. Tonight, the Match Banquets fell apart. Some of you will remember this."

When I go to the window, I see movement.

The Rising is here, no longer hiding. They fly over us in ships; they are among us in black. How many of them came in from the sky? I wonder. How many simply changed a set of clothes? How deeply and well had the Rising infiltrated Central? Why do I know so little about what is taking place? Is that the Society's fault, for making me forget, or the Rising's, for not telling me enough in the first place?

"When the Plague was first developed," the Pilot says, "there were those of us who saw what might happen. We were able to give some of you immunity. For the rest, we have a cure."

And now the Pilot's voice takes on more emotion, more persuasion, *more*. It becomes bigger; it plays on our emptiness, fills our hearts. "We will keep all the good things from the Society, all the best parts of our way of life. We won't lose all the things you've worked so hard to build. But we'll get rid of the sicknesses in the Society.

"This rebellion," the Pilot says, "is different than others throughout history. It will begin and end with saving your blood, not spilling it."

I start to edge toward the door. I need to run. To try to find Ky. He didn't come tonight to the lake; perhaps this is why. He couldn't get away. But he might still be here in Central, somewhere, tonight.

"Our only regret," the Pilot says, "is that we were unable to step in before *any* lives were lost. The Society was stronger than we were, until now. Now, we can save *all* of you."

On the screen, someone in a black uniform opens a case. It is filled with small red tubes.

Like the tubes in the cave, I think again, *only those were lit blue.*

"This is the cure," the Pilot says. "And now, at last, we have made enough for everyone."

The man on the screen reaches inside the case and takes out a tube, pulling off the cap and revealing a needle. With the smooth confidence of a medic, he plunges the needle into the line. I draw in a breath.

"This illness may look peaceful," the Pilot says, "but I can assure you that it is still fatal. Without medical care, bodies shut down quickly. Patients dehydrate and die. Infection can set in. We can bring you back if we find you soon enough, but if you try to run, we cannot guarantee a cure."

The port goes dark. But not silent.

There are likely many reasons they chose this Pilot. But one of the reasons has to be his voice.

Because when the Pilot starts to sing, I stop to hear.

It's the Anthem of the Society, a song I have known all my life, one that followed me into the canyons, one that I will never forget.

The Pilot sings it slow, and sad.

The Society is dying, is dead.

Tears stream down my cheeks. In spite of myself, I find that I am crying for the Society, for its end. For the death of what did keep some of us safe for a very long time.

The Rising told me to wait.

But I am no longer any good at that.

I feel my way along the long underground hallway, crumbles of green moss coming off in my hands, and I wonder at how thick and fast things can grow here, below. Somehow,

I rarely seem to run into anyone going or coming, though the fear of putting out my hand to touch stone and feeling skin instead is always there.

I couldn't find Ky, so I've come to ask the Archivists what they know. They might lean one way or the other—Society or Rising—but it seems to me that they are Archivists above all.

Today, everyone isn't hidden among their own shelves, tucked away in their own trades. The Archivists and traders have gathered in the larger main room and stand in clusters, talking. Of course, the largest group has gathered around the head Archivist. I might have to wait a long time to speak with her. To my surprise, when she sees me, she separates herself out to come talk with me.

"Is the Plague real?" I ask.

"That information is worth quite a bit," she says, smiling. "I should ask for something in exchange."

"All my papers are gone," I tell her.

Her face changes, shows genuine regret. "No," she says. "How?"

"They were stolen," I say.

Her expression softens. She hands me a piece of paper, a curl of white from one of the illegal Archivist ports. As I look around the room, I notice that many of the people hold slips of paper like mine.

"You're not the only one who wanted to know if the Plague was real," she says. "It is."

"*No,*" I breathe out.

"We suspected a Plague even before the stillzone barrier went up," she says. "The Society was able to keep it contained for a long time, but now it's spreading. Quickly."

"Who told you?" I ask. "Was it the Rising?"

She smiles. "We hear things from the Rising *and* the Society. But Archivists have learned to be wary of both." She gestures to the paper I hold in my hand. "We have a code for times like these. We've used it for a long time to warn one another of illness. The lines come from a very old poem."

I look down and read it.

Physic himself must fade.
All things to end are made;
The plague full swift goes by.
I am sick, I must die.

I grip the paper tightly in my hand. "Who is the physic?" I ask, thinking of Xander.

"No one," she says. "Nothing. The important word here is *plague*. The physic isn't anyone special." She tilts her head. "Why? Who did you think it might be?"

"The Leader of the Society," I say, hedging. Even after all my trading with the head Archivist, I'm hesitant to tell her about Xander, or Ky.

She smiles. "There *is* no Leader of the Society," she says. "They rule by committees of Officials from different departments. Surely you've figured that out by now."

She's right. I have. But it's strange to hear confirmation of what I've suspected. "What about the Plague, then?" I ask. "There must be other mentions of it in your Archives."

"Oh, there are," the Archivist says. "Plagues are mentioned everywhere, in literature, histories, even poetry, as you've seen. But they all say the same thing. People die until someone finds a cure."

"Will you tell me if my papers surface somehow?" I ask. "If someone else brings them to trade?"

I already know the answer but it's difficult to hear. "No," she says. "Our job is only to certify authenticity of items and keep track of our own trades. We do not ask anyone to account for the items they bring here."

I knew that, of course. Otherwise, I would have had to explain how I came by my papers in the first place. In a way, I stole them, too.

"I could write some poems," I say. "I've thought of them before—"

The head Archivist interrupts me. "There's no market for that," she says, her voice matter-of-fact. "We deal in old things of established worth. And some new things whose value is obvious."

"Wait," I say, my idea taking hold and making me reckless. I can't help it—I picture it: all of us coming together to trade. For some reason I imagine the scene taking place in a City Hall, under the dome, only instead of wearing bright dresses we are bearing bright pictures, holding colorful words, humming snatches of new melodies under our breaths, unafraid of being caught out, ready to be asked, *What song is this you sing?*

"What if," I say, "we started another line of trading, using *new* things that we've made? I might want someone else's painting. They might want my poem. Or—"

The Archivist shakes her head. "There's no market for that," she says again. "But I *am* sorry about your papers." Her voice rings with the loss only felt by a true connoisseur. She knew what those pages were worth. She saw the words, smelled the faint aroma of rocks and dust that clung to them.

"So am I," I say. And my loss is much deeper, more visceral and essential. I have lost my way to get to Ky, the insurance I always had that if I stopped believing in the Rising, or if things went terribly wrong, I could trade my way to Ky, to my family. Now I have very little left, and even the Thomas poem, which no one else knows, won't be nearly enough to get me there without the actual document.

"You have, of course, two items in transit," the Archivist says. "When those items arrive, you'll be able to take possession of them immediately since you have already paid in full."

Of course. The *I did not reach Thee* poem. Grandfather's microcard. Will they still come through?

"And you may keep running trades for us," the Archivist says, "as long as you prove trustworthy."

"Thank you," I say. At least there's that. The small amount I get as payment for the trades won't be much, but perhaps I can start to accrue something.

"Some things will remain valuable no matter who is in charge," the Archivist tells me. "Others will change. The currency will shift."

She smiles. "It is always," she says, "so interesting to watch."

PART TWO

POET

CHAPTER 9
XANDER

I'm dying," the patient tells me. He opens his eyes. "It's not very hard."

"You're not dying," I assure him, taking a cure from my case. I've seen more and more of this as the weeks go on. People know the symptoms of the Plague now and they often come in before they go down. "And this red? It's the color of the tube, not the cure. It will start working soon." He's old, and when I reach out to pat his hand, the skin feels very fragile. In the Society he could have expected to die in the next few years. Now, who knows? Maybe he's got plenty of time left. All we have to do is get him through this Plague.

"You *promise*," he says, looking right at me. "You give me your word as a physic."

I promise.

I hook up a vital-stats machine to him so that we'll be alerted if his heart stops beating or if he quits breathing. Then I move on to the next patient. We're keeping up, but it takes every minute of every shift.

The outbreak of the Plague happened sooner than the Rising had anticipated. Overall, the takeover of the Society has gone well, but it hasn't been perfect. People have accepted the Rising because they want the cure. We've got their loyalty, for now. But there are still Society sympathizers and those who are just plain scared of what's happening. They don't trust anyone. That's what we're trying to change. The more people who come in sick and go out cured, the better. Then everyone can see that we're here to help.

"Carrow." The head physic's voice comes across my miniport. "We have a new group assembling in the conference hall for their welcome speech."

"Of course," I say. This is another part of my job. "I'll come right away."

I nod to the nurses on duty on my way out the door. Once I finish the speech, my shift's over, so I won't come back here tonight unless there's an emergency. "See you tomorrow," I say to them.

I fall into step with the others walking to the conference room. I haven't gone far when I hear someone say my name: *"Carrow."* There's a crowd of people in black pressing down the hall, and it takes me a second to figure out who called to me, but then I see her.

"Official Lei," I say, before I remember that it's just Lei now. The Rising's done away with titles. We only use last names. The last time I saw her was almost two months ago, back when the Plague first came and she was stuck in quarantine. She couldn't have been in for long—the Rising let everyone in the cells go home as soon as the Boroughs and

Cities were secure. But I still walked away and left her there.

"I'm sorry—" I begin, but she shakes her head.

"You did what you needed to do," she says. "It's good to see you."

"You too," I say. "Especially here. Does this mean you've joined the Rising?"

"I have," she says, "but I'm afraid I need your help to stay here."

"Of course. What can I do?"

"I was hoping you would vouch for me," she says. "If you don't, I can't stay."

Each member of the Rising is only allowed to vouch for three other people. Obviously we want everyone to join eventually, but right now we've got to be careful. Vouching for someone isn't something you can take lightly. I've always assumed that my three people would be my parents and Cassia, if she needed it, in case I was wrong about her being in the Rising.

If someone that you vouch for turns out to be a traitor, you'll be investigated right along with them. So: how much do I trust Lei?

I'm about to ask Lei if there's anyone else she can ask, but something about the tightness around her mouth and the way she stands—her posture even more perfect than usual—makes me realize that no, there isn't. She doesn't look away. I'd forgotten how we're almost exactly the same height.

"Of course," I say. I'll still have two people left. If something happens and I was wrong about Cassia, my brother, Tannen, can vouch for one of our parents. He's probably planning on it anyway. Not for the first time, I wish I'd had a chance to talk to him about the Rising.

Lei puts her hand on my arm, very briefly. "Thank you," she says. Her voice sounds lovely and sincere, and a little surprised. She didn't think I'd do it.

"You're welcome," I say.

"If you're here," I tell the new workers, "it means that you've met the three main qualifications required to work in the medical center. First, you have medical training. Second, you're safe, because you either contracted the Plague immediately and have since been cured, or you received an immunization when you applied to return to work. Third, you've joined the Rising."

I pause and let the silence settle before I begin again.

"You are now a part of this rebellion. You might not have known the Rising existed until you heard the Pilot speak, or you may have only come to believe in the Rising now that you've seen our cure, or because you want our immunity. We don't hold that against you, of course. We're grateful for your assistance. Our immediate goal is to save people from the Plague."

I smile out at them, and almost everyone smiles in return. They're glad to be back at work and part of the solution. Some of them look downright eager.

Then a woman calls out, "If that's true, then why didn't you—I mean we—immunize everyone *before* they got sick? Why wait until they need the cure?"

One of the Rising officers at the back moves forward, but I hold up my hand. The Rising has given me all the information I need to field a question like this. And it's a good question.

"Why didn't we stockpile immunizations as well as cures?" I ask. "That's what you want to know, isn't it?"

"Yes," she says. "It would be easier and more efficient to keep people from getting sick in the first place."

"The Rising had limited resources," I say. "We decided that focusing on the cure was the best use for those resources. There was no way to warn the public about the possibility of the Plague before it happened without causing panic. And the Rising didn't want to immunize you without your permission. We're not the Society."

"But you—we—immunized the babies," she point outs. "Without their permission."

"That's true," I say. "The Rising felt that immunizing the infants was important enough that we diverted some of the resources in that direction. As you all know, infants suffer most during times of illness, and even a cure can't guarantee a positive outcome in all cases with children so small. In this case, the decision was made to immunize without permission. And the result is that we haven't seen anyone under the age of two years come in sick." I let that sink in. "Now that the Rising is fully in power, we've already been able to shift additional resources over to making immunizations. We'll save everyone eventually, one way or another."

She nods, apparently satisfied.

There's another reason, of course, but I don't say it out loud: If the Rising had secretly immunized people, the people wouldn't know whom to thank for saving them. They wouldn't even know they *had* been saved. The Rising didn't start this Plague. They solved it. And the people need to know that. They can't appreciate the solution unless they know there had been a problem.

So, the Rising had to let some people become sick. But in most revolutions, many have to die.

This is much better.

"It's my job to remind you," I say, looking out over the group, "that each of you are here because you have been vouched for by a member of the Rising. They've taken a chance on you, one they believe was warranted. Please don't disappoint them, or us, by trying to sabotage what we're doing here. We're working to save people."

I'm not sure where Lei is in the room and I'm glad. I'm speaking to everyone, not only to her.

"Now," I say. "Let me describe the basic procedures for taking care of the sick. You'll receive more specific instructions and your initial shift assignments as you leave the room. Some of you will go straight to work and others will be assigned to rest and take your turn later."

I run through the basic steps of protocol, reminding the workers about proper antiseptic techniques and procedures like hand washing and disinfecting supplies and equipment. These practices are especially important since this virus can be spread through contact with bodily fluids. I tell them about the admittance system and the initial medical exams, that we're short on pressurized mattresses so we need to turn some patients by hand. I describe the wound vacuums we use for sealing off the lesions to try to stave off infection.

You can hear a pin drop when I get to the part that they all find the most interesting: the cure.

"Administering the cure is very similar to what you saw on the portscreens when the Pilot first spoke to everyone," I say. "A negative reaction is almost unheard of, but if it does occur, it'll take place within the first half hour of cure administration."

"What is the adverse reaction?" a man asks.

"Patients stop breathing," I say. "They have to be intubated. But the cure still works. They just need help breathing for a while. Obviously, only medics are allowed to intubate."

"Have you ever seen a bad reaction?" he asks.

"Three times," I say. "And I've been working at this medical center since the Rising took over here." In some ways it feels like no time at all and in other ways it feels like it's been my whole life.

"How long does it take for the cure to work?" someone else calls out.

"Often, patients are fully alert within three or four days," I say, "and they move to the recovery area of the medical center by day six. They'll stay there for a few more days before going back out to their families and friends. The cure is extremely potent."

Some eyes widen and people look at each other in surprise. They've seen people come out of the medical centers, of course, but they didn't know just how fast the cure kicked in.

"That's all," I say. I smile at everyone. "Welcome to the Rising."

They all start clapping and someone cheers loudly. The room is full of excitement. They're all glad to be back doing something that matters instead of sitting outside the barricade walls. I understand. When I'm giving people the cure, I know I'm doing the right thing.

I stare up at the sleeproom ceiling and listen to everyone breathing. Somewhere out in the medical center, Lei's working with the patients. I'm glad she's part of the Rising now: She'll take good care of the still. I wonder why she didn't join earlier. Maybe she just didn't know about the Rising. People didn't talk openly about the rebellion, after all.

I'm sure Tannen's part of the Rising. Like me, he would have recognized the rebellion as our responsibility the minute he heard about it, and he's immune to the tablet, too. He's a perfect fit.

I never could figure out why Ky didn't join the Rising

right away, back when they first asked us. The Rising could have helped him. But he didn't, and he wouldn't tell me why.

Even before Cassia went out into the Outer Provinces to find Ky, you could tell that she might do something big. Like that day at the pool when she finally decided she was ready to jump: She went into the water without looking back. So I shouldn't have been surprised at the way she fell in love with Ky because it's the way I wanted her to fall in love with me: completely.

The only time I was tempted to try to get out of the Rising was when Cassia and I were Matched. For a few months there, I played both sides in the game, doing what the Rising wanted and acting Society at the same time so that I could stay Matched to Cassia. But it didn't take me long to realize—I wanted Cassia to *choose* me. In some ways, our being Matched is the biggest strike against me. How was she supposed to love me when the Society said she should?

After Cassia told me that she was falling for Ky, I realized that if he left, she'd go too. She'd jump. It wasn't hard to recognize that the Society wouldn't let Ky live in Mapletree Borough forever, and anywhere he went might be dangerous.

I had to send something with her: something that could help her and that would remind her of me.

So I printed out the picture from the port and went outside to get the newrose petals. But those were both things to remind her of the past. I decided that wasn't enough. I wanted to give her something that could help her in the future and that would make her think of me.

It was kind of ironic that Ky was the one who'd told me about the Archivists. Without him, I might not have known how to trade.

All I had to give the Archivists was the silver box from my Banquet. In exchange, they gave me a piece of paper printed from one of their ports—all the information I told them from my official Matching microcard, plus a few changes and additions of my own.

Favorite color: red.

Has a secret to tell his Match when he sees her again.

That was the easy part. Getting the tablets was harder. I didn't fully understand what the Archivists were asking of me when I agreed to the trade.

But it was all worth it. The blue tablets kept Cassia safe. She even told me that on the port: *There's* something *about the blue.*

I roll over onto my side and stare at the wall.

The night of the Banquet, when I waited at the air-train stop with my parents and my brother, I hoped Cassia and I would be on the same train. That way we could at least ride to the City together before everything changed. And she came up the stairs, holding on to the skirt of her green dress. I saw the top of her head first, then her shoulders and the green of the silk against her skin, and finally she looked up and I saw her eyes.

I knew her then and I know her now. I'm almost sure of it.

CHAPTER 10
CASSIA

I hurry along the edge of the white barricade, which runs near the Museum. Before the Rising boarded up the Museum's windows, you could see the stars and scatters of broken glass. People tried to break in the night we first heard the Pilot's voice. I don't know what they hoped to steal. Most of us realized long ago that the Museum holds nothing of value. Except for the Archivists, of course, but they always know when it's time to hide.

In the weeks since the Rising came to power, we have more, and we have less, than we did before.

I am late home every single day, because I always go to trade after work. Though a Rising officer might tell me to hurry along, he or she won't issue me a citation or warn me against what I am doing, so I have a little more freedom. And, we have more knowledge about the Plague and the Rising now. The Rising explained that they made some people immune to the Plague *and* the red tablet from birth. Which explains Ky's and Xander's ability to remember everything, in spite of having taken the red tablet. It also means that, long ago, the Rising did not choose me.

And we have less certainty. What will happen next?

The Pilot says the Rising will save us all, but we have to help it happen. No traveling—we must try to keep the Plague from spreading and focus resources on curing those who are ill. That, the Pilot says, is the most important thing: stopping the Plague so that we can truly begin again. I've been immunized against the Plague now, as have most in the Rising, and soon, one way or the other, we'll all be safe. Then, the Pilot promises, we can truly begin changing things.

When the Pilot speaks to us, his voice is as perfect as it was the first day we heard it on the ports, and now that we can see him too, it's hard to look away from his blue eyes and the conviction they hold. "The Rising," he says, "is for everyone," and I can tell that he means it.

I know my family is all right. I've talked with them a few times through the port. Bram fell ill with the Plague at the beginning, but he has recovered, just as the Rising promised, and my parents were quarantined and immunized. But I can't talk to Bram about how it felt to have the Plague—we still speak guardedly; we smile and don't say much more than we did when the Society was in power. We aren't quite sure who can hear us now.

I want to talk without *anyone* listening.

The Rising has only facilitated communication between immediate family members. According to the Rising, the Matches of those too young to have celebrated their Contracts no longer exist, and the Rising doesn't have time to track down individual friends for every person. "Would you rather," the Pilot asks us, "spend time setting up communications? Or should we use our resources saving people?"

So I haven't been able to ask Xander what his secret is, the one he mentioned on a slip of paper that I read in the Carving. Sometimes I think I've guessed the secret, that it's as simple as his being in the Rising. Other times, I'm not sure.

It's easy to imagine how people must feel when Xander comes to help them. He bends down to listen to them. Takes their hands in his. Speaks in the honest, gentle tone he used in my dream back in the canyons when he told me I had to open my eyes. Patients must feel healed just seeing him.

I sent a message to Ky and Xander after the Plague broke to let them know that I'm all right. That trade cost more than I could afford after the theft at the lake, but I had to do it. I didn't want them to worry.

I haven't heard anything back. Not a word written on a paper or printed on a scrap. And my trades for the *I did not reach Thee* poem and Grandfather's microcard still haven't come through. It's been so long.

Sometimes, I think the microcard must be held in the hands of a trader gone still in a remote place; that it is lost forever. Because Bram would have sent it to me. I believe that.

When I was working in Tana Province, before I ran away to the Carving, Bram was the one who sent me a message about the microcard, and made me want to view it again. In his message, Bram described some of what he'd seen when he viewed the microcard again:

At the very end is a list of Grandfather's favorite memories. He had one for each of us. His favorite of me was when I said my first word and it was "more." His favorite of you was what he called the "red garden day."

Back in Tana, I convinced myself that Grandfather had made a small mistake—that he had meant to say "red garden days," plural, those days of spring and summer and autumn when we sat talking outside his apartment building.

But lately I've been convinced that that is not the case. Grandfather was clever and careful. If he listed the red garden *day*, singular, as his favorite memory of me, then he meant one specific day. And I can't remember it.

Did the Society make me take the red tablet on the red garden day?

Grandfather always believed in me. He's the one who first told me not to take the green tablet, that I didn't need it. He's the one who gave me the two poems—the Thomas one about not going gentle and the Tennyson one about crossing the bar and seeing the Pilot. I still don't know which one Grandfather meant for me to follow, but he did trust me with both.

Someone waits outside the Museum—a woman standing forlornly in the gray of a spring afternoon that has not yet decided for rain.

"I want to find out more about the Glorious History of

Central," she says to me. Her face is interesting, one I'd know if I saw her again. Something about her reminds me a little of my own mother. This woman looks hopeful and afraid, as people often do when they come here for the first time. Word has spread about the Archivists.

"I'm not an Archivist," I say. "But I am authorized to trade with them on your behalf." Those of us who have been sanctioned to trade with the Archivists now wear thin red bracelets under our sleeves that we can show to people who approach us. The traders who don't have the bracelet don't last long, at least not at the Museum meeting place. The people who come here want security and authenticity. I smile at the woman, trying to make her feel at ease, and take a step closer so that she can better see the bracelet.

"Stop!" she says, and I freeze.

"I'm sorry," she says. "But I noticed—you were about to step on this." She points to the ground.

It's a letter written in the mud; I didn't leave it. My heart leaps. "Did you write this?" I ask.

"No," she says. "You see it, too?"

"Yes," I say. "It looks like an *E*."

Back in the Carving I kept thinking I saw my name, which wasn't true until I found the tree where Ky had carved for me. But this is real, too, a letter written deep in the mud with strong, rough strokes, as though the person who wrote also wanted to communicate intent, purpose.

Eli. His name comes to my mind, although as far as

I know he never learned to write. And Eli's not here, even though this is where he grew up. He's out beyond the Outer Provinces, all the way to the mountains by now.

People are *watching*, I think. *Maybe they, too, will put their hands to the stone.*

"Someone can write," the woman says, sounding awed.

"It's easy," I tell her. "You have the shape of things right before you."

She shakes her head, not understanding what I mean.

"I didn't write this, but I do know how," I tell her. "You look at the letters. Make them with your hands. All it takes is practice."

The woman looks worried. Her eyes are shadowed, and there is something restrained about the way she holds herself, something tense and sad.

"Are you all right?" I ask her.

She smiles; she says the answer that we grew accustomed to giving in the Society. "Yes, of course I am."

I look out toward the dome of City Hall and wait. If she wants to say something, she can. I learned that from watching first Ky, and then the Archivists—if you don't walk away from someone's silence, they just might speak.

"It's my son," she says quietly. "Ever since the Plague came, he hasn't been able to sleep. I tell him over and over again that there's a cure, but he's afraid of getting sick. He wakes all night long. Even though he's been immunized, he's still afraid."

"Oh no," I say.

"We are so tired," the woman says. "I need green tablets, as many as this will purchase." She holds out a ring with a red stone in it. How and where did she find it? I'm not supposed to ask. But if it's authentic, it will be worth something. "He's afraid. We don't know what else to do."

I take the ring. We've seen more and more of this, since the Rising took away the tablets and containers the Society gave us. Though I'm glad to see the red and the blue tablets gone, I know there are people who need the green and who are having a hard time going without. Even my mother needed it once.

I think of her, bending over my bed when I couldn't sleep, and it sends an ache through me and reminds me of how she used to lull me to sleep with the descriptions of flowers. *"Queen Anne's lace,"* she'd say, in a slow, soft voice. *"Wild carrot. You can eat the root when it's young enough. The flower is white and lacy. Lovely. Like stars."*

Once, the Society sent her out to see flowers in other Provinces. They wanted her to look at rogue crops that they thought people might be using for food, as part of a rebellion. My mother told me how in Grandia Province there was an entire field of Queen Anne's lace, and how, in another Province, she saw a field of a different white flower, even more beautiful. My mother talked to the growers who'd cultivated the fields. She saw the fear of discovery in their eyes, but she did her job and reported them to the Society because she wanted to keep my family safe. The Society let her remember what she'd done. They didn't take *that* memory.

My mother spent her life growing things. Could the red garden day memory Grandfather talked about have something to do with her?

The spring breeze cuts around me, tearing the last of the old leaves from the branches of the bushes. It pulls on my clothes, and I imagine that if it took them from me, the last of my papers would soar out into the world, and I know it is time for me to stop holding certain things so close.

The woman has turned to look in the direction of the lake, that long stretch of water glinting in the sun.

Water, river, stone, sun.

Perhaps that is what Ky's mother would have sung to him as she painted on the rocks in the Outer Provinces.

I press the ring back into the woman's hand. "Don't give him the tablets," I say. "Not yet. You can sing to him. Try that first."

"What?" she asks, looking at me in genuine surprise.

"You could sing to him," I say again. "It might work."

And then her eyes open a little wider. "I could," she says. "I have music in me. I always have." Her voice sounds almost fierce. "But what *words* would I sing?"

What would Hunter, back in the farmers' settlement, have sung to his child, Sarah, who died? She believed in things that he did not. So what would he have said that could bridge the gap between belief and unbelief?

What would Ky sing? I think of all the places we've been together, all the things we've seen:

Wind over hill, and under tree.
Past the border no one can see.

I wonder, standing there with the mother of the sleepless child, something that I have wondered before—when Sisyphus reached the top of the hill, was there someone for him to see? Was there a stolen touch before he found himself again at the bottom of the hill with the stone to push? Did he smile to himself as he set, again, to rolling it?

I've never written a song, but I have started a poem before, one I could not finish. It was for Ky, and it began:

I climb into the dark for you
Are you waiting in the stars for me?

"Here," I say, and I pull a charred stick from my sleeve and a paper from my wrist.

I write carefully. No words have ever come to me so easily, but I can't make a mistake in writing them out or I'll have to go back to the Archivists for more paper. And I have the poem all in my head, right now, so I write quickly for fear that I might lose some of it.

I always thought my first finished poem would be for Ky.

But this seems right. This poem is between the two of us, but also for others. It is about all the places you find someone you love.

> *Newrose, oldrose, Queen Anne's lace.*
> *Water, river, stone, and sun.*
>
> *Wind over hill, under tree.*
> *Past the border none can see.*
>
> *Climbing into dark for you*
> *Will you wait in stars for me?*

I have turned one of the beginnings I wrote for Ky into an ending. I have written something all the way through. After a moment of hesitation, I write my own name at the bottom of the page as the author.

"Here," I say. "You can put music behind it, and it will be your own." And it strikes me that this is how writing anything is, really. A collaboration between you who give the words and they who take them and find meaning in them, or put music behind them, or turn them aside because they were not what was needed.

She doesn't take it at first. She thinks she has to offer me something in return.

At that moment I realize that the idea I had about trading art was all wrong.

"I am *giving* it to you for your son," I say. "From me. Not from the Archivists. And not as a trader."

"Thank you," the woman says. "That's very kind." She seems surprised and gratified, and she slides the paper up into her sleeve, imitating me. "But if it doesn't work—" she begins.

"Then come back," I say. "I'll get the green tablets for you."

After I leave the woman, I make my way to the Archivists' hiding place to see if they have more work for me, and to check on my things. After the theft of my belongings, I asked the Archivist to store my case for me. They keep it somewhere back in a hidden room, one I've never even seen. Only a few of the Archivists have keys.

They bring me out my case and I look inside. Once filled with priceless pages, my case now holds a roll of paper from a port, a pair of Society-issued shoes, a white shirt that was once part of some Official's uniform, and the red silk dress I wore when I thought I would see Ky at the lake. The poems I have left I keep with me always. Together, everything does not make up an impressive collection, but it's a start. It's only been a few weeks. Either the Rising will take me to the ones I love or I will find a way to do it myself.

"It's all here," I say to the Archivist helping me. "Thank you. Is there any further trading you need me to do today?"

"No," he says. "You're welcome, as always, to wait outside the Museum to see if anyone approaches you."

125

I nod. If I hadn't talked the woman out of the trade earlier today, I'd be on my way to another item for my collection.

I tear off a long strip of port paper from the roll and wrap it around my wrist, under my plainclothes. "That will be all," I say to the Archivist. "Thank you."

The head Archivist catches my eye as I come out from the shelves. She shakes her head. *Not yet.* My poem and the microcard still haven't come through.

Sometimes I wonder if the head Archivist is the *real* Pilot, steering us into the waters of our own want and need and helping us come out safely in little boats filled with different things for each person, the items we need to begin our true, right lives.

It's not impossible.

What better place to run a rebellion than down here?

When I climb the steps and emerge above ground, I smell grass coming up, and feel night coming down.

Back in the City, I'm not sure I can do it. I've held on to the poem for so long. Perhaps I'm spending and giving too much now.

But my biggest regrets are from saving and holding back. I kept my poems too long and they were stolen; I never taught Xander or Bram to write. Why didn't I think to do that? Bram and Xander are smart; they could learn on their own, but sometimes it is good to have someone help you in beginning.

I creep out into the dark and unroll the spool of paper from my wrist. I drape the paper along the smooth, cool metal surface of one of the benches in the greenspace, and then I write, pressing down carefully with a charcoaled stick. They're so easy to make if you know how, a dip of a branch into the incinerator. When I finish, my hands are black and cold and my heart feels red, warm.

The branches of the trees hold out their arms and I drape the paper over them. The wind moves gently, and it seems the trees cradle the words as carefully as a mother would a small child. As carefully as Hunter held Sarah when he carried her to her grave in the Carving.

In the white light of the streetlamps, it feels that this greenspace might only live in a high flight of imagination or the depth of a dream. I wonder if I will wake up and find it all gone. These paper trees, this white night. My dark words waiting for someone to read them.

I know Ky will understand why I have to write this, why there was nothing else that would suffice.

> *Do not go gentle into that good night.*
> *Rage, rage against the dying of the light.*

Even if it's a Society sympathizer who takes them down, he will see the words as he pulls the papers from the tree. Even if he burns them, they will have slipped through his fingers on the way to fire. The words will be shared, no matter what.

> *Good men, the last wave by, crying how bright*
> *Their frail deeds might have danced in a green bay,*
> *Rage, rage against the dying of the light.*

There are many of them in the world, I think, good men and women with their frail deeds. Wondering what might have been, how things might have danced, if we had only dared to be bright.

I have been one of them.

I unwind more paper and see the line

> *Wild men who caught and sang the sun in flight*

I weave the papers through the branches. A long loop. Up and down, my knees bending. My arms above my head, like the girls I saw once in a painting in a cave. There is a rhythm to this, a keeping of time.

I wonder if I am dancing.

CHAPTER 11
KY

Are you jumping today?" one of the other pilots asks me. Our squadron walks along the path next to the river that twists and turns through the City of Camas. At one spot in the river—down near City Hall and the barricade—the river becomes a series of falls. A gray heron slices through the swift waters near us.

"No," I say, not bothering to hide the irritation in my voice. "I don't see the point of it."

"It's a sign of unity," he says. I turn to look at him a little more closely.

"We all work for the Rising, don't we?" I ask. "Isn't that all the unity we need?"

The pilot, Luke, falls silent and walks a little faster, so that I'm alone at the back of our group. We've been given a few hours off and everyone wanted to go into the City. For many of us, it still feels dangerous and exhilarating to walk freely through the streets of a City that used to be Society, even though the Rising has had full power in Camas for some weeks now. As expected, Camas was the first and easiest

Province for the Rising to take over—so many insurgents live and work here.

Indie falls back to walk with me. "You should jump," she says. "They all want you to do it."

Some of the other squadrons have started jumping into the river. Though it's officially spring now, the water comes down from the mountains and it's frigid. I have no plans to go in the river. I'm not a coward, but I'm also not stupid. This isn't the safe, warm blue pool of the Borough. After the Sisyphus, and what happened when Vick died—

I don't trust the water anymore.

Many people walk the river paths today. The sun feels warm on our backs. The Rising has asked everyone to keep to their Society-assigned jobs for now, until the Plague is fully contained, so most people are at work. But still, there are childcare providers bringing little kids to throw stones into the river, and workers with foilware trays, enjoying the new freedom of eating their lunch wherever they want. All of these people must be immune or cured to walk so freely. They're like us. They know they're safe.

I glance at the barricade wall, which also runs near the river. Even though the Rising is firmly in control, there are still restrictions for now as to where we can go. The medics and workers behind the walls can't come out. They eat and sleep and breathe the Plague.

Cassia told me that Xander was assigned to Camas. It's strange that he might be on the other side of that barricade, working in the medical center. Our paths haven't crossed in Camas, though we've both been here for months. I wish I had seen Xander. I'd like to talk to him. I'd be interested to hear what he thinks of the Rising—if he's found it everything he hoped it would be.

I don't wonder if he still loves Cassia. I'm sure that he does.

I haven't heard anything from her since the Plague broke, but they've immunized everyone in the Rising who wasn't already immune. So I think she's safe, one way or the other. But I don't *know*.

I sent her a message as soon as I could, telling her how sorry I was that I couldn't reach her that night at the lake. I asked her if she was all right and told her that I loved her.

I traded four of my foilware pilot meals for that, and it was worth it, though I can't do it too often or I'll get in trouble.

The silence from Cassia is making me crazy. Every time I fly, I have to keep myself from taking off and risking everything to try to get to her. Even if I managed to steal a ship, the Rising would shoot me down. *You won't do her any good if you're dead,* I remind myself.

But I'm not doing her much good by staying alive, either. I don't know how much longer I can wait before I'll have to risk it.

"Why *not* jump?" Indie asks, still needling at me. "You can swim."

"What about you? Are you going in?" I ask Indie.

"Maybe," Indie says. Everyone's still a little perplexed by Indie, but more and more they also respect her. It's hard not to after you've seen her fly.

I'm about to say something more to her, but then I recognize a face in the crowd. One of the traders who used to bring me notes from Cassia. I haven't seen this particular trader in a long time. *Does she have something for me today?*

The way Archivists trade is different now. The Rising closed down the Society's Museums, saying they were filled with nothing more than propaganda. So we have to wait outside of the Museums to make contact or find each other in the crowds.

The handoff is quick, as usual. She passes me, keeping her gaze level and cool, and we bump into each other slightly, the jostling normal on a crowded path. From the outside, I'm sure it all looks perfectly natural, but she's handed off something to me—a message. "I'm sorry," she says, meeting my eyes briefly. "I'm late."

She's acting as if she bumped into me because she's in a hurry to get somewhere on time, but I know what she means. The message is late, likely because she's had the Plague. How did she manage to hold on to the paper? Did anyone else read it while she was still?

My heart races like a rabbit in search of cover out on the plateau. This note has to be from Cassia. No one else has ever sent anything to me. I wish I could read it *now*. But I'll have to wait until it's safe.

"If you could fly anywhere, where would you go?" Indie asks.

"I think you know the answer to that," I tell her. I slip the paper into my pocket.

"Central, then," Indie says. "You'd fly to Central."

"Wherever Cassia is."

Caleb looks back at us and I wonder if he saw the exchange. I doubt it. The trader was fast. I can't figure Caleb out. He's the only one who brings cases back when we're dropping off the cure. None of the other ships are taking on cargo. The commander always tells us it's approved, but I think there's more going on than we know. And I think Caleb has been assigned to work with Indie and me to watch one of us—but I can't figure out which of us it is. Maybe both.

"What about you?" I ask Indie, keeping my tone light. "If you could fly anywhere, where would you go? Back to Sonoma?"

"*No,*" she says, as if the suggestion is ridiculous. "I wouldn't go back to where I'm from. I'd go someplace I've never been."

My fingers close around the paper in my pocket. Cassia told me once that she wears some of the pages against her skin. This is the closest I can get to touching or seeing her right now.

Indie watches me. And then, as she often does, she says something disconcerting. Unexpected. She leans closer and speaks quietly so that the others can't hear. "I've been wanting to ask you. Why didn't you steal any of the tubes when we were in the Cavern? I saw Cassia and Eli each take one. But you didn't."

Indie's right. I didn't take a tube. But Cassia and Eli both did. Cassia took her grandfather's tube. Eli stole the one that had belonged to Vick. Later, both Cassia and Eli gave me their tubes for safekeeping. I hid them in a tree near the stream that led down to the Rising camp.

"I didn't need one," I say.

Indie and I stop. The rest of the group shouts and hollers. They've found the spot where they want to jump, a deep place downriver from one of the falls. It's where the other squadrons have been going in and it's close enough to the path that people can stop and watch.

"Come on," calls Connor, one of the other pilots. He looks right at Indie and me. "You afraid?" he asks.

I don't bother to answer. Connor's competent, arrogant, and mediocre. He thinks he's a leader. I know he's not.

"No," Indie says, and right then she strips out of her uniform, down to the fitted undershirt and shorts that we all wear, and takes a running leap into the water. Everyone cheers as she hits the surface. I catch my breath, thinking how cold it must be.

And then I'm thinking of Cassia, that long-ago day in Oria when she jumped into the warm blue pool.

Indie breaks to the surface, wet and laughing and shivering.

Even though she's beautiful, with a certain wildness in her eyes, I can't help but think, *I wish Cassia were here.*

Indie sees it. A little of the light in her eyes disappears as she looks away from me and pulls herself from the river, reaching for her uniform and slapping hands with the others. Someone else jumps in and the crowd hollers again.

Indie shivers, wringing out her long hair.

And I think, *I have to stop this. I don't have to love Indie the way I do Cassia, but I do have to stop thinking about Cassia when I look at Indie.* I know how it feels when people look right through you, or worse, see you as something or someone other than what you are.

A formation of air ships flies overhead and we all glance at the sky, a reflex now that we spend so much time there.

Indie climbs up on one of the rocks next to the river and watches the others jump in. She leans her head back and closes her eyes. She reminds me of one of the little lizards in the Outer Provinces. They might look lazy, but if you try to catch them, they'll run away, fast as the lightning that breaks the desert sky before the summer thunderstorms.

I climb up next to her and watch the river and all the things that float and swim along it—birds, debris from the mountains. You could build a dozen boats from everything that races past in an hour or two, especially in the spring.

"Wonder if they'll ever let either of you fly on your own," Connor says. His voice is loud, of course, so that everyone can hear, and he comes closer, trying to intimidate us. He's huge and hulking, at least six foot three. I'm only six feet even, but I'm much faster, so I'm not worried about a fight. He won't catch Indie or me if we decide we need to run. "Seems like the Pilot always has the two of you paired up. Like he doesn't think either of you can fly without the other."

Indie laughs out loud. "That's ridiculous," she says. "The Pilot knows I can fly alone."

"Maybe," Connor says, and he's so easy to read, the dirty thing he's ready to say obvious before he can even spit it out, "the reason he has the two of you fly together is because you're—"

"The best," Indie says. "Of course. We are."

Connor laughs. Water drips off him from his jump into the river. He looks soaked and stupid, not fine and shining like Indie. "You think a lot of yourself," he says. "Think you'll be the Pilot one day?" He glances over his shoulder to see if the others are all laughing, too, at how ridiculous this is. But everyone stays quiet.

"Of course," Indie says, as if she can't believe he'd even ask.

"We all hope for that," a girl named Rae says. "Why not? We can dream now."

"But not *you*," Indie says to Connor. "You need a different dream. You're not good enough to be the Pilot. And I don't think you ever will be."

"Really?" he says, leaning in, a sneer on his face. "And how do you know that?"

"Because I've flown with you," she says, "and you never give in to the sky." Connor laughs and starts to say something, but Indie keeps talking over him. "You're always thinking about yourself. How it looks, what you're doing. Who will notice."

Connor turns away from her. Over his shoulder he says something crude about Indie—what he'd do to her and with her if she weren't crazy. I start after him.

"It doesn't matter," Indie says, her tone perfectly unconcerned. I want to tell her that it's dangerous to be so oblivious to people like Connor. But would it do any good?

The fun's over. People start back to the camp for dry clothes. Some of the pilots and runners shiver as they walk. Almost everyone went into the river.

As we walk, Indie begins to braid her long, wet hair. "What if you could bring back anyone who's gone?" she asks me, keeping up her line of questioning from before. "And don't say Cassia," she adds, with a little *huff* of impatience. "She doesn't count. She's not dead."

It feels good to hear Indie say that, even though of course she doesn't know for certain. Although, if Cassia sent me a message, that's a good thing. I close my fingers around the paper again and smile.

"Who would I bring back from the dead?" I ask Indie. "Why would you ask something like that?"

Indie presses her lips together. For a moment I think she's not going to answer, but then she says, "Anything is possible now."

"You think the Rising might be able to do what the Society never could?" I ask. "You think the Rising has figured out how to bring people back to life?"

"Not yet," she says, "but don't you think they will someday? Don't you think that's the Pilot's ultimate purpose? All the old stories and songs talk about him saving us. It might not just mean from the Society or the Plague, but from death itself—"

"No." I speak low. "You saw those samples in the Carving. How could you bring anyone back from *that*? And even if you could use the sample to create someone a lot like the original person, it would never be the person *themselves*. You can't bring anyone back, *ever*. Do you see what I mean?"

Indie shakes her head, stubborn.

Right then I feel a push at my back, shoving me off balance and toward the river nearby. I have barely enough time to reach my hand into my pocket and close my fingers around the paper before I hit water. I hold my hand up high and push off the bottom of the river as hard as I can with my feet.

But I know the paper is still wet.

The others think my fist is raised in some kind of salute, so they start cheering and calling out and raising theirs back. I have to play it off, so I call out, "The Rising!" and they all pick up the cry.

I'm certain it was Connor who pushed me. He watches from the shore with his arms folded.

Camas River runs near our camp, too, and as soon as the others are out of sight changing clothes in the barracks, I run down to the flat stones at the edge of the water, unfolding the paper as I go. *If he ruined her message to me . . .*

Part of the writing at the bottom is ruined. My heart sinks. But most of it is legible, and it's written in Cassia's handwriting. I'd know it anywhere. She's changed our code a little, the way we always do, but it doesn't take long to puzzle it out.

I'm fine, but most of my papers were stolen.

So don't worry if you don't hear from me as often. I'll find my way to you as soon as I can. I have a plan. Ky, I know that you're going to want to come find me, that you're going to want to save me. But I need you to trust me to save myself.

Spring is coming. I can feel it. I still sort and wait, but I've been writing letters everywhere I can.

I was right. This message is old. The Plague has sped things up and slowed others down. Trading isn't as reliable as it used to be. How many weeks ago did she write this? One week after the Plague arrived? Two? Did she ever get my message or is it sitting in the pocket of someone lying still in a medical center?

Sometimes, when I feel that it isn't fair that we're telling each other our stories in bits and pieces again, I remind myself that we are luckier than most, because we can write to each other. That gift, the first of many you've given me, means more to me each day. We have a way to keep in touch until we can be together again.

I love you, Ky.

That's how we always end our messages to each other. But there's more this time.

I couldn't afford to send two separate messages all the way to Camas. I haven't asked this of you before; I've tried to talk to him in different ways so that the two of you wouldn't have to share. But can you find a way for Xander to see this, too? The next part is for him and it's important.

That's when I see that the code switches into numbers partway down the page. It looks like a basic numerical code, and near the bottom of the page it blurs into waves of ink on the paper from when I fell into the river.

I'm tempted to decipher it. She knows I could, but she thinks she can trust me.

She can. I won't ever forget the way she looked at me in that little house in the Carving, when she realized I'd hidden the map to the Rising from her. I promised myself then that I wouldn't let fear make me into someone I didn't want to be. Now I'm someone who can trust and be trusted.

I have to find a way to get this message to Xander, even if

it's incomplete. And even if giving it to him makes it look like I *am* untrustworthy because part of it is ruined.

I pin the paper down on the flat stone with a small rock so that the wind can pull the water from the page. It won't take long for the messages to dry. Hopefully the others won't miss me.

When I turn back, I see Indie walking across the rocks. She's changed into a dry uniform and she sits down next to me. I keep one hand on a corner of the paper, afraid to let go in case the wind picks up and sends the message sailing. For once, Indie doesn't say anything. Doesn't ask any questions.

So *I* do. "What's the secret?" I ask Indie.

She looks at me and raises her eyebrows. *What do you mean?*

"What's the secret to flying like you do?" I ask. "Like that time when the landing gear malfunctioned and you brought the ship in fine." We'd scraped along the asphalt of the runway, the ship's metal belly sending up sparks, and Indie hadn't seemed flustered at all.

"I know how spaces fit together," she says. "When I look at things, they make sense to me."

She's right. She's always had a good sense of proportion and position when it comes to concrete objects. She carried that wasp nest because she liked the way it fit together. When she climbed the walls of the canyon, she made it look easy. But still, excellent spatial reasoning alone—even if it's practically intuition the way it is for her—doesn't account for how good she is at flying and how fast she learned. I'm not bad myself, but I'm nothing like Indie.

"And I know how things move," Indie says. "Like that."

She points to another heron over the water. This one skims along the river, wings outstretched, following a current of air for as long as it lasts. I look at Indie and feel a sharp ache of loneliness for her, like she's the bird. She knows how things fit together and move, but so few people understand her. She's the most solitary person I've ever known.

Has it always been that way?

"Indie," I ask, "did *you* take a tube from the Cavern?"

"Of course," she says.

"How many?" I ask.

"Only one."

"Who?"

"Just someone," Indie says.

"Where did you hide it?"

"I didn't keep it for long. It got lost in the water when we went down the stream to the Rising."

She's not telling the whole truth. I can't tell where the lie comes in, but there's no way to get Indie to talk about something when she's decided to keep her own counsel.

"You and Hunter are the only ones who didn't," Indie says. "Take one of the tubes, I mean."

Of course. Because Hunter and I accept the truth about death.

"I've seen people dead," I tell Indie. "So have you. When

they're dead, they're gone. You can't bring them back."

We are the ones who are alive. Here. With everything to lose.

"What if you needed to get something over the walls of the barricade?" I ask Indie, changing the subject. "Would you say that's impossible?"

"Of course not," she says. Just like I knew she would. "There are lots of ways to do it."

"Like what?" I ask. I'm grinning. I can't help it.

"Climb," Indie says.

"They'll see us."

"Not if we're fast," Indie tells me. "Or we could fly."

"They'd catch us for sure that way."

"Not if it's the Pilot who sends us in," she says.

CHAPTER 12
XANDER

There's always a feeling of excitement in the medical center when the cures come in. It's one of the few times we get to see people who are *really* from outside the barricade. We've got medics and patients coming in all the time, but the pilots and runners who bring the cures are different. They're not tied down to the medical center or even to Camas.

And there's a chance that we might see the Pilot. The rumor is that he brings in some of the Camas City cures himself. Apparently the landing within our barricade is one that only the best pilots can manage.

The first ship drops down from the sky onto the street they use for a runway. The pilot brings the ship to a stop yards away from the marble steps of City Hall.

"I don't know how they do that," one of the other physics says, shaking her head.

"Neither do I," I say. The ship turns and comes toward us. It goes a lot slower on land than it did in the air. As I watch it come in, I wonder if someday I'll have a chance to fly in one of those ships. There are so many things to look forward to after we get everyone cured.

We physics open the cases in the medical storage room and scan the tubes with our miniports. *Beep. Beep. Beep.* The Rising officers from the ships bring in the cases one after another.

I finish scanning the tubes in the first case. As soon as I do, another appears in front of me.

"Thank you," I say, reaching out to take it from the officer. I look up.

It's Ky.

"Carrow," he says.

"Markham," I say. It's odd using his last name. "You're in the Rising."

"Of course," he says. "Always." He grins at me because we both know it's a lie. There are about a thousand things I want to ask him but we don't have time. We've got to keep the supplies moving.

Suddenly that doesn't feel like the most important thing in the world anymore. I want to ask him how and where she is and if he's heard from her.

"It's good to see you," Ky says.

"You too," I tell him. And it is. Ky holds out his hand to shake mine and we grip tightly, and I feel him press a piece of paper into my palm.

"It's from her," Ky says in a low voice so the others can't hear. Before anyone can tell us to get back to work, he heads for the door. After he disappears, I glance over at the rest of the people delivering cures and find a girl with red hair watching me.

"You don't know me," she says.

"No," I agree.

She tilts her head, scrutinizing me. "My name is Indie," she says. She smiles and it makes her beautiful. I smile back and then she's gone, too.

I shove the paper into my pocket. Ky doesn't come back again, at least not that I see. I can't help but feel like we're playing at the tables back in the Borough, when he was throwing the game and I was the only one who knew. We've got another secret. What does it say on that paper? I wish I could read it now, but my shift isn't over. When you're working, there isn't time for anything else.

Ky and I were friends almost from the beginning of his time in the Borough. At first, I was jealous of him. I dared him to steal the red tablets, and he did. After that we respected each other.

I remember another time when Ky and I were younger. We must have been thirteen or so, and we were both in love with Cassia. We stood talking near her house pretending to care what the other was saying but really waiting to see her when she came home.

At some point we both stopped pretending. "She's not coming," I said.

"Maybe she went to visit her grandfather," Ky said.

I nodded.

"She'll come home eventually," Ky said. "So I don't know why it matters so much that she's not here now."

Right then I knew we were feeling the same thing. I knew we loved Cassia, if not exactly the same way, then the same amount. And the amount was: completely. One hundred percent.

The Society said that numbers like that don't exist but neither Ky nor I cared. I respected that about him, too. And I always admired the way he didn't complain or get upset about anything even though life couldn't have been easy for him in the Borough. Most people there saw him as a replacement for someone else.

That's something I've always wondered about: What *really* happened to Matthew Markham? The Society told us that he died, but I don't believe it.

On the night Patrick Markham went walking up and down the street in his sleepclothes, it was my father who went out and talked him into going back home before anyone called the Officials.

"He was out of his mind," my father whispered to my mother on our front steps after he took Patrick home. I listened through the door. "He was saying things that couldn't possibly be true."

"What did he say?" my mother asked.

My father didn't speak for a while. Right when I thought

he wasn't going to tell her, he said, "Patrick kept asking me, *Why did I do it?*"

My mother drew in her breath. I did too. They both turned around and saw me through the screen. "Go back to bed, Xander," my mother said. "There's nothing to worry about. Patrick's home now."

My father never told the Officials what Patrick said. And the neighborhood knew that Patrick wandered the street that night because he was grieving his son's death—no need to give any of us a red tablet to explain that away. Besides, his distress reminded us all of the need to keep Anomalies away from everyone else.

But I remember what my father whispered to my mother later that night when they came down the hall together. "I think I saw something else in Patrick's eyes besides grief," my father said.

"What?" my mother asked.

"Guilt," my father said.

"Because it was at his workplace that everything happened?" my mother asked. "He shouldn't blame himself. He couldn't have known."

"No," my father said. "It was guilt. Real, intelligent guilt."

They went into their room and I couldn't hear anything more.

I don't think Patrick killed his son. But something happened there that I haven't been able to puzzle out.

~

When my shift finally ends, I head for the small courtyard. Each medical wing has one, and it's the only place where we have access to the outdoors. I'm lucky: The only other people here are a man and woman deep in conversation. I walk to the other side of the courtyard to give them privacy and turn my back so they can't see me open the paper.

At first, all I do is stare at Cassia's writing.

It's beautiful. I wish I knew how to write. I wish she'd taught me. A little surge of bitterness goes through me like someone's shot it right into my veins with a syringe. But I know how to get over the feeling: remember that it doesn't do any good. I've been bitter before about losing her and it never gets me anywhere. More importantly, that's not the kind of person I've spent my life trying to become.

It takes me only moments to decipher the code—a basic substitution cipher like we learned back when we were kids and the Society tested us to see who could sort the best. I wonder if anyone else figured it out before the message got to me. Did Ky read it?

Xander, Cassia wrote, *I wanted to tell you that I'm fine, and to tell you some other things, too. First of all, don't ever take one of the blue tablets. I know the Rising has taken the tablets away, but if you come across any of the blue somehow, get rid of them. They can kill.*

149

Wait. I read it again. That can't be right. Can it? The blue tablets are supposed to save us. The Rising would have told me if that weren't true. Wouldn't they? Do they know? Her next sentence tells me that they do.

It seems to be common knowledge within the Rising that the blue tablets are poisonous, but I didn't want to leave it to chance that you would find out on your own. I tried to tell you on the port and I thought you understood, but lately I've been worried that you didn't. The Society told us the tablets would save us, but they lied. The blue makes you stop and go still. If someone doesn't save you, you die. I saw it happen in the canyons.

She saw it happen. So she does know.

There's something *about the blue.* She tried to tell me. I feel sick. *Why didn't the Rising let me know?* The tablets could have killed her. And it would have been my fault. How could I make that kind of mistake?

The couple in the courtyard is talking louder now. I turn my back to them. I keep reading, my mind racing. Her next sentence offers some relief: at least I wasn't wrong about her being in the Rising.

I'm in the Rising.
I tried to tell you that, too.
I should have written to you earlier, but you were an Official. I

didn't want to risk getting you in trouble. And you've never seen my writing. How would you know that the message was from me, even if the Archivists said that it was? And then I realized a way that I could get a message to you—through Ky. He's seen my writing. He can tell you that this is really from me.

I know that you're in the Rising. I understood what you were trying to tell me on the port. I should have realized—you've always been the first of us to do the right thing.

There is something else that I wanted to tell you in person, that I didn't want to put down in a letter. I wanted to speak to you face to face. But now I feel that I should write to you after all, in case it is still some time before we meet.

I know you love me. I love you, and I always will, but—

It ends there. Water damage has made the rest of the message crinkled and illegible. For a second, I see red. How could it be so conveniently destroyed right at the critical spot? What was she going to say? She said she would always love me, *but*—

Part of me wishes the message ended right there, before that last word.

What happened? Did the paper get ruined by accident? Or could Ky have done it on purpose? Ky played fair in the games. He'd better be playing fair now.

I fold the paper back up and put it into my pocket. In the minutes that I've been reading the note the light has gone. The sun must have dipped below the horizon beyond the walls of the barricade. The door to the courtyard opens and Lei comes out, right as the other couple goes inside.

"Carrow," she says. "I was hoping I would find you."

"Is something wrong?" I ask. I haven't seen Lei in several days. Since she wasn't part of the Rising from the beginning, she's not working as a physic but instead as a general medical assistant, assigned to whatever team and shift needs her most.

"No," she says. "I'm fine. It's good to work with the patients. And you?"

"I'm fine, too," I tell her.

Lei looks at me and I see the same question in her eyes that I know was in mine when I had to decide whether to vouch for her or not. She's wondering if she can trust me, and if she really knows me.

"I wanted," she says finally, "to ask you about the red mark that the patients have on their backs. What is it?"

"It's a small infection of the nerves," I say. "It happens along the dermatomes in the back or neck when the virus is activated." I pause, but she's part of the Rising now, so I can tell her everything. "The Rising told some of us to look for it because it's a sure sign of the Plague."

"And it only happens to people who have actually become ill."

"Right," I say. "The dead form of the virus they used in

the immunizations doesn't lead to any significant symptoms at all. But when a person is infected with the *live* Plague virus, it involves the nerves, resulting in that small red mark."

"Have you seen anything unusual?" she asks. "Any variations on the basic virus?" She's trying to figure out the Plague on her own and not taking what the Rising says for granted. Which should make me uneasy about having vouched for her, but it doesn't.

"Not really," I say. "Now and then we do have people who come in before they're completely still. I had one who was talking to me while I gave him the cure."

"What did he say?" Lei asks.

"He wanted me to promise him that he'd be all right," I say. "So I did."

She nods, and it strikes me how exhausted she looks. "Do you have a rest shift now?" I ask her.

"Not for a few hours," she says. "It doesn't matter much anyway. I haven't slept well since he left. I can't dream. In some ways, that's the hardest part of having him gone."

I understand. "Because if you can't dream you can't pretend that he's still here," I say. That's what I do when *I* dream: I'm back in the Borough with Cassia.

"No," Lei says. "I can't." She looks at me and I hear what she doesn't say. *Her Match is gone, and nothing is the same.*

Then she leans a little closer and to my surprise she puts her hand on my face, very briefly. It's the first time someone has done that since Cassia, and I have to resist leaning into Lei's touch. "Your eyes are blue," she says. Then she pulls her hand back. "So are his." Her voice is lonely and full of longing: for him.

CHAPTER 13
CASSIA

At first the area near the Museum seems empty, and I clench my jaw in frustration. How am I supposed to earn my way out of Central if no one's trading? I need the commissions.

Be patient, I remind myself. *You never know when someone might be watching, waiting to decide whether or not they want to speak up.* I'm the only trader here right now, which won't last long. Others will come.

I see movement out of the corner of my eye, and a girl with short blond hair and beautiful eyes comes around the corner of the Museum. Her hands are cupped in front of her, holding something. For a moment I think of Indie and her wasp nest, and how carefully she always carried it in the canyons.

The girl comes closer to me. "Can I talk to you?" she asks.

"Of course," I say. Lately, we've mostly done away with the passwords of asking about the History of the Society. There's not as much need for them anymore.

She holds out her hands and there, sitting inside of them, is a tiny brown-and-green bird.

It's so strange that for a minute I stare at the bird, which does not move in any way, except for the wind tossing its feathers gently.

They're a shade of green I recognize.

"I made it," the girl says, "to thank you for the words you wrote for my brother. Here."

She gives me the bird. It's tiny, sculpted out of mud, and then dried. It feels weighted and earthy in my palm, and the feathers, tiny torn pieces of green silk, only cover the wings.

"It's beautiful," I say. "The feathers—are they—"

"From the square of silk the Society sent me after my Banquet a few months ago," she says. "I didn't think I needed it anymore."

She wore green, too.

"Don't hold the bird too tightly," she says, "it might cut you," and then she pulls me out from under the tree's shadow, and the parts of the bird that aren't feathered turn starry. They glitter in the sun.

"I had to break the glass to get the silk out," she says, "so I thought I might as well use it. I crushed it, and then, when I'd made the bird, I rolled it in the pieces. They were almost as small as sand."

I close my eyes. I did something similar, back in the Borough, when I gave Ky the piece of my dress. I remember clearly the clean *snap* when I broke the scrap free.

The bird shimmers and seems to move. Glitter of glass, feathers of silk.

It looks so close to living that I have a momentary urge to toss it to the sky, to see if it will take wing. But I know I will hear only the thud of clay and see the scatter of green when it hits the ground, the shape that made it *bird, flying thing* destroyed. So I hold it carefully and let this knowledge rise within me like a song.

I am not the only one writing.

I am not the only one creating.

The Society took so much from us, but we still hear rumors of music, hints of poetry; we still see intimations of art in the world around us. They never did keep us from all of it. We took it in, sometimes without knowing, and many still ache for a way to let it out.

I realize all over again that we don't need to *trade* our art—we could give, or share. Someone could bring a poem, someone else a painting. Even if we took nothing away, we would all have more, having looked on something beautiful or heard something true.

The breeze dances the bird's green feathers. "It's too beautiful," I say, "to keep to myself."

"That's how I felt about your poem," she says eagerly. "I wanted to show it to everyone."

"What if we had a way to do that?" I ask. "What if we could gather together, and everyone could bring what they'd made?"

Where?

The Museum is the first place that comes to mind, and I turn and look at its boarded-up doors. If we could find a way inside, the Museum has glass cases and glowing golden lights. They are broken, but perhaps we could repair them. I imagine sliding open a door to one of the cases and pinning my poems inside, then stepping back to look.

A little shiver goes through me. *No.* That's not the place.

I turn back and the girl watches me, her gaze level and measuring. "I'm Dalton Fuller," she says.

We're not supposed to give our names away as traders, but I'm not trading. "My name is Cassia Reyes," I tell her.

"I know," Dalton says. "You signed it on the poem you wrote." She pauses. "I think I have a place that will work."

"No one comes here," she tells me, "because of the smell. But it's starting to get better."

We stand at the edge of the marsh that goes to the lake. We're far enough away that we can only see the shore, not what might be washed up on it.

I've wondered about those dead fish bumping against the dock, my shins, my hands—was it a last-ditch effort on the Society's part to poison more water, the way they did in the Outer Provinces and in Enemy territory? But why would the Society do something like that to their own lake?

As the Rising has cured the Plague, they've made the

stillzone smaller. I've seen air ships lifting the pieces of the barricade back up into the sky, pulling the other pieces in more closely. Some of the buildings that were once within the barricade are now back outside of it.

The Rising brings the unused pieces of the barricade out to this vacant ground near the lake. Taken apart, the white pieces of the wall look like art in themselves—curving and enormous, like feathers dropped to earth by giant beings and then turned to marble, like bones risen from the ground and then turned to stone. They are a canyon shattered, with spaces to walk between.

"I've seen this from up on the air-train stops," I say, "but I didn't know what it looked like up close."

In one place they've dropped two pieces closer together than the others. The pieces form what looks almost like a long hallway, curving toward each other, but not meeting at the top. I walk inside and the space underneath is cool and a little bit dark, with a neat line of blue sky streaming in light from above. I put my hand against a piece of the barricade and look up.

"Rain will still get in," Dalton says. "But it's sheltered enough that I think it would work."

"We could put the pictures and poems on the walls," I say, and she nods. "And build some kind of platform to hold things like your bird."

And if someone knew how to sing, they could come here and we could listen. I stand there for a moment, imagining music echoing along the walls and out over the ruined, lonely lake.

I know I need to keep trading to get to my family, and sorting to keep my place in the Rising, but this also feels like something I have to do. I think Grandfather would understand.

PART THREE

PHYSIC

CHAPTER 14
XANDER

I'm sending a group of new patients your way," the head physic tells me over the miniport.

"Good," I say. "We're ready for them." We have empty beds now. Three months into the Plague, things are finally tapering off, thanks in large part to the increase in immunizations provided by the Rising. The scientists and pilots and workers have all done their best and we've saved hundreds of thousands of people. It's an honor to be a part of the Rising.

I go to the doors to let the transfer medics inside. "Looks like we had a minor outbreak in one of the suburbs," one of the medics says, pushing his way in and holding on to one end of a stretcher. Sweat drips down his face and he looks exhausted. I admire the transfer medics more than almost anyone else in the Rising. Their work is physical and exhausting. "I guess they missed their immunizations somehow."

"You can put him right over here," I say. They move the patient from the stretcher to the bed. One of the nurses begins changing the patient into a gown and I hear her exclaim in surprise.

"What is it?" I ask.

"The rash," the nurse says. She points to the patient and I see red stripes running across his chest. "It's bad on this one."

While the small red mark is more common, now and then we see the rash extending all the way around the torso. "Let's turn him and check his back," I say.

We do. The rash extends to the patient's back. I glance down at my miniport to enter a notation. "Are the others like this?" I ask.

"Not that we noticed," the medic says.

The medics and I examine the rest of the new patients. None of them exhibit the acute rash, or even have the small red marks.

"It's probably nothing," I say, "but I'll call in one of the virologists."

It doesn't take the virologist very long to respond. "What do we have?" he asks, his tone confident. I haven't had much interaction with him, but I know him by sight and reputation as one of the best research medics in the Rising. "A variation?"

"It looks that way," I say. "The acute viral rash, formerly small and localized, is now manifesting on dermatomes all around the torso."

The virologist looks at me in surprise, as if he didn't expect me to use the right language. But I've been here for three months. I know which words to use and, more importantly than that, I know what they mean.

We're already gloved and masked, as per procedure. The virologist reaches into a case and pulls out a cure. "Get me a vital-stats machine," he tells one of the other medics. "And you," he tells me, "draw a blood sample and get a line running."

"It's nothing we didn't anticipate," the virologist says as I slide the needle into the man's vein. The head physic watches us from the main port on the wall. "Viruses change all the time. You can see different mutations of a single virus showing up in different tissues, even in the same body."

I hook up the fluid-and-nutrient bag and start the drip.

"For a mutation to flourish," the virologist says, "there would have to be some kind of selective pressure applied. Something that made the mutation more viable than the original virus."

He's teaching me, I realize, which he doesn't have to do. And I think I understand what he's saying. "Like a cure?" I ask. "Could that be the selective pressure?" Could *we* have given this new virus the opportunity to flourish?

"Don't worry," he says. "What's more likely is that we have an immune system responding uniquely to the virus."

He looks at the patient and makes a notation in the miniport. Since I'm attending, it pops up on my miniport as well. *Rotate patient every two hours to prevent skin breakdown. Clean and seal affected areas to inhibit the spread of infection.* The instructions are the same as those for all the other patients. "Poor fellow," he says. "Maybe it's best he stays under for a while. He's going to hurt before he heals."

"Should we quarantine the patients from this transfer in a separate part of the center?" I ask the head physic over the port.

"Only if you'd prefer not to have them in your wing," he says.

"No," I say. "We can quarantine later if necessary."

The virologist nods. "I'll let you know as soon as we have the results from the samples," he says. "It may be an hour or two."

"In the meantime, start them all on the cure," the head physic tells me.

"All right."

"Nice work drawing the blood," the virologist says as he leaves the room. "You'd think you were still a medic."

"Thanks," I say.

"Carrow," the head physic says, "you're long past due for a break. Take one now while they're running the sample."

"I'm fine," I say.

"You've already extended your shift once," the head physic tells me from the port. "The nurses and medics can handle this."

I've started taking all my breaks in the courtyard. I even bring my food out there to eat. It's a little patch of trees and flowers that are starting to die because no one has time to take care of them, but at least when I'm out there I know whether it's day or night.

Also, I figure if I stay in the same place most of the time, there's more of a chance I'll see Lei and we can talk about our work and what we've noticed.

At first, I think I'm out of luck because she's not in the courtyard. But then, right when I'm finishing my meal, the door opens and Lei comes out.

"Carrow," she says, sounding glad. She must have been looking for me, too, which feels good. She smiles and gestures to the people in the courtyard. "Everyone else has discovered this place."

She's right. I can count at least fourteen other people sitting in the sun. "I've been wanting to talk to you," I say. "Something interesting happened in our last transfer."

"What was it?" she asks.

"A patient came in with a more acute form of the rash."

"What did it look like?"

I tell her about the lesions and what the virologist said. I try to explain selective pressure to her but I do a bad job of it. Still, she catches on. "So it's possible that the *cure* caused the mutation," she says.

"If it even is a mutation," I say. "None of the other patients have a similar rash. Of course, it could be that they haven't had time for it to manifest yet."

"I wish I could see them," she says. At first I think she's talking about the patients, but then I see that she's gesturing in the direction where the mountains would be if the walls didn't block them out. "I always wondered how people lived without mountains to tell them where they were. Now I guess I know."

"I never missed them," I say. All we had in Oria was the Hill and I never really cared about that. I always liked the little places—the lawn at First School, the bright blue of the swimming pool. And I liked the maple trees in the Borough before they took them down. I want to build all those things again, but this time without the Society.

"My other name is Xander," I say to Lei suddenly, surprising us both. "I don't think I ever told you that."

"Mine is Nea," she says.

"That's good to know," I say. And it is, even though we won't break protocol and use each other's first name while we're working.

"What I like best about him," she says, her tone and the change of subject almost abrupt, "is that he is never afraid. Except when he fell in love with me. But even then, he didn't back down."

It takes me longer than usual to think of the right thing to say, and before I can come up with anything, Lei speaks again.

"So what do you like about her?" Lei asks. "*Your* Match?"

"All of it," I say. "Everything." I hold my hands out to my sides. Once again, I'm at a loss for words. It's an unfamiliar feeling and I'm not sure why it's so hard for me to talk about Cassia.

I think Lei's going to get frustrated with me but she doesn't. She nods. "I understand that, too," she says.

My time's up and the break is over. "I've got to get back," I say. "Time to see how they're all doing."

"This all comes naturally to you," Lei says. "Doesn't it?"

"What do you mean?" I ask.

"Taking care of people." She's looking in the direction of the mountains again. "Where were you living last summer?" she asks. "Had you already been assigned to Camas?"

"No," I say. Back then, I was home in Oria, trying to make Cassia fall in love with me. It feels like a long time ago. "Why?"

"You remind me of a kind of fish that comes to the river during the summer," she says.

I laugh. "Is that a good thing?"

She's smiling, but she looks sad. "They come all the way back from the sea."

"That seems impossible," I say.

"It does," she says. "But they do. And they change completely on the journey. When they live in the ocean, they're blue with silver backs. But by the time they get here, they're wildly colorful, bright red with green heads."

I'm not sure what she thinks this has to do with me.

She tries to explain. "What I'm trying to say is that you've found your way home. You were born to help people, and you'll find a way to do that, no matter where you are. Just like the redfish are born to find their way back from the ocean."

"Thank you," I say.

For a second, I think about telling her everything, including what I really did to get the blue tablets. But I don't. "Time for me to get back to work," I say to Lei, and I dump the last of the water in my canteen on the newroses near our bench and head for the door.

I walk along the backs of the houses in Mapletree Borough, near the food delivery tracks. Even though it's late and no meals are being delivered, I can hear the soft scrape-whine of the carts in my mind. When I go past Cassia's house I want to reach out and touch one of the shutters or tap on a window, but of course I don't.

I come to the common area for the Borough, where the recreation areas are clumped together, and before I even have time to wonder where the Archivist is he appears beside me. "We're right behind the pool," he says.

"I know," I tell him. This is my neighborhood and I know exactly where I am. The sharp white edge of the high dive looms in front of us. Our voices whispering in the humid night sound like locust wings grating.

He climbs over the fence swiftly and I follow. I almost say, "The pool's closed. We can't be here," but, obviously, we are.

A group of people waits under the high dive. "All you have to do is draw their blood," the Archivist tells me.

"Why?" I ask, feeling cold.

"We're taking tissue preservation samples," the Archivist says. "We all want control of our own. You knew this."

"I thought we'd be taking the samples the usual way," I say. "With swabs, not needles. You only need a little tissue."

"This way is better," the Archivist says.

"You're not stealing from us the way the Society does," one of the women tells me, her voice quiet and calm. "You're taking our blood and giving it back." She holds out her arm. "I'm ready."

The Archivist hands me a case. When I open it up I see sterile tubes and syringes sealed away in plastic. "Go ahead," he tells me. "It's all worked out. I have the tablets to give to you when you finish. You don't need to know any more than that."

He's right. I don't want to try to understand the complicated system of trades and balancing. And I certainly don't want to know what these people have paid to be here. Is a trade like this even sanctioned by the other Archivists or is this man conducting transactions on the side? What have I stumbled into? I didn't realize that black market blood would be the price of the blue tablets.

"You're going to get caught," I say.

"No," he says. "I won't."

"Please," the woman says. "I want to get home."

I put on a pair of gloves and prepare a syringe. She keeps her eyes closed the whole time. I slide the needle of the syringe into the vein near the crook of her elbow. She makes a startled sound. "Almost done," I say. "Hold on." I pull the syringe back out and hold it up. Her blood is dark.

"Thank you," she says, and the Archivist hands her a square of cotton that she presses against the inside of her arm.

When I've finished, the Archivist gives me the blue tablets. And *then he tells the others, "We'll be here again next week. Bring your children. Don't you want to make sure you have samples for them, too?"*

"I won't be here next week," I tell the Archivist.

"Why not?" he asks. "You're doing them a service."

"No," I say. "I'm not. The science doesn't exist yet to bring people back."

If it did, I thought, I'm sure people would use it. Like Patrick and Aida Markham. If there was a way to bring their son back, they'd do it.

Back at home, using a little scalpel stolen from the medical center, I perform the only surgery I'll likely ever do, slicing very carefully along the back of the tablets, cutting the paper from the Archivists' port into strips, inserting them, and then holding the packages over the incinerator to melt the adhesive back together.

It takes almost all night, and in the morning I wake up to the sound of screaming in the Borough as they take Ky away. Not long after that, Cassia leaves, too, and thanks to me, she's got blue tablets to take with her.

I walk back to my wing to check on the patients. "Any adverse reactions to the cure?" I ask.

The nurse shakes her head. "No," she says. "Five of them are responding well. But the rest, including the patient with the rash, are not. Of course, it's still early." She doesn't need to articulate what we both know: Usually we've seen some sort of response by now. This isn't good.

"Has anyone else manifested with the rash?"

"We haven't checked since they came in," she says. "It's been less than an hour."

"Let's do it now," I say.

We turn one of the patients over carefully. Nothing. We turn another patient. Nothing.

But the third patient's rash circles her entire body. Her lesions aren't yet as red as those belonging to the first patient, but the reaction is certainly atypical. "Call the virologist," I tell one of the medics. Carefully, we turn the woman back over and I catch my breath. Blood seeps from her mouth and nose.

"We have a patient with different symptoms," I tell the head physic over the port. Before he can answer, another voice comes over my miniport. It's the virologist. "Carrow?"

"Yes?"

"I analyzed the viral genome taken from the patient with the circumferential rash," he says. "It reveals an additional copy of the neural-insertion envelope protein gene. Do you understand what I'm saying?"

I do.

We have a mutation on our hands.

CHAPTER 15
CASSIA

At dusk the evening light gilds the white of the barricade into gold, and the sky is cool and blue except for the spot where the sun burns down beyond the horizon. That's when we gather, more of us each day. One person tells two people, and two tell four, and it increases exponentially, and within a few weeks of beginning we have what I think of as an outbreak of our own.

I don't know who started referring to this place as the Gallery, but the name caught on. I'm glad people cared enough to name it. I like it best when I hear the whispers of those who are here for the first time, who stand before the wall with their hands over their mouths and tears in their eyes. Though I could be wrong, I think that many of them feel as I do whenever I come here.

I am not alone.

If I have a little time and can stay for a while, I show whoever wants to learn how to write. Once they've seen me do it, they make their own marks, clumsy at first, then definite, confident.

I teach them printing, not the ornate cursive Ky taught

me. Printing is easier because of the separate, distinct lines. It's the joining together—the writing without ceasing and the continuous movement—that is most difficult to learn, that feels so foreign to our hands. Now and then I do write in cursive so I don't lose the feeling of connection to what I'm putting down, and more importantly, to Ky. When I write without lifting the stick from the ground or the pencil from the paper, I'm reminded of Hunter and his people, how they drew the blue lines on their skin and then onto the next person.

"That's harder," a man says, watching me write in cursive. "But the regular way—it's not bad."

"No," I say.

"So why haven't we been doing it all along?" he asks.

"I think some people have," I say, and he nods.

We have to be careful. There are still pockets of Society sympathizers who want to fight and destroy, and they can be dangerous. The Rising itself hasn't forbidden us to gather like this, but the Pilot has asked that everyone focus attention on completing our work and ending the Plague. He tells us that saving people is what matters most, and I believe that to be true, but I think we are also saving ourselves here in the Gallery. So many people have waited a long time to create, or had to hide what they'd done.

We bring whatever we've made to the Gallery. There are many pictures and poems tacked to the wall with tree sap. They look like tattered flags—paper from ports, napkins, even torn pieces of cloth.

There is a woman who carves patterns on pieces of wood and then darkens them with charred ash and presses the woodcuts against paper, imprinting her world on ours.

There is a man who must have been an Official once, who has taken all his white uniforms and found a way to turn them different colors. He cuts the fabric into pieces and makes clothing in a style different from any I've seen, with angles and flourishes and lines that are unexpected and right. He hangs his creations from the top of the Gallery, and they look like the promises of who we might be in the future.

There is Dalton, who always brings artwork that is beautiful and interesting, fashioned from pieces of other things. Today she's brought a person created out of bits of cloth and paper torn small and then remade into something large, with stones for eyes and seeds for teeth, and it's beautiful and terrible. "Oh, Dalton," I say.

She smiles and I lean in for a closer look. I smell the tangy scent of the tree sap she uses to hold all the pieces of her creations together.

"There's a rumor," Dalton says softly, "that at dark, someone's going to sing."

"Are we sure this time?" I ask. We've heard the rumor before. But it never seems to happen. Poems and artwork are easier to leave; we don't *have* to stand before the others and see their faces as we offer up what it is we have to give.

Before Dalton can answer, someone is at my elbow.

I turn, and there is an Archivist I know. Panic sets in for a moment—how did he find the Gallery? Then I remember that the Archivists are not the Society, and also that we are not competing with the Archivists for trades. This is a place of sharing.

He pulls something white from the inside of his coat and hands it to me. A piece of paper. Could it be a message from Ky? Or Xander?

What did Xander think of *my* message? Those were the hardest words I've ever had to write. I begin to open the paper.

"Don't read it," the Archivist says, sounding embarrassed. "Not when I'm here. I wondered—could you put it up sometime? After I leave? It's a story I wrote."

"Of course," I promise him. "I'll do it tonight." I shouldn't have assumed that he was only an Archivist. Of course he might have something to add to the Gallery, too.

"People come to us asking if there's any value in what they've made," he says. "I have to tell them that there isn't. Not to us. I send them on to you. But I don't know what you call this place."

For a moment, I hesitate, and then I remind myself that the Gallery isn't a secret, it can't be kept. "We call it the Gallery," I say.

The Archivist nods. "You should be careful about gathering in groups," he tells me. "There are rumors that the Plague has mutated."

"We've heard those rumors for weeks," I say.

"I know," he says, "but someday they could be true. That's why I came tonight. I had to write this down in case we ran out of time."

I understand. I have learned that, even without a Plague or a mutation, time is *always* short. That's why I had to write those things to Xander, even though it was almost impossible to do. I had to tell him the truth because, since time is short, it should not be spent waiting:

I know you love me. I love you, and I always will, but things can't hold like this. They have to break. You say you don't mind, that you'll wait for me, but I think that you do mind, and you should. Because we've done too much waiting in our lives, Xander. Don't wait for me anymore.

I hope for love for you.

I hope for this more than anything else, maybe even more than my own happiness.

And in a way, perhaps that means I love Xander best of all.

CHAPTER 16
KY

Where are we going?" Indie asks, climbing into the air ship.

It's my turn to fly, so I sit in the pilot's seat. "No idea," I say. "As usual." Once the Rising began in earnest, we stopped getting our assignments in advance. I start my equipment check. Indie helps me.

"An older ship today," she says. "Good."

I nod in agreement. Indie and I both prefer the older ships, which can be more temperamental than the new ones but which also have a different feel to them. When you're piloting the new ships, sometimes you feel like they're flying you instead of it being the other way around.

Everything is in order so we wait for our instructions. It's raining again and Indie hums, sounding happy. It makes me smile. "It's a good thing they have us flying together," I say. "I never see you in the barracks or the meal hall anymore."

"I've been busy," Indie says. She leans closer to me. "After the Plague is gone," she asks, "are you going to request to train as a fighter?"

Is that why I don't see Indie as much? Is she planning on

changing jobs someday? The fighters, the ones who cover our errand ships as we fly, have to train for years. And, of course, they learn to fight and kill. "No," I say. "What about you?"

Before she can answer, our flight plans start coming through. Indie reaches for them but I snatch them away first and she sticks out her tongue at me like we're kids. I look down at the plans and my heart misses a beat.

"What is it?" Indie asks, craning her neck so she can see.

"We're going to Oria," I say, stunned.

"That's strange," Indie says.

It is. The Rising doesn't like us to pilot into Provinces where we once lived. They think we'll want to try to get the cargo to people we know instead of letting the Rising distribute according to need. "The temptation is too high," the commanders tell us.

"Well, it could be interesting," Indie says. "They say Oria and Central are the places with the most Society sympathizers."

I wonder who still lives there that I would know. Cassia's family was sent to Keya, and my parents were taken away. Does Em's family still live there? What about the Carrows?

I haven't seen Xander since the time I gave him the note from Cassia. A few days after I talked with Indie about getting inside the Camas City barricade, the Rising sent us in to deliver some of the cures. I think Indie had something to do with the assignment, but whenever I ask her about it she shrugs it off. "They probably just wanted to see if we could make the landing," she says, "since it's one of the most difficult ones in a City." But she's got that glint in her eye that means she's not telling the whole story. It worries me, but if Indie doesn't want to tell you something, it's pointless to keep asking.

But we made it inside the walls and helped Caleb with the cargo and I delivered Cassia's message. It was good to see Xander again. He was glad to see me too. I wonder how long that lasted after he saw that part of the letter was ruined.

The main part of the flight is, as usual, all sky.

Then we drop lower. I aim the ship in the direction of the barricade. Though it was the Society who put up the white barriers, the Rising has left them in place for now to keep a line between the sick and the healthy.

"Oria looks like everywhere else," Indie says, sounding disappointed.

I've never thought of it that way. But she's right. That was always Oria's most important characteristic—it was so perfectly Society that it was practically anonymous. Not like Camas, which has the mountains to set it apart, or Acadia, which has a rocky shore to the East Sea, or Central with all its lakes. The middle Provinces—Oria and Grandia, Bria and Keya—look pretty much the same.

Except for one thing.

"We do have the Hill," I tell Indie. "You'll see when we get closer."

I feel hungry for the sight of that forested rise with its green trees. I feel like if I can't see Cassia, the Hill is the next best thing. We stood there together. We hid in the trees and for the first time our lips touched. I can almost feel the wind on my skin and her hand in mine. I swallow.

But when we soar a circle over Oria to prepare for landing, I can't seem to find the Hill in the dusky light of evening.

Indie is the one who sees it. "That brown thing?" she asks. She's right.

That bare, brown place *is* the Hill.

I start to bring the ship down. We get closer and closer to the ground. Trees along the streets turn large. The ground rushes at us. The buildings become familiar instead of generic.

At the last second, I pull the ship back up.

I feel Indie looking at me. I've never done this before in the months we've been running in supplies.

"Landing wasn't right," I say into the speakers. It happens. It will go down on my record as an error. But I have to see the Hill again, closer.

We come up in the opposite direction and head for the Hill, dropping lower than I should so I can get a good look.

"Is something wrong?" one of the fighters asks over the speaker.

"No," I say. "I'm bringing it in."

I've seen what I needed to see. The ground is bare. It's been completely bulldozed. Burned. Butchered. It's like the Hill never knew trees. Parts of the Hill have sloughed downward, no longer anchored by the roots of living things.

The little piece of green silk from Cassia's dress is no longer tied to a tree on the top of the Hill, wearing out into white with wind and rain and sun. Our buried scraps of poems have been exhumed and reburied and pushed farther under.

They've killed the Hill.

I land the ship. Behind me, I hear Caleb open the hold and start dragging out the cases. I sit and stare straight ahead.

I want to be back there, on the Hill, with Cassia. I want it so much I think it might destroy me. All these months have passed and we're still apart. I put my head in my hands.

"Ky?" Indie asks. "Are you all right?" She puts her hand on my shoulder for a second. Then she lets go and, without looking at me, goes down to help Caleb.

I'm grateful to her for both the touch and the solitude, but neither lasts long.

"Ky?" Indie calls out. "Come see this."

"What?" I ask, climbing down into the hold. Indie points at a spot near the floor, concealed earlier by the cases. Someone has scratched into the metal of the ship and carved images into the walls. It reminds me of the pictures back in the Carving.

"They're drinking the sky," Indie says.

She's right. It's not rain that the picture shows, not like one I drew once back in the Borough. It's different—broken pieces of sky falling to the ground and people picking them up and tipping water out of them.

"It makes me thirsty," Indie says.

"Look," I say, pointing to the figure coming down from the sky. "Who do you think this is?"

"The Pilot, of course," she says.

"Did you draw these?" I ask Caleb, who's appeared at the top of the hold, ready for more cargo.

"Draw what?" he asks.

"The pictures carved into the side of the ship."

"No," he says. "It must have been one of the other runners. I'd never vandalize the Rising's property."

I hand up another case.

We finish our delivery and head for the ship. As we walk, Indie falls back. I turn around to see her talking to Caleb. He shakes his head. Indie steps closer to him. She's lifted her chin and I know exactly what her eyes must look like.

She's challenging him about something.

Caleb shakes his head again. His posture looks tense.

"Tell me," I hear Indie saying. "*Now*. We should know."

"No," he says. "You're not even the pilot on this flight. Leave it alone."

"Ky's flying," she says. "He had to come all the way here, back to his home Province. Do you know how hard that must be? What if you had to go back to Keya, or wherever it is that you're from? He should at least know what we're doing."

"We're bringing in supplies," he says.

"That's not all we're doing," she says.

He steps around her. "If the Pilot wanted you to know," he says over his shoulder, "you would."

"You know you're nothing more than a runner, even to the Pilot," Indie says. "He doesn't think of you as his."

Caleb takes a step back and I see hatred on his face for Indie.

Because she's right. She knows what Caleb hopes for. It's the dream of every parentless, orphaned worker of the Rising—to make the Pilot so proud that he'd claim them as his own kin. It's Indie's dream too.

Indie finds me later out in the field near the camp. She sits down and takes a deep breath. At first I think she's going to try to make me feel better by talking about things that don't matter, but Indie has never been very good at that.

"We could try it," she says. "We could make a run for Central if you want."

"It's not an option," I say. "The fighters would shoot us down."

"You'd try it if it weren't for me," Indie says.

"Yes," I agree. "And Caleb." I'm finished with the selfishness that let me leave everyone behind on the plains and take only Vick and Eli into the Carving. Caleb is part of our group.

When I fly, he's my responsibility. I can't risk him either. Cassia wouldn't want other people to die just so I could find her.

And if the Pilot is telling the truth, it doesn't matter. The Plague's under control. Everything will be all right soon, and I can find Cassia and we can be together. I *want* to believe in the Pilot. Sometimes I do.

"Back in camp, when we were training," I say, "did you ever fly with him?"

"Yes," Indie says simply. "That's how I knew he was the Pilot, even before they told us. His flying . . ." She stops, at a loss for words, and then her face brightens. "It was like the picture we saw today carved into the ship," she says. "It felt like I was drinking the sky."

"So you trust him?" I ask.

Indie nods.

"But you'd still run the risk of going to Central with me."

"Yes," Indie says, "if that's what you wanted." She looks at me as if she's trying to see inside me. I'd like her to smile. That beautiful, wide, wise, innocent, devious smile of hers.

"What are you thinking about?" she asks.

"I want to see you smile," I tell her.

And then she does—sudden, delighted—and I grin back.

The grass rustles with the breeze. Indie leans a little closer. Her face is radiant and hopeful and raw. It feels like some new hole has been torn in my heart.

"What's to keep us from flying together?" Indie whispers.

"You and me?" I can barely hear her above the wind rustling the grass, but I know the way this question sounds from her. She's asked something like it before.

"Cassia," I say. "I'm in love with Cassia. You know that." There's no uncertainty in my voice.

"I know," she says, and there's no apology in hers.

When Indie wants something badly enough, her instinct is to jump.

Like Cassia.

Indie breathes in and then she moves.

She moves to me.

Her hands slide into my hair, her lips press against mine.

Nothing like Cassia.

I pull back, breathless. "Indie," I say.

"I had to," she says. "I'm not sorry."

CHAPTER 17
CASSIA

Someone's coming into the Archivists' hiding place; I hear their feet on the stairs. Since I'm waiting in the main area with the others, I shine my flashlight up like the rest. The figure stops, expecting us.

Once I see who it is—a trader I've passed down here before—I drop my light. But many of the others don't. She's trapped there like a moth. A nearby Archivist signals for me to bring my light back up and so I do, blinking, though the girl standing in the doorway is the one caught in the glare.

"Samara Rourke," the head Archivist says. "You should not be here."

The girl laughs nervously. She wears a bulky pack and she shifts it down a little.

"Don't move," the head Archivist says. "We'll escort you out."

"I'm allowed to trade here," Samara says. "*You're* the one who showed me where this place is."

"You are no longer welcome," the head Archivist says. She's somewhere in the shadows, and then she steps forward, pointing the beam of her flashlight right into the girl's eyes.

This is the Archivists' place. They decide who stays in shadows and shades and who has to face the light.

"Why?" Samara asks, her voice finally faltering a little.

"You know why," the Archivist says. "Do you want everyone else to know as well?"

The girl licks her lips. "You should see what I found," she says. "I promise you're going to want to know . . ." She reaches for the pack at her side.

"Samara cheated," the Archivist says, her voice every bit as powerful as the Pilot's. It resonates around the room. None of the lights waver and when I close my eyes I can still see their bright spots and the girl's nervous, blinded expression. "Someone gave an item to Samara to trade on their behalf. She brought it here. We assessed its value, accepted it, and gave an item in return, with a separate, smaller item for the trader fee. And then Samara kept both."

There are crooked traders in the world, plenty of them. But they don't usually dare to try to work with the Archivists.

"You're not out anything," Samara says to the Archivist. "You got your payment." Her attempt at defiance makes me ache with pity. What made her do this? Surely she knew she'd get caught. "If anyone should get to punish me, it's the person I stole from."

"No," the head Archivist says. "You undermine *us* when you steal."

Three of the Archivists drop their lights and move forward.

My heart pounds and I step back a little farther into the shadows. Though I come down here often, I'm not an Archivist. At any time my privileges—which are more than those afforded to most traders—could be revoked.

I hear the click of scissors and the head Archivist steps back, holding Samara's red bracelet up in the air. Samara looks ashen but unharmed, and in the lights still directed on her, I can see her sleeve pulled up and her bare wrist where the bracelet used to be.

"People should know," the Archivist says to the room at large, "that they can trust when they trade with us. What has happened here undermines everything. Now *we* will have to pay the price of the trade." The others have dropped their lights down now and so her voice is the most recognizable part of her; her face is in shadows. "Paying the price for another is not something we like to do." Then her tone changes and the incident is over, finished. "You may all go back to your trades."

I don't move. Who's to say I wouldn't do what Samara did, if something passed through my hands that I needed for someone else? Because I think that's what happened. I don't think Samara risked this for herself.

I feel a hand on my elbow and I turn to see who it is.

It's the head Archivist herself. "Come with me," she says. "There's something I need to show you."

She brings me through rows of shelves and through a long dark hall, her grip firm on my arm. And now we're in another vast room ribbed with metal shelves, but these are all filled. They're lined with everything anyone could ever want, every lost piece of a past, every fragment of a future.

Other Archivists move among the shelves while some stand guard. This room has other lights, strung along the ceiling and glowing faintly. I catch a glimpse of cases and boxes and containers of uneven sizes. You would need a map to find your way through a place like this.

I know where we are before she tells me, even though I've never been here before. The Archives. It's a little like seeing the Pilot for the first time; I've always known of the existence of this place, but to confront it face to face makes me want to sing or weep or run away; I'm not certain which.

"The Archives are filled with treasures," the Archivist says, "and I know every one."

Her hair shines golden in this light, as if she is one of the treasures she guards. Then she turns to look at me.

"Not many people have been here," she says.

Then why me? I wonder.

"There are many stories that have passed through my hands," the Archivist says. "I always liked the one about a girl who was tasked with turning straw into gold. An impossible piece of work, but she managed it more than once. That's what this job is like."

The Archivist walks partway down an aisle and lifts a case from the shelf. She opens it and inside I see rows and rows of paper-wrapped bars. She takes one of them out and holds it up. "If I could," she says,"I would stay in here all day. This is where I began my work as an Archivist. I sorted the items and cataloged them." She closes her eyes and breathes in deeply, and I find myself doing the same.

The scent coming from the case is familiar, a memory, but I can't place it at first. My heart beats a bit more quickly and I have a sudden rush of remembered anger; unexpected, out of place. And then I know.

"It's chocolate," I say.

"Yes," she says. "When was the last time you had any?"

"My Match Banquet," I say.

"Of course," she says. She closes the case and reaches for another and opens it. I see glints of silver that at first I think are boxes from Banquets but instead are forks, knives, spoons. Then another case, this one handled even more gently than the others, and inside I see pieces of china, bone white and fragile as ice. Then we move to another aisle and she shows me rings with red and green and blue and white stones, and over again to another row, where she takes out books with pictures so rich and beautiful I have to hold my hands together so that I won't touch the pages.

There is so much wealth in here. Even if I wouldn't trade for silver or chocolate, I understand why someone else would.

"Before the Society," the head Archivist says, "people used to use money. There were coins—some of them gold—

and crisp green papers. They'd trade it with each other and it represented different things."

"How did it work?" I ask.

"Say I was hungry," the Archivist says. "I'd give someone five of the papers and they'd give me some food."

"But then what would they do with the papers?"

"Use them to get something else," she says.

"Did they have things written on them?"

"No," she says. "Nothing like your poems."

I shake my head. "Why would anyone do that?" Trading the way the Archivists do seems much more logical.

"They trusted each other," the Archivist says. "Until they didn't anymore."

She waits. I'm not sure what she expects me to say.

"What I'm showing you," the Archivist says, "are the things that most people find to be valuable. And we also have cases and cases full of very specific items for more eccentric tastes. We have been doing this for a long time." She leads me back the way we came, to the rows where the jewels were stored. She stops for a moment to take down a case. She doesn't open it, but carries it with her as we walk. "Everyone has a currency," she says. "One of the most interesting ones is knowledge, when people want to *know* things, not possess them. Of course, what people want to know is a similarly varied and intricate business." She stops near the end of one of the shelves. "What is it *you* want to know, Cassia?"

I want to know if my family and Ky and Xander are all right. What Grandfather meant by the red garden day. What memories I've lost.

A pause, in that decadent, deliberate room.

Her flashlight glances off the shelves, sending slants and glints of light in strange places. Her face, when I can see it, looks thoughtful. "Do you know what's extremely valuable right now?" she asks me. "Those tubes that the Society had, the secret ones. Have you heard of them? The samples they take long before the Final Banquet?"

"I've heard of them," I say. I've seen them, too. All rowed and stored in a cave in the middle of a canyon. While we were there in that cave, Hunter broke some of the tubes, and Eli and I each stole one of the others.

"You're not the only one who has," the head Archivist says. "Some people will do anything they can to get their hands on those samples."

"The tubes don't matter," I say. "They're not real people." I'm quoting Ky, and I hope the Archivist can't hear the lie in my voice. Because I stole Grandfather's tube from the Carving and gave it to Ky to hide, and I did that because I can't seem to let go of the idea that those tubes *could* matter.

"That may be," the Archivist says. "But others don't agree with you. They want their own samples, and the ones that belong to family and friends. If they lose a loved one in the Plague, they'll want the tubes even more."

If they lose a loved one in the Plague. "Is that possible?" I wonder, but the minute I speak it I know it is. Death is always possible. I learned that in the Carving.

Almost as if she's reading my mind, the Archivist asks, "You've seen the tubes, haven't you? When you were outside the Society?"

For some reason I want to laugh. *The Cavern you are asking about, yes, I have seen that, with rows and rows of tubes stored neatly in the earth. I have also seen a cave full of papers, and golden apples on dark trees twisted from growing in a place with great wind and little rain, and my name carved in a tree, and paintings on stone.*

And in the Carving I have seen burned bodies under the sky and a man singing his daughter to her grave, marking her arms and his with blue. I have felt life in that place, and I have seen death.

"You didn't bring back any of those tubes to trade, did you?" she asks me.

How much does she know? "No," I say.

"That's too bad," she says.

"What would people trade for the tubes?" I ask.

"Everyone has something," the Archivist says. "Of course, we don't guarantee anything except that the sample belongs to the right person. We don't promise that there's a way to bring anyone back."

"But it's implied," I say.

"It would only require a few tubes to take you anywhere

you wanted to go," the Archivist says. "Like Keya Province." She waits, to see if I rise to the bait. She knows where my family is. "Or home to Oria."

"What about," I say, thinking of Camas, "someplace else entirely?"

We both look at each other, waiting.

To my surprise, she speaks first, and it is then that I know how badly she wants those samples.

"If you are asking for passage to the Otherlands," she says, very softly, "that is no longer possible."

I've never heard of the Otherlands—only the Other Countries, marked on a map back in Oria, places synonymous with Enemy territory. From the way the Archivist speaks of the *Otherlands,* though, I can tell she means someplace entirely different and distant, and a little thrill goes through me. Even Ky, who lived in the Outer Provinces, has never mentioned the Otherlands. Where are they? For a moment, I'm tempted to tell the Archivist *yes*, to try and find out more about places so remote they appear on no map I've ever seen, even the ones belonging to the villagers who once lived in the Carving.

"No," I say. "I don't have any tubes."

For a moment, we're both silent. Then the Archivist speaks. "I've noticed that lately your focus has shifted away from trading," she says. "I've seen the Gallery. It's quite an accomplishment."

"Yes," I say. "Everyone has something worth sharing."

The Archivist looks at me with pity and astonishment in her eyes. "No," she says. "Everything done in the Gallery has been done before, and better. But it's still a remarkable achievement, in its own way."

She is not the Pilot. I know it now. She reminds me of my Official, back in Oria. They both have in common their conviction that they are still learning, still growing, when in fact they have long ago lost that ability.

It's a relief to leave the Archives and go to the Gallery, which is alive and above ground. As I draw closer to the Gallery, I hear something.

Singing.

I don't know the song; it's not one of the Hundred. I can't really understand the words, I'm too far away, but I hear the melody. A woman's voice rises and falls, aches and heals, and then, in the chorus, a man joins in.

I wonder if she knew he was going to sing, too, if it was something they planned, or if she was surprised to suddenly find that she was not alone in her song.

When they stop, at first there is silence. Then a cheer from someone up at the front, and soon we all join in. I press closer through the crowd, trying to see the faces of those who are the music.

"Another?" the woman asks, and we cry out our answer. *Yes.*

This time she sings something else, something short and clear. The tune is full of movement but easy to follow:

> *I, a stone, am rolling,*
> *Up the highest hill*
>
> *You, my love, are calling*
> *Though the winter chills*
>
> *We must keep on going*
> *Now and then and still.*

Could this song be one from the Outer Provinces? It reminds me of the story of Sisyphus, and Ky said they kept their songs longer in the Outer Provinces. But all those people are gone now. That makes it seem like the words should be sad, but with the music behind them, they don't sound that way.

I catch myself humming along, and before I know it, I'm singing and so are the people around me. Over and over we go through the song, until we have the words and the melody right. At first I'm embarrassed when I catch myself moving, and then I don't care anymore, I don't mind, all I wish is that Ky were here and that he could see me now, singing too and dancing in front of the world.

Or Xander. I wish he were here. Ky already knows how to sing. Does Xander?

Our feet thump on the ground, and we can no longer smell even a trace of the fishes' bodies that once bumped up against the shore because they're decayed now, gone to bone, the smell of them lost in the scent of our living, our flesh, the salt of our tears and sweat, the sharpness of green grass and plants trampled underfoot. We're breathing the same air, singing the same song.

CHAPTER 18
XANDER

Over the course of the night, fifty-three new patients come in. Not all of them have the rash and bleeding, but some do. The head physic orders them all quarantined to our wing and assigns me to be the physic over the mutation. I'll be in charge of managing the patients' care from the floor while he watches from the port.

"Doesn't want to risk his own skin," one of the nurses mutters to me.

"It's all right," I tell her. "I want to see it through. But that doesn't mean you have to risk it. I can ask him to reassign you someplace else."

She shakes her head. "I'll be all right." She smiles at me. "After all, you talked him into including the courtyard as part of the quarantine area. That makes a difference."

"We've got the cafeteria, too," I say, and she laughs. None of us spend much time there anymore, except to take delivery of our meals.

The virologist comes in to examine the patients himself. He's intrigued, too. "The bleeding occurs because the virus is destroying platelets," he tells me. "Which means the spleen is likely to become enlarged in the affected patients."

A female medic near us nods. She's conducting a follow-up physical exam of one of the first patients. "His spleen *is* enlarged," she says. "It's protruding beneath the costal margin."

"And the patients are losing the ability to clear the secretions in their lungs and respiratory tracts," another medic says. "We're going to run into trouble with pneumonia and infection if we can't get them better soon."

Farther down the row of patients, we hear a shout. "We've had a rupture!" a medic calls. "I think he's bleeding internally."

I call out over the miniport for a surgic. We all gather around the patient, who has gone pale. The vital-stats machine screams at us as the patient's blood pressure drops and his heart rate speeds up. The medics and surgics yell out instructions.

This patient, and all the rest, lie completely still.

We can't save him. We don't even have time to get him to a surgical room before he dies. I glance around at the patients nearby. I hope they haven't seen too much. What *can* they see? The weight of the patient's death settles over me as I pick up my miniport, which beeps insistently with a private message from the head physic. He's watched the whole thing from the main port.

Sending patient data now. Review immediately.

He wants me to look at data now? When we've just had a

death? The entire team looks rattled. The point of the medical center, and the Rising, is that we save people. We don't lose them like this.

I walk over to the side of the room to check the data. At first I don't understand the urgency. It's data from the patients who've come in sick, and the information looks like basic medical workups. I'm not sure what it's supposed to tell me.

Then I get it. The workups are all recent, from when the patients were immunized. *The patients were immunized, and they still got the mutation, which means a huge segment of the population is at risk.*

"I'm going to have to lock down your wing completely," the head physic says from the miniport.

"I understand," I tell him. There's nothing else they can do. "We're going into lockdown," I tell the team.

They nod, exhausted. They understand. We've all been through this in drills a million times. We're here to save people.

Then I hear footsteps behind me, running. I spin around.

The virologist is heading for the main doors to the wing. Have they had time to lock it down yet? Or is he going to expose an entire new cluster of people to the mutated plague?

I take off, running back down the rows of patients, as fast as I can. He's older than me. It's short work to catch up and I tackle him, throwing us both to the ground. "You don't *run*," I say, not bothering to keep the disgust out of my voice. "You stay to help when people are sick. That's part of your job."

"Listen," he says, struggling to sit up. I let him but I hold on to his arm. "We may not be safe from this mutation. Our immunizations may mean nothing."

"That's exactly why you can't risk exposing anyone else," I say. "You know that better than anyone." I haul him up by the back of his uniform and walk him toward one of the wing's storage closets. I don't want to lock him up, but I'm not sure how else to deal with him right now.

"Unless," the virologist says, sounding either crazy or inspired, "the people with scars are safe. The *small* scars."

I know what he means. "The people who had the first round of the Plague," I say. The Rising told us to look for the marks, and Lei and I talked about them—those small red scars between their shoulder blades.

"Yes," he says eagerly. "They could have had a slightly mutated version of the earlier virus, and their variant is close enough to the mutant form that they're not getting it. But the immunization you and I were given—it was just chopped-up pieces of the original virus. It won't be close enough to this new mutant form to protect us."

I keep hold of him but nod to show that I'm listening.

"We didn't go down with the earlier version of the Plague," he says. "But we were still exposed. Our initial immunity protected us from the worst symptoms, but we could still contract that earlier version of the Plague. That's how an immunization works. It teaches your body how to react to a virus so your system recognizes the virus when it comes again. It's not that you don't get sick at all. But your body knows how to handle it."

"I know," I say. I've figured out this much already.

"*Listen to what I'm telling you,*" the virologist says. "If that happened, if we actually *contracted* the first version of the Plague, the one going around when the Pilot first spoke— then we have the red mark, too, and we're safe. We didn't go down, but we still had the virus. Our bodies just dealt with it. But if we *didn't* catch the earlier virus during that window"— he spreads out his hands—"we can still get the mutation. And we may not have a cure that works for this version."

For a minute he sounds crazy, like he's speaking gibberish, and then it all comes together and I think he might be right.

He twists his arm free from my grasp and starts unbuttoning the top of his plainclothes. Then he pulls down the collar of his black uniform. "Look," he says. "I don't have the small mark. Do I?"

He doesn't.

"No," I say. I resist the urge to pull down my own collar and try to see if the mark is there. I've never thought to look for it on myself. "You're needed here. And if you go out there, you could infect other people. You've been exposed to the mutation already, like the rest of us."

"I'll go out into the woods. People in the Borders have always known how to survive. There are places I can go."

"Like where?" I ask.

"Like the stone villages," he says.

I raise my eyebrows. Is he confused? I don't know what those places are. I've never heard of them before. "And do they have fluid and nutrient bags there?" I ask. "Do they have what you need to stay alive until there's a cure? And don't you care about exposing them to illness?"

He stares up at me with wild-eyed panic. "Didn't you see him?" he asks. "That patient? He died. I can't stay here."

"Was that the first time you've seen anyone die in real life?" I ask.

"People didn't die in the Society," he says.

"They did," I say. "They were just better at hiding it." And I understand why the virologist is afraid. I think about running away too, but only for a second.

The head physic decides to relax the lockdown long enough to send us more patients and more personnel. He's heard everything the virologist told me over the miniport, so he'll decide how to report it all to the Pilot. I'm glad that's not my job.

But I do have one request for the head physic. "When you send in the new personnel," I say, "make sure they know this new form of the virus hasn't responded yet to the cure. We don't need anyone else trying to run. We want them to know what they're getting into."

It's not long before several Rising officers, armed and wearing hazmat suits, escort the new personnel to our wing. The officers take the virologist away with them. I'm not sure where they'll quarantine him—in an empty room on his own, perhaps—but he's become a liability, and we can't keep him here when he's so volatile. I'm so focused on making sure he's taken care of that it takes me a moment to realize that one of the new staff is Lei.

As soon as I can, I find her in the courtyard. "You shouldn't be here," I tell her quietly. "We can't guarantee that it's safe."

"I know," she says. "They told me. They're not sure the cure works on the mutation."

"It's more than that," I say. "Remember when you and I were talking about the small red mark on the people who had the earlier virus?"

"Yes."

"The virologist they took out had a theory about that."

"What was it?"

"He thought that if someone had the red mark, it meant they'd had the virus, like we thought—and he also thought that it meant that they were protected from the new mutation."

"How could that be?" Lei asks.

"The virus changes," I say. "Like those fish you were talking about. It was one thing, now it's different."

She shakes her head.

I try again. "People who had the immunizations had been exposed to one form of the virus, a dead one. Then the first round of the Plague came along. Some of us might have contracted the virus, but we didn't get really sick because we'd already been exposed to it in its weakened form. The immunization did its job and our bodies fought off the illness. Still, we had exposure to the live virus itself, which means we might be safe from this mutation. The dead virus wasn't close enough to the mutation to protect us, but our exposure to the original live version of the Plague might be, as long as we actually contracted it."

"I still don't understand," she says.

I try again. "According to his theory, those who have the red mark are lucky," I say. "They've been exposed to the right versions of the virus at the right times. And that means they're safe from this mutation."

"Like stones in the river," she says, understanding crossing her face. "Going across. You need to step on them in the right order to get safely to the other side."

"I guess so," I say. "Or like the fish you were talking about. They change."

"No," she says, "The fish remain themselves. They adapt; they look completely different, but they're not fundamentally altered or gone."

"All right," I say, though now I'm the one who's confused.

She can tell. "I suppose," she says, "that you have to see them."

"Do you have the mark?" I ask Lei.

"I don't know," she says. "Do you?"

I shake my head. "I'm not sure either," I say. "It's not exactly in an easy place to see."

"I'll look for you," she tells me, and before I can say anything else, she steps around behind me, slides her finger under my collar, and pulls it down. I feel her breath on my neck.

"If the virologist is right, then you're safe," she says, and I can hear the smile in her voice. "You have the mark."

"Are you sure?" I ask.

"Yes," she says. "I am. It's right there." After she takes her hand away I can still feel the spot where her finger pressed against my skin.

She knows what I'm about to ask.

"No," she says. "Don't look. I don't want it to change what I do."

Later, as we leave the courtyard, Lei stops and looks at me. As she does, I realize that not very many people have eyes that are the color of hers: true black. "I changed my mind," she says.

At first I'm not sure what she means but then she sweeps her long hair to the side and says, "I think I want to know." There's a faint tremor in her voice.

The mark. She wants to know if she has it.

"All right," I say, and suddenly I feel awkward. Which is ridiculous, because I've looked at plenty of bodies that are just bodies. I know they're people, and I want to help them, but to some extent they're anonymous all the same.

But her body—will be *hers*.

She turns her back to me and unbuttons her uniform, waiting. For a moment I hesitate, my fingers hovering. Then I take a deep breath and pull her collar down. I'm careful not to brush her skin.

The mark isn't there.

And then without thinking I do touch her. I put my hand on her with my palm flat against the bone at the base of her neck and my fingers curving up into her hair. Like I can hide this from her.

Then I draw in my breath and pull my hand back. *Stupid.* Just because I'm fully immune doesn't mean I can't still carry some form of the mutated Plague. "I'm sorry—" I begin.

"I know," she says. She reaches over and takes my hand down without looking at me, and for a brief moment our fingers lock and hold on.

Then she lets go and pushes open the door, walking inside the building without looking back. And out of nowhere, I think: *So this is how it feels to stand at the edge of a canyon.*

PART FOUR

PLAGUE

CHAPTER 19
KY

The City of Oria looks like it got its teeth kicked out. The barricade here is no longer a neat circle. Instead, it's riddled with gaps. The Rising must have run out of white walls to enclose the stillzone, so they've had to use metal fencing instead. I see the hot glint of it in the spring sun as we fly over. I try not to look in the direction of the Hill.

Others, Rising officers in black, wave up at us. We're flying lower now, and I can see people looting and pushing against weak places in the fence. The barricade is about to be breached. Even from up here, I can feel the panic.

"The situation has deteriorated too much to land," our commander says. "We'll do a supply drop."

I have to admit that there have been times when I wished something bad would happen to the people of the Boroughs in Oria. Like the time the Society took me away and no one but Cassia ran after me. Or when the people laughed during the showings because they didn't understand death. I never wanted to see *them* die, but I would have liked for them to know how it felt to be afraid. I wanted them to know that their easy lives had a cost. But this is terrible to see. Over the past few weeks, the Rising has lost their grip on the people *and* the Plague. They won't say what's happened, but something has. Even the Archivists and traders seem to have completely disappeared. I have no way to get a message to Cassia.

One of these days, I'm not going to be able to resist flying to Central.

"The most secure area is located in front of City Hall," says the commander. "We'll make the drop there."

"Are we dropping all our supplies at City Hall?" I ask the commander. "What about the Boroughs?"

"Everything in front of City Hall," he says. "It's the safest way."

I don't agree. We need to disperse the supplies, or it'll be a bloodbath. People are already trying to break through the barricade. When they see us drop, they're going to want to get inside even more, and I don't know how long the Rising can hold off having to use violence in a situation like this. Will they send the fighters in like they had to do in Acadia?

Indie and I are last in the formation, so we circle around again while the others make their drop. We're outside of the City proper now, moving back in over the Boroughs. As we do, I see people coming out of their homes to watch us fly. They've obeyed the Rising's commands to stay put and wait instead of coming to the barricade.

And it means they'll likely starve, while the others at the walls fight over the supplies we've brought.

I feel a fierce, unexpected surge of sorrow and loyalty to the people of the Boroughs. They try to follow orders and do the right thing. Is it their fault everything is such a mess?

No.

Yes.

"Prepare the drop," the commander says. We've never done this before—left supplies without landing—but we've trained for it. There's a hatch in the belly of the ship where we can let the cargo out.

"Caleb," I say, switching on the speaker that goes down into the hold. "Are you ready?"

There's no answer.

"Caleb?"

"I'm ready," he says, but his voice sounds off.

I'm the pilot this time, so I'm in charge. "Go see what's wrong with him," I tell Indie. She nods and walks over to the hold, her balance perfect even with the motion of the ship. I hear her open the hatch to the hold and go down the ladder.

"Is there a problem?" the commander asks.

"I don't think so," I tell him.

"Caleb doesn't look good," Indie says a moment later, reappearing from the hold. "I think he's sick."

"I'm all right," Caleb says, but his voice still has a hint of strain in it. "I think I'm having a reaction to something."

"Do not drop your cargo," the commander says. "Return

immediately to the base."

Indie looks at me and raises her eyebrows. *Is he serious?*

"I repeat," he says, "do not drop cargo. Report immediately back to the base in Camas."

I look at Indie and she shrugs her shoulders. I ease the ship around and we fly over the people. I was coming in low for the drop and so I can see their faces turned up to watch us. They look like baby birds waiting for food.

"Here," I say to Indie, gesturing for her to take over the controls. I go down to check on Caleb.

He's not strapped in anymore. He stands at the back of the hold, his hands pressed against the side of the ship, his head bent down, every muscle tight in agony. When he looks at me I see fear in his eyes.

"Caleb," I say. "What's happening?"

"Nothing," he says. "It's fine. Go back up above."

"You're sick," I say. But with what? We can't get the Plague. Unless something went wrong.

"Caleb," I say. "What's happening?"

He shakes his head. He won't tell me. The ship shifts a little and he stumbles. "You know what's going on," I say, "but you won't tell me. So how am I supposed to help you?"

"There's nothing you can do," Caleb says. "You shouldn't be here anyway if I'm sick."

He's right. I turn to leave. When I sit down Indie raises her eyebrows at me. "Lock the hold," I say. "Don't go back down."

We're almost back to Camas before Caleb speaks again. We're flying over the long flat fields of Tana and I am, of course, thinking of Cassia and her family when Caleb's voice comes over the speaker.

"I changed my mind," he says. "There is something you can do. I need you to write something down for me."

"I don't have any paper," I say. "I'm flying the ship."

"You don't have to write it now," he says. "Later."

"All right," I say. "But first, you tell me what's happening."

The commander is silent. Is he listening?

"I don't know," Caleb says.

"Then I can't write," I tell him.

Silence.

"Tell me this," I say to Caleb. "What was in those cases you kept bringing back when we delivered the cure?"

"Tubes," Caleb says immediately, surprising me. "We brought out tubes."

"Which tubes?" I ask, but I think I know the answer. They'd fit in the cases perfectly. They're about the same size as the cures. I should have figured it out long ago.

"The tubes with the tissue preservation samples in them," Caleb says.

I'm right. But I don't understand the reasoning. "Why?" I ask Caleb.

"The Rising took over the storage facilities where the Society kept the tubes," he says, "but some members of the Rising wanted their families' samples under their own personal control. The Pilot provided that service for them."

"That's not fair," I say. "If the Rising really is for everyone, they should have given *all* the samples back."

"Pilot Markham," our commander says, "you're engaging in speculation about your commanding officers, which amounts to insubordination. I order you to cease this line of conversation."

Caleb doesn't say anything.

"So does the Rising think they can bring people back?" I ask. The commander starts speaking again, but this time I talk over him and so does Caleb.

"No," Caleb says. "They know they can't. They know the Society couldn't either. They just want the samples. Like insurance."

"I don't understand it," I say. "Someone like the Pilot should have seen enough death to know the tubes aren't worth anything. Why would he waste resources doing something so stupid?"

"The Pilot knows you can't bring people back with the samples," Caleb says. "Not everyone else does. He uses that to his advantage." He exhales. "The reason I'm telling you all this," he says, "is that you need to believe in the Pilot. If you don't, we're going to lose everything."

"I didn't know I was so important," I say.

"You're not," he says. "But you and Indie are two of the best pilots. He'll need everyone he can get before this is all over."

"What's *this*?" I ask. "The Plague? The Rising? You're right. The Pilot does need all the help he can get. He hasn't managed to get anything under control so far."

"You don't even know him," Caleb says. He sounds angry. That's good. There's a little more life in his voice.

"I don't," I say. "But you do, don't you. You knew him before the Rising came to power."

"We're both from Camas," Caleb says. "I grew up on the Army base where he was stationed. He was one of the pilots who flew to the Otherlands. He took more people out to the stone villages than any other pilot. And he never got caught. He was the obvious choice to lead the Rising when it was time for a new Pilot."

"I've lived in the Outer Provinces," I say, "and I've never heard of the stone villages *or* the Otherlands."

"They're real," Caleb says. "The Otherlands are the places *far* past Enemy territory. And the stone villages were built by Anomalies along the edge of the Outer Provinces when the Society came to power. The villages are like stepping-stones in a river. That's how they got their name. They run north to south and they're all built a day's journey apart from one another. When you reach the last one, you have to cross through Enemy territory if you want to go on to the Otherlands. You really haven't heard of the villages?"

"Not by that name," I say, but my mind races. The farmers in the Carving were far away from any other Anomalies, but they did have the map with another village marked in the mountains. *That* village could have been the southernmost of the stone villages, the final one. It's possible.

"So what did the Pilot do?" I ask.

"He saved people," Caleb says. "He and some of the other pilots would run people from the Society out as far as the last stone village. He made citizens pay to get out, and he helped Aberrations and Anomalies, too."

"That's who carved in the ships, isn't it?" I say, understanding. "People who were hiding there when the Pilot flew them out."

"It was stupid of them," Caleb says, a hint of anger in his voice. "They could have gotten the pilots in trouble."

"I think they meant it as a tribute," I say, remembering the picture carved on one of our earlier ships of the Pilot giving the people water. "That's what it looked like to me."

"It was still stupid," Caleb says.

"Do people live in the villages anymore?" I ask.

"I don't know," Caleb says. "They might have all left for the Otherlands by now. The Pilot tried to get them to join the Rising, but they wouldn't."

That sounds like the Anomalies who lived in the Carving.

They wouldn't join the Rising either. It makes me wonder what happened to Anna's people when they reached the village we saw marked on the map. Did they meet the stone villagers there? Did the groups have enough in common to get along? Did the people living in the stone villages help the people from the Carving, or did they drive them away—or worse? What's happened to Hunter and Eli?

"Other kids grew up telling stories about the Pilot," Caleb says. "But *I* grew up watching him fly. I know he's the one who can lead us out of this."

Caleb sounds terrible. The pain's winning out. I can hear it thick in his voice. And I know what's happening.

He's going still.

He was supposed to be immune. Something's happened with the Plague. Is this a new version of it? One our immunity can't protect us against?

"I want you to write down everything I said about the Pilot," Caleb says, "including that I believed in him until the end."

"Is this the end?" I ask.

Silence.

"Caleb?"

Nothing.

"Did he go still?" Indie asks. "Or decide he didn't want to talk anymore?"

"I don't know," I say.

She stands up as if she's about to go down into the hold. "No," I say. "Indie, you can't risk exposure to whatever it is."

"He didn't tell you much," Indie says, sitting back down. "I bet there were plenty of people who knew that about the tubes and the Pilot."

"We didn't," I remind her.

"You believe Caleb because he has those notches on his boots," she says, "but it doesn't mean he was in the camps. Anyone could have cut their boots like that."

"I think he was there," I say.

"But you don't *know* that he was."

"No."

"He *is* right about the Pilot, though," Indie says.

"So you do believe Caleb," I say. "About the Pilot, at least."

"I believe *myself* about the Pilot," Indie says. "I know that he's real." She leans closer to me and for a minute I think she might kiss me again, like she did all those weeks ago. "The villages are real, too," she says, "and the Otherlands. All of it."

Her voice is every bit as impassioned as Caleb's was. And I understand her. Indie loves me, but she's a survivor. When I told her I wouldn't run with her, she turned to something else to keep going. I believe in Cassia. Indie believes in the Rising and the Pilot. We've both found something to pull us through.

"It could have been different," I say, almost under my breath. If I'd kissed Indie again after she kissed me. If I hadn't known Cassia before I met Indie.

"But it's not," Indie says, and she's right.

CHAPTER 20
CASSIA

The world is not well.

I look out the window of my apartment and put my hand on the glass. It's dark. Crowds gather at the barricade, the way they do often now at night, and soon the Rising officers will come in black and disperse them all, petals to the wind, leaves on the water.

The Rising hasn't told us exactly what's happened, but, for the past few weeks, we've all been confined to our apartments. Those of us who can, send in our work over the ports. All communication with other Provinces has ceased. The Rising says that is temporary. The Pilot himself promises that everything will be fine soon.

It has begun to rain.

I wonder what it would have been like to see a flash flood in the Carving from up high like this. I'd like to have stood at the edge of the canyon and felt the rumble; closed my eyes to better hear the water; opened them again to see the world laid to waste, the rocks and trees torn and tumbling down. It would have been something to watch what looked like the end of the world.

Perhaps I am witnessing that now.

A chime sounds from my kitchen. Dinner has arrived, but I am not hungry. I know what the food will be—emergency rations. We have only two meals each day now. Someday they will run out of the rations, too. And then I don't know what they'll do.

If we start to feel sick and tired, we're supposed to send a message on the port. Then they'll come and help us. *But what if you go still while you sleep?* I wonder. The thought makes me lie awake at night. It's become difficult to find any rest.

I pull the meal from the delivery slot. There it is, cold and bland and blank, the Society's stores served to us by the Rising.

I have learned a few things from the Archivists. Food is running out; therefore, it is valuable. So I've used it to trade my way out of my confinement in my apartment. I take the meal out to the Rising guard at the entrance of our building. He's young and hungry, so he understands.

"Be careful," he says, and he holds open the door for me as I slip into the night.

I feel my way down the stones and steps, my hands brushing against the sides and coming away with the familiar green smell and feel of moss. The recent rain has made things slippery, and I have to concentrate, keeping the beam of my flashlight steady.

When I reach the end of the hallway, I'm not blinded, the

way I usually am. No flashlights flicker onto me, no beams swing in my direction as people notice me coming through the door.

The Archivists are gone.

A chill runs up my spine as I remember how this place reminded me of the crypt from the Hundred History Lessons. I close my eyes, imagining the Archivists lying down on the shelves, folding their hands on their chests, holding perfectly still as they wait for death to come.

Slowly I shine my light on the shelves.

They are empty. Of course. No matter what, the Archivists will survive. But they didn't tell me that they were leaving, and I have no idea where they might have gone. Did they leave anything back in the Archives?

I'm about to go look when I hear feet on the stairs and I spin around, swinging up my flashlight to blind whoever has entered.

"Cassia?" the voice asks. It's her. The head Archivist. She came back. I lower the light so she can see.

"I was hoping to find you," she says. "Central is no longer safe."

"What has happened?" I ask.

"The rumors about a mutated Plague," she says, "have been proven to be true. And we've confirmed that the mutation has spread here to Central."

"So you've all run away," I say.

"We have all decided to stay alive," she says. "I have

something for you." She reaches into the pack she carries and pulls out a slip of paper. "This came in at last."

The paper is real and old, printed with dark letters pressed deep into the page, not the slick surface blackness of printing from a port. There are two stanzas; the ones I don't have. Even though time is short and the world is wrong, I can't help but glance down, greedy, to read a bite, a bit of the poem:

The Sun goes crooked—that is night—
Before he makes the bend
We must have passed the middle sea,
Almost we wish the end
Were further off—too great it seems
So near the Whole to stand.

I want to read the rest but I feel the head Archivist's gaze on me, and I look back up. Something has gone crooked here; night is coming. Am I drawing close to the end? It almost feels like it—that there can't be much farther to go, having come so far already—and yet nothing feels finished.

"Thank you," I say.

"I'm glad it came in time," she says. "I've never left a trade unfinished."

I fold the poem back up and put it in my sleeve. I keep my expression neutral, but I know she'll hear the challenge in what I'm about to say. "I'm grateful for the poem, but you've still left a trade unfinished. My microcard never came in."

She laughs a little, the sound echoing through the empty Archives. "That one has come through, too," she says. "You'll receive the microcard in Camas."

"I don't have enough to pay for passage to Camas," I say. *How did she find out that's where I want to go?* Does she really have a way for me to get to Camas, or is she playing a cruel joke on me? My heartbeat quickens.

"There's no fee for your journey," the head Archivist says. "If you go to your Gallery and wait, someone from the Rising will arrive to bring you out."

The Gallery. I've never kept it hidden, but something about it being used like this feels wrong. "I don't understand," I say.

The Archivist pauses. "What you've traded," she says, very carefully, "has been interesting to some of us."

It's like my Official, again. I was not interesting to her, but my data was.

When my Official said that the Society had put Ky into the Matching pool, I saw the flicker of a lie in her eyes. She wasn't sure who had put him in.

I think the head Archivist is keeping something from me, too.

I have so many questions.

Who put Ky in the pool?

Who paid for my passage to Camas?

Who stole my poems?

This, I think I know. *Everyone has a currency.* The Archivist told me that herself. Sometimes, we might not even know what our price is until we are confronted with it, face to face. The Archivist could resist everything else in that treasure trove of the Archives, but my papers, smelling of sandstone and water and just out of reach, were irresistible to her.

"I've already paid my passage," I say. "Haven't I? With my pages from the lake."

It's so quiet, here underneath the ground.

Will she admit to it? I'm certain I'm right. The impassive stone of the Archivist's face looks entirely different from the flicker I saw on the Official's face when she lied to me. But both times, I feel the truth. The Official didn't know. The Archivist took my papers.

"My obligation to you is finished now," she says, turning to leave. "You're aware of the chance for passage to Camas. It is yours to keep or refuse." She moves away from the beam of my flashlight into the dark. "Good-bye, Cassia," she says.

And then she's gone.

Who will be waiting for me at the Gallery? Is the passage to Camas real, or is it one final betrayal? Did she arrange it for me, perhaps out of guilt for taking my papers? I don't know. I can't trust her anymore. I pull off the red bracelet that marked me as one of the Archivists' traders and put it on the shelf. I have no need of it, because it does not mean what I thought it did.

I find my case sitting alone on its shelf. When I open it and see the contents inside, I find I want none of them. They are part of other people's lives, and it feels that they no longer have place in my own.

But I will keep the poem the Archivist gave me. *Because this*, I think, *is real*. The Archivist might have stolen from me, but I cannot believe she would forge something. This poem is true. I can tell.

We step like plush, we stand like snow—

I stop at that line and remember when I stood at the edge of the Carving, in the snow looking out for Ky. And I remember when we said good-bye at the edge of the stream—

The waters murmur now,
Three rivers and the hill are passed,
Two deserts and the sea!
Now Death usurps my premium
And gets the look at Thee.

No.
That can't be right. I read the last two lines again.

Now Death usurps my premium
And gets the look at Thee.

I switch off my light and tell myself that the poem doesn't matter after all. Words mean what you want them to mean. Don't I know that by now?

For a moment, I'm tempted to stay here, hidden among the warren of shelves and rooms. I could go above ground now and then to gather food and paper, and isn't that enough to live on? I could write stories; I could hide from the world and make my own instead of trying to change it or live in it. I could write paper people and I would love them too; I could make them almost real.

In a story, you can turn to the front and begin again and everyone lives once more.

That doesn't work in real life. And I love my real people the most. Bram. My mother. My father. Ky. Xander.

Can I trust anyone?

Yes. My family, of course.

Ky.

Xander.

None of us would ever betray the other.

Before I came here, Indie and I ran a river, and we didn't know if it would poison us or deliver us to where we wanted to go. We took a dangerous, black-water risk; even now, I think I can feel the spray as we went down, the swell as we were swept under.

It was worth it then.

I remember again the Cavern in the Carving. It and the

Archives mingle together in my mind—those muddy fossiled bones and clean little tubes, these empty shelves and vacant rooms. And I realize that I can never stay in these hollowed-out places in the earth for long before I have to come up for air.

This passage to Camas, I tell myself, *is a risk I am willing to run.* You cannot change your journey if you are unwilling to move at all.

I hide in alleys, behind trees. When I wrap my hand around the bark of a small willow in a greenspace, I feel fresh letters carved into it, and they don't spell my name. The tree is sticky with its own blood. It makes me sad. Ky never cut deeply like this when he carved on something living. I wipe my hand on my black plainclothes and wish there were a way to leave a mark without taking.

I'm not even halfway to the lake when I hear and see the air ships.

They soar in overhead, carrying pieces of the barricade back toward the City.

No, I think, *not the Gallery.*

I run through the streets, darting away from lights and people, trying not to count how many times the ships come overhead. Someone calls out to me but I don't recognize the voice, so I keep going. It's too dangerous to stop. There's a reason we are supposed to stay inside—people are angry, and afraid, and the Rising is finding it increasingly difficult to cure and keep peace.

I run out into the dark of the marsh. Rising officers in black climb up to secure cables to the barricade walls while the ships hover over, their blades chopping through the air. I can just make out what's happening from the lights of the ships above and from the steadier beacons of those that have landed in the marsh.

The Gallery is still there, ahead of me, if I can just reach it in time.

I press up against a wall, breathing hard. I'm getting closer. The lake smell of water hits me.

One of the Gallery walls lifts into the sky and I stifle a cry. So much will be lost if the Gallery is gone. All those papers, everything we made, and how will I ever find the person who was supposed to take me to Camas if the meeting place no longer exists?

I am running, running, as hard as I ran into the Carving to find Ky.

They lift the second piece of the Gallery from the ground. *No. No. No.*

Within moments I'm standing there, staring down at the deep grooves in the earth, where papers float in puddles, like sails without boats. Paintings, poems, stories, all drowned. The people who used to meet here—who still have words and songs inside—what will happen to them? And how will I get to Camas *now*?

"Cassia," someone says. "You were almost too late."

I know her instantly, even though I haven't heard her speak in months; I could never forget the voice of the person who piloted me down the river. *"Indie,"* I say, and there she is, wearing black and standing up from her hiding spot among the marsh plants and bracken.

"They sent *you* to bring me to Camas," I say, and I laugh, because now I know I will get there, whatever else happens. Indie and I ran to the Carving, we came down the river, and now—

"We're going to fly," Indie tells me. "But we have to go."

I follow her, running, to her ship on the ground.

"You don't have to worry about any other Rising being on the ship," she says over her shoulder. "I'm the only one who flies alone. But we can't talk on board. The other ships might be listening in. And you have to ride in the hold."

"All right," I say, breathless. I'm glad I have no case to hinder me; it's enough to keep up with Indie as it is, carrying nothing but the lightness of paper.

We reach the ship and Indie scrambles up. I follow, and stand for just a moment in surprise at all the lights in the cockpit that Indie must manage. Our eyes meet and we both smile. Then I hurry and climb down into the hold. Indie shuts the door and I'm alone.

The ship is smaller and lighter than the ones we flew in to the camps. A few tiny lights line the floor, but the hold is largely dark and there are no windows. I am so tired of flying blind.

I run my hands along the walls of the ship, trying to distract myself by discovering all that I can about my surroundings.

There. I think I've found something. A tiny line, scratched into the wall near the floor:

l

An *L*, lowercase?

I smile a little to myself, at how I want to find letters in everything. It could be a scratch, the haphazard scarring and scraping that comes with the loading and shifting of cargo. But the more time I spend running my fingers over it, the more I'm convinced it was carved with intent. I try to feel for more but I can't stretch any farther while I'm still strapped in.

Glancing up at the door to the hold, I unbuckle the strap and move quietly so that I can feel farther down.

There are many of them, carved in a row.

lllll

This letter must mean something, I think, *to write it so many times,* and then I realize; not letters. Notches. Like the ones Ky told me about the decoys cutting into their boots to mark time survived out in the work camps.

I remember what Ky told me about his friend Vick, how every day he marked was a day without the girl he loved.

Ky and I have been marking, too, with flags on the Hill.

With the poetry of others and with words of our own. Whoever carved here was keeping time and holding on.

I do the same, running my fingers across each tiny groove in the metal over and over again, thinking about the pieces of the Gallery lifted up into the sky. I wonder if, when the Rising sets them down again to make a wall, some of the papers will have survived the flight.

The door to the hatch opens and Indie beckons for me to come up.

The ship is flying itself, somehow. Indie sits back down at the controls. She gestures for me to take the seat next to her and I do, my heart pounding. Until now, I've never been able to see while I fly, and I feel a dizzying lightness as I look out at the land below us.

Is this *what I've missed?*

The stars have come to the earth, and the ocean has turned over the ground; dark waves meet the sky. They are unmoving, barely visible but for the light of the sun rising behind them.

Mountains, I realize. That's what the ocean is. Those waves are peaks. The stars are lights in houses and on streets. The earth reflects the sky and the sky meets the earth and, every now and then, if we're lucky, we have a moment to see how small we are.

Thank you, I want to tell Indie. *Thank you for letting me see while I fly. I have wanted it for so long.*

CHAPTER 21
XANDER

*P*atient number 73 exhibits little to no improvement.

Patient number 74 exhibits little to no improvement.

Wait, that's a mistake. I haven't examined Patient 74 yet. I delete the notation and hook the vital-stats machine up to Patient 74. The display lights up with numbers. Her spleen is enlarged, so I turn her very carefully when I perform my exam. When I shine a light into her eyes, she doesn't respond.

Patient number 74 exhibits little to no improvement.

I move on to the next patient. "I'm checking your stats again," I tell him. "Nothing to worry about."

It's been weeks and none of the patients is getting better. The rashes along the infected nerves turn into boils, which would be extremely painful if the still could feel anything. We don't think they can. But we're not certain.

Only a few of us are left who haven't gotten sick. I'm still a physic but because we're so shorthanded I spend most of my time changing the patients' nutrition bags and catheter bags, monitoring their stats, and performing physical exams. Then I sleep for a few hours and do it all again.

They don't bring in new patients very often anymore, except for those who are already here working when they get sick. We don't have room for anyone else because the still don't go home. I used to pride myself on how fast we got patients into recovery. Now my satisfaction comes from keeping as many of them here as long as possible because these days, if a patient leaves, it means they've died.

Once I'm finished with this round, I'll get to rest. I think I'll be able to fall asleep quickly. I'm exhausted. If I didn't know better, I'd think I was coming down with the mutated Plague myself. But this is the same old weariness I've felt for days.

Most of the workers at the medical center have figured out by now that those who have the small red mark are the exceptions among those of us who the Rising initially made immune. The virologist's theory appears to be right. If someone was lucky enough to get exposed to the earlier Plague—the live virus—they're now immune and carry the red mark on their backs. The Rising hasn't told the general public about the mark because our leaders are worried about what will happen. And they've been trying to figure out a cure for the mutation.

It's too much for one Pilot to handle.

Once again, I've been lucky. The least I can do is stick around. It's the people like Lei whom I really admire. They know they're not immune but they stay anyway so they can help the patients.

I move through the rest of the patients, all the way to the last bed, where Patient 100 draws in ragged, wet breaths. I try not to think too much about how the cure might have caused the mutation, or about where my family or Cassia might be. I've already failed them. But I can't fail these hundred.

I don't see Lei in the courtyard when I'm finished, so I break protocol and look in the sleeproom. She's not there either.

She wouldn't have run away. So where is she?

As I pass the darkened cafeteria, I see a flicker of light. The port is on. Who could be inside? Is the Pilot speaking to us? Usually, when he does, they have us watch on one of the larger screens. I open the door to the cafeteria and see Lei silhouetted against the port. When I get a little closer I see that she's going through the Hundred Paintings.

I'm about to say something but then I stop myself and watch her for a second. I've never seen anyone look at the paintings the way she does. She leans forward. She takes a few steps back.

Then she pulls up a painting, and I hear her draw in her breath as she puts her hand right on the screen. She stays there looking at it so long that I clear my throat. Lei whirls around. I can barely see her face in the reflected light from the port.

"Still having trouble sleeping?" I ask.

"Yes," she says. "This is the best remedy I've found. I try to picture the scenes again in my mind when I'm lying down."

"You're taking your time with them," I say, trying to joke with her. "You'd think you hadn't seen the paintings before."

For a moment, I feel like she's about to tell me something. Then: "Not this one," she says, moving aside so I can see the screen.

"It's number Ninety-Seven," I say. The painting shows a girl in a white dress and a lot of light and water.

"I suppose I didn't notice it until now," Lei says, and her voice sounds final, like a door shutting tight. I don't know what I said wrong. For some reason I'm desperate to open that door back up. I talk to everyone here, all the time, patient and medic and nurse, but Lei's different. She and I worked together before we came in.

"What do you like about it?" I ask, trying to get her to keep talking. "I like how you can't tell if she's in the water or on the shore. But what's she doing? I've never been able to figure it out."

"She's fishing," Lei says. "That's a net she's holding."

"Has she caught anything?" I ask, looking closer.

"It's hard to say," Lei tells me.

"So that's why you like it," I say, remembering Lei's story about the fish that come back to the river in Camas. "Because of the fish."

"Yes," Lei says. "And because of this." She touches a little patch of white at the top of the picture. "Is it a boat? The reflection of the sun? And here," she says, pointing to darker spots on the painting. "We don't know what's casting these shadows. There are things going on outside the edges. It leaves you with a sense of something you can't see."

I think I understand. "Like the Pilot," I say.

"No," she says.

In the distance, we hear screaming and calling out. A fighter ship whirs overhead.

"What's going on out there?" Lei asks.

"I think it's the same as usual," I tell her. "People outside the barricade wanting to come in." The orange light of bonfires on the other side of the walls looks eerie, but it isn't new. "I don't know how much longer the officers can hold them."

"They wouldn't want in if they knew what it looked like," she says.

Now that my eyes have adjusted to the light, I can see that Lei's fatigue is actual pain. Her face has a drawn look, and her words, usually so light, sound heavy.

She's getting sick.

"Lei," I say. I almost reach out and take her by the elbow to guide her from the cafeteria, but I'm not sure how she'd feel about the gesture. She holds my gaze for a moment. Then, slowly, she turns away from me and lifts up her shirt. Red lines run around her back.

"You don't have to say it," she says. She tucks her shirt back in and turns around. "I already know."

"We should get you hooked up to one of the nutrient bags," I say. "Right now." Thoughts race through my mind.

You shouldn't have stayed, you should have left like the others did until we knew we had something that worked—

"I don't want to lie down," Lei says.

"Come with me," I tell her, and this time I do take her arm. I feel the warmth of her skin through her sleeve.

"Where are we going?" she asks me.

"To the courtyard," I say. "You can sit on a bench while I go get a line and a nutrient bag." This way, she won't have to be inside when she goes down. She can stay outside as long as possible.

She looks at me with her exhausted, beautiful eyes. "Hurry," she says. "I don't want to be alone when it happens."

When I return with the equipment, Lei waits in the courtyard with her shoulders slumped in exhaustion. It's strange to see her with less-than-perfect posture. She holds out her arm and I slide the needle in.

The fluid begins to drip. I sit down next to her, holding the bag higher than her arm so that the line keeps running.

"Tell me a story," she says. "I need to hear something."

"Which one of the Hundred would you like?" I ask. "I remember most of them."

I hear a faint trace of surprise in her voice under the fatigue. "Don't you know anything else?"

I pause. Not really. The Rising hasn't had time to give us new stories, and it's not like I know how to create. I just work with what I have.

"Yes," I say, trying to think of something. Then I borrow from my own life. "About a year ago, back in the Society, there was a boy who was in love with a girl. He'd watched her for a long time. He hoped she'd be his Match. Then she was. He was happy."

"That's all?" Lei asks.

"That's all," I say. "Too short?"

Lei begins to laugh and for a moment she sounds like herself. "It's you," she says. "It's obvious. That's no story."

I laugh, too. "Sorry," I say. "I'm not very good at this."

"But you love your Match," Lei says, no longer laughing. "I know that about you. You know it about me."

"Yes," I say.

She looks at me. The liquid drips into the line.

"I know an old story about people who *couldn't* be Matched," she says. "He was an Aberration. She was a citizen and a pilot. It was the first of the vanishings."

"The vanishings?" I ask.

"Some people inside the Society wanted to get out," Lei says. "Or wanted to get their children out. There were pilots who would fly people away in exchange for other things."

"I've never heard of anything like this," I say.

"It happened," Lei says. "I saw it. Some of those parents would trade anything—risk everything—because they thought sending their children away was the best way to keep them safe."

"But where would they take them?" I ask. "Into Enemy territory? That doesn't make any sense."

"They'd take them to the edge of Enemy territory," Lei says. "To places called the stone villages. After that, it was up to people to decide whether they'd stay in the villages, or try to cross Enemy territory to find a place known as the Otherlands. No one who went on to the Otherlands ever came back."

"I don't understand it," I say. "How would sending your children out to the middle of nowhere—closer to the Enemy— be safer than staying in the Society?"

"Perhaps they knew about the Plague," Lei says. "But obviously your parents didn't feel that way. Neither did mine." She looks at me. "You almost sound like you're defending the Society."

"I'm not," I say.

"I know," she says. "I'm sorry. I didn't mean to tell you history. I meant to tell you a story."

"I'm ready," I say. "I'm listening."

"The story, then." She lifts her arm and looks at the liquid running in. "This pilot loved the man but she had obligations at home, ones that she couldn't break, and obligations to her leaders, too. If she left, too many people would suffer. She flew the man she loved all the way to the Otherlands, which no one had done before."

"What happened after that?" I ask.

"She was shot down by the Enemy on her way back," Lei says. "She never got to tell people what she had seen in the Otherlands. But she had saved the one she loved. She knew that, no matter what else happened."

In the silence that follows her story, she leans against me. I don't think she even knows she's doing it. She's going down.

"Do you think you could do that?" she asks.

"Fly?" I say. "Maybe."

"No," she says. "Do you think you could let someone go if you thought it was best for them?"

"No," I say. "I'd have to *know* it was best for them."

She nods, as if she expected my answer. "Almost anyone could do that," she says. "But what if you didn't know and you only *believed*?"

She doesn't know if it's true. But she wants it to be.

"That story would never be one of the Hundred," she says. "It's a Border story. The kind of thing that can only happen out here."

Was she a pilot once? Is that where her husband is? Did she fly him out and now she's going down? Is this story true? Any of it?

"I've never heard of the Otherlands," I say.

"You have," she says, and I shake my head.

"*Yes*," she says, challenging me. "Even if you never heard the name, you had to know they existed. The world can't only be the Provinces. And it isn't flat like the Society's maps. How would the sun work? And the moon? And the stars? Didn't you look up? Didn't you notice that they changed?"

"Yes," I say.

"And you didn't think about why that might be?"

My face burns.

"Of course," Lei says, her voice quiet. "Why would they teach you? You were meant to be an Official from the very beginning. And it's not in the Hundred Science Lessons."

"How do *you* know?" I ask.

"My father taught me," she says.

There's a lot I'd like to ask her. What is her father like? What color did she wear when she was Matched? Why didn't I find out all of this before? Now there's not enough time for the little things. "You're not a Society sympathizer," I say instead. "I've always known that. But you weren't Rising at the beginning."

"I'm not Rising or Society," she says. The fluid drips into her arm slowly. It can't keep pace with what's happening to her.

"Why don't you believe in the Rising?" I ask. "Or the Pilot?"

"I don't know," she says. "I wish I could."

"What do you believe?" I ask.

"My father also taught me that the earth is a giant stone," she says. "Rolling and turning through the sky. And we're all on it together. I do believe that."

"Why don't we fall off?" I ask.

"We couldn't if we tried," she says. "There's something

that holds us here."

"So the world is moving under my feet right now," I say.

"Yes."

"But I don't feel it."

"You will," she says. "Someday. If you lie down and hold very still."

She looks at me. We both realize what she's said: *still*.

"I was hoping to see him again before this happened," she says.

I almost say, *I'm here*. But looking at her I know that it's not going to be enough, because I'm not who she wants. I've seen someone look at me this way before. Not through me, exactly, but beyond to someone else.

"I was hoping," she says, "that he'd find me."

After she's still, I find a stretcher left behind by the medics. I lie her down and hang up the bag. One of the head medics comes past. "We don't have room in this wing," he says.

"She's one of ours," I tell him. "We're making room."

He has the red mark, too, so he doesn't hesitate to bend down and look more closely at her. Recognition crosses his face. "Lei," he says. "One of the best. The two of you worked together even before the Plague, didn't you?"

"Yes," I tell him.

The medic's face is sympathetic. "Feels like that was in a whole different world, doesn't it?" he says.

"Yes," I say. It does. I feel strangely detached, like I'm watching myself take care of Lei. It's just the exhaustion, but I wonder if this is what it feels like to be still. Their bodies stay in one place, but can their minds go somewhere else?

Maybe part of Lei is floating around the medical center and going to all the places she knew. She's in the patients' rooms, overseeing their care. She's in the courtyard, breathing in the night air. She's at the port, looking at the painting of the girl fishing. Or, maybe she's left the medical center behind and gone to find him. They could be together even now.

I bring Lei into the room with the others. There are a hundred and one of them now, all staring up at the ceiling or off to the sides. "You're due to sleep now," the head physic tells me from the port.

"I will in a minute," I say. "Let me get her settled." I call for one of the medics to come over to help me perform the physical exam.

"She's all right so far," the medic says. "Nothing's enlarged, and her blood pressure is decent." She reaches out and touches my hand before she leaves. "I'm sorry," she says.

I'm looking into Lei's staring-up eyes. I've talked to lots of other patients, but I'm not sure what to say to her. "I'm sorry," I say, echoing the medic's words to me. It's not enough: I can't do anything for Lei.

Then I get an idea, and before I can talk myself out of it, I take off down the hall for the cafeteria and the port where Lei was looking at the paintings.

"Please have paper, please have paper," I say to the port. If I'm talking to patients who can't answer, why not talk to the port, too?

The port listens. It prints out all of the Hundred Paintings when I enter the command. I gather up those pages full of color and light and take them with me. This is what I did for Cassia when she left me: I tried to give her something I knew she loved to take with her.

Most of the other workers think I'm crazy, but one of the nurses agrees that my idea might help. "If nothing else, it'll give *me* something different to look at," she says, and she finds adhesive tape and surgical thread in the supply closet and helps me hang the pictures from the ceiling, above the patients.

"Port paper deteriorates pretty fast," I say, "so we'll have to print them out every few days. And we should rotate them through. We don't want the patients getting sick of any one painting." I step back to survey what we've done. "It would be better if we had new pictures. I don't want the patients to think they're back in the Society."

"We could make some," another nurse says eagerly. "I've always missed drawing, the way we did in First School."

"What would you use?" I ask. "We don't have any paints."

"I'll think of something," she says. "Haven't you always wanted the chance?"

"No," I say. I think it surprises her, so I smile to take the edge off. I wonder if I'd be a different kind of person, the kind Lei and Cassia could fall in love with, if I had.

"The head physic is going to pull you from your next shift if you don't go to the sleeproom now," the nurse tells me.

"I know," I say. "I heard him on the port."

But there's someone I have to speak to before I go. "I'm sorry," I tell Lei. The words are as inadequate as they were the first time, so I try again. "They'll find a cure, don't you think?" I point to the painting hanging above her. "There's got to be some light in a corner somewhere." I wouldn't have seen the light if she hadn't pointed it out, but once she did, it became impossible to ignore.

On my way to the sleeproom, the door to the courtyard opens and someone in black steps out into the hall, blocking my way. I stop in my tracks. It's a girl I've seen before, but my exhausted mind won't let me place exactly where. Regardless, I know she doesn't belong here in our locked-down wing. The head physic didn't tell me anyone new was coming in, and even if they did, they'd have to come through the main door.

"Oh good," the girl says. "There you are. I've been looking for you."

"How did you get in here?" I ask.

"I flew," she says. Then she smiles, and I know exactly who she is: Indie, the girl who brought the cures in with Ky once before. "I might also have some keycodes for the doors," she says.

"You shouldn't be here," I tell her. "This place is full of people who are sick."

"I know," she says, "but you're not, are you?"

"No," I say. "I'm not sick."

"I need you to come with me," she says. "Now."

"No," I say. This doesn't make any sense. "I'm a physic here." I can't leave all the still, and I certainly can't leave Lei. I reach for the miniport.

"But I'm here to take you to Cassia," Indie says, and I drop my hand. Is she telling the truth? Could Cassia really be close by somewhere? Then fear rushes over me. "Is she in the medical center?" I ask. "Is she sick?"

"Oh no," Indie says. "She's fine. She's outside, on my ship."

All these months I've wanted to see Cassia again, and now I might have the chance. But I can't do it. There are too many still, and one of them is Lei. "I'm sorry," I tell Indie. "I have to take care of the patients here. And you've been exposed to the mutation now. You shouldn't leave. You need to go to quarantine."

She sighs. "He thought you might be hard to convince. So I'm supposed to tell you that if you come with me, you'll be able to help him work on the cure."

"Who are you talking about?" I ask.

"The Pilot, of course." She says it so matter-of-factly that I believe her.

The *Pilot* wants me to help work on the cure.

"He knows you have firsthand knowledge of the mutated Plague," Indie says. "He needs you."

I look back down the hallway.

"*Now,*" Indie says. "He needs you now. There's no time to say good-bye." Her voice is honest and unflinching. "Can any of them hear you anyway?"

"I don't know," I say.

"You trust the Pilot," Indie says.

"Yes."

"But have you ever met him?"

"No," I say. "But you have."

"Yes," Indie says. She enters a code and pushes open the door. It's almost morning now. "And you're right to believe in him."

CHAPTER 22
KY

Ky," she whispers to me. *"Ky."*

Her hand is soft against my cheek. I can't seem to wake up. Maybe it's because I don't want to. It's been too long since I dreamed about Cassia.

"Ky," she says again. I open my eyes.

It's Indie.

She sees in my face that I'm disappointed. Her expression falters a little, but even in the very faint light of early morning I can see triumph in her eyes.

"What are you doing?" I ask her. "You should be in quarantine." After we brought back Caleb, they took him away and locked Indie and me both up in quarantine cells here at the base. At least they didn't put us in City Hall. "How did you get in here?" I ask, looking around. The door to my cell is open. Everyone else that I can see looks asleep.

"I did it," she says. "I've got a ship. And I've got her." She grins. "While you were sleeping, I flew to Central."

"You went to *Central?*" I say, standing up. "And you found her?"

"Yes," Indie says. "She's not sick. She's fine. And now you can run."

Now we can run. We can get out of here. I know it's dangerous but I feel like I can do anything if Cassia's really in Camas. When I stand up, I'm dizzy for a second and I put my hand on the wall for support. Indie pauses. "Are you all right?" she asks.

"Of course," I say. Cassia's no longer in Central. She's here and she's safe.

In unison, Indie and I slip out the door of the cell and start for the fields. The grasses whisper to each other in the pale dark and I start to run. Indie stays next to me, keeping pace.

"You should have seen the landings I did." Indie says. "They were perfect. *Better* than perfect. People are going to tell stories about them someday." Indie sounds almost giddy. I haven't heard her like this before, and it's contagious.

"How does she look?" I ask.

"The same as always," Indie says, and I start laughing and stop running and reach to grab Indie and spin her around and kiss her cheek and thank her for managing the impossible, but then I remember.

I could be sick. So could she.

"Thank you," I tell Indie. "I wish we weren't quarantined."

"Does it really matter?" she asks, coming a tiny bit closer. Her face is full of pure joy and I feel that kiss again on my lips.

"Yes," I say, "it does." Then I'm struck by fear. "You made sure Cassia wasn't exposed to the new virus, didn't you?"

"She rode in the hold almost the whole time," Indie says. "The ship had been sterilized. I didn't really even talk to her."

I'll have to be careful. Wear a mask, stay out of the hold, keep my distance from Cassia . . . but at the very least, I can see her. *Too good to be true,* some instinct within me warns. *You and Cassia together, flying away, just like you imagined? Things don't happen like that.*

If you let hope inside, it takes you over. It feeds on your insides and uses your bones to climb and grow. Eventually it becomes the thing that *is* your bones, that holds you together. Holds you up until you don't know how to live without it anymore. To pull it out of you would kill you entirely.

"Indie Holt," I say, "you are too good to be true."

Indie laughs. "No one's ever called me good before."

"Sure they have," I say. "When you're flying."

"No," she says. "Then they say I'm *great*."

"That's right," I say, "you are," and in unison we're both running again for the ships. They huddle against the morning like a flock of metal birds.

"This one," Indie says, and I follow her. "You first," she says.

I scramble up into the cockpit, turning around to ask, "Who's going to fly?"

"I am," says a familiar voice.

The Pilot emerges from the shadows at the back of the cockpit.

"It's all right," Indie says to me. "He's the one who's going to help you run, all the way to the mountains."

Neither the Pilot nor I say anything. It's strange not hearing his voice again. I'm so used to him talking at us from the screen.

"Is she really here?" I ask Indie quietly, hoping that she lied to me about Cassia being on board. Something about this seems wrong. Can't Indie feel it?

"Go see," Indie says, pointing to the hold. She smiles. Then I know. She doesn't think this is a trap, and Cassia's here. That's clear, even though nothing else is. Something's wrong with me. I can't think right, and when I climb down into the hold, I almost lose my footing.

There she is. After all these months, we're on the same ship. All I want, right here. *Let's take the Pilot down, let's run, let's take each other all the way to the Otherlands.* Cassia looks up at me, her expression strong and wise and beautiful.

But Cassia's not alone.

Xander's with her.

Where is the Pilot taking all of us? Indie trusts him, but I don't.

Indie, what have you done?

"You wouldn't run with me," Indie says, "so I brought her to you. Now you can go to the mountains."

"You're not coming with us," I say, realizing.

"If things were different, I would," Indie says, and when she looks at me, it's hard to hold her honest, longing gaze. "But they aren't. And I still have flying to do." And then, fast, like a fish or a bird, she disappears from the entrance to the hold. No one can catch Indie when it's time for her to move.

CHAPTER 23
CASSIA

We were supposed to meet months ago on a dark early-spring night by the lake, where we could be alone.

Ky's face is drawn with fatigue, and I catch the scent of sage and sand and grass, of the world outdoors. I know that look of stone in his face, that set of his jaw. His skin is rough. His eyes are deep.

We began with his hand around mine, showing me shapes.

In Ky's eyes is such complete love and hunger that it goes through me like the sharp, high note of a bird in the canyon, echoing all the way through my body. I am seen and known, if not yet touched.

The moment sings between us and then everything turns to motion.

"No," Ky says, moving back toward the ladder. "I forgot. I can't be down here with you."

He's too late; the Pilot has closed the hatch above us. Ky pounds on the door as the engines fire up and the Pilot's voice comes through the speakers. "Prepare for takeoff," he says. I grab hold of one of the straps hanging from the ceiling.

Xander does the same. Ky still hammers at the door to the hold.

"I can't stay," he says. "There's an illness out there, worse than the Plague, and I've been exposed to it." His eyes look wild.

"It's all right," Xander tries to tell Ky, but Ky can't hear over the roar of the engines and the pounding of his hands.

"Ky," I say, as loud as I can, between the beats of his fists hitting the metal. "It's. All. Right. I. Can't. Get. Sick."

Then he turns around.

"Neither can Xander," I say.

"How do you know?" Ky asks.

"We both have the mark," Xander says.

"What mark?"

Xander turns around and pulls down his collar so Ky can see. "If you've got this, it means you can't get the mutated Plague."

"I have it, too," I say. "Xander looked for me when we were flying here."

"I've been working with the mutation for weeks," Xander says.

"What about me?" Ky asks. He turns around, and in one fast motion, pulls his shirt over his head. There, in the dim light of the air ship, I see the planes and muscles of his back, smooth and brown.

And nothing else.

My throat tightens. "Ky," I say.

"You don't have it," Xander says, his words blunt but his voice sympathetic. "You should stay away from us, in case your exposure didn't actually infect you. We could still be carriers."

Ky nods and pulls his shirt back over his head. When he turns to us there's something haunted and relieved in his eyes. He didn't expect to be immune; he's never been lucky. But he's glad that I am. My eyes burn with angry tears. Why does it always have to be like this for Ky? How does he stand it?

He keeps moving.

The Pilot's voice comes in through a speaker in the wall. "The flight won't be long," he tells us.

"Where are we going?" Ky asks.

The Pilot doesn't answer.

"To the mountains," I say, at the same time Xander says, "To help the Pilot find a cure."

"That's what Indie told you," Ky says, and Xander and I nod. Ky raises his eyebrows as if to say, *But what does the* Pilot *have in mind?*

"There's something in the hold for Cassia," the Pilot says. "It's in a case at the back."

Xander finds the case first and pushes it toward me. He and Ky both watch as I open it up. Inside are two things: a datapod and a folded piece of white paper.

I take out the datapod first and hand it to Xander to hold. Ky stays on the other side of the ship. Then I lift out the paper. It's slick, white paper from a port, and heavier than it should be, folded in an intricate pattern to conceal something inside. When I peel away the layers, I see Grandfather's microcard in the center.

Bram sent it after all.

He sent something else, too. Radiating out from the middle of the paper are lines of dark writing. A code.

I recognize the pattern in the writing—he's made it look like a game I once made for him on the scribe. *This is my brother's writing.* Bram taught himself to write, and instead of just deciphering my message, he's put together a simple code of his own. We thought he couldn't pay attention to detail, but he can, when it interests him enough. He would have been a wonderful sorter after all.

My eyes fill with tears as I picture my exiled family at their home in Keya. I only asked for the microcard, but they sent more. The code from Bram, the paper from my mother—I think I see her careful hand in the folding. The only one who didn't send anything is my father.

"Please," the Pilot says, "go ahead and view the micro-card." His tone remains polite, but I hear a command in his words.

I slide the microcard into the datapod. It's an older model, but it only takes a few seconds for the first image to load. And there he is. Grandfather. His wonderful, kind, clever face. I haven't seen him in almost a year, except in my dreams.

"Is the datapod working?" the Pilot asks.

"Yes," I say, my throat aching. "Yes, thank you."

For a moment, I forget that I'm looking for something specific—Grandfather's favorite memory of me. Instead I'm distracted by the pictures of his life.

Grandfather, young, a child standing with his parents. A little older, wearing plainclothes, and then with his arm around a young woman. My grandmother. Grandfather appears holding a baby, my father, with my grandmother laughing next to him, and then that too is gone.

Bram and I appear on the screen with Grandfather.

And vanish.

The screen stops on a picture of Grandfather at the end of his life, his handsome face and dark eyes looking out from the datapod with humor and strength.

"In parting, as is customary, Samuel Reyes made a list of his favorite memory of each of his surviving family members," the historian says. "The one he chose of his daughter-in-law, Molly, was the day they first met."

My father remembered that day, too. Back in the Borough, he told me how he went with his parents to meet my mother at the train. My father said they all fell in love with her that day; that he'd never seen anyone so warm and alive.

"His favorite memory of his son, Abran, was the day they had their first real argument."

There must be a story behind this memory. I'll have to ask my father about it when I see him again. He rarely argues with anyone. I feel a little pang. Why didn't Papa send me something? But he must have approved of their sending the microcard. My mother would never have gone behind my father's back.

"His favorite memory of his grandson, Bram, was his first word," the historian says. "It was 'more.'"

Now, my turn. I find myself leaning forward, the way I did when I was small and Grandfather told me things.

"His favorite memory of his granddaughter, Cassia," the historian says, "was of the red garden day."

Bram was right. He heard the historian correctly. She did say *day*. Not days. So did the historian make a mistake? I wish they'd let Grandfather speak for himself. I'd like to hear *his* voice saying these words. But that's not the way the Society did things.

This has told me nothing except that Grandfather loved me—no small thing, but something I already knew. And a red garden day could be any time of year. Red leaves in the fall, red flowers in the summer, red buds in the spring, and even, sometimes, when we sat outside in the winter, our noses and cheeks turned red from the cold and the sun set crimson in the west. Red garden days. There were so many of them.

And for that, I am grateful.

"What happened on the red garden day?" the Pilot asks, and I look up. For a moment, I'd forgotten that he was listening.

"I don't know," I say. "I don't remember."

"What does the paper say?" Xander asks.

"I haven't decoded it yet," I tell him.

"I can save you the time," the Pilot says. "It reads, '*Cassia, I want you to know that I'm proud of you for seeing things through, and for being braver than I was.*' It's from your father."

My father *did* send me a message. And Bram encoded it for him, and my mother wrapped it up.

I glance down at Bram's code to make sure the Pilot has translated the note correctly, but then the Pilot interrupts me.

"This trade didn't come through until recently," the Pilot says. "It appears that after it left your family's hands, the trader involved fell ill. When it did come through, we found the microcard intriguing, and the message as well."

"Who gave this to you?" I ask.

"I have people who watch out for things they know might interest me," the Pilot says. "The head Archivist in Central is one of those people."

She has betrayed me again. "Trades are supposed to be secret," I say.

"In a time of war, different rules apply," the Pilot says.

"We are not at war," I say.

"We are *losing* a war," the Pilot says, "against the mutation. We have no cure."

I look at Ky, who doesn't have the mark, who isn't safe, and I understand the urgency of the Pilot's words. We can't lose.

"You are either helping us to find and administer the cure," the Pilot says, "or you are hindering our efforts."

"We want to help you," Xander says. "That's why you're taking us to the mountains, isn't it?"

"I *am* taking you to the mountains," the Pilot says. "What happens to you when you arrive there is something I haven't determined yet."

Ky laughs. "If you're spending this much time deciding what to do with the three of us when there's an incurable virus raging through the Provinces, you're either stupid or desperate."

"The situation," the Pilot says, "is long past desperate."

"Then what can you possibly expect *us* to do?" Ky asks.

"You will help," the Pilot says, "one way or the other." The ship turns a little and I wonder where we are in the sky.

"There are not very many people I can trust," the Pilot says. "So when two of them tell me contradictory things, that worries me. One of my associates thinks that the three of you are traitors who should be imprisoned and questioned away from the Provinces, out where I'm certain of the loyalty of the people. The other thinks you can help me find a cure."

The head Archivist is the first person, I think. *But who is the other?*

"When the Archivist drew my attention to this trade," the Pilot says, "I was interested, as she knew I would be, both by the name on the microcard and the message included on the paper. Your father did not side with the Rising. What, exactly, did you do that he didn't dare to do? Did you take things one step further and strike *against* the Rising?

"And then when I looked more closely, I found other things worthy of notice."

He begins reciting the names of flowers to me. At first, I think he's gone crazy, and then I realize what he's saying:

Newrose, oldrose, Queen Anne's lace.

"You wrote that and distributed it," the Pilot says. "What does the code represent?"

It's not a code. It's just my mother's words, turned into a poem. Where did he find it? Did someone give it to him? I meant for it to be shared, but not like this.

"*Where* is the place over the hill, under the tree, and past the border no one can see?"

When he asks the question like that, it sounds complicated, like a riddle. And it was only supposed to be simple, a song.

"Who were you meeting there?" he asks, his voice clear and even. But Ky's right. The Pilot *is* desperate. There's no undertone of fear when he speaks; but the questions he's asking, the way he's gambling some of his precious time on the three of us—it all makes me cold with fear. If the Pilot doesn't know how to save us from the new Plague, who does?

"No one," I say. "It's a poem. It doesn't have to have a literal meaning."

"But poems often do," the Pilot says. "You know this."

He's right. I've thought about the poem with the Pilot's name in it and whether that was the one Grandfather really meant me to find. He gave me the compact, he told me the stories of hiking the Hill, of his mother, who sang forbidden poems to him. What *did* Grandfather want me to do? I've always wondered.

"Why did you gather people at the Gallery?" the Pilot asks.

"So they could bring what they'd made."

"What did you talk about there?"

"Poetry," I say. "Songs."

"And that's all," the Pilot says.

His voice can be as cold or as warm as a stone, I realize. Sometimes it sounds generous and welcoming, like sandstone under sun, and other times it's as unforgiving as the marble of the steps at City Hall.

I have a question of my own for him. "Why did my name interest you *now*?" I ask. "People in the Rising must have seen it before. It meant nothing to them."

"Things have happened since you first joined the Rising several months ago," the Pilot says. "Poisoned lakes. Mysterious codes. A Gallery built where people could gather and exchange things they'd written. It seemed your name was worth a second look. And when we looked again, there was a great deal to find." And now his voice is *very* cold.

"Cassia's not fighting against the Rising," Xander says. "She's part *of* the Rising. I can vouch for her."

"So can I," Ky says.

"That might mean something to me," the Pilot says, "if

it weren't for the confluence of data around the three of you. There's enough to make *all* of you suspect."

"What do you mean?" I ask. "We did whatever the Rising wanted us to do. I came back to Central to live. Ky flew ships for you. Xander saved patients."

"Your small obediences did serve to camouflage your other actions to those in the Rising with less authority and information," the Pilot tells me. "They initially had no reason to report you to me. But after you were brought to my attention, I saw things and made connections that were unavailable to others. As the Pilot, I have access to more information. When I looked closely, I found the truth. People died wherever you went. The decoys in your camp, for example, many of whom were Aberrations."

"We didn't kill those decoys," Ky says. "You did. When the Society sent people out to die, you sat back and watched."

The Pilot continues, relentless. "A river near the Carving was poisoned while you were in the area. You detonated wiring in the Carving, destroying part of a village that belonged to Anomalies. You destroyed tubes in a storage facility in the canyons, a facility that the Rising had infiltrated. You conspired to obtain and carry blue tablets. You even killed a boy with them. We found his body."

"That's not true," I say, but in a way, it is. I didn't mean to kill that boy by giving him the blue tablets, but I did. And then I realize why the Archivist asked me about locations where tissue preservation samples might be stored. "You're the one who wanted to know how much I knew about the tubes," I say. "Do you really trade them?"

"You *trade* the tubes?" Ky asks.

"Of course," the Pilot says. "I'll use whatever I need to secure loyalty and resources for finding the cure. The samples are a currency that works when almost nothing else will."

Ky shakes his head, disgusted. I can't help but be grateful that we were able to get Grandfather's tube away from the Cavern. Who knows what the Pilot would have used it for.

"There's something more," the Pilot says. "The Cities where you lived were among those who suffered contaminated water supplies."

The lake. I remember those dead fish. But I don't understand what he means. The three of us look at each other. *We have to figure this out.*

"The Plague spread too quickly," Xander says, his eyes lighting up. "It stayed contained in Central for a long time, and then all of a sudden it was widespread. Until the virus went into the water, we had an epidemic—people getting sick from transferring it to one another. After the water supplies were contaminated, we had a pandemic."

And now Ky and I are right there with Xander, putting together the pieces. "It's a waterborne Plague," Ky says. "Like the one they sent to the Enemy."

The numbers of the Plague make sense to me now. "The sudden outbreak we saw at the beginning of the Rising— widespread contamination in several different Cities and

Provinces—means that someone added the virus to water sources to hurry up the process." I shake my head. "I should have realized. So that's why the illness was everywhere, all at once."

"And that's why we were stretched so thin at the medical center," Xander says. "The Rising didn't anticipate the sabotage. But we handled it anyway. Everything would have been fine, except for the mutation."

"You can't think the three of us could coordinate all of that," Ky says.

"No," the Pilot says. "But the three of you were a part of it. And it's time to come clean with what you know." He pauses. "There's something else for Cassia on the datapod."

I look back at the screen and see a second file embedded. Inside I find a picture of my mother, and one of my father. The screen flashes back and forth between the two of them.

"No," I say. *"No."* My parents look up from the screen, glassy-eyed. They are both still.

"They have the mutation," the Pilot says. "There is no cure. They are both in a medical center in Keya." He anticipates my next question before I ask it. "We have been unable to locate your brother."

Bram. Is he lying somewhere where no one can find him? Is he dead like that boy in the Carving? No. He's not. I won't believe it. I can't imagine Bram still.

"Now," the Pilot says, "you have an incentive to tell us

everything you can. Who do you work for? Are you Society sympathizers? Someone else? Did your group introduce the mutation? Do you have a cure?"

For the first time, I hear him lose control while he speaks. It's only on the last word, *cure*, and I can tell how truly desperate and driven he is. He wants this cure. He will do anything he can to find it.

But we don't have a cure. He's wasting his time with us. What should we do? How can we convince him?

"I know you can do the right thing," the Pilot says. The break in his voice is gone, and now he sounds coaxing, gentle. "Your father may have sided with the Society and refused to join the Rising, but your grandfather worked for us. You are, of course, the great-granddaughter of Pilot Reyes. And you've helped us before, though you don't remember it."

I barely hear the last thing he says because—

My great-grandmother. *She* was the Pilot.

She was the one who sang the poems to my grandfather, even when the Society had told her she could only choose a hundred. She was the one who saved the page I burned.

"I never met Pilot Reyes in person," the Pilot says. "She came before my predecessor. But as the Pilot, I am one of the only people who knows the names of the Pilots who came before. And I know her from her writings. She was the right Pilot at the right time. She preserved records and gathered what we needed to know to take action later. But one thing is the same for *all* Pilots: We have to understand what it means to be the Pilot. Your great-grandmother understood that if you don't save, you fail. And she knew that the smallest rebel who does their job is as great as the Pilot who leads. She didn't just believe that. She *knew* it."

"We haven't done anything—" I begin, but the ship drops suddenly, down, down.

Ky loses his balance and slams into the cases against the wall. Both Xander and I move to help him.

"I'm fine," Ky says. I can barely hear him over the sounds of the ship, and then we hit the ground hard. My whole body snaps with the impact.

"When he opens the hold," Ky says, "we're going to run. We'll get away."

"Ky," I say, "wait."

"We can get past him," Ky says. "There are three of us and only one of him."

"Two of you," Xander says. "I'm not going."

Ky stares at Xander in astonishment. "Have you been listening at all?"

"Yes," Xander says. "The Pilot wants a cure. So do I. I'll help him however I can." Xander looks at me and I see that he still believes in the Pilot. He's choosing the Pilot over everything else, in this at least.

Why wouldn't he? Ky and I left Xander behind; I never taught him to write. And I never asked Xander for *his* story because I thought I already knew it. Looking at him now, I realize that I didn't know it all then, and I certainly don't know it all now. He has traveled through canyons of his own and come through changed.

And he's right. All that matters is the cure. That is what we have to fight for now.

I'm the vote in the balance. They both wait for me. And this time, I choose Xander, or at least, I choose his side. "Let's talk to the Pilot," I tell Ky. "Just a little more."

"Are you sure?" Ky asks.

"Yes," I say, and the Pilot opens the door to the hold. I follow Ky up the ladder, Xander coming after, and I hand the Pilot the datapod with my parents' pictures on it.

"The Gallery was a place for meeting and poetry," I tell him. "The blue tablets were an accident. We didn't know they killed. We used the wiring in the Carving to seal off the cave so that the Society wouldn't take the villagers' stores. The poisoned streams and water—that's the Society's signature, and we are not the Society, nor do we sympathize with them."

For a moment everything is as quiet as it can be in a ship in the mountains. The wind moves in the trees outside, and under that is the breathing of those of us who are not still, not yet.

"We're not trying to take down the Rising," I say. "We believed in it. All we want is a cure." And then I realize who the other person the Pilot trusts must be—the pilot he asked to gather us together when he couldn't spare the time or the risk. "You should listen to Indie," I say. "We *can* help you."

The Pilot doesn't seem surprised that I've figured it out.

"Indie," Ky says. "Does she have the mark?"

"No," the Pilot says, "but we'll do our best to keep her flying."

"You lied to her," Ky says. "You used her to bring us all in."

"There is no stone I won't overturn," the Pilot says, "to find the cure."

"We can help you," I tell the Pilot again. "I can sort data. Xander has been working with the sick and has seen the mutation firsthand. Ky—"

"May be the most useful of all," the Pilot says.

"I'll be a body," Ky says. "Just like in the Outer Provinces." Ky walks away from me, closer to the door. He moves slower than usual, but with the same fluidity that I've always associated with him; his body belongs to him more than most people's do, and I ache at the thought that it might have to stop, be still.

"You don't know that, yet," I say, my heart sinking. "You might not be sick." But Ky's expression is resigned. Does he know more than he's saying? Can he feel the mutation inside of him, running through his veins, making him ill?

"Either way, Ky's been exposed to the virus," Xander says. "You don't want to risk him exposing the people you have working on the cure to the mutation."

"There's no risk," the Pilot says. "The villagers are immune."

274

"So *that's* why you're looking here for a cure," Xander says, and he smiles. His voice fills with hope. "There *is* a chance we'll find it."

"But if you knew about the red mark, why didn't you bring some of those who had it out here earlier?" I ask the Pilot. "Maybe our data could be useful." If I'm immune, they could correlate my data with that of the villagers from the mountain.

The moment the words leave my mouth, I shake my head. "It won't work," I say, answering my own question, "because our data is compromised. All the immunizations, the exposures we've had—you need a pure sample group to find the cure."

"Yes," the Pilot says, looking at me with a measuring expression. "We can only use those who have lived outside of the Society since birth. Others can help us work on the cure, but we can't use their data."

"And you must give more weight to data from those who have lived longest outside of the Society," I say. "For second-generation, and third-generation villagers. Their information will have greater importance."

"We've come by some additional data recently," the Pilot says. "A second group of villagers has also proved to be immune, though they only arrived in the mountains recently."

The farmers from the Carving. It must be. I remember the small dark house, the symbol for *settlement*, that we saw marked on the mountains of the farmers' map. They didn't know the name of the village or if anyone still lived there, but that was where the farmers fled when the Carving was no longer safe.

Ky is looking at me. He's had the same thought. *What if we can see Eli again? Or Hunter?*

"When the people from the Carving arrived, the villagers of Endstone let them build a settlement of their own nearby," the Pilot says. "We weren't sure at first if the people from the Carving would also be immune to the mutation. They lived in a very different climate and had had no contact with those living in Endstone for many years. But they were immune. Which was a huge boon to us because—"

"—then you could correlate *their* data," I say, understanding instantly. "You could look for commonalities between the two groups. It would save you time."

"How close *are* you?" Xander asks.

"Not as close as we'd like," the Pilot says. "There were many commonalities in the diets and habits of the two groups. We're ruling out each possibility as fast as we can, but it takes time, and people to try the cure on."

He's looking at the three of us. Have we convinced him?

Xander watches me, too. When our eyes meet he smiles and I see the old Xander in him again, the one who used to smile at me exactly this way to try to get me to jump in the pool, to join in the games. When I turn back to Ky, I see that his hands are shaking just a little, his fine hands that taught me to write, that touched me when we went through the canyons.

Long ago on the Hill, Ky warned me about a situation like this, where we might be caught. He told me about the prisoner's dilemma and how we would have to keep each other safe. Did he ever think that there might be three of us, not two?

Here, between Xander's smile and Ky's hands, I come to my own understanding, that the only way to keep one another safe is to find the cure.

"We can help you," I say again to the Pilot, hoping that this time he will believe me.

Grandfather believed in me. In my palm, I hold the microcard. It is wrapped in a paper from my mother that is covered in my father's words, written by my brother's hand.

PART FIVE

PRISONER'S DILEMMA

CHAPTER 24
XANDER

Outside the ship, Ky paces the clearing while we wait for the villagers to come down to meet us. "You should rest," I tell him. "There's no evidence that continued motion delays the onset of the illness."

"You sound like an Official," Ky says.

"I used to be one," I say.

"The reason you don't have any evidence that this works," Ky says, "is because you never had anyone try it."

He and I are talking and joking, using the same tone we did when we played at the game tables. Once again Ky is going to lose and it's not fair. He shouldn't have to be still.

But he hasn't lost Cassia. The way the two of them look at each other is like touching. I'm caught in the middle of it.

There's no time to think about that now. A group of people emerges from the trees. There are nine of them. Five carry weapons and the rest have stretchers.

"I don't have any patients for you today," the Pilot says. "Nor supplies, I'm afraid. Just these three."

"My name is Xander," I say, trying to put the villagers at ease.

"Leyna," says one of the women. Her hair is in a long blond braid and she looks young, like us. None of the others move to introduce themselves, but they all appear strong. I see no signs of illness among them.

"I'm Cassia," Cassia says.

"Ky," Ky says.

"We're Anomalies," Leyna says. "Probably the first you've ever seen." She waits for our reaction.

"We knew other Anomalies in the Carving," Cassia says.

"Really?" Leyna asks, her voice full of interest. "When was this?"

"Right before they came here," Cassia says.

"So you know Anna," says one of the men. "Their leader."

"No," Cassia says. "We came after she left. We only knew Hunter."

"We were surprised when the farmers came to Endstone," Leyna says. "We thought everyone in the Carving had died long ago. We believed that those of us in the stone villages were all that was between the Society and the rest of the world."

She's very good at this. Her voice is warm but strong, and she takes in our measure as she looks at us. She'd make a good physic. "What can they do for us?" she asks the Pilot, addressing him not as her leader but as her equal.

"I'm a body," Ky says. "I've got the mutation. I just haven't gone down yet."

Leyna raises her eyebrows. "We haven't seen anyone

standing," she says to the Pilot. "All the other patients were already still."

"Ky is a pilot," Cassia says. I can tell she doesn't like the way Leyna is talking about Ky. "One of the best."

Leyna nods, but she keeps watching Ky. Her eyes are shrewd.

"Xander's a medic," Cassia says, "and I can sort."

"A medic and a sorter," Leyna says. "Excellent."

"I'm not actually a medic anymore," I say. "I've been working in administration. But I've seen a lot of the sick and I've been assisting with their care."

"That will be useful," Leyna says. "It's always good to speak to someone who has seen the virus and how it works in the Cities and Boroughs."

"I'll return as soon as I can," the Pilot says. "Is there anything new to report?"

"No," Leyna says, "but there will be soon." She gestures to one of the stretchers. "We can carry you if you need it." She's speaking to Ky.

"No," Ky says. "I'll keep going until I drop."

"You trust the Pilot very much," I say to Leyna as we climb up the path to the village. Cassia and Ky walk ahead of us, keeping a steady but slow pace. I know Leyna and I are both watching them. Others in the group keep looking at Ky, too. Everyone's waiting for the moment when he goes still.

"The Pilot isn't our leader," she says, "but we trust him enough to work with him, and he feels the same way about us."

"And you're really immune?" I ask. "Even to the mutation?"

"Yes," she says. "But we don't have a mark. The Pilot told us that some of you do."

I nod. "I wonder why there's a discrepancy," I say. In spite of what I've seen it do to people, the workings of the Plague and its mutation fascinate me.

"We're not sure," Leyna says. "Our expert in the village says that viruses and immunity are incredibly complex. His best explanation is that whatever causes our immunity simply prevents infection from ever being established at all, which means we don't get the mark."

"And it also means that you'd better not change your diet or environment too much before you find out *what* makes you immune, or you could get sick," I say.

She nods.

"That must have taken courage to volunteer for exposure to the mutation," I say.

"It did."

"How many people live in the village?" I ask.

"More than you would think," Leyna says. "The stones are rolling."

What does she mean?

"When the Society began rounding up the Aberrations and Anomalies to send to the decoy camps," Leyna explains, "more and more of them started escaping to these places, the stone villages. Have you heard of them?"

"Yes," I say, remembering Lei.

"Now we're all gathering together in one village, the last one," Leyna says. "It's called Endstone. We're pooling our resources to try to turn our immunity into your cure."

"Why?" I ask. "What have those of us who live in the Provinces ever done for you?"

Leyna laughs. "Not much," she says. "But the Pilot has promised us something in return if we succeed."

"What is it?" I ask.

"If we find a cure," she says, "he'll use his ships to take us to the Otherlands. It's what we want most, and the cure is what *he* wants most, so the trade is fair. And if it turns out that our immunity changes when we leave, we will certainly want cures to take with us to the Otherlands as a precaution."

"So the Otherlands *do* exist," I say.

"Of course," she says.

"If you let everyone in the Provinces die, you could take the Pilot's ships yourselves," I say. "Or you could wait until everyone was gone and then go in and take their Cities and houses for your own."

For the first time, her easy, charming mask slips a little and I see the contempt underneath. "You're like rats," she says, her voice still pleasant. "Even if most of you die, there are too many of you for us to overcome. We're ready to leave you all behind and go someplace you haven't touched."

"Why are you telling me all of this?" I ask her. We've just met, so it can't be that she trusts me yet.

"It's good for you to understand how much we have to lose," she says.

And I do understand. With so much at stake, she can't and won't tolerate anything that might compromise her goal. We'll need to watch our step here. "We have the same objective," I say. "To find a cure."

"Good," Leyna tells me. She lowers her voice and looks at Ky. "So tell me," she says, "when is he going to go down?"

Ky's pace has picked up a little. "It won't be long now," I say. Cassia is electric, lit up simply because Ky is near her, even though she's worried that he might be ill. *Would it be worth it to have the mutation if I knew she loved me?* I wonder. *If I could trade places with him right now, would I do it?*

CHAPTER 25
CASSIA

When it happens, everything feels sudden and slow at the same time.

We're walking along the narrow path when Ky goes down to his knees.

I crouch beside him, put my hands on his shoulders.

His eyes, unfocused at first, find me. "No," he says. "Don't want you to see this."

But I don't look away. I hold on and I ease him down until he's lying on the spring grass and I keep my hands underneath his head. His hair is soft and warm; the grass is cool and new.

"Indie," Ky says. "She kissed me." I see the pain in his eyes.

I should feel shock, I know. But it doesn't matter. What matters is here, now, his eyes looking at me, my fingers holding on to him and touching earth. I almost tell Ky this, that it doesn't matter, but then I realize that it *does* to him or he wouldn't be telling me. "It's all right," I say.

Ky sighs out in relief and exhaustion. "Like the canyons," he says.

"Yes," I say. "We'll come through them."

Xander kneels down too. The three of us look at one another; my eyes meet Xander's briefly, then Ky's.

Can we trust one another? Can we keep one another safe?

Near the edge of the path, the grass gives way to wildflowers, some pink, some blue, some red. The wind stirs the grass around our feet, sending a clean smell of blossoms and dirt into the air.

Ky follows my gaze. I reach over and snap off one of the buds and roll it around in my hand. It's so ripe in tint and texture that I half expect to look down and see my palm turned red, but it isn't. The bud keeps its color.

"You told me once," I say to Ky, holding up the bud for him to see and then pressing it into his hand, "that red was the color of beginning."

He smiles.

The color of beginning. For a moment, a memory flickers in and out. *It is a rare moment in spring when both buds on the trees and flowers on the ground are red. The air is cool and at the same time warm. Grandfather watches me, his eyes bright and determined.*

Spring, then. The red garden day Grandfather mentioned on the microcard was in the spring, to have both red tree buds and red flowers at the same time, to feel the way it did. I'm certain of this. But what did Grandfather and I talk about?

I don't know that, yet. But as I feel Ky's fingers tighten around mine, I think how this is always the way he is, giving me something even when most would think there was nothing left to do but let go.

CHAPTER 26
KY

K y," Cassia says. I wonder if this will be one of the last times the sound of her voice reaches me. Can the still hear anything at all?

I knew I was sick when I couldn't keep my balance on the ship. My body didn't move when instinct said it should. My muscles feel loose and my bones feel tight.

Xander kneels next to me. I catch a glimpse of his face. He thinks he's going to find a cure. Xander's not blind. Just believing. It's so damn painful to see.

I look back to Cassia. Her eyes are cool and green. When I look into them I feel better. For just a second the pain is muted.

Then it's back.

I know now why people might not try to fight very long.

If I stopped fighting the pain, fatigue would win, and that seems preferable. I'd rather be asleep than feel this. The Plague was much kinder than the mutation, I realize. The Plague didn't have the sores that I can feel forming around my torso and curving across my back.

Small red-and-white flashes of light appear in my vision as the villagers lift me onto a stretcher. I have another thought. *What if you give in to the exhaustion, let yourself go still, and then the pain comes* back?

Cassia touches my arm.

We were free in the canyon. Not for long, but we were. She had sand on her skin and the smell of water and stone in her hair. I think I smell rain coming. When it arrives, will I be too far gone to remember?

It's good to know that Xander's here. So that when I go down, she won't be alone.

"You walked through the Carving to find me," I tell Cassia softly. "I'm going to walk through this to reach you."

Cassia holds on to one of my hands. In the other, I can feel the flower she gave me. The air in the mountains is cool. I can tell when we pass underneath the trees. Light. Dark. Light. It's almost nice to have someone else carrying my body. This damn thing is so heavy.

And then the pain gets worse. It turns red all through me and that's the only thing I can see—bright red in front of my eyelids.

Cassia's hand disappears from mine.

No, I want to shout. *Don't go.*

Xander's voice is here instead. "The important thing," he tells me, "is that you remember to breathe. If you don't clear your lungs, that's when pneumonia can settle in." A pause. Then he says, "I'm sorry, Ky. We'll find a cure. I promise."

Then he's gone and Cassia's back, her hand a softer pressure now on mine. "What the Pilot was saying on the ship," she tells me, "was a poem I wrote for you. I finally finished it."

She speaks to me gently, almost singing. I breathe.

Newrose, oldrose, Queen Anne's lace.
Water, river, stone, and sun.

Wind over hill, under tree.
Past the border none can see.

Climbing into dark for you
Will you wait in stars for me?

I will.

And no matter what, she'll remember me. No one, not Society or Rising or anyone else, can take that from her. Too much has happened. And too much time has passed.

She'll know that I was here. And that I loved her.

She'll always know that, unless *she* chooses to forget.

CHAPTER 27
XANDER

The village isn't still at all. People are everywhere. Kids run the paths and play on an enormous stone in the center of the village. Unlike the sculptures in the Society's greenspaces, this stone isn't carved smooth. It's rough and jagged where it broke away from the side of the mountain years ago. You can tell the people built the village around it. The children turn to look at us as we come past, and their eyes are curious, not afraid, which is nice to see.

The infirmary is a long wooden building across from the village stone. Once we're inside, we carefully transfer Ky from his stretcher to a cot.

"We need to take both of you back to the research lab and interview you," Leyna says to Cassia and me. Around us, the villagers' versions of medics and nurses take care of the still. I do a quick count and see that Ky is the fifty-second patient. "We need Xander's information about the Plague and its mutation, and we need Cassia to take a look at the data we've gathered. You'll be more useful there." Leyna smiles to ease the blow of what she's saying. "I'm sorry. I know he's your friend, but really the best way to help him—"

"Is to work for the cure," Cassia says. "I understand. But surely we have breaks now and then. I could come visit him."

"That's up to Sylvie," Leyna says, gesturing to an older woman standing near us. "I'm in charge of overseeing the cure as a whole, but she supervises the infirmary."

"I don't mind as long as you scrub in and wear a mask and gloves," Sylvie says. "It might be interesting to see. None of the others here have anyone to visit them. Maybe he'll recover more quickly."

"Thank you," Cassia says, her face bright with hope. I don't want to tell her, *Actually, talking to them and staying with them seems to make no difference at all.* I kept talking to the patients myself. It's instinct. And maybe the right person *could* make a difference. Who knows? I hope someone back at the medical center is talking to Lei. Would it have been better for me to stay there?

The door slams open. Cassia and I both turn, startled, and a man comes through the entrance. He's tall and rail-thin, staring at us with shrewd dark eyes that peer out from under shaggy white eyebrows. His head is brown and smooth and bald. "Where is he?" he demands. "Colin told me there's someone here who went down within the hour."

"Here," Leyna says, pointing to Ky.

"It's about time," the man says, hurrying over to us. "What have I been telling the Pilot all along? Bring them to me when they're still fresh and I might have a chance of getting them back."

Cassia doesn't move away from Ky. She stays there, looking protective.

"I'm Oker," the man says to us, but he doesn't offer to shake hands. He carries a plastic bag full of liquid and his knotted hands grip it so tightly that it bulges and seems as if it might burst. "Damn it," he says, noticing, and he holds it out to Sylvie. "Take it from me," he says. "I'm seizing up. Don't break my fingers."

Sylvie pries the bag out of his grip.

"Hook it up now," he says, nodding toward Ky. "I just made this. It's fresh. As fresh as he is." Then he laughs.

"Wait," Cassia says. "What is it?"

"Better stuff than what the Rising gives them," Oker says. "Go on," he tells Sylvie. "Hurry up."

"But what's in it?" Cassia asks.

Oker huffs and glares at Sylvie. "Take care of this. I don't have time to go through all the ingredients." He pushes the door open with his shoulder and leaves the infirmary. I hear his shoes on the path outside as the door squeaks shut. He moves fast. His hands might be twisted, but there's nothing wrong with his legs.

"He's right," Sylvie says. "At first, we used the nutrient

bags the Pilot brought in from the Provinces, but then we ran out before the Pilot could deliver more. Oker made his own mixture to keep the patients alive and it seemed to work better, so we've been using it ever since."

"But won't that compromise the cure?" I ask. "This isn't what the patients back in the Provinces are getting."

"That may change," Sylvie says. "Oker recently gave the Pilot the formula for the solution in the bags. If the Pilot can, he's going to try to change what they use in the Provinces."

"What do you think?" Cassia asks me quietly.

"They do look better," I say. "Their color is good. Hold on." I listen to one of the patients breathe. His lungs sound clear of fluid. I feel near his ribs—the spleen seems to be normal size.

"I think Oker's telling the truth," I say. I wish we'd had this formula earlier. Maybe it would have made a difference for our patients.

Cassia kneels down next to Ky. He looks ashier than the others, though he's the most recently still. She sees it. "All right," she says.

Sylvie nods and hooks up the bag that Oker brought in. Cassia and I watch Ky's face to see if there is any change, which is stupid. Not many things work that fast.

But Oker's stuff does. After only a few minutes, Ky does look a little bit better. It reminds me of the way the cure worked on the first Plague.

"It seems too good to be true," Cassia breathes. She looks worried. "What if it is?"

"We don't have a lot to lose," I say. "What the Rising is doing in the Provinces isn't working."

"You've never seen anyone come back?" Cassia asks.

"No," I say. "Not from the mutation."

We both stand there for a moment longer, watching the liquid drip into Ky's line. We avoid each other's eyes.

Cassia draws in a deep breath and I wonder if she's going to cry. But then she smiles. "Xander," she says.

I don't even try to stop myself. I reach out and pull her close and she lets me. It feels good and for a moment I don't say anything. Her arms go around me and I can feel her breathing.

"Are you all right?" she asks.

"I'm fine," I say.

"Xander," Cassia asks. "Where have *you* been? While I was in the canyons and in Central, what happened to you?"

I'm not really sure how to tell her. *Well, I didn't go through any canyons, but I gave tablets to babies on their Welcoming Days. And, I took tissue samples from old people at their Final Banquets. I did make one real friend, but I couldn't keep her from going still. No one I took care of came back.*

"We need to go," Leyna says. "Colin's gathering together people to question you. I don't want to keep them waiting."

"I'll tell you later," I say, smiling at Cassia. "Right now, we have to find a cure."

She nods. I don't mean to seem like I'm trying to get even with her for all the times she left me in the dark about what was happening. But it's strange to realize that she knows as little about me right now as I did about her for all these months. She's the one who has to wonder.

I don't want us to have to wonder about the other anymore. I'd like us to *know* what's going on because we've been together. I'm hoping that finding this cure can be the beginning of that.

"Can you," one of the villagers asks me, "give us any specific numbers regarding the way you were treating the still?"

The room is filled with people. I couldn't tell right away from looking at them which of them might be people like us, brought here by the Pilot to help with the cure, or who might be the Anomalies from the village. But after a few minutes, I think I can tell who has lived in the Society at one point or another.

Oker sits on a chair near the window, his arms folded, listening to me. Some of the village's sorters are here to take down the information. Oker's the only person in attendance without a datapod, except for me.

Leyna sees me noticing the datapods. "The Pilot brought them for us," she explains. "They're very useful, but not as dangerous as miniports. We don't allow *any* miniports in the village." I nod. Datapods can record information but they don't transmit location the way a miniport can.

"I have treatment and patient data for the regular Plague and for the mutation," I tell the group. "I've been working inside the medical center since the night the Pilot came over the ports to announce the Plague."

"And when did you leave?" someone else asks.

"Early this morning," I say.

They all lean forward at once. *"Really,"* one says. "You've been working on the mutation that recently?"

I nod.

"Perfect," says another, and Leyna smiles.

The medics want to know everything I can remember about each patient: the way they looked, their ages, the rate of infection, how long it took until they went still, which people's illnesses progressed more rapidly than others.

I'm careful to tell them when I'm not certain.

But for the most part, I remember. So, I talk and they listen, but I wish it were Lei here working with me on the cure. She always knew the right questions to ask.

I talk for hours. They all take notes, except for Oker, and I realize that he can't manage the datapod with his hands the way they are. I expect him to interrupt like he did when he came into the infirmary, but he remains perfectly quiet. At one point, he leans his head back against the wall and appears to fall asleep. My voice starts to wear out right when I'm explaining about the mutation and the small red mark.

"Now this," Leyna says, "we already know. The Pilot told us." She stands up. "Let's give Xander a rest for a few minutes."

The room clears out. Some of the people look back over their shoulders like they're worried I'm going to vanish. "Don't worry," Leyna says. "He's not going anywhere. Will one of you bring back something for him to eat? And more water." I finished the pitcher they'd brought in for me long ago.

Oker is still asleep at the back of the room. "It's hard for him to rest," Leyna says. "He catches a catnap when he can. So we'll leave him alone."

"Are *you* a medic?" I ask Leyna.

"Oh no," Leyna says. "I can't take care of sick people. But I'm good at managing the live ones. That's why I'm in charge of finding the cure." She pushes her chair back a little and then leans closer to me. I'm reminded again of an opponent at one of the game tables back in the Society. She's drawing me in, getting ready to make some kind of move. "I have to admit," she says, smiling, "that this is all rather humorous."

"What is?" I ask, leaning forward so that there's not much space between us.

Her smile widens. "This whole situation. The Plague. Its mutation. You being here now."

"Tell me," I say. "I'd like to be in on the joke." I keep my voice easy, conversational, but I've seen too many still to think that anything about what's happened to them is funny.

"You all called us Anomalies," Leyna says. "Not good

enough to live among you. Not good enough to marry you. And now you need us to save you."

I smile back at her. "True," I say. I lower my voice. I'm not entirely sure that Oker is asleep. "So," I say to Leyna, "you've asked me plenty of questions. Let me ask you one or two."

"Of course," she says, her eyes flickering. She's enjoying this.

"Is there any chance at all you can find a cure?"

"Of course," she says again, perfectly confident. "It's only a matter of time. You'll be helpful to us. I won't lie. But we'd have found the cure without you. You'll just help us speed up the process, which is valuable, of course. The Pilot's not going to take us to the Otherlands if too many people die before we can save them."

"What if your immunity provides no clues?" I ask. "What if it turns out to be a matter of genetics?"

"It's not," she says. "We know that. The people in the village come from many different places. Some came generations ago, some more recently. The Pilot doesn't want us to include the recent arrivals in the data, so we don't, but we're *all* immune. It must be environmental."

"Still," I say, "an immunity and a cure aren't the same thing. You might not figure out how to bring people back. Maybe you'll only find out how to keep them from getting the virus in the first place."

"If so," Leyna says, "that's still an extremely valuable discovery."

"But only if you make it in time," I say. "You can't

immunize people if they've already gotten the virus. So we're *very* useful to you, actually."

I hear a snort from the corner. Oker stands up and walks over toward us.

"Congratulations," Oker says to me. "You're not just a Society boy after all. I'd been wondering."

"Thank you," I say.

"You were a physic in the Society, weren't you?" Oker asks.

"I was," I say.

He waves one knotted hand in my direction. "Assign him to my lab when you're done," he tells Leyna.

She doesn't like it, I can tell, but she nods. "All right," she says. It's a sign of a good leader when they know the most important player in their game, and if Oker is it, she should make sure he has what he needs to try to win.

It takes them almost all night to finish questioning me. "You should get some rest," Leyna says. "I'll show you where you'll sleep."

She walks with me through the village and I hear the crickets singing. Their music sounds different up here than it did in the Borough, like it matters more. There aren't many other sounds to cover it up, so you have to listen.

"Did you grow up in this village?" I ask her. "It's beautiful."

"No," Leyna says. "I used to live in Camas. Those of us in

the Border Provinces were the last to go. They used to let us work at the Army base sometimes. We left for the mountains when the Society tried to gather in the last of the Anomalies and Aberrations."

She looks off in the distance. "The Pilot was the one who warned us that we should go," she says. "The Society wanted us all dead. Those who didn't come along were picked up by the Society and sent out to the Outer Provinces to die."

"So that's why you trust the Pilot," I say. "He warned you."

"Yes," she says. "And he'd been part of the vanishings. I don't know if you've heard about them."

"I have," I say. "People who escaped from the Society and ended up either here or in the Otherlands."

She nods.

"And no one has ever returned from the Otherlands?"

"Not yet," she says. She stops at a building with bars on the windows. A guard stands at the door and nods to her. "I'm afraid this is the prison," she says. "We don't know you well enough to trust you on your own without supervision, so there are times when we will need to keep you here, especially at night. Some of the other people the Pilot brought have been less cooperative than you have. They're here full-time."

It makes sense. I'd do the same thing, if I were in charge of this situation. "And Cassia?" I ask. "Where will she stay?"

"She'll have to sleep here, too," Leyna says. "But we'll

come for you soon." She gestures for the guard to take me inside.

"Wait," I say. "I'm trying to understand."

"I thought it was clear," she says. "We don't know you. We can't trust you alone."

"It's not that," I say. "It's about the Otherlands, and why you want to go there. You're not even sure that they exist."

"They do," she says.

Does she know something I don't? It's possible that she might not be telling me everything. Why would she? As she's pointed out, she doesn't know me and she can't trust me yet. "But no one ever came back," I say.

"People like you see that as evidence that the Otherlands aren't real," Leyna tells me. "People like me see it is evidence that it's a place so wonderful no one would ever *want* to come back."

CHAPTER 28
CASSIA

Where are you, Ky?

This is it, my greatest fear. What I've been afraid of ever since the Carving when I saw those people, dead, out under the sky. Someone I love is leaving me.

The lead sorter, Rebecca, is about my mother's age. She has me complete a few test sorts. After she goes through my work, she smiles at me and tells me that I can start right away.

"You'll find that the way we work here is different from what you're used to," she says. "In the Society, you sort alone. Here, you will need to talk to Oker and the medics about everything." She puts the datapod down on the table. "If we make an error and leave something out, miss some pattern, then it could be critical."

This *will* be different from any sorting I've done before. In the Society, we were not supposed to know what the data was attached to, what it really looked like; everything remained encoded.

"I've made a data set with the people in our village and

those from the Carving who have lived outside of the Society their entire lives."

I want to tell her that I know some of those who lived in the Carving—I want to find out how Eli and Hunter are doing. But right now I have to focus on the cure and on Ky and my family.

"We have information about diet, age, recreational habits, occupations, family histories," Rebecca says. "Some of the data is corroborated by other sources, but most of it is self-reported."

"So it's not the most reliable data set," I observe.

"No," she says. "But it's all we have. Commonalities are everywhere in the data, of course. But we've been able to narrow certain things down by extrapolating from what we have. For example, our data indicates an environmental or dietary exposure."

"Do you want me to work on sorting the elements for the cure now?" I ask hopefully.

"I will," Rebecca says, "but I have another project for you first. I need you to solve a constrained optimization problem."

I think I already know what she means. It's the problem that's been on my mind since I realized there was no cure for the mutation. "You want me to find out how long it will be before the Rising starts unhooking people," I say. "We need to know how much time we have."

"Yes," she says. "The Pilot won't fly us out if there's no

one left to save. I want you to work on that while I continue sorting for the cure. Then you can help me." She pushes a datapod across the table. "Here are the notes from Xander's interview. They include information regarding rate of infection, rate at which the resources were being expended, and patient attributes. We have additional data from the Pilot about these same things."

"I'm still missing some information," I say. "I don't know the initial quantity of the resources or the population of the Society as a whole."

"You'll have to extrapolate the initial quantity of resources from the rate of expenditure," she says. "As for the population of the Provinces as a whole, the Pilot was able to give us an estimate of twenty-point-two million."

"That's all?" I ask, stunned. I thought the Society was much larger than that.

"Yes," she says.

The Rising will be trying to figure out how to best allocate resources and personnel. People have to take care of the still, obviously. Others have to work to keep food coming through, to make sure the buildings in the Cities and Boroughs have power and water. And even if a small pocket of people is safe due to contracting the initial Plague, there are only so many of them, and they're the ones who are going to have to care for everyone else.

I need to know how many of them are out there—how

many people are likely to be immune. I will have to figure out how many people are likely to go still, what percentage of those sick the immune can reasonably keep alive, and how quickly that percentage will decrease.

"Oker's estimate is that five to ten percent of the population is generally immune to any plague," Rebecca says. "So there will be that group, as well as the very small group of people like your friend Xander, who were initially immune and then contracted the live virus at precisely the right time. You'll need to take both of those groups into account."

"All right," I say. And, as I have had to do so often before, when I sort the data I must put Ky out of my mind. For a faltering, fragile moment, I want to leave this impossible task behind, let the numbers fall where they might, and walk over to the little room where Ky is and hold him, the two of us together in the mountains now after having come through the canyons.

That can *happen,* I tell myself. *Only a little farther now.* Like the journey in the *I did not reach Thee* poem:

> *We step like plush, we stand like snow—*
> *The waters murmur now,*
> *Three rivers and the hill are passed,*
> *Two deserts and the sea!*
> *Now Death usurps my premium*
> *And gets the look at Thee.*

But I will rewrite the last two lines. Death will not take the people I love. Our journey *will* end differently.

It takes me a long time, because I want to get it right.

"Are you finished?" Rebecca asks quietly.

For a moment I can't look up from my result. Back in the Carving, I wished for a time like this, a collaboration with people who have lived out on the edges. Instead we found an empty village in a beautiful place, peopled only by papers and pages left in a cave, things treasured up and left behind.

We are always fighting against going quiet, going gentle.

"Yes," I say to Rebecca.

"And?" she asks. "How long before they start letting people go?"

"They will have already begun," I say.

CHAPTER 29
KY

Someone comes inside. I hear the door open and then footsteps crossing the floor.

Could it be Cassia?

Not this time. Whoever this is doesn't smell like Cassia's flowers-and-paper scent. This person smells like sweat and smoke. And they breathe differently than she does. Lower. Louder, like they've been running and they're trying to hold it in.

I hear the person reach for the bag.

But I don't need new fluid. Someone just changed it. Where are they now? Do they know what's happening?

I feel a tug on my arm. They've unhooked the bag from my line and started to drain it. The liquid drips into some kind of bucket instead of into me.

I'm turned toward the window so the wind rattling the panes is even louder now.

Is this happening to everyone? Or only to me? Is someone trying to make sure I don't come back?

I can hear my own heart slowing down.

I'm going deeper.

The pain is less.

It's harder to remember to breathe. I repeat Cassia's poem to myself, breathing with the beats.

New. Rose. Old. Rose. Queen. Anne's. Lace.

In. Out. In. Out. In. Out. In.

Out.

CHAPTER 30
XANDER

I must have fallen asleep, because I jump when the prison door opens. "Get him out," someone says to the guard, and then Oker appears in front of my cell, watching the guard unlock the door. "You," Oker says. "Time to get back to work."

I glance at the cell across from me. Cassia hasn't come in. Did she spend the whole night watching over Ky? Or have they made her work all this time? All the other prisoners are quiet. I can hear them breathing, but no one else seems to be awake.

When we get outside, I see that it's dark: not even early morning yet. "You're working for me," Oker says, "so you keep the same hours I do." He points to the research lab across the way. "That's mine," he says. "Do what I say, and you can spend most of your day in there instead of locked up."

If Leyna's the physic of this village, then I think Oker is the pilot.

"Follow my instructions exactly," he tells me. "All I need are your hands since mine don't work right."

"Oker isn't much for introductions," one of the assistants says after Oker's left. "I'm Noah. I've worked with Oker since

312

he came here." Noah looks to be somewhere in his mid-thirties. "This is Tess."

Tess nods to me. She's a little younger than Noah and has a kind smile.

"I'm Xander," I say. "What's all this?" One of the walls of the lab is covered with pictures of people I don't know. Some are old photos and pages torn from books, but most look like they might have been drawn by hand. Did Oker do that before his hands stopped working right? I'm impressed, and it makes me think of that nurse back in the medical center. Maybe I *am* the only one who can't make things—pictures, poems—without any training.

"Oker calls them the heroes of the past," Noah says. "He believes we should know the work of those who came before us."

"He trained in the Society, didn't he," I say.

"Yes," Tess says. "He came here ten years ago, right before his Final Banquet."

"He's *ninety*?" I ask. I've never known anyone so old.

"Yes," Noah says. "The oldest person in the world, as far as we know."

The office door slams open and we all get back to work.

A few hours later, Oker tells the assistants to take a break. "Not you," he says to me. "I need to make something and you can stay and help me with it."

Noah and Tess send me sympathetic looks.

Oker sets a bunch of neatly labeled boxes and jars in front of me and hands me a list. "Put this compound together," he says, and I start measuring. He goes back over to the cabinet to rummage through more ingredients. I hear them clinking together.

Then, to my surprise, he starts talking to me. "You said you saw approximately two thousand patients while you worked in the medical center in Camas," he says. "Over the course of four months."

"Yes," I say. "There were many more patients that I didn't treat, of course, in other parts of the center and other buildings in Camas."

"Out of all the ones you *did* see, how many looked better when they were still than my patients here?" he asks.

"None," I say.

"That's a fast answer," he says. "Take your time to think it over."

I think back on all of my patients. I can't remember everyone's face, but I can call up the last hundred. And Lei, of course.

"None," I say again.

Oker folds his arms and sits back, satisfied. He watches me measure a few more ingredients. "All right," he says. "Now *you* can ask a question."

I didn't expect this opportunity, but I'm going to take advantage of it. "What's the difference between the bags you make and the ones the Rising uses?" I ask.

Oker pushes a container toward me. "Have you ever heard of Alzheimer's disease?"

That's a question, not an answer. But I go along with it. "No," I say.

"Of course not," Oker says. "Because I cured it before you were born."

"*You* cured it," I say. "Just you. No one else?"

Oker taps a couple of the pictures on the wall behind him. "Not by myself. I was part of a research team in the Society. That disease clogged up the brain with extra proteins. Others before us had worked on the project, but *we* figured out a way to control the level of expression of those proteins. We shut them down." He leans a little closer to look at the compound I've made. "So, to answer your first question, the difference is that I know what I'm doing when I put together the medication. Unlike the Rising. I know how to help keep some of the proteins from the mutation from accumulating because they act in ways that are similar to the disease we cured. And I know how to keep the patients' platelets from accumulating in the spleen so patients don't rupture and bleed internally. The other difference is that I don't include as many narcotics in my solutions. My patients feel some pain. Not agony, more like discomfort. It reminds them to breathe. More likely to get them back that way."

"But is that a good thing?" I ask. "What if they can feel all the pain of the boils?"

Oker snorts. "If they feel something, they fight," he says.

"If you were in a place with no pain, why would you want to come back?"

He slides a tray of powder in my direction. "Measure this out and distill it in the solution."

I look down at the instructions and measure two grams of the powder into the liquid.

"Sometimes I can't believe this," Oker mutters. I can't tell if he's talking to himself or not, but then he glances in my direction. "Here I am, working on a cure for that damn Plague again."

"Wait," I say. "You worked on the first cure?"

He nods. "The Society knew about the work we'd done in protein expression. They pulled my team to work on the cure for the Plague. Before the Society sent it out to the Enemy, they wanted to make sure we had a cure—in case the Plague came back."

"So the Rising lied," I say. "The Society *did* have a cure."

"Of course they did," Oker says. "Not enough for a pandemic, so the Rising does get credit for making more. But the Society came up with the cure first. I bet your Pilot didn't mention that."

"He didn't," I say.

"I paid a considerable amount for my escape here," Oker says. "The current Pilot is the one who brought me out." Oker walks over to look for something else in the cupboard. "That was before he was the Rising's Pilot," he says, his voice muffled. "When the Rising asked him to lead, I told him not to believe them. They're no rebellion. They're Society, with a different name, and they just want you and your followers, I said. But he was so sure it would work." Oker comes back to the table. "Maybe he wasn't *that* sure," he says. "He kept note of where I was here in Endstone."

So Oker was part of the vanishings that Lei told me about. "Did that bother you?" I ask. "Him keeping track of you like that?"

"No," Oker says. "I wanted to be out of the Society, and I was. I don't mind feeling useful now and then. Here." He hands me the datapod. "Scroll through this list for me."

As I do, he grumbles. "Can't they narrow it down any more? We all assume that it's something environmental. Well, we eat anything we can find or grow. It's a long list. We'll find something to help them. But it might not be in time."

"Why didn't the Pilot bring you into Camas or Central?" I ask. "That would be a better place to work on the cure. They could bring you supplies and plants from the mountain. In the Provinces, you'd have access to all the data, the equipment . . ."

Oker's face is rigid. "Because I agreed to work with him on one condition only," he says. "That I stay right here."

I nod.

"Once you get out," Oker says, "you don't go back."

His hands look so old, like paper covering bone, but the veins stand out, fat with life and blood. "I can tell you have another question," he says, his voice annoyed and interested at the same time. "Ask it."

"The Pilot told us that someone contaminated the water supplies," I say. "Do you think they also created the mutation? They both happened so fast. It seems like the mutation could have been manipulated, just like the outbreak was."

"That's a good question," Oker says, "but I'd bet that the mutation occurred naturally. Small genetic changes take place regularly in nature, but unless there is an advantage conferred by a mutation, it is simply lost because other nonmutated versions predominate." He points to another jar, and I take it down for him and unstop the lid. "But if some kind of selective pressure is present and confers an advantage to a mutation, that mutation ends up outgrowing and surviving the nonmutated forms."

"That's what a virologist back in Camas told me," I say.

"He's right," Oker says. "At least to my thinking."

"He also told me that it was likely the cure itself that applied the selective pressure and caused the mutation."

"It's likely," Oker says, "but even so, I don't think anyone planned that part. It was, as we who live outside of the Society sometimes say, bad luck. One of the mutations was immune to the cure, and so it flourished and caught on."

Oker's confirmed it. The cure caused the real pandemic.

"I've gotten ahead of myself," Oker says. "I haven't yet told you the way a virus works. You've figured some of it out for yourself. But the best way to explain it," and his tone is dry, "is to refer to a story. One of the Hundred, in fact. Number Three. Do you remember it?"

"Yes," I say, and I actually do. I've always remembered it because the girl's name—Xanthe—sounds a little like my own.

"Tell it to me," Oker says.

The last time I tried to tell a story was to Lei and it didn't go well at all. I wish I'd done better for her. But I'll try again now, because Oker asked me to do it and I think he's going to be the one to figure out the cure. I have to try to keep from smiling. *It's going to happen. We're going to do it.*

"The story is about a girl named Xanthe," I say. "One day she decided she didn't want to eat her own food. When the meal delivery came she snatched her father's oatmeal and ate it instead. But it was too hot, and all day long Xanthe felt sick and feverish. The next day she stole her mother's oatmeal, but it was too cold, and Xanthe shook with chills. On the third day she ate her own meal and it was just right. She felt fine." I stop. It's a pretty stupid story, meant to remind Society kids to do what they're told. "It goes on and on like that," I tell Oker. "She ends up with three citations for improper behavior before she realizes the Society knows what's right for her."

To my surprise, he nods. "Good enough," he says. "The only part you forgot was the part about her hair."

"Right," I say. "It was gold. That's what the name Xanthe means."

"Doesn't matter anyway," Oker says. "The important

319

thing is the idea that something could be too hot, too cold, and just right. That's what you need to remember about the way a virus works. It uses something I think of as the Xanthe strategy. A virus doesn't want to run out of targets too quickly. It kills the organism it infects, but it can't kill too fast. It needs to be able to transfer to another organism in time."

"So if the virus kills everything too quickly," I say, "it's too hot."

"And if it doesn't move to another organism fast enough, it dies," Oker says. "Too cold."

"But somewhere in the middle," I say, "is just right."

Oker nods. "This mutation," he says, "was just right. And not only because of the Society and the Rising and what they each did. They contributed to some of the conditions, yes. But the virus mutated on its own, as viruses have done for years. There have been Plagues all through history and that won't end with this one."

"So we're never really safe," I say.

"Oh no, my boy," Oker says, almost gently. "That might be the Society's greatest triumph—that so many of us ever believed that we were."

CHAPTER 31
CASSIA

I should go to see Ky.

I should stay here and work on the cure.

When I let myself really think, I am torn between two places and become lost, adrift in worry, accomplishing nothing and helping no one. So I *don't* think, not that way. I think about plants and cures and numbers and I sort through the data, trying to find something that will bring back the still.

Comparing the lists isn't as simple as it sounds. They don't only include names of the things that the villagers and the farmers ate, but also the frequency with which the foodstuffs were consumed; the type of ground where they were cultivated, if they were plant or animal goods, and a myriad of other information that needs to be taken into account. Just because something was eaten often doesn't mean that it provides immunity; conversely, something eaten only once is unlikely to produce immunity.

People go in and out—medics examining patients and returning to report, Oker and Xander doing their work, the sorters taking breaks, Leyna checking in to see our progress. I become accustomed to the comings and goings and eventually I don't even look up when I hear the wooden door opening, closing; I barely notice when the mountain breeze slips in and rustles my hair.

A woman's voice breaks into my concentration. "We thought of a few more things," she says. "I want to make certain we included them all on our list."

"Of course," Rebecca says.

Something about the woman's voice seems familiar. I glance up.

She looks older than her voice sounds, her hair completely gray and twisted in complicated braids and knots up high on her head. She has weathered skin and a gentle way of moving her hands, holding up a list on a piece of paper. Even from here, I can tell that it's handwritten, not printed.

"Anna," I say out loud.

She turns to look at me. "Have we met?" she asks.

"No," I say. "I'm sorry. But I've seen your village, and I know Hunter and Eli." I want to see Eli. But because I've been visiting Ky and working on the cure, I haven't taken the time to go looking for the farmers' new settlement, even though I know it's not far from the main village. Guilt washes over me, although I don't know if Leyna and others would let me go, even if I asked. I *am* here to work on the cure.

"You must be Cassia," Anna says. "Eli has always talked about you."

"I am," I say. "Tell Eli that Ky is here, too." Has Eli told Anna about Ky? From the flash of recognition in Anna's eyes, I think that Eli has. "But Ky is one of the patients."

"I'm very sorry," Anna says.

I grip the edges of the rough-hewn table, reminding myself not to think too deeply of Ky, or I'll break down and be no good to him at all. "Hunter and Eli—they're fine?"

"They are," Anna says.

"I've wanted to come see them—" I begin.

"It's all right," Anna says. "I understand."

Rebecca moves slightly and Anna takes the hint. She smiles at me. "After I'm finished, I'll tell Eli that you're here. He'll want to see you. And so will Hunter."

"Thank you," I say, not quite believing that I've met her. This is *Anna*, the woman who I heard about from Hunter and whose writings I saw in the cave. When she begins reading her list, I can't tune out the sound of her voice.

"Mariposa lily," Anna says to Rebecca. "Paintbrush flowers, but only in small quantities. It can be toxic otherwise. We used sage to season, and ephedra for tea . . ."

Words as beautiful as songs. And I realize why I knew Anna's voice. It sounds the smallest bit like my mother's. I pull a scrap of paper toward me and write down the names Anna says. My mother might already know some of them, and she will love to learn the others. I'll sing them back to her when I bring her the cure.

"It's time for you to rest for a little while." Rebecca presses a piece of flatbread wrapped in cloth into my hand. The bread is warm and the smell of it makes my stomach rumble. They make their own food here. What would that be like? What if I had time to learn that, too? "And here," she says, handing me a canteen. "You should eat while you visit him."

She knows where I'm going, of course.

As I walk down the path to the infirmary, I breathe in the forest. Wildflowers grow in all the places where people don't walk; purple and red and blue and yellow. The clouds, a stirring and startling pink, soar in the sky above the trees and peaks of the mountains. And a conviction comes to me in this moment: *We can find a cure.* I have never felt it so strongly.

When I arrive, I sit down next to Ky and look at him, touch his hand.

The victims of the Plague don't close their eyes. I wish that they did. Ky's look flat and gray; not the colors I'm used to seeing, blue, green. I put my hand on his forehead, feeling the smooth expanse of skin and the understructure of bone. He seems hot. Could he be infected? "He doesn't look good," I say to one of the medics on duty. "His nutrient bag is already empty. Do you have the drip turned up too high?"

She checks her notes. "This patient should still have one working."

I don't move. It's not Ky's fault something went wrong. After a moment she stands up and goes to get a new bag to attach to his line. She seems harried. There are only two medics on duty. "Do you need more help in here?" I ask.

"No," she says sharply. "Leyna and Oker only want those of us with medical training to work with the still."

After she finishes, I sit next to Ky and rest my hand on his, thinking of how alive he was on the Hill, in the canyons, and, for a moment, in the mountains. And then he was gone. I think of how I spent all that time puzzling out the color of his eyes when I started to fall in love with him. I found him changeable and difficult to put into one finite set, one clear description.

The door opens and I turn, expecting to see someone coming to tell me that my time's up, that I need to return to work. And I don't want to leave. It's strange. When I was sorting, I felt certain it was the most important thing I could be doing. When I'm here, I know that being with the still matters most.

But it's not someone from the research lab. It's Anna.

"May I come in?" Anna asks. After she's washed her hands and put on her face mask, she comes toward me. I stand up, ready to offer her my chair, but she shakes her head and sits on the floor near the bed. It's strange to be looking down at her.

"So this is Ky," she says. He's turned on his side and she looks into his eyes and touches his hand. "Eli wants to see him. Do you think it's a good idea?"

"I don't know," I say. It might be a good idea for Eli to come because then Ky could hear more than only my voice speaking to him, calling him back. But would it be good for Eli? "You would know better than I." It's hard to say, but of course it's true. I only knew Eli for days. She has known him for months.

"Eli told me that Ky's father was a trader," Anna says. "Eli didn't know his name, but he remembered that Ky told him his father learned to write in our village."

"Yes," I say. "Do you remember him?"

"Yes," Anna says. "I wouldn't forget him. His name was Sione Finnow. I helped him learn to write it. Of course, he wanted to learn his wife's name first." She smiles. "He traded for her whenever he could. He brought her those paintbrushes even when he couldn't afford paint."

I wonder if Ky can hear this.

"Sione traded for Ky, too," Anna says.

"What do you mean?" I ask.

"Some of the traders used to work with the rogue pilots," Anna says. "The ones who flew people out of the Society. Sione did that, once."

"He tried to trade to get Ky out?" I ask, surprised.

"No," she says. "Sione executed a trade on another's behalf to bring someone—his nephew—to the stone villages. We farmers never assisted in any of that, of course. But Sione told me about it."

My mind is whirling. *Matthew Markham. Patrick and Aida's son. He isn't dead?*

"Sione performed that trade with no fee, because it was a family member who wanted it. It was his wife's sister. Her husband knew something was rotten in the Society. He wanted his child out. It was an extremely delicate, dangerous trade."

She looks past me, remembering Ky's father, a man I never met. *What was he like?* I wonder. It's impossible not to picture him as an older, more reckless version of Ky: bright, daring. "But," Anna says, "Sione managed it. He thought that the Society would prefer word of a death getting around to news of an escape, and he was right. The Society made up a story to explain the boy's disappearance. They didn't want rumors to spread about the vanishings, as they were called. They didn't want people to think they could escape."

"He risked a great deal for his nephew," I say.

"No," Anna says. "He did it for his son."

"For Ky?"

"Sione couldn't change who he was. He couldn't Reclassify himself. But he wanted a better life for his son than he could provide."

"But Ky's father was a rebel," I say. "He believed in the Rising."

"And in the end, I think he was also a realist," Anna says. "He knew the chances of a rebellion succeeding were slim. What he did for Ky was an insurance policy. If something went wrong and Sione died, then Ky would have a place in the Society. He could go back to live with his aunt and uncle."

"And he did," I say.

"Yes," Anna says. "Ky was safe."

"No," I say. "They sent him out to the work camps eventually." *I* sent him out to the work camps.

"But much later than they would have," she says. "He likely lived longer where he was in the Society than he would have if he'd been trapped in the Outer Provinces."

"Where is that boy now?" I ask. "Matthew Markham?"

"I have no idea," Anna says. "I never met him, you understand. I only knew of him from Sione."

"I knew Ky's uncle," I say. "Patrick. I can't believe he would send his son out here to live where he knew nothing and no one."

"Parents will do strange things when they see a clear danger to their children," she says.

"But Patrick didn't do the same for Ky," I say, angry.

"I suspect," Anna says, "that he wanted to honor Ky's parents' request for their child, which was that he have a chance to leave the Outer Provinces. And eventually, I'm sure Ky's aunt and uncle didn't want to give him up. Sending one son out would have almost killed them. And then, when nothing terrible happened for years, they would have wondered if they'd done the right thing in sending him away." Anna takes a deep breath. "Hunter may have told you that I left him behind, along with his daughter. My granddaughter. Sarah."

"Yes," I say. I saw Hunter bury Sarah. I saw the line on her grave—*Suddenly across the June a wind with fingers goes.*

"Hunter never blamed me," Anna says. "He knew I had to take the people across. Time was short. The ones who stayed *did* die. I was right about that."

She looks up at me. Her eyes are very dark. "But I blame myself," she says. Then she holds out her hand, flexing her fingers, and I think I see traces of blue marked on her skin, or perhaps it's her veins underneath. In the dim light of the infirmary, it's hard to tell.

She stands up. "When is your next break?" she asks.

"I don't know," I say.

"I'll try to find out and bring Eli and Hunter to see you." Anna bends down and touches Ky's shoulder. "And you," she says.

After she leaves, I lean down to Ky. "Did you hear all that?" I ask him. "Did you hear how much your parents loved you?"

He doesn't answer.

"And I love you," I tell him. "We are still looking for your cure."

He doesn't stir. I tell him poems, and I tell him that I love him. Over and over again. As I watch, I think the liquid dripping into his veins helps; there is a warming to his face, like sun on stone, when the light comes up.

CHAPTER 32
KY

Her voice comes back first. Beautiful and gentle. She's still telling me poetry.

Then the pain comes back, but it's different now. My muscles and bones used to hurt. But now I ache even deeper than that. Has the infection spread?

Cassia wants me to know that she loves me.

The pain wants to eat me away.

I wish I could have one without the other, but that's the problem with being alive.

You don't usually get to choose the measure of suffering or the degree of joy you have.

I don't deserve either her love or this illness.

That's a stupid thought. Things happen whether you deserve them or not.

For now, I'll ride out the pain on the song of her voice. I won't think about what will happen when she has to leave.

Right now, she's here and she loves me. She says it over and over again.

CHAPTER 33
CASSIA

Xander finds me there next to Ky. "Leyna sent me to bring you back," he says. "It's time to get to work again."

"Ky's drip was out," I say. "I wanted to stay until he looked better."

"That shouldn't have happened," Xander says. "I'll let Oker know."

"Good," I say. Oker's anger will carry much more weight with the village leaders than mine will.

"I'll be back," I tell Ky, in case he can hear. "As soon as I can."

Outside of the infirmary, the trees grow right up to the edge of the village buildings. Branches scrape and sing along one another when the wind comes through them. So much life here. Grasses, flowers, leaves, and people walking, talking, living.

"I'm sorry about the blue tablets," Xander says. "I—you could have died. It would have been my fault."

"No," I say. "You didn't know."

"You never took one, did you?"

"Yes," I say. "But I'm fine. I kept going."

"*How?*" he asks.

I kept going by thinking of Ky. But how can I tell Xander that? "I just did," I say. "And the scraps in the tablets helped."

Xander smiles.

"The secret you mentioned on one of the scraps," I say. "What was it?"

"I'm a part of the Rising," Xander says.

"I thought that might be what you meant," I say. "You told me on the port. Didn't you? Not in words, I know, but I thought that's what you were trying to say. . . ."

"You're right," Xander says. "I did tell you. It wasn't much of a secret." He grins, and then his expression sobers. "I've been meaning to ask you about the red tablet."

"I'm not immune," I say. "It works on me."

"Are you sure?"

"They gave it to me in Central," I say. "I'm certain of it."

"The Rising promised me that you were immune to the red tablet, and to the Plague," Xander says.

"Then they either lied to you or made a mistake," I say.

"That means you would have been vulnerable to the original version of the Plague," Xander says. "Did you go down with it? Did they give you a cure?"

"No." I understand what's puzzling him. "If the red tablet works on me, then I was never given the initial immunization when I was a baby. So I should have gone down sick with the original Plague. But I didn't. I just got the mark."

Xander shakes his head, trying to figure it out. I am

sorting through, too. "The red tablet works on me," I say. "I've never taken the green. And I walked through the blue."

"Has anyone else ever walked through the blue?" Xander asks.

"Not that I know of," I say. "I had Indie with me, and she helped me keep going. That might have made a difference."

"What else happened in the canyons?" Xander asks.

"For a long time, I wasn't with Ky at all," I say. "We started in a village full of other Aberrations. Then three of us ran to the Carving; me, the boy who died, and Indie."

"Indie is in love with Ky," Xander says.

"Yes," I say. "I think she is, now. But first it was you. She used to steal things. She took my microcard and someone else's miniport and she used to look at your face whenever she could."

"And in the end, it was Ky she wanted," Xander says. I detect a note of bitterness in his voice; it's not something I've heard often before.

"They flew in the same Rising camp," I say. "She saw him all the time."

"You don't seem angry at her," Xander says.

And I'm not. There was the moment of shock and hurt when Ky said that she'd kissed him, but it vanished when Ky went still. "She makes her own way," I say. "She does what she wants." I shake my head. "It's hard to stay upset with her."

"I don't understand," Xander says.

And I don't think he can. He doesn't really know Indie; has never seen her lie and cheat to get what she wants, or realized how among all of that is a strange inexplicable honesty that is only hers. He didn't see her push through the silver water and bring us to safety against the odds. He never knew how she felt about the sea or how badly she wanted a dress made of blue silk.

Some things cannot be shared. I could tell him everything that happened in the Carving and he still won't have been there with me.

And it's the same for him. He could tell me all about the Plague and the mutation that followed and what he saw, but I still wasn't *there*.

Watching Xander's face, I see him realize this. He swallows. He's about to ask me something. When he does, it's not what I expect. "Have you ever written anything for me? Besides that message, I mean."

"You did get it," I say.

"All except for the end," he says. "It got ruined."

My heart sinks. So he doesn't know what I said, that I told him not to think of me anymore in that way.

"I wondered," Xander says, "if you'd ever written a poem for me."

"Wait," I say. There is no paper here, but there is a stick and dark dirt on the ground and it is, after all, how I learned to write. I hesitate for a moment, glancing back at the infirmary, but then I realize *The time for keeping this to ourselves is long past. And if I tried to share it with everyone out in Central, why would I keep it from Xander?*

All the same, it feels intimate to write for Xander. It means more.

I close my eyes for a moment, trying to think of something, and then it comes to me, an extension of the poem with a word that made me think of Xander. I begin to write. "Xander," I say, pausing.

"What?" he asks. He doesn't lift his eyes from my hands, as if they're capable of a miracle and he can finally witness what it is.

"I thought about *you* in the Carving, too," I say. "I dreamed of you."

Now he does look at me and I find I can't hold his gaze; something deep I feel makes me look down, and I write:

Dark, dark, dark it was
But the Physic's hand was light.
He knew the cure, he held the balm
To heal our wings for flight.

Xander reads it over. His lips move. "Physic," he says softly. His expression looks pained. "You think I can heal people," he says.

"I do."

Just then, some of the children from the village come down the path across from us. As if we're one person, Xander and I stand up at the same time to watch them go by.

They are playing a game I've never seen before, one where

they pretend to be something else. Each child is dressed as an animal. Some used grass to make fur, others used leaves for feathers, and there are still more with wings lashed together, made of branches and of blankets that will be used again to warm at night. The repurposing of nature and scraps for creation reminds me of the Gallery, and I wonder if the people back in Central have found another place to gather and share, or if they don't have time at all for this anymore, with a mutation on the loose and no cure in sight.

"What would it have been like if we could do that?" Xander asks.

"What?" I ask.

"Be whatever *we* wanted," he says. "What if they'd let us do that when we were younger?"

I've thought about this, especially when I was in the Carving. *Who am I? What am I meant to be?* I think how lucky I am, in spite of the Society, to have dreamed so many, such wild things. Part of that is, of course, because of Grandfather, who always challenged me.

"Remember Oria?" Xander asks.

Yes. Yes. I remember. All of it. It's all clear and close again; the two of us, Matched, holding hands on the air train on the way home from the Banquet. My hand on the nape of his neck as I dropped the compass down his shirt so he could save Ky's artifact from the Officials. Even then, the three of us were doing our best to keep faith with one another.

"Remember that day planting newroses?" he asks.

"I do," I say, thinking of that kiss, the only one we've had, and my heart aches for us both. The air here in the mountains is sharp even in the summer. It bites at us, twists our hair, puts tears in our eyes. Standing here with Xander among the mountains is everything and nothing like standing with Ky out at the edge of the Carving.

I reach out my hand to take Xander's. My palm is streaked with dirt from writing with the stick, and as I look at it and think of Xander and newrose roots hanging down, the wind moves and the children dance toward the village stone, and light as air another cottonwood seed of memory comes to me:

My mother's hands are printed black with dirt, but I can see the white lines crossing her palms when she lifts up the seedlings. We stand in the plant nursery at the Arboretum; the glass roof overhead and the steamy mists inside belie the cool of the spring morning out.

"Bram made it to school on time," I say.

"Thank you for letting me know," she says, smiling at me. On the rare days when both she and my father have to go to work early, it is my responsibility to get Bram to his early train for First School. "Where are you going now? You have a few minutes left before work."

"I might stop by to see Grandfather," I say. It's all right to deviate from the usual routine this way, because Grandfather's

Banquet is coming soon. So is mine. We have so many things to discuss.

"Of course," she says. She's transferring the seedlings from the tubes where they started, rowed in a tray, to their new homes, little pots filled with soil. She lifts one of the seedlings out.

"It doesn't have many roots," I say.

"Not yet," she says. "That will come."

I give her a quick kiss and start off again. I'm not supposed to linger at her workplace, and I have an air train to catch. Getting up early with Bram has given me a little extra time, but not much.

The spring wind is playful, pushing me one way, pulling me another. It spins some of last fall's leaves up into the air, and I wonder, if I climbed up on the air-train platform and jumped, if the spiral of wind would catch me and take me up twirling.

I cannot think of falling without thinking of flying.

I could do it, I think, if I found a way to make wings.

Someone comes up next to me as I pass by the tangled world of the Hill on my way to the air-train stop. "Cassia Reyes?" the worker asks. The knees of her plainclothes are darkened with soil, like my mother's when she's been working. The woman is young, a few years older than me, and she has something in her hand, more roots dangling down. Pulling up or planting? I wonder.

"Yes?" I say.

"I need to speak with you," she says. A man emerges from the Hill behind her. He is the same age as she is, and something about them makes me think, They would be a good Match. I've never had permission to go on the Hill, and I look back up at the riot

of plants and forest behind the workers. What is it like in a place so wild?

"We need you to sort something for us," the man says.

"I'm sorry," I say, moving again. "I only sort at work." They are not Officials, nor are they my superiors or supervisors. This isn't protocol, and I don't bend rules for strangers.

"It's to help your grandfather," the girl says.

I stop.

"Cassia?" Xander asks. "Are you all right?"

"Yes," I say. I'm still staring down at my hand, wishing I could close it tight around the rest of the memory. I know it belongs with the lost red garden day. I'm certain of this, though I can't say why.

Xander looks like he's about to say something more, but the children are coming back again in their game, having circled all the way around the village stone. They are loud and laughing, as children should be. A little girl smiles at Xander and he smiles back, reaching out to touch her wing as she passes, but she turns at the wrong moment and he catches nothing.

CHAPTER 34
XANDER

Oker's so driven, it's almost inhuman. I feel the same way—we *have* to find the cure—but his focus is something else. It doesn't take many days before I'm accustomed to the routine in the research lab, which is: we work when Oker says to work and we rest when Oker says to take a break. Sometimes I catch a glimpse of Cassia in the sorting rooms, but for the most part I spend my time compounding formulas according to Oker's instructions.

Oker eats his meals right here in the lab. He doesn't even sit down. So that's what the rest of us do, too: we stand around and watch each other chew our food. It's probably the stress of the situation and the late hours, but something about it always makes me want to laugh. The mealtime conversations are a measure of how well things are going with the cure trials. Oker's different from most people because when things are going well he won't talk. When things are going badly, he'll say more.

"What is it about the Otherlands," I ask him today, "that makes all of you want to go there so much?"

Oker snorts. "Nothing," he says. "I'm too old to start over. I'll be staying right here. And I'm not the only one."

"Then why work on the cure if you're not sharing the reward?" I ask.

"Because of my inherent altruism," Oker says.

I can't help but laugh at that and he glares at me. "I want to beat the Society," Oker says. "I want to find the cure first."

"It's not the Society anymore," I remind him.

"Of course it is," he says, tipping back his canteen to drink. He wipes off his mouth with the back of his hand and glares at me. "Only fools think that anything has changed. The Rising and the Society have infiltrated each other so thoroughly that they don't even know who's who anymore. It's like a snake eating its own damn tail. This—out here—is the only true rebellion."

"The Pilot believes in the Rising," I say. "He's not a fraud."

Oker looks at me. "Maybe not," he says. "But that doesn't mean you should follow him." Then his gaze turns sharp. "Or me."

I don't say anything because we both know I'm already following the two of them. I think the Pilot's the way to revolution, and that Oker's the way to the cure.

The patients here still look much better than the ones back in the Provinces. Oker's cured all the secondary symptoms from the mutated Plague, like the platelet accumulation and the lung secretions. But he keeps muttering about proteins and the brain, and I know he hasn't figured out how to prevent or reverse the mutation's effect on the nervous system. But he'll get there.

Oker swears. He's spilled some of the water from the canteen onto his shirt. "The Society was right about one thing," Oker says. "Damn hands stopped working a year or two after eighty. Of course, my mind still functions better than most."

Cassia's already in her cell when I get there, but she's waited up for me. I can't see her very well because it's night, but I can hear her when she talks to me. Someone down the hall shouts out at us to be quiet but everyone else seems to have fallen asleep.

"Rebecca says all the research medics like you," Cassia says. "She also says that you're the only one who talks back to Oker."

"Maybe I should stop," I say. I don't want to alienate any of the workers. I've got to stay inside the research lab working on that cure.

"Rebecca says it's good," Cassia says. "She thinks Oker likes you because you remind him of himself."

Is that true? I don't think I'm as proud as Oker is, or as smart. Of course, I have always wondered if *I* could be the Pilot someday. I like people. I want to be around them and make things better for them.

"We're getting closer," Cassia says. "We have to be." Her voice sounds a little bit farther away. She must have moved back to sit on her bed instead of standing right at the front of the cell. "Good night, Xander," Cassia says.

"Good night," I tell her.

CHAPTER 35
CASSIA

Sometimes, when I am tired, it seems that I have never lived anywhere else. I have never done anything but this. Ky has always been still, and Xander and I have always been working on a cure. My parents and Bram are lost to me, and I have to find them, and the task at hand seems very large, too large for any one person or any group of people.

"What are you doing?" one of the other sorters asks. She gestures to the datapod, and to the tiny scraps of paper and the charcoaled stick I've been using for notes. I've found that sometimes I have to write things down by hand to understand the data I see on the datapod's screen. Writing clears my mind. And lately, I've been trying to draw by hand from the descriptions recorded in the datapod, because I can't picture the things they've described as being possible components for the cure. The sorter's eyes crinkle with laughter as she looks at my attempt at drawing a flower, and I pull the paper closer to me.

"There aren't any pictures on the datapod," I say. "Only written descriptions."

"That's because *we* all know what they look like," another sorter says, sounding annoyed.

"I know," I say softly, "but I don't. And it's affecting the sorts we do. They're wrong."

"Are you saying we're not doing our job correctly?" the first sorter asks, her voice cold. "We know the data could have errors. But we're sorting it in the most efficient way we can."

"No," I say, shaking my head. "That's not what I mean. It's not the beginning or the end of the sort—it's not the data or the way we're sorting it. Something's not coming together in the middle, in the correlation of the lists. It's as if there's an underlying phenomenon that we're not observing, some latent variable that we're not measuring in the data." I'm sure that our understanding of the relationship between these two sets of data isn't right. As sure as I am that I'm missing the middle of the red garden day memory.

"The important thing," says the other sorter, "is that we keep getting the lists to Oker." Every day, we send him suggestions of what might contribute to the cure, weighted according to the best information we have about the patients and taking into account what hasn't worked.

"I don't know how much Oker listens to us anyway," I say. "I think there's one person Oker trusts, and that's himself. But if we can come to some kind of consensus on what should be the most important ingredients and give that to him—he might be more likely to take what we say into account if our analysis lines up."

Leyna is watching me.

"But that's what we're doing," one of the sorters protests.

"I don't feel like I'm doing it *right*," I say. Frustrated, I push back my chair and stand up, holding the datapod in my hand. "I think I'll take my break now."

Rebecca nods.

"I'll walk you to the infirmary," Leyna says, surprising me. She works very, very hard, and I know the Otherlands are to her what Ky is to me, the best, most beautiful place, not fully realized, but full of promise.

We cross the village circle and pass the enormous stone set there. In front of it are two narrow troughs.

"What do you use these for?" I ask Leyna.

"Voting," she says. "It's how we choose. The farmers, too. Each person in the village has a little stone with his or her name written on it. Those troughs are where people cast their stones. The choice, or trough, with the most votes wins."

"And are there always only two choices?" I ask.

"Usually," Leyna says. Then she gestures for me to follow her around to the other side of the stone. "Look back here."

There are tiny names on the stone, arranged in columns. Someone has chipped and carved them in. They start at the top and come down to the bottom, where there is only a little room left.

"This column," Leyna says, "is a list of all those who have died in this village, in Endstone. And this," she adds, pointing to another part of the stone, "is a list of people who have gone on to the Otherlands. This is the jumping-off place, so to speak, so anyone who came through here on their way to the

346

Otherlands—no matter where they came from originally—has their name carved here."

I stand there for another moment, looking at the names on the stone in the Otherlands column, hoping to find someone. At first my eyes slide right over his name, not daring to believe he's there, but then I look back and it hasn't disappeared.

Matthew Markham.

"Did you know him?" I ask Leyna eagerly, touching the name.

"Not well," she says. "He was from another village." She looks at me with interest. "Do *you* know him?"

"Yes," I say, my heart pounding. "He lived in the Borough. His parents sent him out of the Society." I should have thought to ask about this sooner; I can't wait to tell Ky that his cousin was here once, that he might be alive somewhere, even if it's in a place from which people do not come back.

"A lot of those who vanished went on to the Otherlands," she says. "Some of them—and I can't remember if Matthew was this way—felt that, if their parents didn't want them in the Society, they'd get even farther away than their families intended. For some, it was almost like revenge." Then she puts her hand on his name, too. "But you say he used this name in the Borough?"

"Yes," I say. "It's his real name."

"That's something, then," she says. "Many of them changed their last names. He didn't. That means he didn't want to erase the trail completely if someone wanted to look for him eventually."

"They had no ships," I say. "So they would have had to walk all the way to the Otherlands."

She nods. "That's why they don't come back," she says. "The journey is too long. Without ships, it takes *years*." Then she points to the bottom of the stone. "There's just enough space for the rest of our names," she says. "It's a sign that we should go."

"I understand," I say. The stakes are high, almost impossibly so, for every single one of us.

When I get to the infirmary, I tell Ky all about the stone. "It's proof that Anna's right, that he didn't die in Oria," I say, "unless there's another Matthew Markham, but the likelihood of that is . . ." I stop calculating and breathe out. "I think it's him. I feel it."

I try to remember Matthew. Dark-haired, older than me, handsome. He looked enough like Ky that you could tell they were cousins, but different. Matthew wasn't as quiet as Ky; he had a louder laugh, a bigger presence in the Borough. But he was kind, like Ky.

"Ky," I say, "when we find the cure, I'll take you to see the stone. And then we can go back and tell Patrick and Aida."

I'm about to say more when the door opens. Anna has brought Eli to see me at last.

Eli has grown, but he still lets me hold him the way I hope Bram will when I see him again, pulled close and tight. "You made it," I say. He smells like the outdoors, a scent of pine and dirt, and I am so glad he's well that tears stream down my cheeks even though I smile.

"Yes," Eli says.

"I lived in your city," I say. "In Central. I thought of you all the time and wondered if I was walking on the streets where you lived, and I saw the lake."

"I miss it sometimes," Eli says. He swallows. "But it's better here."

"Yes," I say. "It is."

When Eli pulls away, I look over at Hunter. He still wears blue markings up and down his arms, and his eyes are very tired.

"I want to see Ky," Eli says.

"And you're sure Eli's immune?" I ask Anna.

She nods. "He doesn't have the mark," she says, "but none of us do."

I step away from the cot so Eli can go around to the other side. He crouches down next to Ky and looks right into his eyes. "I live in the mountains now," he tells Ky, and I have to turn away.

Anna points to my datapod. "Are you any closer to a cure?" she asks.

I shake my head. "I'm not helping," I say. "I don't know enough about the things on the lists. I can read the descriptions, but I don't know what the plants and animals you eat *look* like."

"And you think that matters?" Anna asks.

"I do," I say.

"I can draw some pictures for you," she says. "Show me the items on the list that you've never seen before."

I pull out a scrap of paper and write them all down for her. It's a long list and I feel embarrassed. "I'll work on it right away," she says. "Where should I begin?"

"Flowers first," I say. It feels right. "Thank you, Anna."

"I'm glad to do it," she says.

"And thank you for coming to see Ky," I tell Hunter. He shakes his head as if to say, *It's nothing.* I want to ask him how he is, to find out more about what his life has been like here in the mountains, but he nods to me and leaves. I should go, too. I have more sorting to do, always, until we find a cure.

CHAPTER 36
KY

Every time she leaves, Cassia always promises that she'll be back.

It feels like it's been a long time since she was here, but I can't really tell. Now that she's gone, I hear other voices, like I heard Vick's after he died on the bank.

This time it's Indie talking to me, but that can't be right because she's not here.

"Ky," she says. "I brought Cassia to Camas for you."

"I know," I say. "I know, Indie."

I can't see her. But her voice is so clear it's hard to believe that it's actually me, making this up. Because Indie can't be here talking to me. Can she?

"I'm sick," she says. "So I had to run. There's still no cure."

"Where are you running?" I ask.

"As far as I can before I go down," she says.

"No," I say. "No, Indie. Go back. They'll find a cure. And you might have the old version of the illness. Maybe they can help you." I can't believe I'm telling her to do this, but what other choice is there?

She's not going to listen to me.

"No," she says. "It's the mutation."

"You can't be certain," I tell her.

"I can," she says. "I've got red marks around my back. It hurts, Ky. So I'm running." She laughs. "Or flying, you could say. I took a ship from the Pilot."

I'm saying her name, over and over again, trying to stop her. *Indie, Indie, Indie.*

"Even when I hated you, I liked your voice," she says.

"Indie—" I say one more time, but she doesn't let me go on.

"Am I the best pilot you've ever seen?" she asks.

She is.

"I am," she says, and I can tell from her voice that she's smiling. She's always so beautiful when she smiles.

"Remember how I used to think the Pilot would come on the water?" Indie asks. "Because my mother sang me that song." Then Indie's singing it for me, her voice strong and plain. *"Any day her boat might fly /Across the waves and to the shore."* A pause. "I thought she might be trying to tell me that I could be the Pilot someday. So I built the boat and tried to escape."

"Turn around," I tell Indie. "Go back. Let them hook you up to keep you alive."

"I don't *want* to die," Indie says. "Either they'll shoot me down or I'll get somewhere I can land and then I'm going to *run* until I can't anymore. Don't you understand? I'm not giving up. I'm just running until the end. I can't go back again."

And now I don't know what to say.

"He's not the Pilot," Indie tells me. "I know that now." She breathes out shakily. "Remember when I thought *you* were the Pilot?"

"Yes," I say.

"Do you know who the Pilot *really* is?" Indie asks.

"Of course," I say. "You do, too."

She catches her breath and for a moment I think she might be crying. When she speaks I hear the tears in her voice, but I can also tell she's smiling again. "It *is* me," she says.

"Yes," I say. "Of course it is."

For a little while there is silence.

"I think you kissed me back," she says.

"I did," I say.

I'm not sorry anymore.

When Indie kissed me, I felt all her pain and longing and want. It cut me up to know how she felt and to know how much I loved her, too, but not in a way that could work. The way I feel about Indie is an understanding so painful and elemental that it would tear me apart.

The strange thing is that what she felt for me held her together.

I could do for her what Cassia does for me. I knew that and it's why I kissed Indie back.

It feels as though I'm running with her—I see moments from her life. Water filling a boat in Sonoma as the Officials sink it before her. Her triumphant run down the river to the

Rising that didn't save her. Our kiss. A flight, a landing, a run, step after step after step, running when anyone else would go still—

Then nothing but black.

Or maybe it was red.

CHAPTER 37
XANDER

O ker," Leyna says, "the sorters have made a new list for you."

"Another one?" Oker asks. "Put it over there." He gestures to one end of the long table.

In theory, Oker needs the lists from the sorters because their input is valuable. The sorters try to discover which factors are most likely to contribute to the immunity. Oker has to figure out what that means in the real world. If eating some kind of plant seems to be a factor, what component of the plant is it that's important? How do you put that into a cure? In what concentration? The collaboration is supposed to save everyone time and increase the chances that we'll find an effective cure quickly.

But Oker never seems inclined to drop what he's doing and read through the list right away. I know how hard Cassia has been working on sifting through the information. It's valuable. I clear my throat to say something but Leyna speaks first.

"You need to look at it," Leyna tells him. "The sorters have been through all the data again with the latest information from the infirmary and from your own observations. They've modeled the likelihood that each of these ingredients could effectively treat the disease."

"Right," Oker says. "You've said all this before." He starts for his office, holding his datapod.

"*Oker,*" Leyna says. "As the cure administrator, I need to insist that you look at this list. Or I will remove you from your duties."

"Ha," Oker says. "There's not another fully trained pharmic in this place."

"Your assistants are perfectly competent," Leyna says.

Oker mutters something and comes over. He picks up the datapod. "They're always sending lists," he says. "What's so urgent about this one?"

"We have another sorter now," Leyna reminds him. "And you can be sure that those back in the Provinces are using sorters to help decide on the next cure."

"Of course that's what they're doing," Oker says. "They used to be Society. They're not capable of any originality of thought. They can't act without numbers."

Leyna tries again. "The new sorter, Cassia—"

Oker waves his hand. "I don't need to know about the sorters. I'll go look at it now." He walks back to his office, taking the datapod and the list, and shuts the door hard behind him.

After only a few moments, I hear the door to Oker's office open. I expect him to say something caustic about it being time for Leyna to leave, but instead he stands there as if frozen, his eyes narrowed in thought. "Camassia," he says.

"It's Cassia," I begin, thinking that he's trying to remember the names of the sorters for some reason, but then he cuts me off.

"No," he says. "*Camassia*. It's a plant. We haven't done much with that one yet." Now he's muttering, as if he doesn't remember that we can hear him. "It's edible. Nutritious, even. It tastes like potatoes, only sweeter. The flower is purple. It's where Camas Province gets its name." His eyes snap back into focus and he looks right at me. "I'll go dig some."

"Camassia is not ranked very high on the sorters' list," Leyna says.

"*This isn't the Society,*" Oker growls. "We don't have to go by the numbers. We have room for intuition and intelligence in this village, don't we? We can find a cure faster than the people in the Provinces, but only if we stop thinking the way they would."

Leyna shakes her head. I know she must be trying to decide on the best way to deal with this, and she's asking herself the same questions she's had to ask before: Is Oker a valuable enough asset that she can let him do what he wants, even when it's in direct opposition to what she thinks is best?

"How about this," Oker says. "You gather the other ingredients and I'll make the cures you want, too." He looks at Noah and Tess. "You stay and keep the bags going."

"We have extra," Noah points out.

"We're going to need a lot more," Oker says impatiently. "Do *not* let any of the patients run out, especially that newest one." Then he turns to me. "Come on. You can help me dig."

"We only have seven patients available for trial now," Leyna says as Oker points out things he wants me to put in a bag—clean burlap straps, canteens, and two small shovels. "The other patients still need time to get the most recent cure trial out of their systems."

"Then we'll only use seven patients," Oker says, barely able to control his frustration.

"The Pilot will need more evidence than a few cured patients—" Leyna begins.

"Then give them all *my* cure," Oker says. He pushes open the door. "We're talking in circles. I'll make the cures. You decide who gets them. Just make sure someone takes mine. And that I get the one most recently still to try my cure." Then he glances over his shoulder at Leyna. "You should ask the sorters to calculate the odds that we're going to figure this out before the people back in the Provinces do. We're not the Pilot's best hope. He's throwing everything he can into the air on the chance that something might take flight. And we're the smallest, weakest bird."

"Your medications made a difference," Leyna says firmly. "The Pilot knows that."

"I didn't say we couldn't still be the ones to figure it out," Oker says. "But only if you let me do what I need to do."

"We have camassia in our stores," Leyna says, one final

protest. "You don't need to walk all the way to the camassia fields."

"I want it fresh from the ground," Oker tells her.

"Then I'll send someone out to glean the field," Leyna says. "That will be faster than you going yourself."

"*No,*" Oker says. "No." He takes a deep breath. "I don't want anything to compromise this cure. I'll see it through from start to finish."

Now that sounds like something a real Pilot would say. I follow Oker out the door.

I don't trick myself that Oker's picked me to come with him because he trusts me the most. He can count on Noah and Tess to prepare the medicated nutrient bags for the patients, but he can't trust me to manage that yet without supervision. He just needs someone to dig for him.

And he likes to talk to me about the mutation because I'm the most recent person to work firsthand with the still. I've seen the mutation up close. Of course this would all be intriguing to him. He's the one who came up with the first cure. He knew about the Plague before almost anyone else.

"How far are we going?" I ask.

"A few miles," he says. "The field I want isn't near here. It's closer to the other stone villages, toward Camas."

I follow him. It all looks like grass and rock to me. Nothing stands out as a pathway. "People must not go to the other villages often anymore," I say to Oker.

"Not after this last gathering to Endstone," Oker says. "We've sent people out to harvest different wild crops since then, but it doesn't take long for the mountain to reclaim the path."

Every now and then we pass a round stone pressed flat into the ground. Oker says the stones indicate we are on the right track. "I walked all the way out here," Oker says. His voice sounds peaceful, contemplative, but he moves as fast as he can. "Back then, the pilots often flew you as far as the first stone village and then it was up to you where you went after that. I decided on Endstone since it was the farthest away. Thought I might not make it, since according to the Society I was old enough to be dead, but I kept going." He laughs. "I walked through the day of my own Final Banquet."

"That's what my friend tried to do," I say to Oker. "He tried to keep walking through the mutation. He was convinced that if he kept moving, he wouldn't go still."

"Where'd he get an idea like that?" Oker asks.

"I think it's because Cassia walked through a blue tablet once. She took one and kept on going."

I expect him to say that's impossible, but instead he says, "Maybe your friends are right. Stranger things have happened." Then he smiles. "Cassia is an unusual name. It's botanical. The bark is used as a spice."

"Is it any relation to the plant we're looking for now?" I ask. "The names sound so similar."

"No," Oker says. "Not to my knowledge."

"She helped with that list," I say. "You should look at it again after we're done with the camassia." I don't bring up the fact—yet—that she, not Oker, should be the one who decides which cure Ky gets.

Oker stops to get his bearings. I could go faster than this, but he's in excellent shape for someone so old. "The camassia should be near here," he says. "This is where the villagers come to harvest. But they won't have taken it all. Always have to leave some to grow for next year, even if you hope you won't be here." He leaves the path and starts down through a stand of trees.

I follow him. The trees on the mountainside are pines and some others I don't know. They have white bark and thin green leaves. I like the sound when we walk under them.

Oker points down. "See it?"

It takes me a moment, but I do. The flowers are a little dead and dry, but they're purple like he said.

"You can dig here," he says. "Don't take them all. Dig up every other plant. We don't need the flowers, just the roots. Wrap the roots in burlap and wet them at the stream." He points to a tiny rivulet of water winding through the grass, turning it marshy. "Be as fast as you can about it."

I kneel down and start digging around the plant. When I pull up the bulb, it's brown and dirty, with tangles of roots coming out. It reminds me of Cassia, and how the two of us planted those flowers the day we kissed in the Borough. That kiss has kept me going for months.

At the stream, I wet the strips of burlap and wrap up the bulbs one after the other. I keep digging, and the sun shines down on me, and I decide that I like the smell of the dirt. My back aches a little, so I stand up to stretch it out. I'm almost out of space in the bag.

Oker's impatient for me to finish. He crouches down next to me and starts sawing at a plant, his motions clumsy. The flowers bob back and forth, back and forth. He pulls up the roots, fumbling with his twisted hands, and then gives the plants to me. "Can't wrap it," he says. "You'll have to do it for me."

I wrap up Oker's harvest and finish filling our bags. When I start to sling his bag over my shoulder with mine—I should carry it for him now that it's full—Oker shakes his head. "I can carry my own."

I nod and hand it over. "Do you think this camassia is really the cure?"

"I think there's a very good chance," Oker says. "Let's go."

Oker has to stop and rest on the way back to the village. "Forgot to eat this morning," he says. It's the first time I've seen him worn out. He leans up against a rock, his face twisted into a scowl of impatience as he waits for his heart to stop racing.

"I've been wondering something," I say. Oker grunts but doesn't tell me I can't ask, so I go ahead. "How did the villagers know that they were immune to the Plague in the first place, before the mutation?"

"They've known about their immunity to the original Plague for years," Oker says. "When the Society first sent it out to the Enemy, one of the pilots who dropped the virus ran away from his Army base and came to the first stone village, the one nearest Camas."

Oker takes a moment to catch his breath. "What the idiot didn't realize when he came," Oker says, "is that he himself had caught the Plague. He thought it could only come through water, because that's how he'd distributed it in the Enemy's rivers and streams. But it can also be transmitted from person to person, and he'd had contact with some of the Enemy. Apparently he'd tried to help them before he came to the stone village."

"Why did he run to the village?" I ask.

"He was one of the pilots who took part in the vanishings," Oker says, "so he knew the people in the village and they knew him. A week after he took refuge there, he became sick." Oker pushes himself away from the rock. "Let's get going."

Birds chatter in the trees around us and the grass grows so long over the path that it *whisk-whisks* against our pant legs. "Of course, the Society had cures for any of their workers who happened to contract the disease," Oker says. "But since the pilot didn't go back to the Society, he didn't get the cure. He came to the stone villages, and he died."

"Because the villagers didn't have a cure," I say, "or because they killed him?"

Oker looks at me, his glance sharp. "They left him out in the woods with food and water, but they knew he'd die."

"They had to," I say. "They thought he could infect their whole village."

Oker nods. "When the pilot became sick, he told them about the Plague and the Enemy and what had happened. He begged the villagers to go back into the Society and get him a cure. By that time, he'd already exposed most of the village. The entire community thought they were going to die, and they knew they'd never get their hands on the cure in time. They had to try to do what they could." Oker laughs. "Of course, at the time they had no idea that they would turn out to be immune."

"Did they exile anyone else?" I ask.

"No," Oker says. "They quarantined those who'd been exposed, but no one ever got sick."

I breathe out a sigh of relief.

"Their immunity wouldn't have mattered to the Society, of course," Oker says, "since they already had a cure. But it meant something to the villagers. They knew that if the Society tried to put the Plague in the villagers' waters, they wouldn't die. For the most part, they kept their immunity a secret. Someone told the Pilot, but he didn't do anything with the knowledge until the mutation happened."

"And then he wondered if the villagers might be immune to the mutation, too," I say.

"Right," Oker says. "He came out here to ask if anyone was willing to test their immunity, and to find out if we could help discover a cure."

"I know people volunteered to be exposed to the mutated virus," I say. "Why?"

"Foilware meals," Oker says, sounding disgusted. "He brought us an entire cargo hold full of them and said that he could bring more."

"Why would anyone want those?" I ask. "The food here is so much better."

"For the trip to the Otherlands," he says. "Those meals last for years. They'd be perfect for the journey. The Pilot promised he could get enough for *all* the travelers to take, if only a few of us would volunteer for exposure to the virus. They injected people with the mutation and had them go stay in one of the other villages just in case. But no one got sick." Now Oker's grinning from ear to ear. "You should have seen the look on the Pilot's face. He couldn't believe there was a chance. That's when he offered us the ships if we could find a cure."

Oker steps over a puddle of blue flowers growing right in the center of the path. "Your friends who try to walk through the illness are closer to the truth about the virus and the blue tablets than you might think. Those tablets aren't poison. They're a trigger."

"A trigger?" I ask.

"When the Society made the Plague to use on the Enemy," Oker says, "they engineered several other viruses as experiments. One of them had a very similar effect to what the Plague does—it made people stop and go still—but it couldn't be transmitted from person to person. It only affected the person who had direct contact with the tablet. The Society decided not to use that particular virus on the Enemy. They used it on their own people instead."

Oker glances over his shoulder to look back at me. "The Society named the viruses," he says. "That one was called the Cerulean virus."

"Why?"

"It's another word for blue," Oker says, "and they used blue labels for that virus in the lab so they could easily tell it apart from the others. I wonder sometimes if that's what gave the Officials the idea to use it in the blue tablet. The Society modified the Cerulean virus and put it in the babies' immunizations. Then, if they needed to, they could trigger the virus later with the blue tablet."

"It's perfect Society logic," I say. "While they're protecting you, they also implant a virus so that they can still control you if they need to. But why didn't more people go still before now?"

"Because it's latent," Oker says. "It works its way into your DNA, but then it lies dormant. The virus doesn't become active until you take the trigger, which is the blue tablet. If you take one, you'll go still until the Society helps you, if they find you in time. If they don't, you die. They had a cure for the Cerulean virus as well as the Plague. But that was the limit of their science. They haven't found a cure for the mutation."

"Why are you telling me all of this?" I ask.

"Because I could drop dead at any minute," Oker says. "Someone needs to know what's going on."

"And why'd you pick me?" I ask. "You don't even know me."

"You know people who have the mutation," Oker says. "You've got family or friends on the inside, and that friend of yours here now. You want people to get better for personal reasons. And you know that if you don't get your friend cured, you'll always wonder who she would have chosen out of the two of you."

Oker's right, of course. He's noticed more than I thought he would have, although I shouldn't be surprised. A true pilot would have to be that way.

We don't talk the rest of the way back.

When we get to the lab, we sling the bulbs out on the table. "Wash them," Oker tells Tess and Noah. "But don't scrub them. We just want them clean from dirt."

They nod.

"I'll sort out the best bulbs," he says to me, pushing through the assortment with his knuckles. "You gather equipment. We need knives, a cutting board, and mortar and pestle. Make sure it's all sterilized."

I hurry to get the equipment ready. Oker's already finished sorting by the time I'm done. He taps a little pile of bulbs. "These are the best ones," he says. "We'll start with them." He pushes one toward me. "Cut it open. You're going to have to do this part. I can't."

So I make the incision down the middle of the bulb. When we've laid it open, I draw in my breath. It's layered like an onion inside, and the color is beautiful: a pearly, almost glittery white.

Oker hands me the mortar and pestle. "Pulverize it," he says. "We're going to need enough for everyone."

The door to Oker's lab slams open. "There you are," Leyna says, her face pale. "I sent someone out of the village to find you."

"We just got back," I say. "We must have missed them."

"What is it?" Oker asks.

"It's the still," Leyna says. "They've started to die."

The room goes completely silent. "Is it one of the patients from that first group the Pilot brought in?" Oker asks.

"Yes," Leyna says. I exhale in relief. That means it isn't Ky.

"This had to happen eventually," Oker says. "That first group has been holding on for weeks now. Let's go see what we can do."

Leyna nods. But before we go, Oker has me wrap the bulbs back up and lock them away. "Get back to the bags," he tells Noah and Tess. "But I don't want anyone working on the actual cure unless I'm here."

They nod. Oker takes the key back from me. Only then do we follow Leyna toward the infirmary, where people have gathered outside. The crowd parts for Oker and Leyna to come through. I follow behind them, acting like I belong here, and I'm lucky as usual, because no one stops me or asks me what I'm doing. If they did, I'd tell them the truth and say that I've found my real Pilot, and I'm not letting him out of my sight until we've got the cure.

CHAPTER 38
CASSIA

I was in the infirmary when the first person died.

It wasn't a good way to go. And it wasn't still.

I heard a commotion at the other end of the infirmary. "Pneumonia," one of the village medics said to another. "His lungs are full of infection." Someone pulled a curtain back and everyone hurried to gather around and try to save the patient, who was breathing with awful, wet, gasping breaths that sounded like he'd swallowed an entire sea. Then he coughed and a spatter of blood came out of his mouth. I saw it even from far away. It was bright red on his clean white sheet.

Everyone was too busy to tell me to go. I wanted to run, but I couldn't leave Ky. And I didn't want him to hear the sounds of people trying to save the man, or how Ky's own breathing sounded labored.

So I crouched down in front of Ky and covered one of his ears with my shaking hand, and then I leaned right up close to his other ear and I sang to him. I didn't even know I knew how.

I'm still singing when Leyna brings Oker and Xander in. I have to keep singing because someone else has started choking.

One of the village medics walks over to Oker and gets right in his face. "This is your fault for keeping them coherent," he says to Oker. "Come see what you've done. He knows what's happening. There's no peace in his eyes."

"He came back?" Oker asks, and I hear excitement in his voice. It makes me sick.

"Only enough to know that he's dying," the medic says. "He's not cured."

Xander stops and crouches down next to me. "Are you all right?" he asks.

I nod. I keep singing. He can see in my eyes that I'm not crazy. He touches my arm, very briefly, and goes to stand with Oker and the others over by the patients.

I understand that Xander needs to see what's happening. And he's found a Pilot in Oker. If *I* had to choose someone as the Pilot, I'd pick Anna.

But I also know we can't plan on anyone else rescuing us. We have to do it ourselves. There can be no one Pilot. We have to be strong enough to go without the belief that someone can swoop down and save us. I think about Grandfather.

"Do you remember what I said once about the green tablet?" he asks.

"Yes," I say. "You said I was strong enough to go without it."

"Greenspace, green tablet," he says, quoting himself from that long ago day. "Green eyes on a green girl."

"I'll always remember that day," I tell him.

"But you're having a hard time remembering this one," he says. His eyes are knowing, sympathetic.

"Yes," I say. "Why?"

Grandfather doesn't answer me, at least not outright. "They used to have a phrase for a truly memorable day," he says instead. "A red-letter day. Can you remember that?"

"I'm not sure," I say. I press my hands to my head. I feel foggy, not quite right. Grandfather's face is sad, but determined. It makes me feel determined, too.

I look around again at the red buds, the flowers. "Or," I say, something sharpening in me, "you could call it a red garden day."

"Yes," Grandfather says. "A red garden day. A day to remember."

He leans closer. "It's going to be hard to remember," he says. "Even this, right now, won't be clear later. But you're strong. I know you can get it all back."

I remembered another part of the red garden day. And I can get it *all* back. Grandfather said so. I tighten my fingers around Ky's and keep singing.

Wind over hill, and under tree.
Past the border no one can see.

I will sing to him until people stop dying and then I will figure out the cure.

CHAPTER 39
KY

Past the border
No one can see.

I'm in the sea.

I go in and out. Over and under. And under. And under.

Indie's there in the sea.

"You are *not* supposed to be here," she says, annoyed. Exactly like I remember. "This is my place. I'm the one who found it."

"All the water in the world can't be yours," I say.

"It is," she says. "And the sky. Everything that's blue is mine now."

"The mountains are blue," I tell her.

"Then they're mine."

Up and down we go, on the waves next to each other. I start to laugh. Indie does, too. My body has stopped hurting. I feel light. I might not even have a body anymore.

"I like the ocean," I tell Indie.

"I always knew you would," Indie says. "But you can't follow me." Then she smiles. She slips below the waves and is gone.

CHAPTER 40
CASSIA

"Cassia," Anna says, standing in the doorway of the infirmary, "come with us."

"I can't," I say, paging through my notes, looking up the flowers Anna mentioned. *Mariposa lily. Ephedra. Paintbrush.* Anna said she'd bring me pictures of the flowers. Did she forget? I'm about to ask her when she speaks again.

"Not even to see the vote?" The people of the village and the farmers have gathered outside to decide what to do with the cures Oker and Xander and the other assistants have made. There's some disagreement about what to try first and how to proceed.

"No," I tell Anna. "I need to keep thinking. There's something I've missed. And I have to do it here. Someone's been taking the medicine from Ky. I'm not leaving."

"Is that true?" Anna asks one of the medics.

He shrugs unhappily. "It could be," he says. "But I don't see how. We always have medics in attendance. And who in the village would want to harm the patients? We all want to find a cure."

Neither Anna nor I state the obvious. Perhaps not everyone in the village feels this way.

"I made your stone myself," Anna says to me. She hands me a tiny stone with my name written on it. *Cassia Reyes.* I glance up at her for the first time and see that she has the blue lines painted all over her face and arms. She notices my glance. "On a voting day, I dress with the ceremonial marks," she tells me. "It's a Carving tradition."

I take the stone from her. "I have a vote?" I ask.

"Yes," Anna says. "It was decided by the village council that you and Xander could each have one stone, just like everyone else."

The gesture touches me. The people here have come to trust the two of us. "I don't like to leave Ky," I say. "Can someone put my stone in for me?"

"They could," Anna says, "but I think you should see the vote. It's something every leader should witness."

What does Anna mean? I'm not a leader.

"Would you trust Hunter to stay here and keep watch?" Anna asks. "Just for a few moments, so you can cast your vote?"

I look at Hunter. I remember the first time I saw him. He was burying his daughter, and he put that beautiful poem to mark her place. "Yes," I say. It won't take long, and this way I can ask Anna about the flowers again.

Hunter hands his stone to Anna. "I vote with Leyna," he says.

Anna nods. "I'll put it there for you."

Anna was right.

What I see is so extraordinary, I almost forget to breathe.

Everyone has come with a choice in hand. Some, like Anna, carry two stones, because they have been asked by someone else to cast a vote by proxy. So much trust must exist for this to work.

Oker and Leyna stand near the troughs, and others, including Colin, watch to make certain no one moves stones from one place to another. There are two choices today: to vote with Oker or to vote with Leyna. Some stand in indecision, but most walk right up and cast their stones into the trough near Oker. They think we should give Oker's camassia cure to *all* of the eligible patients. The more cautious ones cast their stones with Leyna, who wants to try several different cures.

Oker's trough is almost full.

The decision is made in the shadow of the large village rock, and as everyone clutches their little named stones, I think of Sisyphus, and of the Pilot story, the one I traded the compass for months ago. Beliefs and myths are tied so closely together that you're never sure which is tale and which is true.

But perhaps that doesn't matter. Ky said that once, after he'd told me the Sisyphus story on the Hill. *Even if Sisyphus didn't live his story, enough of us have lived lives just like it. So it's true anyway.*

Xander makes his way through the crowd to find me. He looks both exhausted and illuminated, and when I reach out with my free hand to hold his, he grips my fingers tight. "Have you voted already?" I ask.

"Not yet," he says. "I wanted to ask you how certain you are about the list you last sent us."

We're close enough to Oker that he can hear what we say, but I answer Xander honestly anyway. "Not certain at all," I say. "I missed something." I see a little flash of relief cross Xander's face; my saying this has made his choice easier. Now it's not as if he has to choose between Oker and me.

"What do you think you missed?" Xander asks.

"I'm not sure yet," I say, "but I think it has something to do with the flowers."

Xander tosses his stone into the trough near Oker. "What will you do?" Xander asks.

I'm not ready to vote yet. I don't know enough about the choice I'd be making. Maybe for the next vote I'll be ready, if I'm still here. So I reach into my pocket and take out the paper that my mother gave me and I put the stone inside, next to the microcard. "I'm saving mine." I'm careful to preserve the shape, to fold along the lines my mother made. When I look back up, my gaze meets Oker's. His expression is sharp and thoughtful, a little disconcerting. I look away, to Xander.

"Which way do you think Ky would have voted?" Xander asks.

"I don't know," I say.

"The plan is to give the cure that wins to Ky," Xander says gently. "Because he's the most recently still."

"No," I say. "They can try it on the other patients first." But how will I stop them?

"I think this cure will work," Xander says. "Oker was so certain. I think—"

"Xander," Oker says, his voice cutting between us. "Let's go."

"Aren't you staying for the flooding?" Leyna asks Oker, sounding surprised.

"No," Oker says.

"The farmers will see it as a slight," she says. "This is their part of the voting ceremony."

Oker waves a hand in the air, already moving. "No time," he says. "They'll understand."

"You'll be in the infirmary?" Xander asks me.

"Yes," I say. I will stay with Ky, protecting him, until I *know* we have a cure that works. But I can't seem to leave. I have to see the way this plays out.

Colin moves forward and holds up his hand to silence the crowd. "The last stone has been cast," he says.

It's clear that Oker's won. There are far more stones in his trough than in Leyna's. But Colin doesn't announce that yet. Instead, he stands back as some of the farmers come forward, holding buckets of water. Their arms are marked in blue. Anna follows them.

"The farmers vote with stones, too," Eli whispers to me, "but they also use the water. The villagers have added it as part of their voting ceremony now."

Anna stands in front of the crowd and speaks to us. "Like the floods that came through our canyon home," she says, "we acknowledge the power of our choice, and we follow the water."

The farmers pour the water into both troughs at the same time.

The water rushes down, floods flashing through. Some of it slips through the rocks at the end. Even Oker's trough lets some out. But it has the most stones; it holds the most water.

"The votes have been cast," Colin says. "We'll try Oker's cure first."

I slip through the crowd as fast as the water through the rocks, racing for the infirmary to protect Ky from the cure.

When I push open the door to the building, I don't understand what's happening. It's raining, *inside*. I hear a sound like water hitting the floorboards.

The bags are all unhooked, and they drip onto the floor.

All of them, not only Ky's. I go straight to Ky. He takes a shallow, watery breath.

The line has been pulled out and then looped neatly over the pole next to his bed. It drips out onto the floor. *Drip. Drip. Drip.*

And it's happening to everyone else. For a moment, I don't know what to do. Where are all the medics? Did they leave for the vote? I don't know how to hook Ky's line back up.

I hear a movement at the other end of the room and I turn. It's Hunter, down near the patients who the Pilot first brought to the village. Hunter stands there, a dark shadow at the back, and he doesn't move. "Hunter," I say, walking toward him slowly, "what happened?"

I hear someone at the door behind me and I turn to see who it is.

Anna.

Her face is stricken. She stops a few feet away from me and stares at Hunter. He doesn't look away, and his eyes are full of pain.

Then I notice the crumpled bodies of the medics near him. Are they dead?

"You tried to kill everyone," I say to Hunter, but as soon as the words are out of my mouth, I know I'm wrong. If he wanted to kill them, it would have been easy while we were all gone.

"No," Hunter says. "I wanted to make it fair."

I don't understand what he means. I thought I could trust him, and I was wrong. Hunter sits down and puts his head in his hands, and I hear the sounds of Anna crying and the bags dripping onto the floor.

"Keep him away from Ky," I say to Anna, my voice harsh. She nods. Hunter is much stronger than she is, but he looks broken now. I don't know how long that will last, though, and I need to find people to help the still. I need Xander.

He and Ky are the only people here that I can trust. How could I forget?

CHAPTER 41
XANDER

Oker locks the doors behind us in the lab. "I need you to do something for me," he says, picking up the bag he used when we dug camassia bulbs and sliding it over his shoulder.

"Where are you going?" I ask.

Oker peers out the window. "I have to leave now. They're all still distracted."

"Wait," I say. "Won't you need me to help you?" He can't dig on his own. Is that what he has in mind?

"I want you to stay here," Oker says. He reaches into his pockets and takes out the metal ring with the keys to the cabinets where he's locked the camassia cure. "Destroy all of the cures. I'll be back with something else we can use."

"But you won the vote," I say.

"This cure won't work," Oker says. "But now I know what will."

"We don't have to destroy everything," I say.

"Yes, we do," Oker says. "The people voted on this cure. They're not going to take a substitute. Do it. Dump it all down the sink. Get rid of the cures Leyna had me make, too. They're *all* useless."

I don't move because I can't believe what he's saying. "You were so sure about the camassia. We can still try it on some of them."

"It won't work," Oker spits. "We'll waste time. We'll waste lives. They're already dying. Do what I tell you."

I don't know if I can. We worked so hard on the cure, and he was so sure.

"You think I'm the Pilot, don't you," Oker says, watching me. "Do you want to know what the *real* Pilot is?"

I'm not sure that I do anymore.

"We used to laugh at the Pilot stories back when I worked in the Society," Oker says. "How could people think that someone was going to come from the sky to save them? Or from the water? Stupid stories. Crazy. Only weak-minded people would need to believe in something like that." He drops the keys to the cabinet into my hand. "I told you the Society named the viruses."

I nod.

"When we found out that we'd be dropping it from the sky and sending it on the water, we thought it would be funny to name the Plague after the people's stories. So we called the Plague the 'Pilot.'"

The Plague *is the Pilot.*

Oker didn't only help engineer the cure. First, he helped

create the Plague. The Plague that is now mutated and turning everyone still.

"You see," Oker says, "I *have* to find a cure."

I do see. It's the only thing that can redeem him. "I'll destroy the camassia cure," I say. "But before you go, tell me: What plant is it you're going to find?"

Oker doesn't answer. He walks over to the door and glances over at me. I realize he can't let go of being the only pilot for the cure. "I'll be back," he says. "Lock the door behind me."

And then he's gone.

Oker believes I'll do what he told me to do. He trusts me. Do I trust him? Is this the wrong cure? Would it set us too far back to try it out?

He's right that we're out of time.

I unlock the cabinet. Did the Rising know the Plague was once called the Pilot? How were we *ever* going to succeed against these odds?

The Rising was never going to work.

I don't know if I can do this, I think.

What can't you do, Xander, I ask myself.

Can't keep going.

You're not even still. You have to keep going.

I do the right thing. I don't give up. I do it all with a smile on my face. I've always believed that I'm a good person.

What if I'm not?

There's no time to think like that now. I trusted Oker and when it comes down to it, I trust myself to make the right call.

I open the cabinet and pull out a tray of cures. When I unseal the first one and pour it down the sink, I find myself biting down so hard on the inside of my lip that I taste blood.

CHAPTER 42
KY

It's raining. So I should remember.

Something.

Someone.

The water is gathering inside of me.

Who do I remember?

I don't know.

I'm drowning.

I remember to breathe.

I remember to breathe.

I remember.

I.

CHAPTER 43
CASSIA

People still mill about in the village circle, talking about the result of the vote, so I hurry around the back of the buildings at the edge of the village to try to get to Xander. It's dark and dank here, hemmed in by trees and mountain, and as I come up behind the research lab, I almost step on something twisted in the mud. Not something, someone—

Oker is here.

He's lying on the ground, his face caught in a grimace or a smile; it's hard to tell with his skin stretched tight over his old sharp bones.

"No, no," I say, and I stop and bend down to touch him. No air comes out of his mouth and when I put my ear to his chest I don't hear his heart beating, even though he is still warm. *"Oker,"* I whisper, and I look at his open eyes, and I see that one of his hands is muddy. *Why?* I wonder, irrationally, and then I see that he made something there in the mud, a shape that seems familiar.

It looks like he pressed his knuckles into the earth three times, making a sort of star.

I sit back on my heels, my knees dirty and my hands

shaking. There's nothing *I* can do for him. But if anyone can help Oker, it's Xander.

I stand up and stagger the last few steps to the research lab, pleading, *Xander, Xander, please be here.*

The door is locked. I pound and pound and call out his name. When I stop to take a breath, I hear the villagers coming up the path on the other side of the building. Have they heard me?

"Xander," I cry out again, and he opens the back door.

"I need you," I say. "Oker's dead. And Hunter disconnected all of the still." I'm about to say more, but then Leyna and the others come around the back of the building and stop short.

"What has happened?" Leyna asks, looking down at Oker. Her face doesn't change at all and I understand why, because this is beyond comprehension. Oker *cannot* be dead.

"It looks like a heart attack," says one of the medics, his face ashen. He kneels in the mud next to Oker. They try to bring him back by breathing for him and pushing on his chest to get his heart beating again.

Nothing works. Leyna sits back on her heels, wiping her face with her hand. She's muddy now. She pulls the bag from Oker's shoulder and searches inside. The bag is empty, except for a dirty shovel and traces of soil. "What was he doing?" she asks Xander.

"He wanted to go find something," Xander says. "He

didn't tell me what it was. He wouldn't let me come with him."

For a moment, it is completely silent. Everyone stares down at Oker. "The still in the infirmary," I say. "They've all been unhooked."

The medic looks up. "Are any of them dead?" he asks me.

"No," I say. "But I don't know how to start their lines again. *Please*. And you shouldn't go alone. The medics there were attacked."

Colin signals to several of the others, who then leave with the medic. Leyna stays behind, looking at Xander with the same flat expression she's had since she first saw Oker.

I want to run to be with Ky. But I suddenly have a terrible feeling that Xander is the one in the most danger now, and I can't leave him alone.

"Everything isn't lost," Leyna says. "Oker left us the cure." This strikes me as funny, though nothing should in a moment like this. Minutes ago we were voting between Leyna's plan and Oker's, and now Leyna has come around to believing that we should do what Oker suggested. His death changed her mind.

I have to sort out what has happened with Xander, and I have to find out what can cure Ky, and why Hunter was letting patients go, and what Oker was trying to tell us with the star he made in the mud that the villagers have now trampled into oblivion and no one but me has seen.

"Let's get the cure," Leyna says to Xander, and I take one of his hands and hold on tight as he walks back into the research lab. He lets me touch him but something is wrong. He doesn't hold on to me like he used to, and his muscles are tensed.

"What have you done?" Leyna asks. For the first time since I've known her, her voice sounds small. And shocked.

"Oker asked me to get rid of them," Xander says.

The sink is full of empty tubes.

"Oker told me that he'd been wrong about the camassia cure," Xander says. "He was planning to make something new, and he didn't want us to waste time trying out anything else before he had his new cure ready."

"So what was he going to put in this new cure?" Colin asks. He wants to know. He, at least, appears to be listening, instead of automatically assuming that Xander destroyed the cures for his own reasons. Anna would listen, too, if she were here. *What is she doing now? What's going to happen to Hunter? How is Ky?*

"I asked Oker," Xander says, "but he wouldn't tell me."

But then, saying this, he loses Colin. "You're saying that Oker trusted you enough to ask you to ruin all the cures, but he didn't trust you enough to tell you what he was going to find? Or how he planned to make the new cure?"

"Yes," Xander says. "That's what I'm saying."

For a long moment, Leyna and Colin look at Xander. In the sink, one of the empty tubes clinks and settles.

"You don't believe me," Xander says. "You think I killed Oker and ruined the cure on my own. Why would I do that?"

"I don't have to know why you did it," Colin says. "All I know is that you've cost this village time, which we don't have."

Leyna turns to the other two assistants. "Can you make more of the camassia cure?"

"Yes," Noah says. "But it's going to take some time."

"Get started," Leyna says. "Now."

The villagers take both Xander and Hunter to the prison building. The medics in the infirmary weren't dead; only unconscious. None of the other still have died, but the villagers will hold Hunter accountable for the earlier two deaths, and for disconnecting the other patients and compromising their health.

And Xander, of course, has destroyed the camassia cure, the villagers' best and last chance at the Otherlands. Some believe that Xander harmed Oker, but since there's no evidence to support that, Xander is only being held accountable for the cures. The people look at him like he's killed something, which I suppose to them, he has, even if it is only the cure and not its creator. It's true that the still, and the chance of saving them, seems much further away with Oker gone.

"What are you going to do to Xander and Hunter?" I ask Leyna.

"We'll have another vote after we've had time to gather evidence," Leyna says. "The people will decide."

Out in the village circle, I see the villagers and farmers taking back their stones. The water in the troughs spills away.

CHAPTER 44
KY

CHAPTER 45
CASSIA

Suspicions trickle through the village, cold and creeping like winter rain. The farmers and the villagers whisper to each other. *Did anyone help Hunter disconnect the still? How much did Cassia know about Xander destroying the cure?*

The village leaders decide to keep Xander and Hunter locked away while evidence is gathered. The next vote will decide what happens to them.

I am split into three segments, like Oker's muddy star. I should be with Ky in the infirmary. I should be with Xander in the prison. I should be sorting for a cure. I can only try to do all three and hope these pieces of myself are enough to find something that can make whole.

"I'm here to visit Xander," I say to the prison guard.

Hunter looks up as I pass and I stop. It seems wrong to walk by. Besides, I would like to talk to him. So I face him through the bars. His shoulders are strong and his hands are, as always, marked in blue. I remember how he snapped those tubes in the Cavern. *He looks strong enough to break through these bars here,* I think. Then I realize that he's past breaking through—he seems broken, in a way I didn't see even in the Carving when Sarah had just died.

"Hunter," I say, very gently, "I just want to know. *Were* you the one who disconnected Ky all those times?"

He nods.

"Was he the only one?" I ask.

"No," he says. "I disconnected the others, too. Ky was the only one who had someone visiting him often enough to notice."

"How did you get past the medics?" I ask.

"It was easiest at night," Hunter says. I remember how he used to track and kill and stay hidden in a canyon to survive, and I imagine that the infirmary and the village were child's play to him. And then, left alone in broad daylight, something snapped.

"Why Ky?" I ask. "You came out of the canyon together. I thought the two of you understood each other."

"I had to be fair," Hunter says. "I couldn't disconnect everyone else and leave Ky alone."

The door opens behind me, letting in light. I turn a little. Anna has come in, but she stays out of Hunter's line of view. She wants to listen.

"Hunter," I say, "some of them *died*." I wish I could get him to answer me, to tell me *why*.

Hunter stretches out his arms. I wonder how often he does the markings to keep them so bright. "People dying is what happens if you don't have the right medicines to save them," Hunter says.

And now I do understand. "Sarah," I say. "You couldn't get the medicine for her."

Hunter's hands tighten back into fists. "Everyone—Society, Rising, even people here in the village—we're all doing everything to help these patients from the Society. No one did anything for Sarah."

He's right. No one did, except Hunter himself, and it wasn't enough to save her.

"And if we find the cure, then what?" Hunter asks. "Everyone flies away to the Otherlands. There's been too much of that, people going away."

Anna comes a little closer so that Hunter can see her. "There has," she agrees.

Then tears come to his eyes and he puts his head down and weeps. "I'm sorry," he says.

"I know," she tells him.

There's nothing I can do. I leave them and go to Xander.

"You left Ky alone in the infirmary," Xander says. "Are you sure that's safe?"

"There are medics and guards watching," I say. "And Eli won't leave Ky's side."

"So you trust Eli?" Xander asks. "The way you trusted Hunter?" There's an uncharacteristic edge to Xander's voice.

"I'll go back soon," I say. "But I had to see you. I'm going to try to figure out what the cure could be. Do you have any idea what Oker was looking for?"

"No," Xander says. "He wouldn't tell me. But I think it was a plant. He took the same equipment that we used when we gathered the bulbs."

"When did he change his mind about the cure?" I ask. "When did he decide that the camassia was wrong?"

"During the vote," Xander says. "Something happened while we were out there that made him change his mind."

"And you don't know what it is."

"I think it was something you said," Xander tells me. "You talked about how you felt like you were missing something, and said it had to do with the flowers."

I shake my head. How could that have helped Oker? I reach into my pocket to make sure that I still have the paper from my mother. It's there, and so are the microcard and the little stone. I wonder if the villagers will still let me vote.

"It's lonely," Xander says.

"What is?" I ask him. Does he mean that it's lonely in the research lab now that Oker is gone?

"Death," Xander says. "Even if someone is with you, you still have to do the actual dying all alone."

"It is lonely," I say.

"*Everything* is," Xander says. "I'm lonely with you sometimes. I didn't think it could ever be that way."

I don't know what to say. We stand there looking at each other, sorrowful, seeking. "I'm sorry," I say finally, but he shakes his head. I've missed the point somehow; whatever it was he wanted to say, I did not listen the way he had hoped.

～

The light coming in through the infirmary windows is gauzy, gray. Ky's face looks very still. Very gone. The bag drips neatly into his veins. He and Xander are both trapped. I have to find a way to free them.

And I don't know how.

I look at the lists again. I've gone over them so many times. Everyone else is working on re-creating Oker's camassia cure. But I think Oker was right, and that we were all wrong. The sorters, the pharmics—we have all missed something.

I'm so tired.

Once, I wanted to watch the floods coming into a canyon, to stand on the edge and see it happen, on ground that was safe but shaking. *I'd like to hear the trees snap away and see the water come higher,* I thought, *but only from a place where it couldn't reach me.*

Now I think it might be a terrifying, bright relief to stand on the canyon floor and see the wall of water coming down, and to know *this is it, I am finished,* and before you could even complete the thought, you would be swallowed, and whole.

As evening falls, Anna comes to sit beside me in the infirmary. "I'm sorry," she says, looking at Ky. "I never thought that Hunter—"

"I know," I say. "Neither did I."

"The vote will be tomorrow," she tells me. For the first time, Anna sounds *old*.

"What will they do?" I ask.

"Xander will likely be exiled," she says. "He could also be found innocent, but I don't think that will happen. The people are angry. They don't believe Oker told Xander to destroy the cure."

"Xander's from the Provinces," I say. "How is he supposed to survive in exile?" Xander's smart, but he's never lived out in the wild before, and he will have nothing when they send him away. I had Indie.

"I don't think," Anna says, "that he is supposed to survive."

If Xander is exiled, what will I do? I'd go with him, but I can't leave Ky. And we need Xander for the cure. Even if I do find the right plant, I don't know how to make a cure, or the best way to give it to Ky. If this is to work, it will take all three of us. Ky, Xander, me.

"And Hunter?" I ask Anna, very softly.

"The best we can hope for Hunter," she says, "is exile." Though I know she has other children who came with her from the Carving, her voice sounds as sad as if Hunter were her own child, the very last of her blood.

And then she hands me something. A piece of paper, *real* paper, the kind she must have carried with her all the way from the cave in the Carving. It smells like the canyons, here in the mountains, and it makes me ache a little and wonder how Anna could stand to leave her home.

"These are pictures of the flowers you wanted," she says. "I'm sorry it took me so long. I had to make the colors. I just finished them now, so you'll have to be careful not to smear the paints."

I'm stunned that she did this, with everything else that must have been on her mind tonight, and I'm touched that she still believes me capable of sorting for the cure. "Thank you," I say.

Under the flowers she has written their names.

Ephedra, paintbrush, mariposa lily.

And others, of course. Plants and flowers.

I'm crying, and I wish I weren't. I wrote that lullaby for so many people. And now we may lose almost all of them. Hunter. Sarah. Ky. My mother. Xander. Bram. My father.

Ephedra, Anna wrote. Underneath she drew a spiky-looking bush with small, cone-like flowers. She painted it yellow and green.

Paintbrush. Red. This one I've seen, in the canyons.

Mariposa lily. It's a beautiful white flower with red and yellow coloring deep down inside its three petals.

My hands know what I've seen before my mind does; I'm reaching into my pocket and pulling out the paper my mother sent, recognizing the meaning in its shape. I remember Indie's wasp nest, how it had space inside, and I pull the edges of the paper out and then I *know.*

I hold a paper flower in my hand. My mother made this. She cut or tore the paper carefully so that three pieces fan out from the middle, like petals.

It is the same as the flower in the picture; white, three-petaled, the edges crimped in and pointed like a star. I realize that I also saw it printed in the earth.

This is what Oker was trying to find.

He saw me take out the paper flower when I put the voting stone inside.

Anna's picture tells me that the name of this flower is *mariposa lily*. But I never heard my mother speak that name. And it's not a newrose or an oldrose or a sprig of Queen Anne's lace. What other flowers did she tell me about?

I'm back in the room in our house in Oria, where she showed me the blue satin square from the dress she wore to her *Banquet. She's recently returned from traveling out into different Provinces to investigate rogue crops for the Society. "The second grower had a crop I'd never seen before, of white flowers even more beautiful than the first," she says. "Sego lilies, they called them. You can eat the bulb."*

"Anna," I say, my heart racing, "does mariposa lily have another name?" If it does, that might account for the problem in the data. We've been counting this flower as two separate data points, but it was, in fact, a single variable.

"Yes," Anna says, after a pause. "Some people call it the sego lily."

I pick up the datapod and search for the name. There

it is. The properties are all the same. One flower, reported under two different names. Now, with its names combined, it rises right to the top of potential ingredients. It was a critical, elemental mistake made by those gathering the data, but we should have noticed it earlier. How did I miss it before? How could I fail to recognize the name, when my mother had told it to me? *You only heard it once,* I remind myself, *and that was long ago.* "Where does it grow?" I ask.

"We should be able to find some not far from here," Anna says. "It's early in the season, but it could be in bloom." She looks at the paper flower in my hand. "Did you make that?"

"No," I say. "My mother did."

It's almost dark when we finally find them, in a little field away from the village and the path.

I drop down to my knees to look closer. I've never seen a flower so beautiful. It's a simple white bloom, three curved petals coming out from a sparsely leaved stalk. It's a little white banner, like my writing, not of surrender but of survival. I pull out the crumpled paper flower.

Though my hands shake, I can tell that it's a match. This flower growing in the ground is the one my mother made before she went still.

The real thing is much more beautiful. But that doesn't matter. I think of Ky's mother, who painted water on stone, who believed the important thing was to create, not capture.

Even though the paper lily isn't a perfect rendering, it's still a tribute to its beauty that my mother tried.

I don't know whether she intended the flower as art or message, but I choose to take it as both.

"I think," I say, "that this might be the cure."

CHAPTER 46
XANDER

I can't see Cassia herself, but the solar-cell lamps cast her shadow on the prison wall. Her voice carries from the entryway to my cell. "We think we have found a possible cure," she tells the guards. "We need Xander to make something for us."

The guard laughs. "I don't think so," he says.

"I'm not asking you to release Xander," Cassia says. "We just need to give him the equipment and have him prepare the cure."

"And then what are you going to do with it?" another guard asks.

"We're going to give it to one patient," she says. "*Our* patient. Ky."

"We can't go against Colin," one of the guards says. "He's our leader. And we'd lose our chance at the Otherlands."

"This *is* your chance at the Otherlands," Cassia says. Her voice is low, quiet, full of conviction. "This is what Oker was going to find." She pulls something out of her bag. "Mariposa lily." I can see from her shadow that she's holding a flower. "You eat the bulb, don't you? You eat it when it blooms in the summer, and store it for the winter."

"Are they already in bloom?" one of them asks. "How many did you pull up?"

"Only a few," Cassia says.

Another shadow moves into view and I hear Anna's voice. "We had these flowers in the Carving, too," Anna says. "We also used them for food. I know how to gather them so that they'll come back again next year."

"What does it matter if they take all the plants, anyway?" one of the guards says to the other. "If we're gone to the Otherlands, we won't need to harvest."

"No," Anna says. "Even if everyone is gone, the flower must come back. We cannot take it all and leave nothing."

"The bulbs are so small," another guard says dubiously. "I don't see how it could be a cure."

Cassia comes into view, and I see that she holds the real flower and the paper that her mother sent her. They're a perfect match. "Oker saw me take out this flower—the paper one—during the vote. I believe *this* is the flower he was going to find." She sounds confident that she's sorted everything. She could be right: Oker did change his mind right after he saw her take out the paper.

"Please," Cassia says to the guards. "Let us try." Her voice is gentle, persuasive. "You can feel it, can't you?" she asks, and now she sounds wistful. "The Otherlands are getting farther and farther away."

Everything goes quiet as we realize that Cassia's right. I do feel the Otherlands receding for me, like the real world probably did for Lei and Ky when they went still. I feel everything slipping out of my grasp. I've followed the Pilot, Oker, and Cassia, but things didn't go as I'd hoped. I thought I'd see a rebellion, find a cure, and have someone love me back.

What if they all left? What if everyone else flew to the Otherlands or went still and I was here alone? Would I keep going? I would. I can't seem to treat this life I have as anything but the only thing.

"All right," one of the guards says. "But hurry."

Anna has thought of everything. She's brought equipment from the lab: a syringe, a mortar and pestle, clean water that's been boiled and treated, and some of Oker's base mixtures, with a list of the ingredients in each. "How did you know what we'd need?" I ask her.

"I didn't," she says. "Tess and Noah did. They think it's possible that Oker changed his mind. They're not sure they believe you, but they're not sure that they don't, either."

"They *gave* all of this to you?" I ask.

She nods. "But if anyone asks, we stole it. We don't want to get them in trouble."

Cassia holds the flashlight for me while I scrub my hands with the sterilizing solution. I use the edge of the pestle to split the bulb in half. "It's beautiful," Cassia says.

The inside of the bulb looks white and luminescent like

the camassia bulbs. I grind it down, pulverizing the bulb until it's a paste. Then Anna hands me a tube. Cassia watches and I find myself hesitating. Maybe it's the memory of the night back in Oria when I traded for the blue tablets. I took blood when I shouldn't have, and when I did, I implied promises that no one was in a position to keep. I did exactly what the Society and the Rising have done—I took advantage of people's fears so that I could have something I wanted.

Am I doing that again by making this cure? I look at Cassia. She trusts me. And she shouldn't. I killed that boy in the Carving with the blue tablets. I didn't do it on purpose, but if it wasn't for me, he would never have had the tablets in the first place.

I haven't let myself think about this, even though I've known about it since we came in on the ship. Panic and bile rise together in my throat and I want to run away from what I've been asked to do. I can't make a cure: I've made the wrong call too many times.

"You know that I can't guarantee that this will work," I tell Cassia. "I'm not a pharmic. I might not put in the right amount, or there might be a reacting agent in the base that I don't know about—"

"There are a lot of ways it could go wrong," she agrees. "I might not have found the right ingredient. But I think that I have. And I know you can make the cure."

"Why?" I ask.

"You always come through for the people who need you," she says, and her voice sounds sad. Like she knows this is going to cost me but she's asking me to do it anyway and it breaks her heart.

"Please," she says. "One more time."

CHAPTER 47
CASSIA

Inside the infirmary, Anna distracts the medics while I inject the cure into Ky's line. It doesn't take long; Xander told me how to do this. Before, I might have been afraid to try, but after seeing Xander compound a cure in a prison cell and Ky labor to breathe on through the stillness, there is no room left for my own fears.

I cover the needle back up and slide it and the empty vial that held the cure into my sleeve, next to the poems I always carry. As I sit down next to Ky, I pick up the datapod. I pretend to keep sorting, though my eyes are really on Ky, watching, waiting. He is taking the biggest risk; it's his veins the cure runs through. But we all have so much to lose.

I have sometimes seen the three of us as separate, discrete points, and of course we are that, each individuals. But Ky and Xander and I all have to believe in one another to keep each other safe. In the end, I had to trust Xander to make a cure for Ky, and Ky trusted us to bring him back, and Xander trusted my sorting, and around and around we go, a circle, the three of us, connected, always, in the turning of days and the keeping of promises over and over again.

CHAPTER 48
KY

not in the water anymore
   why not
   where is Indie
   tiny lights come in and out of the darkness.
   I hear Cassia's voice.
   She's been waiting in the stars for me.

CHAPTER 49
CASSIA

K y," I say. I've seen a lightening like this on his face before, but this time it keeps coming, growing brighter, as he returns to us.

> *I did not reach Thee,*
> *But my feet slip nearer every day;*
> *Three Rivers and a Hill to cross,*
> *One Desert and a Sea—*
> *I shall not count the journey one*
> *When I am telling thee.*

Ky and I took the journey in our own order. We began with the Hill, together. We crossed a desert to get to the Carving and streams and rivers inside the canyons and again when we came out. There has been no sea, no ocean, but there has been a great expanse for both of us to navigate without the other. I think that counts.

And I think, looking at him, that the poem is wrong. He will count this journey, and so will I.

Anna comes in later and hands me several more cures from Xander. "He says it will take more than one dose," she whispers. "This is all he could manage for now. He says to give the next dose as soon as possible."

I nod. "Thank you," I say, and she slips back out the door, nodding to the medics as she goes.

They're conducting their morning rounds. One of the village medics turns Ky from his side to his back to change the areas of pressure on Ky's body. "He's looking better," the medic says, sounding surprised.

"I think so, too," I say, and right then we hear something outside. I turn to the window, and through it I see that the guards are bringing Hunter and Xander out to the village circle.

Hunter.

Xander.

They both walk on their own to stand in front of the voting troughs, but their hands are tied and they're flanked by guards. I wish I could see Xander's eyes from here, but all I can see is the way he walks and how tired he seems. He's been up all night making cures.

"It's time for the vote," says one of the medics.

"Open the window," the other says, "so we can hear."

For a split second they are both engaged with pushing open the window and that's when I empty the syringe into

Ky's line. When I finish slipping the evidence into my sleeve, I glance up to find one of the medics watching me. I can't tell what he saw, but I don't miss a beat. Xander would be proud. "Why are they having the trial so soon?" I ask.

"Colin and Leyna must feel that they've gathered enough evidence," the medic says. He looks at me for a second longer and, as the morning smell and fresh air from the window rush in, Ky takes a deep breath. His lungs sound better. He's not all the way back yet, but he's coming, I can tell. I feel him, more than I did before; I know he listens even if he can't yet speak.

People fill the village circle. I'm not close enough to see the stones in their hands, but I hear Colin call out, "Is there anyone here who will stand with Hunter?"

"I will," Anna says.

"The rules are that you may only stand with one person," the medic tells me. And I understand what he's saying: if Anna stands with Hunter, she can't stand with Xander.

Anna nods. She walks up to the front and faces out to the crowd. As she speaks, I notice them drawing closer to her. "What Hunter did was wrong," Anna says, "but he didn't mean to kill. If that was his intent, he could have done it easily and escaped. What Hunter wanted was to make things fair. He felt that since the Provinces denied Anomalies access to any of *their* medications for years, we should do the same for their patients."

Anna doesn't play on the crowd. She says the facts and

lets the crowd weigh them. Of course, we all know that the world isn't fair. But we all understand how it feels to wish that it were. Many of these people know too well what it's like to be tossed aside—or worse, sent out to die—by the Society. Anna says nothing of all the losses Hunter has suffered that would lead him to this point. She doesn't have to. They're written on his arms and in his eyes.

"I know you can require more," Anna says, "but I ask for exile for Hunter."

The lesser of the two sentences. Will the crowd give it?

They do.

They drop their stones in the trough near Anna's feet instead of the one near Colin's. The farmers come with the buckets and pour the water. The decision holds.

"Hunter," Colin says, "you must leave now."

Hunter nods. I can't tell if he feels anything. Someone hands him a pack and there's a disturbance as Eli comes running for Hunter, wrapping his arms around Hunter to say good-bye. Anna embraces them both, and for a moment they are a little family, three generations, connected not by blood but by journeys and farewells.

Then Eli steps back. He will stay with Anna, who must remain with the rest of her people. Hunter walks straight into the forest, not taking the path, not looking back. Where will he go? To the Carving?

And now the crowd murmurs and Xander comes forward.

In that moment, I realize that the people have spent their mercy on Hunter. They lived and worked with him for the past few months. They knew his story.

But they don't know Xander.

He stands in front of the village stone, alone.

Xander will do anything for those he loves, whatever the cost. But, looking at Xander now, I think the cost has become too high. *He looks like Hunter,* I realize. *Like someone who has been driven too far and seen too much.* Hunter kept himself together long enough to deliver Eli safely to the mountains. For a long time, he did what he had to do to help others, but then he broke.

I can't let that happen to Xander.

CHAPTER 50
XANDER

Who will stand with Xander?" Colin asks.

No one answers.

Anna looks at me. I can tell that she's sorry, but I understand. Of course she had to use everything she had for Hunter. He's like a son to her, and it was right for her to have spent everything on him.

But there is no one else. Cassia has to stay in the infirmary with Ky, to give him the cure and make sure he wakes up. Ky would stand with me: but he's still.

People shuffle their feet and look in Colin's direction. They're impatient with him for letting the moment go on so long. I'd like it to be over, too. I close my eyes and listen to my heart, my breathing, and the wind high up in the trees.

Someone calls out: a voice I know. "I will." I open my eyes to see Cassia pushing her way through the crowd. She came after all. Her face is all lit up. The cure must be working.

Something's wrong with me. I should be glad that Cassia's here and that the cure could be viable. But all I can think about are the patients in the Provinces, and Lei when she went down, and I worry that it's too late. Will we be able to bring enough people back? Will the cure work again? How will we find enough bulbs? Who will decide which people get the cure first? There are a lot of questions and I'm not sure we can find the answers fast enough.

I've never felt this worn out before.

CHAPTER 51
CASSIA

People come up to take their stones back from the vote they cast for Hunter. The stones are still wet and they drip a little onto the villagers' clothes, leaving small, dark spots. Some of the people roll the rocks in their hands as they wait.

"This trough," Colin says, pointing to the one nearest him, "is for the maximum penalty. The other," the one closer to Xander's feet, "is for the lesser penalty."

He doesn't specify what the penalties are. Does everyone already know? Anna guessed that the worst sentence Xander would receive would be exile, because his crime wasn't as great as Hunter's. No one died.

But for Xander, exile would *mean* death. He has nowhere to go. He can't live out here alone, and it's a long journey through rough terrain back to Camas. Perhaps he could find Hunter.

But then what?

I look up at Xander. The sun has crept through the trees and shines gold on his hair. I've never had to wonder what color his eyes are, the way I did with Ky; I've always known that Xander's are blue, that he would look at you from a place of kindness and clarity. But now, though the color hasn't changed, I know that Xander has.

"I'm lonely with you sometimes," he told me in the infirmary earlier. *"I didn't think it could ever be that way."*

Are you lonely *now*, Xander?

I don't even have to ask.

There are birds in the trees; there are stirrings in the crowd, and wind in the grasses and coming down the path, and yet all I feel is his silence—and his strength.

He turns to the crowd, straightening his shoulders and clearing his throat. He can do this, I think. He'll smile that smile and his voice will ring out over the crowd like the Pilot he could be someday, and they'll see how good he is and they won't want to destroy him anymore—they'll want to circle around and gather close to smile back up at him. That's how it's always been with Xander. Girls in the Borough loved him; Officials wanted him for their departments; people who became ill wanted him to heal them.

"I promise," Xander says, "that I only did what Oker asked me to do. He wanted the cures destroyed because he realized he'd made a mistake."

Please, I think. *Please believe him. He's telling the truth.*

But I hear how hollow his voice sounds, and when he glances back at me, I see how his smile isn't quite the same. It's not because he's lying. It's because he has nothing left right now. He took care of the still for months without relief. He saw his friend Lei go down. He believed in the Pilot, then he believed in Oker, and they asked him to do impossible things. *Find a cure,* the Pilot said. *Destroy the cure,* Oker ordered.

And I'm no less guilty. *Make another cure,* I told him. *Try again.* I wanted a cure as much as anyone else, whatever the cost. We all asked and Xander gave. In the canyons, I saw Ky get healed. Here in the mountains, I see Xander broken.

A stone clatters into the trough next to Colin's feet.

"Wait," Colin says, bending down to pick it up. "He hasn't had a chance to finish speaking yet."

"Doesn't matter," someone says. "Oker's dead."

They loved Oker and now he's gone. They want someone to blame. When the stones settle, it might not be exile Xander receives. It might be something worse. I glance over at the guards who brought Xander here and who let him make the cures. They won't meet my gaze.

Suddenly, I see the other side of choice. Of all of us having it.

Sometimes we will choose wrong.

"No," I say. I reach into my sleeve to pull out one of the cures Xander made. If I show them this, and the flower that my mother sent and Oker saw, they *have* to understand. We should have done this first, before the trial even began. "Please," I begin, "listen—"

Another stone rattles into the trough, and at the same time, something enormous passes across the sun.

It's a ship.

"The Pilot!" someone calls out.

But instead of moving down the mountain to the landing meadow, the ship hovers over us, the blades rotating so that it can stay suspended in the air. Eli flinches, and some in the crowd duck instinctively. They're remembering firings in the Outer Provinces. Someone else moans, far back in the crowd.

The ship dips down slightly and then comes back up. The intent is clear, even to me. He wants us to move so that he can land in the village circle.

"He said he'd never try to land here," Colin says, his face pale. "He promised."

"Is the circle large enough?" I ask.

"I don't know," Colin says.

And then everyone moves. Xander and I turn to each other and he grabs my hand. We race away from the circle, our feet flying over the grass and ground, the air whipping above us. The Pilot is coming down. He might not survive the landing, and we might not either.

What would drive the Pilot to do this? It's only a short walk from the landing meadow up to the village. Why can't he spare the time? What is happening back in the Provinces?

The ship dips and tilts; the air is always moving in the mountains. The ship's blades churn and the wind whips around us, so we hear nothing but a howl and a scream as the

Pilot comes down, down, down, crashing through the trees, ship turning to the side.

He's not going to be able to land it, I think, and I turn to look at Xander. We're pressed up against the wall of a building for shelter and Xander's eyes are closed, as if he can't bear to see what comes next.

"Xander," I say, but he can't hear me.

Again the ship tips, turns, shudders down closer and closer to us, too near the edge of the circle. There's nowhere else to run. There's not enough time or space to go around the building. These thoughts flash fast through my mind.

I close my eyes, too, and I press against Xander as if either of us can keep the other safe. He puts his arms around me and his body feels warm and sound, a good place to be at the finish. I wait for scraping metal, for breaking stone and cracking wood, for fire and heat and an end as sudden as a flood.

CHAPTER 52
KY

Cassia's not here anymore," I say. My voice is a whisper. Weak and dry.

I don't feel like I do when I've been asleep. I know time has passed. I know I've been here and that there was a time when I was gone. I try to move my hand. Do I succeed?

"Cassia," I say. "Can someone find Cassia?"

No one answers me.

Maybe Indie will do it, I think, and then I remember.

Indie's gone.

But I've come back.

CHAPTER 53
XANDER

When I open my eyes, the air ship fills the village circle. Cassia is tucked into my arms, holding on tight. Neither of us moves as the Pilot climbs out of his ship and stands almost exactly where I stood moments ago, over by the troughs.

Colin strides forward into the circle. "What do you think you're doing?" he asks, furious. "You almost destroyed part of the village. Why didn't you go to the landing meadow?"

"There's not enough time for that," the Pilot says. "The Provinces are falling apart and I need every minute I can get. Do you have a cure?"

Colin doesn't answer. The Pilot looks past Colin in the direction of the research lab. "Find Oker," he says. "Let me talk to him."

"You can't," Leyna says. "He's dead."

The Pilot swears. "How?"

"We think it was a heart attack," Colin says.

Everyone looks over at me. They still think I'm responsible for what happened to Oker.

"Then there's no cure," the Pilot says, his voice flat. "And no chance for one." He starts back to the ship.

"Oker left us a cure," Leyna says. "We're about to try it on the patients—"

"I need a cure that works *now*," the Pilot says, turning around. "I don't know if I'm going to be able to come back here again. This is the end. Do you understand?"

"You mean—" Leyna begins.

"There's a faction in the Rising that wants to remove me from my position," the Pilot says. "They've already taken control of the patient disconnections and the rations. If they succeed with my removal—which they will—I won't have *any* access to ships or a way to get you to the Otherlands. We have to have a cure. *Now*." The Pilot pauses. "The Rising has ordered disconnections of a certain percent of the still."

"What *is* the rate?" Cassia asks. She walks out into the village circle as if she has every right to be there. Leyna narrows her eyes at Cassia but lets her speak. "We projected that they'd start releasing around two percent of the still to preserve the maximum amount of life while still freeing up others to work."

"That's where they began," the Pilot says. "But they've increased it. They're recommending twenty percent, with a further increase to come."

One in five. Who would they pick to cut off first? The ones who went still early? Or later? What's happening to Lei?

"It's too many," Cassia says. "It's not necessary."

"The algorithm assumed that people would be willing

to help," the Pilot says. "That they wouldn't leave the still behind. And the Rising has released the sample storage. They're giving out tissue samples to people if they'll agree to let their loved ones be disconnected to save space."

"People aren't actually agreeing to such a thing, are they?" Cassia asks.

"Some are," the Pilot says.

"But they can't bring anyone back," Cassia says. "No one has that technology. Not the Society, not the Rising."

"The tubes have never been about bringing people back," the Pilot says. "They've always been used to control the people who are here. So I'll ask again. *Do you have a cure?*"

"We need more time," Leyna says. "Not much."

"There is no more time," the Pilot says. "We're getting low on food. People are running away from the Cities and into the Boroughs, where they attack those who are left, or they take off for the country, where they die of the mutation because we can't get to them in time. We're running out of the ingredients Oker recommended for inclusion in the fluid and medication bags, and none of the scientists in the Provinces has found a cure."

"There *is* a cure," Cassia says. "Xander can show your pharmics how to make it." She holds out a tube to the Pilot. She's at the game table and she's throwing down all her cards.

For a second I think Leyna and Colin aren't going to let Cassia get away with it, but neither of them says anything. Everyone watches to see what Cassia will do next.

"How many people have you tried it on?" the Pilot asks, taking the cure from Cassia.

"Only one," Cassia says. "Ky. But we can make more."

That makes the Pilot laugh. "One person," he says. "And how do I know Ky really got cured? When I last saw him, he wasn't even still."

"He was sick," Cassia says. "You saw him yourself. Everyone here will vouch for his illness."

"Of course they will," the Pilot says. "They want passage to the Otherlands. They'll agree with anything you say."

"If this is your last chance to come to the village," Cassia says, "then you should at least see what we have. It won't take long."

Leyna moves closer, smiling, as if she's been in on this all along. But when she gets near enough to Cassia that the Pilot can't hear, Leyna hisses, *Who*? Who helped you?"

Cassia doesn't answer that question. She's protecting the people who helped with the cure: me, the guards, Anna, Noah, and Tess. "It's Oker's base," she says loudly. She's looking at the Pilot but speaking to everyone, trying to get them to go along with her in this. "And it's the ingredient he wanted in it. This is Oker's *real* cure, and it's working." She starts down the path to the infirmary. "It would be a shame," she calls back to the Pilot, "if you came all this way and then didn't get what you needed."

The Pilot follows her across the village circle, and so do the rest of us. Cassia pushes open the door to the infirmary as if she's perfectly confident that everything inside is fine. But I see how her lips tremble when Ky looks up at her, his eyes clear and aware. She didn't know it was working, at least not this well. And then, for a second, it's like none of the rest of us are here. They're the only two in the world. *"Ky,"* she says.

"Can we run yet?" he asks her. His voice is barely a whisper. Everyone, including Leyna and Colin, leans in to hear Ky, even though what he's saying isn't meant for the rest of us.

"No," she says. "Not yet."

"I know," he says, and there's a half smile on his face. She bends down to kiss him, and his trembling hand reaches for hers, but he can't move it far enough yet. So I lift up his hand and put it on hers. I help him to reach her. For a moment, I'm a part of it all. Then I'm just apart.

The Pilot looks down at Ky and then up at me. Does he believe us? His expression doesn't give anything away. "Oker said this was what you should use?" He's asking me directly. It's my turn to convince him now. Cassia and Ky have done what they could.

"Oker told me about his work in the Society," I say. "I know that he was part of the team that originated the viruses. I know how much he wanted to find the cure. And I think he did."

"If what you say is true," the Pilot says, "we'd need to do a full trial of the cure somewhere else."

"How secure is the medical center in Camas where Indie found me?" I ask.

"We still have control over it," the Pilot says. It's a strange feeling to have someone I once believed in deciding whether or not he believes in me. I meet his gaze, the two of us standing face to face.

He knows I'm not telling him everything, but he decides it's enough. "I can fly the three of you out now," the Pilot says. "Seeing Ky might convince some of the pharmics and medics to start a trial. Where can we find more of the plant you used? Do you have stock on hand?"

"Yes," Anna says. "I stayed out digging them all night."

"And I may know where we can get more," Cassia says. "My mother saw a field with this flower once. The Society destroyed that field and Reclassified the grower, but there might be something left. If we can bring my mother back, she'll remember where she saw the flowers."

"Let's go, then," the Pilot says. "Get Ky on the ship." He turns on his heel and walks out the door without looking back at us.

"Thank you," Ky says to me as we bring him onto the ship, Cassia close behind.

"You would have done the same," I say.

Cassia looks around as if she's expecting to see someone else, but the Pilot flies alone.

"Where is Indie?" she asks the Pilot as we climb into our seats. "Is she all right?"

"No," the Pilot says. "She got the mutation and she ran until she had no fuel left. Her ship went down in the old

Enemy territory. We couldn't spare anyone to retrieve her body."

Indie is dead. I look at Ky first to see how he's taking it and his face is full of pain, but he's not surprised. Somehow, he already knew. Cassia looks shocked, as if she can't believe this is true. But of course it is. I know that a virus doesn't think or feel, but it still seems as if this one likes to take down those who were the most alive.

CHAPTER 54
CASSIA

Two impossible things have happened. Ky, cured.

And Indie, dead?

I have so many pictures of Indie in my mind. Indie climbing the walls of the Carving, piloting the boat down the river, holding the wasp nest carefully in her hands. How can she be gone? She can't. It's impossible.

But Ky believes it.

Ky is back.

There's no time to linger over the miracle, to watch him return, to sit and hold his hand and talk with him.

Instead there's the race and rush to get us on board, and within minutes of the Pilot landing in the village, we are lifting off. I don't have a chance to thank Anna for the bulbs, to say good-bye to Eli, to look back at Leyna and Colin and the other villagers as they watch us leave, hoping we will return someday, this time with ships that can take them all the way to the Otherlands.

Xander sits in the copilot's seat and we strap Ky's stretcher down in the hold, where it will be the most secure. Xander told Tess and Noah what he'd added to the cure, and they gave him Oker's formula for the base we used. This way, we can tell those in the Provinces what we used, and the villagers can begin curing the still left behind. A collaboration, again, all of us doing something together that would take us much more time alone.

"It will be like an extra trial of the cure," Leyna told the Pilot. "When you return to take us out, we'll have cured all of these patients, and you can bring them back to their families." She sounded as if she'd never doubted Xander; as though they hadn't planned to sentence him to exile, or worse, for destroying the camassia cure. But it's true that the cure belongs to the village. Anna and Oker, Colin and Leyna, Tess and Noah, the guards—they are also the pilots of the cure.

I sit in the runner's seat for takeoff, but as soon as we're stable I unbuckle the straps and kneel down next to Ky, holding his hand tightly. He looks up at the side of the ship and I see something drawn there, a real picture, not notches or markings. There are people standing and looking up at the sky, which seems to be falling down upon them. But some of the people—not all—have picked up the pieces and are tipping them back to their mouths.

"Drinking the sky," Ky says. "That's what Indie said they

were doing. We had a picture like this in one of our ships, too." He takes a deep breath. His voice sounds stronger already. "It's a picture of you bringing water to the Enemy to help them survive the Plague," he says to the Pilot. "Isn't it?"

For a few minutes, the Pilot doesn't answer. Then I hear his voice coming through the speaker in the hold. It is quiet and sad, and I think that we are, for the first time, hearing his true voice. "The Society told us the Plague would make the Enemy ill and easy to defeat," the Pilot says. "They said we'd bring the Enemy in as prisoners. But when the Plague started to work, our orders were to leave the Enemy where they were."

"And you saw them die," Xander says.

"Yes," the Pilot says. "When a few of us ran the risk of flying in water, most of the Enemy wouldn't drink it even though there was a drought. They didn't trust us. Why would they? We'd been killing one another for years."

I think of those thirsty, dying people, unable to drink anything but the rain which did not come.

"So there really was an Enemy," Ky says. "But after they were gone, the Rising stepped in to act their part. Did you kill the farmers on top of the Carving to keep your cover?"

"No," the Pilot says. "That was the Society. For years, they used the people in the Outer Provinces as a buffer between the main Provinces and the Enemy." He clears his throat. "So I should have realized that we were no longer a true rebellion when we let the farmers, and so many other Anomalies and Aberrations, die. We told ourselves that the timing wasn't right to reveal ourselves, but we still should have tried."

Ky's hand, warm in the dark, tightens on mine. If the Rising had stepped in, so many might have been saved. Ky's family, Vick, the boy who took the blue tablet.

"You should know that the Rising *was* real," the Pilot says. "The scientists who came up with the immunity to the red tablet were true rebels. So was your great-grandmother. And so were many of the others, especially those of us in the Army. But then, the Society realized that their power was slipping and discovered that they had a rebellion in their midst. At first, they tried to take back control by getting rid of the Aberrations and Anomalies. Then the Society began to infiltrate us the way we had infiltrated them. Now I don't know who is who anymore."

"Then who put the Plague in the Cities' water supplies?" I ask. "Who tried to sabotage the Rising, if it wasn't people working for the Society?"

"It appears," says the Pilot, "that the water supplies were contaminated by well-intentioned supporters of the Rising who felt that the rebellion wasn't happening quickly enough and decided to move it along."

For a few long moments, none of us speak. When things like this happen—when what was meant to help results in harm, when a salve brings pain instead of healing—it is clear how wrong even choices intended to be right can become.

"But why didn't the Society destroy the Rising outright if they knew you existed?" Xander asks, breaking the silence. "The Society could have cured everyone on their own—Oker told me that they *always* had the cure. Why didn't the Society make enough cures so that *they* could let the Plague come in and administer the cure themselves?"

"The Society decided that it would be easier to *become* the Rising," Ky says. "Didn't they?"

As soon as he says this, I know that he's right. That's why the transition of power was so smooth, with so little fighting.

"Because if they became the Rising," I say, "they could predict the outcome."

The final predicted outcome. That's what my Official said back in Oria at the Museum. That's what she wanted to see in my case, and what the Society always took into account.

"The Society had discovered that we'd been making people immune to the red tablet," the Pilot says.

"So more and more people couldn't forget," I say, understanding. "People were showing signs of wanting a change, a rebellion. This way, they got one, and the Society stayed in power without the people—including many of those who participated in the Rising—knowing what had really happened. They'd make a few changes, but for the most part, things would go on as they had." The Society must have known that people become restless eventually. They may even have predicted it. Why *not* have a rebellion, if they could calculate the outcome and secure their power again under a different name? Why not use the Rising, a real rebellion in the beginning, to make things seem authentic? The Society knew people believed in the Pilot, and they took advantage of that.

But it didn't turn out as the Society intended. The Plague mutated. And the people know more and want more than the Society thought they did, even people who weren't chosen for immunity to the red tablet. People like me.

The Society *is* dead, even if they don't know it yet.

I believe in a new beginning. And so do many others out there—those writing on scraps to hang in the Gallery, those who continue to work hard to take care of the sick, those who dare to believe that we can *all* be the pilots of something new and better.

We step like plush, we stand like snow—
The waters murmur now,
Three rivers and the hill are passed,
Two deserts and the sea!

I look at Ky and rewrite the end of the poem in my mind.

But I must count this journey, all
For it has brought me thee.

The door to the hold opens and Xander comes down, the light from the cockpit flooding in behind him. "I thought I should check on Ky," he says, and I smile at Xander and he smiles back and for a moment it is all as it was, it is the same. Xander looks at me with longing and pain in his eyes; we are flying wild through a world that could belong to anyone, and I know why Ky kissed Indie back.

And then it is gone, and I know for a certainty that it is too late for us, for Xander and me, in that way. Not because I can't still love him, but because I can no longer reach him.

"Thank you," I say to Xander, and I mean those words as much as *I love you*, as much as anything I've ever said. And I feel a heavy, low, longing note of regret. For in the end, I didn't fail him because I didn't love him back, because I *do* love him back. I failed him because I cannot do for him what Ky does for me. I can't help Xander sing.

When we land in Camas, I find that I am soon to fly again. We pause only long enough for Xander to make more of the cure so that I can bring it with me to Keya. And though this is a journey that I long to take, it is hard to leave Ky and Xander behind.

"I'll be back soon," I promise the two of them, and I will, in a matter of hours, instead of days or weeks. But I see the worry in Ky's eyes that I know is in mine. We are haunted by other good-byes, so many of them.

And so is Xander. Hunter was right about one thing. There has been too much of leaving.

〜

We land in a long field, not even a runway, near the small town where my parents lived in Keya. As the pilot, the medic, and I leave the ship, I see several figures on the ground walking to meet us. One of them, smaller than the others, breaks into a run and I begin running, too.

He throws his arms around me. He's grown, but I am still taller, and the oldest, and I was not here to protect him. "Bram," I say, and then my throat aches so much I can't speak anymore.

A Rising officer comes up behind Bram. "We found him right before you were due to land."

"Thank you," I manage, and then I pull back to look at Bram. He stares up at me. He's so dirty, very thin, and his eyes have changed and darkened. But I still know him. I turn him around and breathe a sigh of relief when I find the red mark on his neck.

"They both got sick," Bram says. "Even with the immunizations."

"We think we found a cure," I say. I take a deep breath. "Is it too late? Do you know where they are?"

"Yes," Bram says, and then he shakes his head. His eyes fill with tears, and I can tell he's pleading with me not to speak any more, not to ask which question he's answering.

"Follow me," he says, and he begins again to run, just as

he always wanted to do, right out in the open, down the streets of the town. No Official stops him, or the rest of us, as we hurry through the empty streets under a brilliant, careless sun.

To my surprise, Bram takes me to the town's tiny Museum, not to the medical center. Inside the Museum, the display cases have all been broken into, and the glass swept up. Any artifacts that were stored are now gone; the map of the Society has been drawn on, altered. I would like to look closely to see what is marked there now, but we don't have time.

There are many of the still, lying on the floor throughout the room. A few people look up when we come in, and their faces relax slightly at the sight of Bram. He belongs here.

"They ran out of space at the medical center," Bram says, "so I had to bring her here. I was lucky, because I had things to trade. Other people had to do the best they could at their homes. Here, at least they have the nutrient bags some of the time."

Her. My mother. But what about *him*? What about my father?

Bram kneels down.

She looks very gone. I try not to panic. Her face is so pale against her scattering of freckles; there is more gray in her hair than I remember, but she looks young with her eyes open like this, young and lost to us.

"I turn her every two hours like they told me," Bram says, "and her sores have healed. They were bad, though."

He speaks very fast. "But look. She has one of the bags now. That's good, isn't it? They're expensive."

"Yes," I say. "It's very good." I pull him close again. "How did you manage it?" I ask.

"I traded with the Archivists," Bram says.

"I thought the Archivists were all gone," I say.

"A few came back," Bram says. "The ones that had the red mark started to trade again." I shouldn't be surprised. Of course some of the Archivists would not have been able to resist coming back, seeing the void into which they could bring their trades and their trinkets.

I lean closer to Bram so that I can whisper to him. "We're taking her back with us," I say.

"Is it safe?" Bram whispers back.

"Yes," the Rising medic says. "She can be transported. She's stable, and shows no sign of infection."

"Bram," I say softly, "we don't have very much of the cure yet. The Rising thinks Mama might be able to help them, so they agreed she could be one of the first to have it." I glance over at my mother, with her staring-ahead eyes. "And I bargained for him, too, since we were coming here. But where is he? Where is Papa?"

Bram doesn't answer my question. He looks away.

"Bram," I say again, "where is Papa? Do you know? He can come with us to have the cure—they promised—but we don't have much time. We have to find him *now*."

And then Bram starts to sob, great heaving sighs. "They bring the dead out to the fields," he says. "Only those of us who are immune can go out to check on them." He looks up at me with tear-filled eyes. "That's what I've been doing for the Archivists," he says. "I can go out and look for faces."

"No," I say in horror.

"It's better than selling the tubes," he says. "That's the other job that pays well." His eyes are different—so much older, having seen so much more—and still the same, with that obstinate glint that I know well. "I won't do that. Selling the tubes is a lie. Telling people whether or not their friends or family are dead is the truth."

He shudders. "The Archivists let me choose," he says. "They have people coming all the time wanting information or tubes or to know where the people they love are. So I helped them. I could find the people, if they gave me a picture. And then they paid me with what I needed for me. And for her."

He did everything he could to take care of our mother, and I'm glad he saved her, but the cost was so high. What has he seen?

"I wasn't in time for him," Bram says.

I almost ask Bram if he's sure; I almost tell him that he might be wrong, but he knows. He saw.

My father is gone. The cure is too late for him.

"We need to leave," the medic tells me as he helps the Rising officer lift my mother onto a stretcher. "Now."

"Where are you taking her?" someone asks from across the room, but we don't answer.

"Did she die?" someone else calls out. I hear their desperation.

We pass through the still and those who tend them, leaving them behind, and my heart aches. *We'll be back,* I want to tell them. *With enough cures for everyone, next time.*

"What do you have?" someone asks, pushing through. An Archivist. "Do you have a different kind of medicine? How much is it worth?"

The officer takes care of him while we hurry through the doors out of the Museum.

On the ship, Bram climbs down into the hold with me and with the medic, who starts a line for my mother. I pull Bram close and he cries, and cries, and cries, and my heart breaks, and I think his tears will never end. And then they do and it is worse, a shivering and shuddering that shakes his whole body, and I do not know how I can feel this much pain and survive, and at the same time know how much I have to live. *Please,* I think, *let Bram feel that second part, somewhere inside his despair, because we are still together, we still have each other.*

When Bram falls asleep, I take my mother's hand. Instead of singing her the names of flowers, as I had planned, I say her name, because that is what my father would have done.

"Molly," I say. "We're here." I press the paper flower into her palm and her fingers twitch a little. Did she know this lily would cure us? That it was important somehow? Was she simply finding a way to send me something beautiful?

Whatever the case, it worked.

But not soon enough for my father.

CHAPTER 55
XANDER

T his all comes naturally to you," Lei said once before. *"Doesn't it?"* I wonder if the medics watching me inject the cure into the line think the same thing. The patient getting the cure went still within the same time frame that Ky did— that's a requirement for this first trial of the cure.

"That's all you've got to do," I tell the medics. "Inject the solution and wait for it to work."

The medics nod. They've done this before. *I've* done this before, back during the original Plague when I first gave cures and speeches at the medical center. There aren't many of us left now. "These hundred patients are the only ones we have on this trial," I tell the medics. "We're trying to find more of the plant, but it won't be in flower much longer. We know the structure of the parent compound, so we've got people working around the clock to find the synthetic pathway so we can make it in the lab. But all *you* have to worry about is taking care of the patients.

"You'll need to give new doses every two hours." I gesture to where the supplies are stored, in a locked cabinet guarded by several armed officers. I don't know their allegiance, except that it's to the Pilot. "You might see some improvement by the time of the second dose. If their rate of recovery is as quick as our initial subject's was, they'll start speaking and talking again after only a few hours, and walking within two days. But I don't anticipate that rate of recovery here. Be sure not to waste any of the cure."

As if they need the warning. What we need are more flowers, and Cassia's mother to come back. She was still for weeks, a lot longer than Ky was, and it's taking her more time than it did him. The Rising has not yet been able to find her report on the rogue crops in the Society's database, so we need her help desperately.

Meanwhile, the Pilot has teams scouring the fields and meadows near the city of Camas, with instructions not to pull up everything so that the flowers can grow back in case we need them again.

I wonder if they'll be able to resist. It's not exactly easy to save things for the future when the present is so uncertain.

"You sound like you're sure this will work," one of the medics says. Their uniforms are dirty and they all look exhausted. I remember some of them from when I was here before. It feels like years have passed instead of weeks.

"I don't know how much longer I could have done this," one of the medics says. "Now there's a reason to keep going."

I wish I could stay and help, but I'm due back at the lab

to oversee the Rising pharmics who are making more of the cure. "I'll be back to check on the patients later," I say.

The medics start down the rows with the cures. I'm finished here for now, and I think I have just enough time to visit my old wing.

Lei's eyes are very glassy and she smells of infection. But she's been turned recently, and her long sweep of black hair has been braided back out of the way. And the paintings still hang above each patient. The medics here have been doing their best.

It doesn't always come naturally to me, I want to tell her as I inject the cure into her line. *Not right now. Please come back. If you were here, it would help.*

This is one of the cures I made in the village. I didn't turn them all over to the research team trying to synthesize the ingredients in the lab. I saved some for her. She didn't go down that much earlier than Ky, so there's a chance. Of course, she didn't have Oker's medicine in the bags.

I hear footsteps behind me and I turn to look. It's one of the medics who worked here back when I did. "I didn't know we were getting any of the new cure up here," he says.

"You're not," I say. "The group they're using had to fall still within a certain time frame. She was just outside of it." I finish emptying the syringe and turn to look at him. "But I had a few extra." I hold several of the vials. "I might not be able to come here for a little while. I'm supposed to get back to work on making more of this."

The medic slips the vials into the pocket of his uniform. "I'll give them to her," he says.

"Every two hours," I say. I can't seem to leave her alone like this. I know how Cassia felt in the infirmary. Can I trust the medic? I'm sure there's someone else he'd like to cure if he could.

"I'm not going to try to sneak it to someone else," he says. "I want to see if it works first."

"Thank you," I tell him.

"*Does* it work?"

"On one hundred percent of the first trial group," I say. I leave out the fact that the trial group only included a single person.

"I have to ask," he says. "Are you the Pilot?"

"No," I say. I stop at the door for a second and look back at Lei. You're not supposed to do what we've done with this cure and Ky and let one patient take on so much significance. It's just one person. Of course, one person can be the world.

We get the first set of data: *They're coming back. They look better.*

According to the numbers, fifty-seven of the hundred can now track movement with their eyes. Three have spoken. Eighty-three patients total exhibit some kind of improvement:

if not speech or sight, then better color, increased heart rate, and breathing that comes closer to normal levels. It's taken them twice as long as it took Ky to exhibit these initial improvements, but at least the cure is working.

"Seventeen aren't responding at all," the head medic tells me. "We think they may have been still longer than we previously thought. There might have been a mistake in the record keeping."

"Keep trying to get them back," I say. "Give them the full two days of medication."

The medic nods. I pick up the miniport and relay the information to the Pilot. "What do you think?" he asks me.

"I don't think we should wait any longer," I say. "I've trained the others here to make the cure. They can oversee their own labs in other Cities if we set them up. But we haven't figured out how to synthesize it yet. Do you have enough bulbs?"

"We've found enough to begin," he says. "We need more."

"You've seen the data we're getting," I say. "Time matters."

"What do you think we should we do first?" he asks. "Send it out to the other Cities now, or start here and then work outward?"

"I don't know," I say. "Ask Cassia. She can sort it out best. I'm going back to the medical center to see the patients for myself."

"Good," the Pilot says.

I walk over to the medical center. There's another patient I need to see whose data wasn't included in the initial report. They haven't been tracking her because they don't know about her. The other medics nod to me when I come in but they leave me alone, and I'm glad.

The painting above her is the same one, that picture of the girl fishing. Lei stares up at the water, and I smile just in case. "Lei," I say. That's all I can get out before her eyes move the slightest bit and focus on me.

She's here.

She sees me.

CHAPTER 56
CASSIA

Don't ask your mother about your father or the flowers right away," Xander told me. "Give her a little time. I know everyone says we don't *have* any time, but she's been under much longer than Ky. We've got to be careful."

So I take his advice. I ask her no questions, I am only there, with Bram, holding her hands and telling her we love her. And the cure works on my mother. She seems glad that I am here, and to see Bram, but she is in and out, a different return than Ky's. She was longer gone.

But she is strong. After a few days, she speaks, her voice a whisper, a little seed. *"You're both all right,"* she says, and Bram puts his head down next to her on the bed and closes his eyes.

"Yes," I say.

"We sent something to you," she tells me. "Did you get it?" She looks at the medic who has come to change her line, and I can tell that she doesn't want to speak too openly in front of him. And she doesn't mention my father. Is she afraid to ask because she doesn't want to know?

"It's all right," I tell her. "We can talk here. And I did get

it. Thank you for sending the microcard. And the flower—"
I pause for a moment, not wanting to rush her, but the
time seems right. She brought up the gift. "It's a sego lily,
isn't it?"

She smiles. "Yes," she says. "You remembered."

"I've seen them growing in the wild," I say. "They're as
beautiful as you said they would be."

She is holding on tight to this talk of flowers, as I did
before, when I was afraid and alone. If you sing and speak of
blooms and petals that come back after a long time of being
winter-still, you don't have to think about things that don't.

"You were in Sonoma?" she asks. "When?"

"I wasn't there," I say. "I saw it growing someplace else.
Was it in Sonoma that you saw the flowers?"

"Yes," she says, no hesitation, no uncertainty. "In Sonoma's
Farmlands, just outside of a small city called Vale."

I look back at the medic and he nods to me before he
slips out of the room to relay the information. The crop was
in Sonoma. My mother remembered.

There is so much I want to ask her, but that is enough
for now. "I'm glad you're back," I say, and I put my head on
her shoulder, and the three of us are together without him.

"Do you still have the microcard?" she asks later. "Could I see
it again?"

"Yes," I say. I pull my chair closer to the bed and hold up
the datapod so that she can see the screen.

There they are again, the pictures: Grandfather with his parents, with my grandmother, my father.

"In parting, as is customary, Samuel Reyes made a list of his favorite memory of each of his surviving family members," the historian says.

"The one he chose of his daughter-in-law, Molly, was the day they first met." The historian's voice sounds full and proud, as if this is a confirmation of the validity of Matching, which I suppose in a way it is. But it is also a confirmation of love. Of my grandfather letting go of my father and letting him choose what he wanted.

Tears stream down my mother's cheeks. They are all gone now, the others from that meeting. My grandmother, who said that my mother still had the sun on her face. My grandfather. My father.

"His favorite memory of his son, Abran, was the day they had their first real argument."

This time, I find the button to pause the microcard. Why would Grandfather choose a memory like that? I have so many memories of my father—his laugh, his eyes brightening as he talked about his work, the way he loved my mother, the games he taught us. My father was, first and foremost, a gentle man, and in spite of the poem advising otherwise, I hope that is the way that he went into the night.

"Why?" I ask softly. "Why would Grandfather say that about Papa?"

"It seems strange, doesn't it," my mother says, and I look

over to see her watching me with tears slipping down her cheeks. She knows he's gone, even though she hasn't asked and I haven't told.

"Yes," I say.

"That memory happened before I knew your father," my mother says. "But he told me about it." She pauses, puts her hand flat against her chest. She finds it hard to breathe without him, I think, something in her is still drowning a little from loss. "Your father told me that your grandfather gave the poems to you, Cassia," she says. "He tried to give them to your father, too."

Now *I* cannot breathe. *"He did?"* I whisper. "Did Papa read them?"

"Just once," my mother says. "Then he gave them back. He didn't want them."

"Why?"

My mother shakes her head. "He always told me that it was because he was happy in the Society. He wanted everything to be safe. He wanted what the Society could offer. That was his choice."

"What did Grandfather do?" I ask. I imagine giving someone such a gift and then having it returned. Parents are always giving things that are not taken. Grandfather tried to give my father the poems and to tell him about the rebellion. My mother and father tried to give me safety.

"That was when they argued," my mother says. "Your great-grandmother had saved the poems. And there was a certain legacy of rebellion attached to them. But Abran thought it was too dangerous, that your grandfather took too many risks. Eventually, Grandfather accepted your father's decision." She brings her hand down from her chest and breathes in more deeply.

"Did you know Grandfather would give the poems to me?" I ask.

"We thought he might," my mother says.

"Why didn't you stop him?"

"We didn't want to take away your choices," my mother says.

"But Grandfather never did tell me about the Rising," I say.

"I think he wanted you to find your own way," my mother says. She smiles. "In that way, he was a true rebel. I think that's why he chose that argument with your father as his favorite memory. Though he was upset when the fight happened, later he came to see that your father was strong in choosing his own path, and he admired him for it."

I see why my father had to honor Grandfather's last request—to destroy his sample—even though my father didn't agree with the choice. It was his turn to give that back; to be the one to respect and honor a decision made. And my father also extended that gift to me. I remember what he said in his note: *Cassia, I want you to know that I'm proud of you for seeing things through, and for being braver than I was.*

"That's why the Rising didn't make us immune to the red tablet," Bram says to me. "Because they thought our father was weak. They thought he was a traitor."

"*Bram,*" I say.

"I didn't say I believe them," Bram says. "The Rising was wrong."

I look at my mother. Her eyes are closed. "Please," she says. "Play the rest."

I press the button on the datapod and the historian speaks again.

"His favorite memory of his grandson, Bram, was his first word," the historian says. "It was 'more.'"

Bram smiles a little.

"His favorite memory of his granddaughter, Cassia," the historian says, and I lean forward to listen, "was of the red garden day."

That's all. The datapod goes blank.

My mother opens her eyes. "Your father is gone," she says, her lips trembling.

"Yes," I say.

"He died while you were still," Bram says to my mother. His smile is gone, and his voice sounds heavy and sad, weary with telling this terrible news.

"I know," my mother says, smiling through her tears. "He came to say good-bye."

"How?" Bram asks.

"I don't know," she says. "But he did. When I was still, I saw him. He was there, and then he went away."

"I saw him dead, but not the way you saw him," Bram says. "I found his body."

"Oh, Bram, *no*," my mother says, her voice a whisper of agony. "No, no," she says, and she gathers my brother close. "I'm sorry," she tells him. "I'm so sorry."

My mother holds Bram tightly. I draw in a ragged breath, the kind you take when the pain is too deep to cry, when you can't cry because all you are is pain, and if you let some of it out, you might cease to exist. I want to do something to make this better, even though I know that nothing can change the fact of my father gone and under ground.

My mother looks at me and her gaze is pleading. "Can you bring me something," she says, "*anything*, that is growing?"

"Of course," I say.

I don't know plants the way my mother does, so I'm not even sure what it is I dig up in the little courtyard of the medical center. It could be a weed, it could be a flower. But I think she'll be happy with either—she just wants, *needs*, something to combat the sterility of her room and the emptiness of a world without my father.

I fold the foilware container I brought with me into a kind of cup, scoop the soil inside, and pull out the plant.

The roots dangle down, some thick, others so thin that the breeze goes through them as easily as it does the leaves.

When I stand up, my knees are dusty, my hands are dark with dirt. I am bringing my mother a plant because there is no way I can bring my father back for her. I understand why people wanted the tubes; I am also desperate for something to hold on to.

And then, standing there with roots dripping dirt on my feet, the middle of the red garden day memory comes back to me. My mother, my father, Grandfather, his tissue sample, cottonwood seeds, flowers growing wild and made of paper, red buds folded up tight, the green tablet, Ky's blue eyes, and suddenly I can follow Grandfather's red garden day clue, I can take it and follow it up to leaves and branches *and* all the way down to the roots.

And I catch my breath with remembering . . .

Everything.

My mother's hands are printed black with dirt, but I can see the white lines crossing her palms when she lifts up the seedlings. We stand in the plant nursery at the Arboretum; the glass roof overhead and the steamy mists inside belie the cool of the spring morning out.

"Bram made it to school on time," I say.

"Thank you for letting me know," she says, smiling at me. On the rare days when both she and my father have to go to work early, it is my responsibility to get Bram to his early train for First School. "Where are you going now? You have a few minutes left before work."

"I might stop by to see Grandfather," I say. It's all right to deviate

from the usual routine this way, because Grandfather's Banquet is coming soon. So is mine. We have so many things to discuss.

"Of course," she says. She's transferring the seedlings from the tubes where they started, rowed in a tray, to their new homes, little pots filled with soil. She lifts one of the seedlings out.

"It doesn't have many roots," I say.

"Not yet," she says. "That will come."

I give her a quick kiss and start off again. I'm not supposed to linger at her workplace, and I have an air train to catch. Getting up early with Bram has given me a little extra time, but not much.

The spring wind is playful, pushing me one way, pulling me another. It spins some of last fall's leaves up into the air, and I wonder, if I climbed up on the air-train platform and jumped, if the spiral of wind would catch me and take me up twirling.

I cannot think of falling without thinking of flying.

I could do it, I think, if I found a way to make wings.

Someone comes up next to me as I pass by the tangled world of the Hill on my way to the air-train stop. "Cassia Reyes?" the worker asks. The knees of her plainclothes are darkened with soil, like my mother's when she's been working. The woman is young, a few years older than me, and she has something in her hand, more roots dangling down. Pulling up or planting? I wonder.

"Yes?" I say.

"I need to speak with you," she says. A man emerges from the Hill behind her. He is the same age as she is, and something about them makes me think, They would be a good Match. *I've never had permission to go on the Hill, and I look back up at the riot*

of plants and forest behind the workers. What is it like in a place so wild?

"We need you to sort something for us," the man says.

"I'm sorry," I say, moving again. "I only sort at work." They are not Officials, nor are they my superiors or supervisors. This isn't protocol, and I don't bend rules for strangers.

"It's to help your grandfather," the woman says.

I stop.

"There's been a problem," she says. "He may not be a candidate for tissue preservation after all."

"That can't be true," I say.

"I'm afraid that it is," the man says. "There's evidence that he's been stealing from the Society."

I laugh. "Stealing what?" I ask. Grandfather has almost nothing in his apartment.

"The thefts occurred long ago," the woman says, "when he worked at Restoration sites."

The man holds out a datapod. It's old, but the pictures on the screen are clear. Grandfather, younger, holding artifacts. Grandfather, burying the artifacts in a forested area. "Where is this?" I say.

"Here," they say. "On the Hill."

The pictures cover a span of many years. Grandfather ages as I scroll through them. He did this for a very, very long time.

"And the Society has only now found these pictures?" I ask.

"The Society doesn't know," the woman says. "We'd like to keep it that way, so he can still have his Banquet and his sample taken. *We need you to help us in return. If you don't, we'll turn him in.*"

I shake my head. "*I don't believe you,*" I say. "*These pictures—they could have been altered. You could have made all of this up.*" But my heart pounds a little more quickly. I do not want Grandfather to get into trouble. And the thought of his sample is the only thing that makes the pain of the upcoming Banquet manageable.

"*Ask your grandfather,*" the man says. "*He'll tell you the truth. But you don't have much time. The sort we need help with happens today.*"

"*You have the wrong person,*" I say. "*I'm only in training. I don't even have my final work assignment yet.*"

I should ignore them completely, or report them to the Society. But they've unsettled me. What if they take their story—true or not—to the Society? Then a wild hope comes to mind: if they do, will the Society delay Grandfather's Banquet while they investigate? Could we have a little more time? But then I realize that won't happen. The Society will have the Banquet and take the sample as planned, and then if there's enough evidence, they might decide to destroy it.

"*We need you to add data to the sort,*" the man says.

"*That's impossible to do,*" I say. "*When I work, I only sort existing data. I don't enter anything new.*"

"*You don't have to enter anything,*" the woman says. "*All you have to do is access an additional data set and transfer some of that data.*"

"That's also impossible," I say. "I don't have the correct passkeys. The only information I see is what I've been given."

"We have a code that will allow you to pull more data," the man says. "It will help you access the Society's mainframe simultaneously as you're sorting their information."

I stand there, listening, as they tell me what they want me to do. When they finish, I feel strange and spinning, as though the wind did after all pick me up and set me turning. Is this really happening? Will I do what they've asked of me?

"Why did you pick me?" I ask.

"You fit all the criteria," he says. "You're assigned to the sort today."

"Also, you're one of the fastest," the woman says. "And the best." Then she says something else, something that sounds like, "And you'll forget."

After they finish explaining what they want me to do, I have very little free time left. But I still climb off at the stop near Grandfather's apartment. I have to speak with him before I decide my course of action. And the people at the Arboretum are right. Grandfather will tell me the truth.

He's out in the greenspace, and when he sees me, surprise and happiness cross his face. I smile back but I have no time to waste. "I have to go to work," I say. "But there's something I need to know."

"Of course," he says. "What is it?" His eyes are sharp and keen.

"Have you ever," I ask him, "taken something that didn't belong to you?"

He doesn't answer me. I see a flicker of surprise in his eyes. I can't tell if he's surprised at the question or that I know to ask it. Then he nods.

"From the Society?" I whisper, so quietly I can barely hear myself.

But he understands. He reads the words on my lips. "Yes," he says.

And looking at him, I know that he has more to tell me. But I don't want to hear it. I've heard enough. If he admits even to this, then what they say could be true. His sample could be in danger.

"I'll come back later," I promise, and I turn and run down the path, under the red-bud trees.

Work is different today. Norah, my usual supervisor, is nowhere to be found, and I don't recognize many of the people at the sorting center.

An Official takes charge of the room as soon as we are all in our places. "Today's sort is slightly different," he says. "It's an exponential pairwise sort, using personal data from a subset of the Society."

The people from the Arboretum were right. They said this was the kind of sort I'd do today. And they told me more than the Society does now. The woman at the Arboretum said that the data was for the upcoming Match Banquet. My Banquet. The

Society should not be sorting this close to the Banquet. And the people from the Arboretum said that some of those who should be included in the Matching pool had been left out, on purpose, by the Society. These people's data exists in the Society's database, but isn't going to be in the pool. If I do what the man and woman from the Arboretum ask, I will change that.

The man and woman said that these other people belong in the pool, that it's unfair to leave them out. Just as it's unfair to leave Grandfather out from having his sample preserved.

I'm doing it for Grandfather, but I'm also doing it for me. I want to have my real Match, with all the possibilities included.

When I access the additional data and nothing happens, no alarm sounds, I breathe a tiny inward sigh of relief. For myself, that I am not yet caught, and for whomever it is that I have put back into the pool.

The data is in numbers, so I don't know their names or even what the numbers correspond to; I only know what's ideal, which ones should go with the others, because the Official has told us what to look for. I'm not changing the procedure of the sort itself, just adding to the data pool.

The Society should have special sorters to do this, in Central. But they're not using them, they're using us. I wonder why. I think of the criteria the Arboretum workers said made me perfect for what they wanted me to do. Could the Society have used the same criteria? I'm fast, I'm good, and I'll . . . forget? What does that mean?

"Won't they trace the sort back to me?" I asked the people at the Arboretum.

"No," the woman said. "We've infiltrated the Matching logs and can reroute your selections so that it will substitute a false identification number instead of yours. If someone decides to investigate later, it will be as if you were never there at all."

"But my supervisor will know me," I protested.

"Your supervisor will not be present for this sort," the man told me.

"And the Officials—"

The woman interrupted me. "The Officials won't remember names or faces," she said. "You're machines to them. If we substitute a false identification code and a false picture, they won't remember who was really there."

And this, I realized, is why the Society doesn't trust technology. It can be overridden and manipulated. Like people, whom the Society also does not trust.

"But the other sorters—" I began.

"Trust us," the man said. "They won't remember."

We've finished at last.

I finally look up from the screen. For the first time, my eyes meet those of the other people who have been working on this sort. And I feel nervous. The man and woman from the Arboretum were wrong. Today has been different, out of the ordinary, for all of the sorters in this room. No matter what, I will remember the other workers here—that girl's freckles, that man's tired eyes. And they'll remember me.

I'm going to get caught.

"Please," says one of the male Officials at the front of the room, *"remove your red tablets from the containers. Do not take the tablet until we come by to observe you."*

The room collectively draws a breath. But we all do as he says. I tap the tablet out into my palm. For years, I've heard rumors about the red tablet. But I never really thought I'd have to take it. What will happen when I do?

The Official stands in front of me. I hesitate, on the edge of panic.

"Now," he says, and I drop the tablet into my mouth, and he watches me swallow it down.

There's a faint taste of tears in my mouth and I am sitting on the air train home without having much recollection of how I got here or what has happened this day.

Something doesn't feel right. But I know I have to go to Grandfather. I have to find him. That's all I can think of. Grandfather. Is he all right?

"Where have you been?" he asks when I arrive.

"Work," I say, because I know I came from there. But I feel out of focus; I'm not sure what exactly happened. Being here feels good, though. It is beautiful out.

It is a rare moment in spring when both buds on the trees and flowers on the ground are red. The air is cool and at the same time warm. Grandfather watches me, his eyes bright and determined.

"Do you remember what I said once about the green tablet?" he asks.

"Yes," I say. "You said I was strong enough to go without it."

"Greenspace, green tablet," he says, quoting himself from that long ago day. "Green eyes on a green girl."

"I'll always remember that day," I tell him.

"But you're having a hard time remembering this one," he says. His eyes are knowing, sympathetic.

"Yes," I say. "Why?"

Grandfather doesn't answer me, at least not outright. "They used to have a phrase for a truly memorable day," he says instead. "A red-letter day. Can you remember that?"

"I'm not sure," I say. I press my hands to my head. I feel foggy, not quite right. Grandfather's face is sad, but determined. It makes me feel determined, too.

I look around again at the red buds, the flowers. "Or," I say, something sharpening in me, "you could call it a red garden day."

"Yes," Grandfather says. "A red garden day. A day to remember."

He leans closer. "It's going to be hard to remember," he says. "Even this, right now, won't be clear later. But you're strong. I know you can get it all back."

And I have. Because of Grandfather. He tied the red garden day like a flag to my memory, the way Ky and I used to tie red strips of cloth to mark obstacles on the Hill.

Grandfather couldn't give me back all of the memory, because I'd never told him what I'd done, but he could give me a part of it, could help me to know what I'd lost. A clue. *The red garden day.* I can build the rest back like stepping-stones to take me to the other side of forgetfulness, to find the memory on the other bank.

Grandfather believed in me, and he thought I could rebel. And I did, always, do little things, even though I believed in the Society, too. I think of how I made a game for Bram on his scribe when we were small. How angry I was when I swallowed that bite of cake at the Banquet. How Xander and I didn't tell the Officials about his tablet container that day he lost it at the pool. How we broke the rules for Em when we gave her the green tablet.

From what I know now, I think it must have been the Rising who approached me. I did what they asked because they threatened Grandfather. I added people to the Matching pool. Back then, I didn't know who those people were. I didn't know they were Aberrations.

The Rising and the Society both used me, because they knew that I would forget. The Society knew I'd forget the sort and its proximity to the Match Banquet, and the Rising knew I could not betray them if I didn't remember what I'd done. The Pilot even made mention of that when he was flying us to Endstone. "You've helped us before," he said, "though you don't remember it."

But I remember *now*.

Why did the Rising have me add the Aberrations to the pool? Did the Rising hope that it would function as a kind of Reclassification for those who made it through? Or were they simply trying to disrupt the Society?

And why did the Society use me, and the other sorters, that day? Were the sorters in Central already beginning to fall ill with the Plague?

Another memory comes to the surface, tugged by this one.

I Matched another time, in Central.

That's what happened that day when I found the paper where I'd written a single word—*remember*—in my sleeve. The Society was having trouble because of the Plague; they couldn't keep up with the people going still. How long did the Society use people like me to sort for the Banquets and then give us the red tablets so that we'd forget the rush, the eleventh-hour aspect of it all?

My Official didn't know who put Ky into the Matching pool.

But I do know that part of it. At least, I can sort through the data and guess.

It was me.

I put him in without knowing what I was doing. And then

someone—myself, or one of the others in the room—paired him, and Xander, with me.

Did my Official ever find out? Could she have predicted this as the final outcome? Did she even survive the Plague and the mutation?

Out of all the people in the Society, were Ky and Xander really the two I fit best with? Wouldn't the Society have noticed that I had two Matches, or have some fail-safe to catch such an occurrence? Or did the Society not even have a procedure in place for something like that, believing that it would never happen, trusting in their own data and their belief that there could be only *one* perfect Match for each person?

So many questions, and I may never have the answers.

I don't want to ask too much of my mother, now that she's just come back, but she is strong. So was my father. I realize now how much courage it takes to choose the life you want, whatever it might be.

"Grandfather," I say. "He was a member of the Rising. He stole from the Society."

My mother takes the plant from me and nods. "Yes," she says. "He took artifacts from the Restoration sites where he worked. But he didn't steal from the Society on behalf of the Rising. That was his own personal mission."

"Was he an Archivist?" I ask, my heart sinking.

"No," my mother says, "but he did trade with them."

"Why?" I ask. "What did he want?"

"Nothing for himself," my mother says. "He traded to arrange for passage for Anomalies and Aberrations out of the Provinces."

No wonder Grandfather seemed so surprised when I told him about the microcard and how I'd been Matched with an Aberration. He hoped they'd all been saved.

The irony is impossible to ignore. Grandfather was trying to help those people by getting them *out* of the Society; I sorted them *in* to the Matching pool. We both thought we were doing the right thing.

The Society and the Rising used me when they needed me, dropped me when they didn't. But Grandfather *always* knew I was strong, always believed in me. He believed I could go without the green tablet, that I could get my memories back from the red. I wonder what he'd think if he knew that I also walked through the blue.

CHAPTER 57
KY

W e have a lead," the Pilot says.

I don't need to ask *On what?* The lead is always for the same thing—a potential location for the flower that provides the cure.

"Where?" I ask.

"I'm sending you the coordinates now," the Pilot says. The printer on my control panel begins spitting out information. "It's a small town in Sonoma."

That's the Province where Indie was from. "Is it near the sea?" I ask.

"No," the Pilot says, "the desert. But our source was sure of the location. She remembered the name of the town."

"And the source of the information . . ." I say, though I think I already know.

"Cassia's mother," the Pilot says. "She came back."

As I fly in from the east, I see a long stretch of fields, away from the city, where the earth is all turned over. It's morning. There is dew on the dirt of the fields, so they shine a little like a sea when the sun hits just right.

Don't get your hopes up, I tell myself. *We've thought we had curefields before, and then there were only a few flowers.*

The lines from the Thomas poem come to my mind:

Good men, the last wave by, crying how bright
Their frail deeds might have danced in a green bay,
Rage, rage against the dying of the light.

This might be the last wave by, the last chance we have to cure a significant amount of people before they go too far under. These deeds—our flying, Cassia's sorting, Xander's curing—will either be frail or bright.

Two ships sit near the field.

On the outside, I don't hesitate—I start to bring the ship down. But inside I always have a catch when I see other ships waiting. Who's piloting them? Right now the Society seems dormant, and the Pilot and *his* rebellion securely in charge, thanks to the cure he brought back from the mountains. His people keep order; under their supervision, workers distribute the last of the food stockpiles. People who aren't sick stay in their homes, the immune help tend the still, and a tenuous and impermanent order exists. For now, the Pilot has enough respect from all the pilots and the officers to keep control, and the Society has drawn back from the Rising, allowing them to proceed in finding more flowers for the cure. But someday they'll be back. And someday, the people are going to have to decide what it is that they want.

We just have to cure enough of them first.

I bring my ship down on the long deserted road where the others landed.

The Pilot comes to meet me, and in the distance I see an air car hovering in from the direction of the city.

"The officers think they've found someone who can help us," the Pilot says. "A man who knew the person who planted these fields and is willing to talk about it."

The two of us cross the grassy ditch between the field and the dusty road. Spirals of barbed wire fence in the area. But I can already see the lilies.

They stick out at awkward angles from the little hills and valleys of turned-over dirt, but there they are—white flowers waving banners over the cure. I reach through the wire and turn one toward us; its shape is perfect. Three curved petals make up the bloom, with a trace of red on the inside.

"The Society plowed them under last year," the man from the town says, coming up behind us. "But this spring, they all came up." He shakes his head. "I don't know how many of us even noticed or thought to come out here, with the Plague."

"You can eat the bulb for food," the Pilot says. "Did you know that?"

"No," the man says.

"Who planted the fields before the Society bulldozed them over?" the Pilot asks.

"A man named Jacob Childs," the man says. "I'm not supposed to remember that the fields were plowed under, but

475

I do. And I'm not supposed to remember that they took Jacob away. But they did."

"We need to arrange a careful harvest of these bulbs," the Pilot says. "Can you help us with that? Do you know people who would be willing to work?"

"Yes," says the man. "Not many. Most are sick or hiding."

"We'll bring our own people in, too," the Pilot says. "But we need to get started immediately."

A slight wind ruffles the flowers. They're little waves dancing in their green bay of grass.

Days later, I'm on my way back from taking another round of cures to Central when the Pilot's voice comes over the speaker again. His voice startles me and so does the timing of his communication—does he know what I have planned? My flying shouldn't have given him any indication yet. The path he assigned me was perfect, close enough to where I need to be that I can do what I have to do.

"There's no record of the man named Jacob Childs," the Pilot says. "He's vanished."

"That's not surprising," I say. "I'm sure the Society didn't waste any time Reclassifying him and sending him out to die."

"I also had them run a search for Patrick and Aida Markham," the Pilot tells me. "They are nowhere in the databases, Society or Rising."

"Thank you for taking the time to look," I say. There are

plenty of us who want to know about family, but we have limited resources for searching, even through the data.

"I can't have you looking for them now," the Pilot says. "We still need you and your ship for the cure."

"I understand," I say. "I'll look for them on my own time."

"You don't have any of your own time right now," the Pilot says. "Your rest hours are intended to be exactly that. We can't have you flying exhausted."

"I have to find them," I tell him. I owe them everything. Through Anna, I learned what Patrick and Aida traded and sacrificed—even more than I'd originally thought. I ask the Pilot something that I could never have questioned him about before. "Isn't there anyone," I say, "that *you* still have to find?"

I've gone too far. The Pilot doesn't answer.

I look down at the dark land below and the bright lights coming into view, right where they should be.

In the weeks that I've been flying out the cure, I've stopped in every Province in the Society several times over.

Except Oria.

The Pilot won't let any of us land in the Provinces where we're from, because we'll know too many people there and we'll be tempted to change the pattern of the cure.

"There were people I had to find," the Pilot says finally, "but I knew where I needed to look. This is like trying to find a stone in the Sisyphus River. You don't even know where to begin. It would take too long. Now. But later, you can."

I don't answer him. We both know that *later* often means *too late*.

The cure works, and so does Cassia's sorting, telling us where to go next. We're saving the optimal amount of people. She tells us what she thinks we should do, the computers and other sorters corroborate it—her mind is as fine and clear as anything in this world.

But we're not saving everyone. Of the still who go down, about eleven percent do not come back at all. And other patients succumb to infections.

I bring the ship in lower.

"I thought I made it clear that you couldn't look for them now," the Pilot says.

"You did," I say. "I'm not going to make people die while I hunt for something I might not find."

"Then what are you doing?" the Pilot asks me.

"I need to land here," I say.

"They're not in Oria," the Pilot says. "Cassia found it extremely unlikely that they would be anywhere in that Province."

"She put the highest likelihood that they died out in the Outer Provinces," I say. "Didn't she?"

The Pilot pauses for a moment. "Yes," he says.

I circle until I see a good place for a landing. Over the Hill I go, and I wonder where the green silk from Cassia's dress is now—a little tattered banner under the sky buried in the ground. Or bleaching out in the sun. Bleeding away in the rain. Blowing away on the wind.

"Oria's still volatile, and you're a resource," the Pilot says. "You need to come in."

"It won't take long," I repeat, and then I bring the ship around and drop down. This ship isn't like the one the Pilot flies. Mine can't switch over to propellers and a tighter landing the way his can.

The street will barely be long enough but I know every bit of it. I walked it for all those years. With Patrick and Aida, and they were usually holding hands.

The wheels hit the ground and the metal sails of the ship shift, creating drag and slowing me down. Houses rush past, and at the end of the street I stop the ship right in time. Through my window, I could see into the ones of the house in front of me if the people inside didn't have their shutters drawn tight.

I climb out of the ship and move as fast as I can. I only have a few houses to go. The flowers in the gardens haven't been weeded. They grow thick and untended. I pause at the door of the house where Em used to live. The windows are broken. I look inside, but it's empty, and has been for a long enough time that there are leaves on the floor. They must have blown in from another Borough, since ours no longer has trees.

I keep going.

When I was still, I heard what Anna said about my parents

and about Patrick and Aida and Matthew. My mother and father couldn't get me out. So, when they died, they sent me in as close as they could and hoped that would work. And Patrick and Aida welcomed me and loved me like their own.

I'll never forget Aida's screams and Patrick's face when the Officials took me away, or how they kept reaching for me and for each other.

The Society knew what they were doing when they Matched Patrick and Aida.

If I'd been the one Matched with Cassia, if I'd known I could have eighty years of a good life and most of it spent with her, I wonder if I would have had the strength to try to take the Society down.

Xander did.

I walk up the pathway and knock on the door of the house where he used to live.

CHAPTER 58
XANDER

In the past few weeks we've had several breakthroughs in administering the cure. First were the fields Cassia's mother told us about, which allowed us to make more of the cure and get it out to people quickly. Then we figured out how to synthesize the proteins of the sego lily in the laboratory. The best minds left in the Rising and the Society have come together to try to make this work.

So far, it has. People are getting better. And if the mutation comes back, we have a cure. Unless, of course, the virus changes again. But, for now, the data says that the worst has passed. I wouldn't trust the data except that Cassia's the one who sorted it.

Now we're heading toward a different time: once people are well, they will need to choose what kind of world it is that they want to live in. I don't know that we're going to come through that as well as we came through the Plague.

"You saved the world," my father likes to say.

"It was luck," I tell him. "We've always been lucky."

And we have. Take a look at my family. My brother went back to the Borough from Oria City when the Plague first broke, and they all managed to keep from getting sick until near the end. And even when they did fall ill, Ky arrived just in time to bring them back here so we could heal them.

"We tried to hold the Borough together," my father says.

To his credit, they did. They rationed and shared the food and looked after each other for as long as they could.

It's not like they did anything wrong. My family has always believed that if you worked hard and did the right thing, you were likely to have it all work out. And they're not stupid. They know it doesn't *always* go that way. They've seen terrible things happen and it's torn them up. But that's as close as they've been to real suffering.

Also, I'm a hypocrite, because nothing bad has really happened to me either. Ky's family has disappeared entirely. Cassia's family lost her father. But not us, not the Carrows. We're all fine. Even my brother, who never did join the Rising. I was wrong about him. I've been wrong about a lot of things.

But the cure we made does work.

When it's time for my break, I leave the medical center and walk out toward the river that goes through the center of the City of Camas. Now that the barricade's down and the mutation is under control, people have taken again to walking along the river. There's a set of cement steps cut into the embankment not far from the medical center.

Ky and Cassia go there sometimes, when he's back from

an errand, and once I found him there alone watching the water.

I sat down beside him. "Thank you," I said. It was the first time I'd seen him since he'd brought my family in for the cure.

Ky nodded. "I couldn't bring my own family back," he said. "I hoped I'd find yours."

"And you did," I said, trying to keep the bitterness out of my voice. "Exactly where the Society left them."

Ky raised his eyebrows.

"I'm glad they're back," I told him. "I'll owe you for the rest of my life for bringing them in. Who knows how long it would have taken for them to get the cure otherwise."

"It was the least I could do," Ky said. "You and Cassia are the ones who cured me."

"How did you know you loved her?" I asked Ky. "When you first fell for her, she didn't really know you. She didn't know anything about where you'd been."

Ky didn't answer right away. He looked out at the water. "I had to put a body in a river once," he said finally, "before all of this. An Aberration died in camp, earlier than the Society planned, and the Officers made us get rid of the evidence. That's when I met my friend Vick."

I nodded. I'd heard them talk about Vick.

"Vick had fallen in love with someone he wasn't supposed to have," Ky said. "He ended up dying for it." Then Ky looked at me. "I wanted to stay alive after my family died," he said. "But I didn't feel like I was living again until I met Cassia."

"But you didn't feel like she really *knew* you, did you?" I asked again.

"No," Ky said, "but I felt like she could."

I start down the wide steps to the water. Ky's not there this time but I see someone else I know. It's Lei, with her long black hair.

It's been days since I've seen her, even in passing. After she recovered, she went back to work, and our paths have rarely crossed since. When they have, we've both nodded and smiled and said hello. She likely knows that I'm working on the cure but I haven't had a chance to talk with her.

I hesitate, but she looks up at me and smiles, gesturing for me to come closer. I sit down next to her and I feel like a fool. I don't know where to begin.

But she does. "Where did you go?" she asks me.

"To the mountains," I say. "The Pilot took some of us there. That's where we found the cure."

"And you were the one to do it," she says.

"No," I say. "Cassia figured it out."

"Your Match," she says.

"Yes," I say. "She's alive, and she's fine. She's here."

"I think I've seen her," Lei says, "talking with you." Her eyes search mine, trying to learn what I haven't said.

"She's in love with someone else," I say.

Lei puts her hand on mine very gently for a moment. "I'm sorry," she says.

"What about *your* Match?" I ask. "Have you been able to find him?"

She turns her face away then, and as her hair swishes across her back and neck, I remember when we checked each other for the mark during those days in the medical center. "He died," she says. "Before the Plague came."

"I'm sorry," I say.

"I think I knew before they told me," Lei says. "I think I could feel him, gone." I am struck again by the sound of her voice. It's very beautiful. I would like to hear her sing. "That must sound ridiculous to you," she says.

"No," I say, "it doesn't."

Something jumps in the river and I start a little.

"A fish," Lei says, looking back at me.

"One of the ones you told me about?" I ask.

"No," she says. "That one was silver, not red."

"Where did *you* go?" I ask Lei.

She knows what I mean: *Where did you go when you were still?*

"I was swimming most of the time," she says. "Like those fish, one of the ones I told you about, and I had a different body. I knew I wasn't *really* a fish, but it was easier than thinking about what was happening."

"I wonder why everyone thinks about the water," I say. Ky did the same. He told us he was on an ocean with that girl who died. Indie.

"I think," Lei says, "because the sky seems too far. It doesn't feel like it will hold you the way the water can."

Or because your lungs are filling with fluid that you can't always clear. But neither of us gives the medical explanation, though we both know it.

I don't know what to say. When I look at Lei I think she might be the kind of person who could do what she said the water could: hold someone up. I imagine pulling her close and kissing her and I can picture letting go, going under, with her.

Her face changes. She must be able to see what I'm thinking.

I stand up, disgusted with myself. I'm not in any condition to love someone, and she's just lost her Match and come back from the mutation. We're both alone.

"I have to go," I say.

CHAPTER 59
CASSIA

I hesitate for a moment at the top of the steps, hidden behind one of the trees along the embankment, waiting for Xander to pass by. He doesn't notice me.

Before I can lose my courage, I go down, toward the water and the girl. I sit down next to her and she turns to look at me. "I'm Cassia," I say. "I think we both know Xander."

"Yes," she says. "I'm Lei. Nea Lei."

I study her face while trying not to seem like I'm doing it. She's not much older than us, but something about her seems wise. She speaks very clearly; but her words are clean, not clipped. She is lovely, in a way that is all her own; very dark hair, very deep eyes.

"We both know Xander," she says, "but you're in love with someone else."

"Yes," I say.

"Xander told me a little about you," she says. "When we worked together. He always talked about his Match, and I talked about mine."

"Is your Match—" I don't dare finish.

"My Match is gone," she says. Tears slip down her cheeks and she brushes them away with the heels of her hands. "I'm sorry," she says. "I've suspected it for months. But now that I know, I can't seem to stop crying whenever I talk about him. Especially here. He loved the water."

"Is there someone I can help you find?" I ask. "Any family—"

"No," she says. "I don't have any family. They're gone. I'm an Anomaly."

"You are?" I ask, stunned. "How did you hide from the Society?"

"Right in front of their eyes," she says. "Data can be forged, if you know the right person, and my parents did. My family used to believe in the Pilot, but after they saw how many Anomalies he let die, they decided I would be safest in the Society after all. They gave everything they had to buy me a perfect set of falsified data. I came into the Society and became an Official shortly after." She smiles a little. "The Society might be surprised to know that they made an Anomaly an Official so quickly." She stands up. "If you see Xander, will you tell him good-bye for me?"

"You should tell him in person," I say, but she keeps going.

"Wait," I say. She stops. There's something I don't understand. "If you weren't a citizen until recently, you wouldn't have had a Match Banquet. So how did you—"

"I never needed the Society," she says, "to Match me."

She looks down at the water. And in that moment, I think I know exactly who she is.

"Your name," I say. "Was it the same, or did you change it when you came into the Society?"

"I didn't change it entirely," she says. "I only reversed it."

I run back to the medical center to find Xander. He's working in the lab, and I pound on the window to get his attention.

Xander's father, who also works in the lab, sees me first. He smiles at me but on his face I also see wariness. He doesn't want me to hurt his son.

And he knows that Xander *is* hurt.

I didn't do it all, I want to tell Mr. Carrow. *But Xander has changed. He's been through so much—the loss of his faith in the Rising, those dark days working in the medical center, the time out in the mountains.*

"Your friend," I tell Xander as soon as he opens the door. "Lei. She's going somewhere else. She told me to tell you good-bye."

And you have to find her. Because she's already lost too much, and so have you. It all came together when she stood there by the river, when she spoke about not needing the Society to Match her. She told me that she didn't even need to change her name, just reverse it. Nea Lei. Lei Nea. When you say it out, it sounds like Laney. Ky had never seen it spelled when

489

he carved the name of the girl Vick loved. Neither, perhaps, had Vick.

Xander takes a step forward. "Did she say where she was going?" The expression on his face tells me everything I need to know.

And what I was going to say doesn't matter the way I thought it would. Because her story, with Vick, is not mine to tell. It's hers—Lei's. And it may or may not become part of her story with Xander, but that is not for me to decide.

"No," I say. "But, Xander, you can catch up with her. You can find out."

For a second, I think he will. Then he sits down at his workstation. He leans forward, his back perfectly straight, his expression a mask of confidence and determination.

How is it that he's so good at reading others but he's not paying attention to himself?

Because he doesn't want to be hurt again.

"There's more," I tell him, leaning closer so that the others won't hear. "The Pilot has decided that it's time to take the villagers to the Otherlands."

"Why now?" he asks.

"It's coming time for the people to vote," I say. "He won't be able to spare the ships then. He'll need them to keep order. There are rumors that people from the Society are going to try to take control."

"He can't spare the ships *now*," Xander says. "We need them to transport the cure."

"He's not going to send many out," I say. "A few of the cargo transports, not the fighters. They're going to Endstone and they'll take the villagers as far as they can. Ky and I are going to the village, to talk to Anna and bring her back here to Camas with us, if she'll come. I wanted to tell you."

"Why?"

"I didn't want you to worry," I say. *I didn't want you to feel like we'd left you behind again.*

"Will the Pilot let other people go on to the Otherlands in addition to the villagers?" he asks.

"If there's room, I think he would," I say.

"The villagers might let me go with them," he says, and then he grins and I see a little bit of the old Xander, and I miss him so much. "They might trust me now that they know I was right about the cure."

"No," I say, stunned. "Xander, *you* can't go to the Otherlands. We need you."

"I'm sorry," Xander says, "but I can't let that keep me here anymore."

CHAPTER 60
KY

Cassia and I wait for the Pilot's command.

It is just the two of us on the ship. We're flying alone this time, carrying supplies in and, hopefully, some of the villagers out. Cassia's decided that we need Anna to stand up for the vote. "She can lead people," Cassia told me. "She's proved it for years."

"How many ships have to take off before we go?" Cassia asks now.

"Ten," I say. "We're one of the last."

"So we have a little time," she says.

Time. It's what we've always wanted, what we rarely have.

She's sitting in the copilot's chair and she turns it so that she faces me. There's mischief in her bright green eyes and I catch my breath.

Cassia slides her hands behind my neck and I lean forward.

I close my eyes and remember her standing as beautiful as snow when she came out of the canyons. I remember holding the green silk against her cheek on the Hill. I remember her skin and sand in the canyons, and her face looking down on me in the mountains, bringing me back.

"I love you," she whispers.

"I love you," I say back.

I choose her again, and again, and again. Until the Pilot interrupts us and it's time to fly.

Into the sky we go. The two of us together. As the wisps of clouds go by, I pretend that they're my mother's paintings, evaporated up from the stone. Drifting even higher on their way to something new.

CHAPTER 61
CASSIA

He takes us up higher and the air ship shudders and groans, and my heart beats fast, and I am not afraid.

There are the mountains, enormous blue and green against the sky, and then less, and less, below us, and it is blue all around.

In the blue, there is white and gold, white wisps of cloud trailing across the sky like the cottonwood seed I once gave Grandfather. *"Clouds of glory,"* I whisper, remembering, and I wonder where he found those words and if this is a journey he made after he died, coming up to be warmed by the sun, his fingers catching hold of these bits of sky, letting go.

And then where? I wonder. *Could there be anywhere else as glorious as this?*

Maybe this is where the angels went when they flew up. Perhaps it is where my father is now, drifting in the sun. Maybe it would be a cruel thing to bring him back and weigh him down. Or maybe when they are light, they are lonely.

I look over at Ky. His face is as I have rarely seen it before, perfectly serene.

"Ky," I say. "You're the Pilot."

He smiles.

"You are," I say. "Look how you fly. It's like Indie."

His smile turns sad.

"You must think of her when you fly," I say, a little sharp pain cutting through me even though I understand. There are places, times, when I will always think of Xander. Whenever I see a blue pool, a red newrose, the roots of a plant pulled up from the ground.

"Yes," Ky says. "But *all* the time, I think of you."

I lean over and press my hand against his cheek, not wanting to distract him too much from what he's doing.

The flight, with the man I love, is gorgeous, glorious. But there are so many people trapped below.

We drop lower, out of the clouds, and the mountains wait for us. The evening light on their faces turns white snow pink and gray rock gold. Dark trees and water, flat at first and then glinting and gaining dimension as we come closer, cling to the sides of the mountain; ravines of tumbled stone cut into green foothills.

Hand in hand, we walk up the path from the landing meadow to the village to find and speak with Anna and Eli. *I hope they'll come with us,* I think. *We need them in the Provinces.* But they might want to go to the Otherlands, or stay in the mountains, or go out to look for Hunter, or back to the Carving. There are many choices now.

Ky stops on the path. "Listen," he says. "Music."

At first I hear only the murmur of the wind through those tall pine trees. And then I hear singing from the village.

We all quicken our pace. When we come into the village, Ky points at someone. "Xander," Ky says. He's right. Xander's ahead of us—I see his blond hair, his profile. He must have flown in on one of the other ships.

He's going to try to go to the Otherlands.

Xander must know we're here, somewhere, but he's not looking for us. All he's doing, right now, is listening.

The villagers aren't just singing, they are also dancing around the stone, in a farewell. Fire dances, too, and somehow, with things carved of wood and strung with string, the villagers are making music.

One of the officers moves to break it up, but Ky stops him. "They saved us," he reminds the officer. "Give them a little time."

The officer nods.

Ky turns to me. I brush my fingers along his lips. *He's so alive.* "What now?"

"Dance with me," he says. "I told you I would teach you."

"I already learned how," I say, thinking of that time back at the Gallery.

"I'm not surprised," Ky whispers. His hands go down around my waist. Something sings inside me and we begin to move. I don't ask if I'm doing this right. I know I am.

"Cassia." He says the word like a song. His voice has always had that music in it.

He says my name, over and over as we move together, until I'm caught in a strange place between weak and strong, between dizziness and clarity and need and satiety and give and take and . . . *"Ky,"* I say back.

For so long, we cared about who saw us. Who might be watching, who might be hurt. But now, we are only dancing.

I come back to myself as the song ends, when the strings make a sound like hearts breaking. And then I can't help but look for Xander. When I find him, I see that he watches us, but there's no jealousy in his gaze. There is nothing but longing, but it's not for me anymore.

You will find love, Xander, I want to tell him. The firelight flickers across Leyna's face. She is very beautiful, very strong. Could Xander love Leyna? Someday? If they go to the Otherlands together?

"We could stay out here," Ky says, low in my ear. "We don't have to go back."

It's a conversation we've had before. We know the answer. We love each other, but there are others to think of, too. Ky has to look for Patrick and Aida, in case they are still alive. I have to be with my family.

"When I was flying," Ky says, "I used to imagine that I came down and gathered everyone up and flew us all away."

"Maybe we can do that someday," I say.

"It might be," Ky says, "that we won't have to go so

far to look for a new world. Maybe the vote really *will* be a beginning."

It is the most hopeful I have ever heard him sound.

Anna walks over to Xander and says something to him, and he follows her toward Ky and me. The light from the fire shades and lightens, flickers and holds, and when it does, I see that Anna holds a piece of blue chalk in her hand. "You did it," she says to the three of us. "You found the cure, and you each had a part." Anna takes Ky's hand and draws a blue line on it, tracing one of his veins. "The pilot," she says. She lifts my hand and draws the line from Ky to me. "The poet." Then Anna takes Xander's hand and draws the line from me to him. "The physic," she says.

Evening in the mountain, with its fresh pine and burning wood smells, its lights and music, gathers around us as Anna steps back. I hold on to Xander and Ky at the same time, the three of us standing in a little circle at the edge of the known world, and even as the moment exists I find myself mourning its passing.

The little girl Xander and I saw in the village dances over, wearing the wings we saw her in before. She looks up at the three of us. It's plain she wants to dance with one of the boys, and Ky lets her lead him away, leaving me alone with Xander to say good-bye.

The music, this time lively, runs along us, over us, into us, and Xander is here with me. "You can dance," he says. "And you can sing."

"Yes," I say.

"I can't," Xander says.

"You will," I say, taking his hands.

He moves smoothly. Despite what he thinks, the music is in him. He's never been taught to dance, and yet he's guiding me. He doesn't notice because he's concentrating so hard on what he doesn't have—what he thinks he can't do.

"Can I ask you about something?"

"Of course," he says.

"I remember something I shouldn't," I say. "From a day when I took the red tablet." I tell him about the way I reclaimed the red garden day memory.

"How could I get part of my memory back?" I ask him.

"It might have something to do with the green tablet," Xander says. His voice sounds very kind and very tired. "Maybe your not taking it, ever, means you could get your memories back somehow. And, you walked through the blue. Oker told me that the blue tablet and the Plague are related. Maybe you helped yourself become immune." He shakes his head. "The Society made the tablets like a puzzle. Everything is a piece. I'm learning from the pharmics and scientists how complicated it all is. The way medications work together, and the ways they work differently in different people—it's something you could spend your whole life trying to figure out."

"So what you're saying," I tell him, "is that I might never know."

"Yes," he says. "You might always have to wonder."

"*'It's all right to wonder,'*" I say. Besides the words on the microcard, that was the last thing Grandfather said to me before he died. He gave me the poems. And he told me that it was all right to wonder. So it's fine that I don't know which poem he meant for me to follow. Perhaps that's even what he intended. It's all right that I can't figure everything out right here, right now.

"It might also just be you," Xander says. I think he's smiling. "You've always been one of the strongest people I know."

Eli has joined Ky and the little girl in their dance. They have linked hands and are laughing, the firelight shimmering on the girl's wings. She reminds me of Indie—the abandoned way she moves, the way the fire turns her hair to red. *I wish Indie was here,* I think, *and my father, and everyone else we've lost.*

Xander and I stop dancing. We stand very close and still in the middle of people moving. "Back in the Borough," he says, "I asked you, if we could choose, would you ever have chosen me?"

"I remember," I say. "I told you that I would."

"Yes," he says. "But we can't go back."

"No," I agree.

Xander's journeys happened in those walled rooms and long hallways of the sick, when he worked with Lei. When I saw him again in the Pilot's air ship, Xander had already been places I would never go and become someone else.

But I didn't see it. I believed him unchanging, a stone in all good senses of the word, solid, dependable, something and someone you could build upon. But he is as we all are: light as air, transient as wisps of cloud before the sun, beautiful and fleeting, and if I ever did truly have hold of him, that has ended now.

"Xander," I say, and he pulls me close, one last time.

The ships lift into the sky, dark on stars. The bonfire burns; some of the villagers, mostly those from the Carving, have decided to stay in the mountains.

Xander is going out to a place that is Other, a place so distant I can't even be certain there is a coming back.

CHAPTER 62

XANDER

It sounds like a million birds beating their wings against the sky, but it's only the ships flying above me. At the last minute, I realized I couldn't go with them to the Otherlands. But I also couldn't make myself go back to Camas. I'm stuck here in the middle, as always.

Morning comes. I climb up to the stream near the field where Oker and I dug the camassia, skirting the village so I don't have to talk to anyone. Later, I'll come back and ask them if there's something I can do: maybe work in Oker's old lab.

Roots from the trees at the edge of the stream dangle down into the water. They are tiny and red. I never knew roots could be that color.

And then I see a larger glimpse of red. Another. Another. They're almost hideous—strange jaws, round eyes—but the color is so brilliant.

They're the redfish Lei told me about. I'm seeing them at last.

My throat aches and my eyes burn. I come down closer to the water.

Then I hear something behind me. I turn around, change my expression to a grin, ready to talk to whatever villager found their way out here.

"Xander," she says.

It's Lei.

"Are they back?" she asks me. "The redfish?"

"Yes," I say.

"I didn't know you were here," she says. "I didn't see you on the ships from Camas."

"We must not have been on the same ship," I say. "I meant to go to the Otherlands."

"I did, too," she says. "But I couldn't leave."

"Why not?" I ask, and I don't know what I hope the answer will be, but my heart pounds in my chest and in my ears there's a sound like rushing water or those ships lifting into the sky.

She doesn't answer, but she looks toward the stream. Of course. The fish.

"*Why* do they come all the way back?" I ask her.

"To find each other." Her eyes meet mine. "We used to come to the river together," she says. "He looked a little like you. He had very blue eyes."

The rushing in my ears is gone. Everything feels very quiet. She came back because she couldn't leave the country where she knew him. It has nothing to do with me.

I clear my throat. "You said these fish are blue in the ocean," I say. "Like a completely different animal."

"Yes and no," she says. "They have changed. We're allowed to change." She's very soft with me. Her voice is gentle.

And then Lei is the one to close the distance. She moves right to me.

I want to say something I've never said before, and it won't be to Cassia, the way I always thought it would be. "I love you," I say. "I know you still love someone else, but—"

"I love you," she says.

It's not all gone. She loved someone before and so did I. The Society and the Rising and the world are all still out there, pressing against us. But Lei holds them away. She's made enough space for two people to stand up together, whether or not any Society or Rising says that they can. She's done it before. The amazing thing is that she's not afraid to do it again. When we fall in love the first time, we don't know anything. We risk a lot less than we do if we choose to love again.

There is something extraordinary about the first time falling.

But it feels even better to find myself standing on solid ground, with someone holding on to me, pulling me back, and know that I'm doing the same for her.

"Remember the story I told you?" Lei asks. "The one about the Pilot and the man she loved?"

"Yes," I say.

"Who do you think had to be more brave?" she asks. "The

Pilot who let him go, or the man who had to start all over in a new world?"

"They were both brave," I say.

Her eyes are level with mine. So I see when she closes them and lets herself fall for me: right when my lips meet hers.

CHAPTER 63
CASSIA

Ky and I stand together at the top of the steps of City Hall, holding hands and blinking in the brightness of an end-of-summer day in Camas. No one notices us. They have other things to think about on their way up the stairs. Some look uncertain, others excited.

An older woman stops at the top of the steps and glances at me. "When do we write our names?" she asks.

"Once you get inside to vote," I tell her.

The woman nods and disappears into the building.

I look at Ky and smile. We have just finished putting *our* names to paper, making a choice about who we want to lead.

"When people chose the Society, it was almost the end of us," I say. "It might be the end of us again, forever this time."

"It might be," Ky agrees. "Or we might make a different choice."

There are three candidates offering to lead the people. The Pilot represents the Rising. An Official represents the Society.

And Anna represents everyone else. She and Eli came

back to Camas with us. "What about Hunter?" Ky asked Anna, and she said, "I know where he's gone," and smiled, sadness and hope mixed together in her expression, a feeling I know all too well.

This voting is such a large and impossible task, such a beautiful and terrible experiment, and it could go wrong in so many ways. I think of all those little white papers inside, all those people who have learned to write, at least their names. What will they choose? What will become of us, and our lands of blue sky and red rock and green grass?

But, I remind myself, *the Society can't take it all again unless we let them. We can get our memories back, but we will have to talk with each other and trust one another. If we'd done that before, we might have found the cure sooner. Who knows why that man planted those fields? Perhaps he knew we'd need the flowers for a cure. Maybe he just thought they were beautiful, like my mother did. But we do find answers in beauty, more often than not.*

This is going to be very difficult. But we came through the Plague and its mutation together, all of us. Those who believed in the Rising and those who believed in the Society and those who believed in something else entirely all worked side by side to help the still. Some didn't. Some ran and some killed. But many people tried to save.

"Who did you vote for?" I whisper to Ky as we walk down the steps.

"Anna," he says. He smiles at me. "What about you?"

"Anna," I say.

I hope she wins.

It's time for the Anomalies and Aberrations to have their turn.

But will we let them?

In the debates on the ports, the Official was clear and concise, statistical. "Don't you think we've seen this before?" she asked. "Everything you do has been done before. You should let the Society help you again. This time, of course, we will allow for greater increase of expression. Give you more choices. But, left too much to your own devices, what would happen?"

I thought, *We'd write something. We'd sing something.*

"Yes," said the Official, as if she knew my thoughts, as if she knew what everyone in the Society was thinking. "Exactly. You would write the same books that other people have written. You'd write the same poems: they'd be about love."

She's right. We would compose poems about love and tell stories that have been heard in some form before. But it would be *our* first time feeling and telling.

I remember what Anna called the three of us.

The Pilot. The Poet. The Physic.

They are in *all* of us. I believe this. That every person might have a way to fly, a line of poetry to put down for others to see, a hand to heal.

Xander sent a message to let us know where he is now.

He wrote it out by hand. It was the first time I ever saw his writing, and the neat rows of letters brought tears to my eyes.

I'm in the mountains. Lei's here, too. Please tell my family that I'm fine. I'm happy. And I'll be back someday.

I hope that's true.

My mother and Bram wait for us on the steps down to the river.

"You're finished voting," Bram says. "How was it?"

"Quiet," I say, thinking back to that large Hall full of people and the sounds of pencils on paper, names being written slowly and carefully.

"I should be able to vote," Bram says.

"You should," I agree. "But they decided on seventeen."

"Banquet age," Bram says. "Do you think I'm going to have a Banquet?"

"You might," I say. "But I hope not."

"I have something for you," Ky says. He holds out his hand and there is Grandfather's tube, the one we found in the Cavern, the one that Ky hid for me in a tree.

"When did you get this?" I ask.

"Yesterday," Ky says. "We were in the Outer Provinces again, looking for survivors." After the mutated Plague was under control, the Pilot let Ky and some of the others try to find those who are still lost, like Patrick and Aida. The hope was that some of them might have found their way to the Rising's old camp, the one on the map near the lake.

So far, we're still looking.

"I brought this back, too," he says. "It's the one Eli saved." He holds out his hand and I see the label on the tube. *Roberts, Vick.*

"I thought you didn't believe in the tubes," Bram says.

"I don't," Ky says. "But I think this one should be given to someone who loved him so they can decide what to do."

"Do you think she'll take it?" I ask Ky. He's talking about Lei, of course.

"I think she'll take it," Ky says, "and then let it go."

Because she loves Xander now. She's chosen to love again.

Sometimes, I felt angry that Grandfather hadn't told me exactly which poem he wanted me to find. But now I see what he did give me. He gave me a choice. That's what it always was.

"It's hard to do this," I say, holding Grandfather's tube. "I wish I'd kept the poems. That would make it easier. I'd have something of him left."

"Sometimes paper is only paper," my mother says. "Words are just words. Ways to capture the real thing. Don't be afraid to remember that."

I know what she means. Writing, painting, singing—it cannot stop everything. Cannot halt death in its tracks. But perhaps it can make the pause between death's footsteps sound and look and feel beautiful, can make the space of waiting a place where you can linger without as much fear. For we are all walking each other to our deaths, and the journey there between footsteps makes up our lives.

"Good-bye," I say to Grandfather, and to my father, and I hold the tube in the river and pause a moment. We hold the choices of our fathers and mothers in our hands and when we cling on or let them slip between our fingers, those choices become our own.

Then I unstop the tube and hold it in the water, letting it take the last little bit of Grandfather away, just as he wanted and asked my father to do.

I wish the two of them could see all of this: green field planted with cures for the future; blue sky; a red flag on top of City Hall signaling that it is time to choose.

"Like climbing the Hill," Ky says, catching my eye and pointing to the flag.

"Yes," I say, remembering the feel of his hand on mine as we tied the scraps to the trees to mark where we had been.

Beyond the City of Camas, the mountains rise blue and purple and white in the distance.

Ky and I climbed the Hill, together. Xander is in the mountains.

Even though Xander is gone, even though all cannot be as everyone would wish, there is satisfaction in knowing that something good and right and true was part of you. That you had the blessing, gift, good fortune, perfect luck, to know someone like this, to pass through fire and water and stone and sky together and emerge, all of you, strong enough to hold on, strong enough to let go.

I can already feel some things slipping through my fingers like sand and water, like artifacts and poems, like everything you want to hold on to and can't.

But we did it. Whatever happens next, we managed to help find a cure and begin a vote.

The river looks alternately blue and green as it reflects grass and sky, and I catch a glimpse of something red swimming in it.

Ky leans in to kiss me and I close my eyes to better feel the moment of waiting and want before our lips meet.

There is ebb and flow. Leaving and coming. Flight and fall.

Sing and silent.

Reaching and reached.

AUTHOR'S NOTE

Throughout the Matched trilogy, I have mentioned and/or quoted from several works of art. While most of the works are attributed in the text, I wanted to include a completed list here for those who are interested in reading or seeing more of these artists' beautiful work.

PAINTINGS:

Chasm of the Colorado, by Thomas Moran
(referred to as Painting Nineteen of the Hundred Paintings)

Girl Fishing at San Vigilio, by John Singer Sargent
(referred to as Painting Ninety-Seven of the Hundred Paintings)

POETRY:

"Do Not Go Gentle Into That Good Night"
                      by Dylan Thomas

"Poem in October" by Dylan Thomas

"Crossing the Bar" by Alfred Lord Tennyson

"They Dropped Like Flakes" by Emily Dickinson

"I Did Not Reach Thee" by Emily Dickinson

"In Time of Pestilence, 1593" by Thomas Nashe

In *Crossed,* I also mention Ray Bradbury and Rita Dove, whose work, along with that of Wallace Stegner and Leslie Norris, inspired me during the writing of this series.

ACKNOWLEDGMENTS

I would like to thank:

My husband, who sees beauty in both poetry and equations, and who never fails to believe and build up;

Our four children, who are the how and why of everything I write;

My parents and my brother and sisters;

Dr. Gregory F. Burton, (who generously let me use his Goldilocks/Xanthe analogy in the text, and who helped me with the immunology involved in the story) and Dr. Matthew O. Leavitt (who lent his expertise as a pathologist). Any science that works regarding the Plague, its mutation, and the tablets is due to Dr. Burton and Dr. Leavitt—the fiction is all my fault;

Ashlee Child, R.N., who answered many questions about nursing and patient care;

Dale Hepworth, fisheries biologist, who sent me information and photos of sockeye salmon (the "redfish" Lei tells Xander about in *Reached*);

My cousin Peter Crandall, a commercial airline pilot, who helped me with the flying scenes in the novel, and introduced me to the Osprey, the inspiration for the Pilot's ship;

My ancestor, Polly Rawson Dinsdale, and the other

pioneers who ate sego lily bulbs to survive hard times and inspired the use of that flower in this story;

Josie Lauritsen Lee, Lisa Mangum, and Robison Wells, who waded through early drafts and gave valuable and empowering feedback;

Lizzie Jolley, Mikayla Kirkby, and Mylee Sanders, who were unfailingly patient and kind with my children and with me;

My agent, Jodi Reamer, who piloted this series from beginning to end, guiding always with gusto and good humor back to where we needed to be (and on to places I hadn't dreamed of);

My editor, Julie Strauss-Gabel, who served as physic and poet, nurturing the manuscript and shaping it with her unparalleled intelligence and perception;

The wonderful team at Writers House, including Alec Shane and Cecilia de la Campa;

The fantastic people at Penguin: Scottie Bowditch, Erin Dempsey, Theresa Evangelista, Felicia Frazier, Erin Gallagher, Anna Jarzab, Liza Kaplan, Lisa Kelly, Eileen Kreit, Rosanne Lauer, Jen Loja, Shanta Newlin, Emily Romero, Irene Vandervoort, and Don Weisberg;

And you, the reader, for taking this journey with Cassia, Ky, and Xander, and with me.

ALLY CONDIE

is the author of the Matched trilogy.
Before becoming a writer, she taught high school English
in Utah and upstate New York. She lives with her husband
and four children outside of Salt Lake City, Utah.

Visit her online at www.allycondie.com.